PRAISE FOR FLASHFORWARD

"Sawyer is on the shortlist of writers to watch."
—*Science Fiction Chronicle*

"It's hard to think of a modern science fiction author with dreams as vast as those of the internationally acclaimed Robert J. Sawyer."
—*The Toronto Star*

"Sawyer writes sharp, clear, seemingly effortless prose."
—*SFRA Review*

"If Robert J. Sawyer were a corporation, I would buy stock in him. He's on my (extremely short) buy-on-sight list, and belongs on yours."
—Spider Robinson

"Robert J. Sawyer can hold his own in SF anywhere in the world."
—*Edmonton Journal*

"Sawyer is a brilliant stylist who depicts daily life events with a shattered world view."
—*The Gainesville Sun*

"Robert J. Sawyer is a skillful, even daring storyteller."
—*Amazing Stories*

"Sawyer writes with a sense of wonder that hasn't prevailed in American SF since the days of Heinlein."
—*Books in Canada*

BOOKS BY ROBERT J. SAWYER

NOVELS
Golden Fleece (Aurora winner)*
End of an Era (Seiun winner)*
The Terminal Experiment (Nebula and Aurora winner)
Starplex (Hugo and Nebula finalist, Aurora winner)
Frameshift (Hugo finalist, Seiun winner)*
Illegal Alien (Seiun winner)
Factoring Humanity (Hugo finalist)*
Flashforward (Aurora winner)*
Calculating God (Hugo finalist)*
Mindscan (John W. Campbell Memorial Award winner)*
Rollback*
Wake

THE NEANDERTHAL PARALLAX
Hominids (Hugo winner)*
Humans (Hugo finalist)*
Hybrids*

THE QUINTAGLIO ASCENSION
Far-Seer*
Fossil Hunter*
Foreigner*

COLLECTIONS
Iterations (introduced by James Alan Gardner)
Relativity (introduced by Mike Resnick)
Identity Theft (introduced by Robert Charles Wilson)

ANTHOLOGIES
Tesseracts 6 (with Carolyn Clink)
Crossing the Line (with David Skene-Melvin)
Over the Edge (with Peter Sellers)
Boarding the Enterprise (with David Gerrold)

*published by Tor Books

(Reader's group guides available at www.sfwriter.com)

Flashforward

Robert J. Sawyer

A TOM DOHERTY ASSOCIATES BOOK
NEW YORK

This is a work of fiction. All the characters and events portrayed in this book are either products of the author's imagination or are used fictitiously.

FLASHFORWARD

Copyright © 1999 by Robert J. Sawyer

All rights reserved.

Edited by David G. Hartwell

A Tor Book
Published by Tom Doherty Associates, LLC
175 Fifth Avenue
New York, NY 10010

www.tor-forge.com

Tor® is a registered trademark of Tom Doherty Associates, LLC.

ISBN 978-0-7653-6383-1
Library of Congress Catalog Card Number: 99-21935

First Edition: November 1999
First Mass Market Edition: April 2000
Second Mass Market Edition: September 2009

Printed in the United States of America

0 9 8 7 6 5 4 3 2

Richard and I first met in high school in 1975. Back then, we each envisioned very different futures for ourselves. But one thing seemed absolutely clear: no matter how many years would pass, we'd always be friends. It's now a quarter-century later, and I'm delighted that at least that part turned out exactly as planned.

ACKNOWLEDGMENTS

Sincere thanks to my agent Ralph Vicinanza, and his associate Christopher Lotts; my editor at Tor, David G. Hartwell, and his assistant, James Minz; Chris Dao and Linda Quinton, also of Tor; Tor publisher Tom Doherty; Rob Howard, Suzanne Hallsworth, Heidi Winter, and Harold and Sylvia Fenn of my Canadian distributor, H. B. Fenn and Company, Ltd.; Neil Calder, Head of the Media Service, European Organization for Particle Physics (CERN); Dr. John Cramer, Professor of Physics, University of Washington; Dr. Shaheen Hussain Azmi, Asbed Bedrossian, Ted Bleaney, Alan Bostick, Michael A. Burstein, Linda C. Carson, David Livingstone Clink, James Alan Gardner, Richard M. Gotlib, Terence M. Green, John-Allen Price, Dr. Ariel Reich, Alan B. Sawyer, Tim Slater, Masayuki Uchida, and Edo van Belkom; my father, John A. Sawyer, for letting me repeatedly borrow his vacation home at Bristol Harbour Village where much of this novel was written; and especially my lovely wife, Carolyn Clink.

BOOK I

*He who foresees calamities
suffers them twice over.*

—Beilby Porteus

1

❖

Day One: Tuesday, April 21, 2009

A SLICE THROUGH SPACETIME . . .

The control building for CERN's Large Hadron Collider was new: it had been authorized in A.D. 2004 and completed in 2006. The building enclosed a central courtyard, inevitably named "the nucleus." Every office had a window either facing in toward the nucleus or out toward the rest of CERN's sprawling campus. The quadrangle surrounding the nucleus was two stories tall, but the main elevators had four stops: the two above-ground levels; the basement, which housed boiler rooms and storage; and the minus-one-hundred-meter level, which exited onto a staging area for the monorail used to travel along the twenty-seven-kilometer circumference of the collider tunnel. The tunnel itself ran under farmers' fields, the outskirts of the Geneva airport, and the foothills of the Jura mountains.

The south wall of the control building's main corridor was divided into nineteen long sections, each of which had been decorated with a mosaic made by an artist from one of CERN's member countries. The one from Greece depicted Democritus and the origin of atomic theory; the one from Germany portrayed the life of Einstein; the one from Denmark, that of Niels Bohr. Not all of the mosaics had physics as their themes, though: the French one depicted the skyline of Paris, and the Italian one showed a vineyard with thousands of polished amethysts representing individual grapes.

The actual control room for the Large Hadron Collider was a perfect square, with wide, sliding doors positioned precisely in the centers of two of its sides. The room was two stories tall, and the upper half was walled with glass, so that tour groups could look down on the proceedings; CERN offered three-hour public tours Mondays and Saturdays at 09h00 and 14h00. Hanging flat against the walls below the windows were the nineteen member-state flags, five per wall; the twentieth spot was taken up by the blue-and-gold flag of the European Union.

The control room contained dozens of consoles. One was devoted to operating the particle injectors; it controlled the beginnings of experiments. Adjacent to it was another with an angled face and ten inlaid monitors that would display the results reported by the ALICE and CMS detectors, the huge underground systems that would record and attempt to identify the particles produced by LHC experiments. Monitors on a third console showed portions of the gently curving underground collider tunnel, with the I-beam monorail track hanging from the ceiling.

Lloyd Simcoe, a Canadian-born researcher, sat at the injector console. He was forty-five, tall, and clean-shaven. His eyes were blue and his crewcut hair so dark brown that one could get away with calling it black—except at the temples, where about half of it had turned gray.

Particle physicists weren't known for their sartorial splendor, and Lloyd had until recently been no exception. But he'd agreed a few months ago to donate his entire wardrobe to the Geneva chapter of the Salvation Army, and let his fiancée pick out all-new things for him. Truth be told, the clothes were a little flashy for his taste, but he had to admit that he'd never looked so sharp. Today, he was wearing a beige dress shirt; a coral-colored jacket; brown pants with exterior pouches instead of interior pockets; and—in a nod to fashion tradition—black Italian leather shoes. Lloyd had also adopted a couple of universal status symbols that also happened to be bits of local color: a Mont Blanc fountain pen, which he kept clipped to his jacket's inside pocket, and a gold Swiss analog watch.

Seated on his right, in front of the detector console, was the master of the makeover herself, his fiancée, engineer Michiko Komura. Ten years Lloyd's junior at thirty-five, Michiko had a small, upturned nose and lustrous black hair that she had styled in the currently popular page-boy cut.

Standing behind her was Theo Procopides, Lloyd's research partner. At twenty-seven, Theo was eighteen years younger than Lloyd; more than one wag had compared the conservative middle-aged Lloyd and his fiery Greek colleague to the team of Crick and Watson. Theo had curly, thick, dark hair, gray eyes, and a prominent, jutting jaw. He almost always wore red denim jeans—Lloyd didn't like them, but no one under thirty wore blue jeans anymore—and one of an endless string of T-shirts depicting cartoon characters from all over the world; today he had on the venerable Tweety Bird. A dozen other scientists and engineers were positioned at the remaining consoles.

Moving up the cube . . .

Except for the gentle hum of air conditioning and the soft whir of equipment fans, the control room was absolutely silent. Everyone was nervous and tense, after a long day of preparing for this experiment. Lloyd looked around the room then took a deep breath. His pulse was racing, and he could feel butterflies gyrating in his stomach.

The clock on the wall was analog; the one on his console, digital. They were both rapidly approaching 17h00—what Lloyd, even after two years in Europe, still thought of as 5:00 P.M.

Lloyd was director of the collaborative group of almost a thousand physicists using the ALICE ("A Large Ion Collider Experiment") detector. He and Theo had spent two years designing today's particle collision—two years, to do work that could have taken two lifetimes. They were attempting to re-create energy levels that hadn't existed since a nanosecond after the Big Bang, when the universe's temperature was 10,000,000,000,000,000 degrees. In the process, they hoped to detect the holy grail of high-energy physics, the long-sought-after Higgs boson, the particle whose interactions endowed other particles with mass. If their experiment worked, the Higgs, and the Nobel that would likely be awarded to its dis-coverers, should be theirs.

The whole experiment was automated and precisely timed. There was no great knife switch to pull down, no trig-ger hidden under a spring-loaded cover to push. Yes, Lloyd had designed and Theo had coded the core modules of the program for this experiment, but everything was now under the control of a computer.

When the digital clock reached 16:59:55 Lloyd started counting down out loud with it. "Five."

He looked at Michiko.

"Four."

She smiled back encouragingly. God, how he loved her—

"Three."

He shifted his gaze to young Theo, the *wunderkind*—the kind of youthful star Lloyd had hoped to have been himself but never was.

"Two."

Theo, ever cocky, gave him a thumbs-up sign.

"One."

Please, God . . . thought Lloyd. *Please.*

"Zero."

And then—

And then, suddenly, everything was different.

There was an immediate change in the lighting—the dim illumination of the control room was replaced with sunlight coming through a window. But there was no adjustment, no discomfort—and no sense that Lloyd's pupils were contracting. It was as if he were already used to the brighter light.

And yet Lloyd couldn't control his eyes. He wanted to look around, to see what was going on, but his eyes moved as if under their own volition.

He was in bed—naked, apparently. He could feel the cotton sheets sliding now over his skin as he propped himself up on one elbow. As his head moved, he caught a brief glimpse of dormer windows, looking out apparently from the second floor of a country house. There were trees visible, and—

No, that couldn't be. These leaves had turned, frozen fire. But today was April 21—spring, not autumn.

Lloyd's view continued to shift and suddenly, with what should have been a start, he realized he wasn't alone in bed. There was someone else with him.

He recoiled.

No—no, that wasn't right. He didn't physically react at all; it was as if his body were divorced from his mind. But he *felt* like recoiling.

The other person was a woman, but—

What the hell was going on?

She was old, wrinkled, her skin translucent, her hair a white gossamer. The collagen that had once filled her cheeks had settled as wattles at the sides of her mouth, a mouth now smiling, the laugh lines all but lost amongst the permanent creases.

Lloyd tried to roll away from the hag, but his body refused to cooperate.

What in God's name was happening?

It was spring, not autumn.

Unless—

Unless, of course, he was now in the southern hemisphere. Transported, somehow, from Switzerland to Australia . . .

But no. The trees he'd glimpsed through the window were maples and poplars; it *had* to be North America or Europe.

His hand reached out. The woman was wearing a navy-blue shirt. It wasn't a pajama top, though; it had buttoned-down epaulets and several pockets—adventure clothing made of cotton duck, the kind L. L. Bean or Tilley sells, the kind a practical woman might wear to do her gardening. Lloyd felt his fingers brushing the fabric now, feeling its softness, its pliancy. And then—

And then his fingers found the button, hard, plastic, warmed by her body, translucent like her skin. Without hesitation, the fingers grasped the button, pushed it out, slipped it sideways through the raised stitching around the buttonhole. Before the top fell open, Lloyd's gaze, still acting on its own initiative, lifted again to the old woman's face, locking onto her pale blue eyes, the irises haloed by broken rings of white.

He felt his own cheeks drawing tight as he smiled. His hand slipped inside the woman's top, found her breast. Again he wanted to recoil, snapping his hand back. The breast was soft and shriveled, the skin hanging loosely on it—fruit gone bad. The fingers drew together, following the contours of the breast, finding the nipple.

Lloyd felt a pressure down below. For a horrible moment, he thought he was getting an erection, but that wasn't it. Instead, suddenly, there was a sense of fullness in his bladder; he had to urinate. He withdrew his hand and saw the old woman's eyebrows go up inquisitively. Lloyd could feel his shoulders rise and fall, a little shrug. She smiled at him—a warm smile, an understanding smile, as if this were the most natural thing in the world, as if he often had to excuse himself at the outset. Her teeth were slightly yellow—the simple yellow of age—but otherwise in excellent shape.

At last his body did what he'd been willing all along: it rolled away from the woman. Lloyd felt a pain in his knee as he did so, a sharp jab. It hurt, but he outwardly ignored it. He swung his legs off the bed, feet slapping softly against the cool hardwood floor. As he rose, he saw more of the world outside the window. It was either mid-morning or mid-afternoon, the shadow cast by one tree falling sharply across the next. A bird had been resting in one of the boughs; it was startled by the sudden movement in the bedroom and took wing. A robin—the large North American thrush, not the small Old World robin; this was definitely the United States or Canada. In fact, it looked a lot like New England—Lloyd loved the fall colors in New England.

Lloyd found himself moving slowly, almost shuffling across the floorboards. He realized now that this room wasn't in a house, but rather a cottage; the furnishings were the usual vacation-home hodgepodge. That night table—low-slung, made of particle board with a wallpaper-thin veneer of fake woodgrain on top: he recognized it, at least. A piece of furniture he'd bought as a student, and had eventually put in the guest room at the house in Illinois. But what was it doing here, in this unfamiliar place?

He continued along. His right knee bothered him with each step; he wondered what was wrong with it. A mirror was hanging on the wall; its frame was knotty pine, covered over with clear varnish. It clashed with the darker "wood" of the night table, of course, but—

Jesus.

Jesus Christ.

Of their own accord, his eyes looked into the mirror as he passed, and he saw himself—

For a half-second he thought it was his father.

But it was him. What hair was left on his head was entirely gray; that on his chest was white. His skin was loose and lined, his gait stooped.

Could it be radiation? Could the experiment have exposed him? Could—

No. No, that wasn't it. He knew it in his bones—in his *arthritic* bones. That wasn't it.

He was *old.*

It was as if he'd aged twenty years or more, as if—

Two decades of life gone, excised from his memory.

He wanted to scream, to shout, to protest the unfairness, protest the loss, demand an accounting from the universe—

But he could do none of that; he had no control. His body

continued its slow, painful shuffle to the bathroom.

As he turned to enter the room, he glanced back at the old woman on the bed, lying now on her side, her head propped up by an arm, her smile mischievous, seductive. His vision was still sharp—he could see the flash of gold on the third finger of her left hand. It was bad enough that he was sleeping with an old woman, but a *married* old woman—

The plain wooden door was ajar, but he reached a hand up to push it open the rest of the way, and out of the corner of his eye he caught sight of a matching wedding ring on his own left hand.

And then it hit him. This hag, this stranger, this woman he'd never seen before, this woman who looked nothing like his beloved Michiko, was his wife.

Lloyd wanted to look back at her, to try to imagine her as she would have been decades younger, to reconstruct the beauty she might have once had, but—

But he continued on into the bathroom, half turning to face the toilet, leaning over to lift the lid, and—

—and, suddenly, incredibly, thankfully, amazingly, Lloyd Simcoe was back at CERN, back in the LHC control room. For some reason, he was slumped in his vinyl-padded chair. He straightened himself up and used his hands to pull his shirt back into position.

What an incredible hallucination it had been! There would be hell to pay, of course: they were supposed to be fully shielded here, a hundred meters of earth between them and the collider ring. But he'd heard how high-energy discharges could cause hallucinations; surely that had been what had happened.

Lloyd took a moment to reorient himself. There had been no transition between *here* and *there:* no flash of light, no sense of wooziness, no popping of his ears. One instant, he'd been at CERN, then, in the next, he'd been somewhere else, for—

what?—two minutes, perhaps. And now, just as seamlessly, he was back in the control room.

Of course he'd never left. Of course it had been an illusion.

He glanced around, trying to read the faces of the others. Michiko looked shocked. Had she been watching Lloyd while he was hallucinating? What had he done? Flailed around like an epileptic? Reached out into the air, as if stroking an unseen breast? Or just slumped back in his chair, falling unconscious? If so, he couldn't have been out for long—nowhere near the two minutes he'd perceived—or surely Michiko and others would be looming over him right now, checking his pulse and loosening his collar. He glanced at the analog wall clock: it was indeed two minutes after five P.M.

He then looked over at Theo Procopides. The young Greek's expression was more subdued than Michiko's, but he was being just as wary as Lloyd, looking in turn at each of the other people in the room, shifting his gaze as soon as one of them looked back at him.

Lloyd opened his mouth to speak although he wasn't sure what he wanted to say. But he closed it when he heard a moaning sound coming through the nearest open door. Michiko evidently heard it too; they both rose simultaneously. She was closer to the door, though, and by the time Lloyd reached it, she was already out in the corridor. "My God!" she was saying. "Are you okay?"

One of the technicians—Sven, it was—was struggling to get to his feet. He was holding his right hand to his nose, which was bleeding profusely. Lloyd hurried back into the control room, unclipped the first-aid kit from its wall mount, and ran to the corridor. The kit was in a white plastic box; Lloyd popped it open and began unrolling a length of gauze.

Sven began to speak in Norwegian, but stopped himself after a moment and started over in French. "I—I must have fainted."

The corridor was covered with hard tiles; Lloyd could see a carnation smear of blood where Sven's face had hit the floor. He handed the gauze to Sven, who nodded his thanks then wadded it up and pressed it against his nose. "Craziest thing," he said. "Like I fell asleep on my feet." He made a little laughing sound. "I had a dream, even."

Lloyd felt his eyebrows climbing. "A dream?" he said, also in French.

"Vivid as anything," said Sven. "I was in Geneva—over by Le Rozzel." Lloyd knew it well: a Breton-style *crêperie* on Grand Rue. "But it was like some science-fiction thing. There were cars hovering by without touching the ground, and—"

"Yes, yes!" It was a woman's voice, but not in response to Sven. It was coming from back inside the control room. "The same thing happened to me!"

Lloyd re-entered the dimly lit room. "What happened, Antonia?"

A heavyset Italian woman had been talking to two of the other people present, but now turned to face Lloyd. "It was like I was suddenly somewhere else. Parry said the same thing happened to him."

Michiko and Sven were now standing in the doorway, right behind Lloyd. "Me, too," said Michiko, sounding relieved that she wasn't alone in this.

Theo, standing next to Antonia now, was frowning. Lloyd looked at him. "Theo? What about you?"

"Nothing."

"Nothing?"

Theo shook his head.

"We all must have passed out," said Lloyd.

"I sure did," said Sven. He pulled the gauze away from his face, then touched it against his nose again to see if the bleeding had stopped. It hadn't.

"How long were we out?" asked Michiko.

"And—Christ!—what about the experiment?" asked Lloyd. He sprinted over to the ALICE monitoring station and tapped a couple of keys.

"Nothing," he said. "*Damn.*"

Michiko blew out air in disappointment.

"It should have worked," said Lloyd, slapping an open

palm against the console. "We should have got the Higgs."

"Well, *something* happened," said Michiko. "Theo, didn't you see *anything* while the rest of us were having—having visions?"

Theo shook his head. "Not a thing. I guess—I guess I *did* black out. Except there was no blackness. I was watching Lloyd as he counted down: five, four, three, two, one, zero. Then it was like a jump cut, you know, in film. Suddenly Lloyd was slumped over in his seat."

"You saw me slump over?"

"No, no. It's like I said: one instant you were sitting up, and the next you were slumped over, with no movement in between. I guess—I guess I *did* black out. No sooner had it registered on me that you were slumped over than you were sitting back up, and—"

Suddenly, a warbling siren split the air—an emergency vehicle of some sort. Lloyd hurried out of the control room, everyone following. The room on the opposite side of the corridor had a window in it. Michiko, who had got there first, was already hoisting the venetian blind; late-afternoon sun streamed in. The vehicle was a CERN fire truck, one of three kept on site. It was racing across the campus, heading toward the main administration building.

Sven's nose had apparently at last stopped bleeding; he was now holding the bloody mass of gauze at his side. "I wonder if somebody else had a fall?" he said.

Lloyd looked at him.

"They use the fire trucks for first aid as well as fires," said Sven.

Michiko realized the magnitude of what Sven was suggesting. "We should check all the rooms here; make sure everyone is all right."

Lloyd nodded and moved back to the corridor. "Antonia, you check everyone in the control room. Michiko, you take Jake and Sven and go down that way. Theo and I will look up this way." He felt a brief pang of guilt at dismissing Michiko, but he needed a moment to sort out what he'd seen, what he'd experienced.

The first room Lloyd and Theo entered contained a downed woman; Lloyd couldn't remember her name, but she worked in public relations. The flatscreen computer monitor in front of her showed the familiar Windows 2009 three-dimensional desktop. She was still unconscious; it was clear from the massive bruise on her forehead that she'd pitched forward, hitting her head on the metal rim of her desk, knocking herself out. Lloyd did what he'd seen done in countless movies: he took her left hand in his right, holding it so that the back of her hand was face up, and he patted it gently with his other hand while urging her to wake up.

Which, at last, she did. "Dr. Simcoe?" she said, looking at Lloyd. "What happened?"

"I don't know."

"I had this—this dream," she said. "I was in an art gallery somewhere, looking at a painting."

"Are you okay now?"

"I—I don't know. My head hurts."

"You might have a concussion. You should get to the infirmary."

"What are all those sirens?"

"Fire trucks." A pause. "Look, I've got to go now. Other people might be hurt, as well."

She nodded. "I'll be all right."

Theo had already continued on down the corridor. Lloyd left the room and headed down, as well. He passed Theo, who was tending to someone else who had fallen. The corridor made a right-hand turn; Lloyd headed along the new section. He came to an office door, which slid open silently as he approached it, but the people on the other side all seemed to be fine, although they were talking animatedly about the different visions they'd had. There were three individuals present: two women and a man. One of the women caught sight of Lloyd.

"Lloyd, what happened?" she asked in French.

"I don't know yet," he replied, also in French. "Is everyone okay?"

"We're fine."

"I couldn't help overhearing," said Lloyd. "The three of you had visions, too?"

Nods all around.

"They were vividly realistic?"

The woman who hadn't yet spoken to Lloyd pointed at the man. "Not Raoul's. He had some sort of psychedelic experience." She said it as if this was only to be expected given Raoul's lifestyle.

"I wouldn't exactly say 'psychedelic,' " said Raoul, sounding as though he needed to defend himself. His blond hair was long and clean, and tied together in a glorious ponytail. "But it sure wasn't realistic. There was this guy with three heads, see—"

Lloyd nodded, filing this bit of information away. "If you guys are all fine, then join us—some people took nasty falls when whatever it was happened. We need to search for anyone who might be hurt."

"Why not go on the intercom, and get everyone who can to assemble in the lobby?" said Raoul. "Then we can do a head count and see who's missing."

Lloyd realized this made perfect sense. "You continue to look; some people might need immediate attention. I'll go up to the front office." He headed out of the room, and the others rose and entered the corridor as well. Lloyd took the shortest path to the office, sprinting past the various mosaics. When he arrived, some of the administrative staff were tending to one of their own who'd apparently broken his arm when he fell. Another person had been scalded when she pitched forward onto her own steaming cup of coffee.

"Dr. Simcoe, what happened?" asked a man.

Lloyd was getting sick of the question. "I don't know. Can you operate the PA?"

The man looked at him; evidently Lloyd was using a North Americanism the fellow didn't know.

"The PA," said Lloyd. "The public-address system."

The man's blank look continued.

"The intercom!"

"Oh, sure," he said, his English harshened by a German accent. "Over here." He led Lloyd to a console and flipped some buttons. Lloyd picked up the thin plastic wand that had the solid-state microphone at its tip.

"This is Lloyd Simcoe." He could hear his own voice coming back at him from the speaker out in the corridor, but filters in the system eliminated any feedback. "Clearly, something has happened. Several people are injured. If you yourself are ambulatory—" He stopped himself; English was a second language for most of the workers here. "If you yourself can walk, and if people you're with can walk as well, or at least can be left, please come at once to the main lobby. Someone could have fallen in a hidden place; we need to find out if anyone is missing." He handed the microphone back to the man. "Can you repeat the gist of that in German and French?"

"*Jawohl*," said the man, already switching mental gears. He began to speak into the mike. Lloyd moved away from the PA controls. He then ushered the able-bodied people out of the office into the lobby, which was decorated with a long brass plaque rescued from one of the older buildings that had been demolished to make room for the LHC control center. The plaque spelled out CERN's original acronym: *Conseil Européenne pour la Recherche Nucléaire*. These days, the acronym didn't actually stand for anything, but its historical roots were honored here.

The faces in the lobby were mostly white, with a few—Lloyd stopped himself before he mentally referred to them as melanic-Americans, the term currently preferred by blacks in the United States. Although Peter Carter, there, was from Stanford, most of the other blacks were actually directly from Africa. There were also several Asians, including, of course, Michiko, who had come to the lobby in response to the PA announcement. Lloyd moved over to her and gave her a hug.

Thank God she, at least, hadn't been hurt. "Anybody seriously injured?" he asked.

"A few bruises and another bloody nose," said Michiko, "but nothing major. You?"

Lloyd scanned for the woman who had banged her head. She hadn't shown up yet. "One possible concussion, a broken arm, and a bad burn." He paused. "We should really call for some ambulances—get the injured to a hospital."

"I'll take care of that," said Michiko. She disappeared into the office.

The assembled group was getting larger; it now numbered about two hundred people. "Everyone!" shouted Lloyd. "Your attention, please! *Votre attention, s'il vous plaît!*" He waited until all eyes were on him. "Look around and see if you can account for your coworkers or office mates or lab staff. If anyone you've seen today is missing, let me know. And if anyone here in the lobby requires immediate medical attention, let me know that, too. We've called for some ambulances."

As he said that, Michiko re-emerged. Her skin was even paler than normal, and her voice was quavering as she spoke. "There won't be any ambulances," she said. "Not anytime soon, anyway. The emergency operator told me they're all tied up in Geneva. Apparently every driver on the roads blacked out; they can't even begin to tally up how many people are dead."

2

CERN WAS FOUNDED FIFTY-FIVE YEARS PRE-
viously, in 1954. Its staff consisted of three thousand people
of which about a third were physicists or engineers, a third
were technicians, and the remaining third were split evenly
between administrators and craftspeople.

The Large Hadron Collider was built at a cost of five billion American dollars inside the same circular underground
tunnel straddling the Swiss-French border that still housed
CERN's older, no-longer-used Large Electron-Positron collider; LEP had been in service from 1989 to 2000. The LHC used
10-Tesla dual-field superconducting electromagnets to propel
particles around the giant ring. CERN had the largest and
most powerful cryogenic system in the world, using liquid
helium to chill the magnets to just 1.8 Celsius degrees above
absolute zero.

The Large Hadron Collider was actually two accelerators
in one: one accelerated particles clockwise; the other, counterclockwise. A particle beam going in one direction could be
made to collide with another beam going in the opposite direction, and then—

And then $E=mc^2$, big time.

Einstein's equation said simply that matter and energy are interchangeable. If you collide particles at high enough velocities, the kinetic energy of the collision may be converted into exotic particles.

The LHC had been activated in 2006, and during its first few years of work it did proton-proton collisions, producing energies of up to fourteen trillion electron-volts.

But now it was time to move on to Phase Two, and Lloyd Simcoe and Theo Procopides had led the team designing the first experiment. In Phase Two, instead of colliding protons together, lead nuclei—each two hundred and seventeen times more massive than a proton—would be rammed into each other. The resulting collisions would produce eleven hundred and fifty trillion electron volts, comparable to the energy level in the universe only a billionth of a second after the big bang. At that energy level, Lloyd and Theo should have produced the Higgs boson, a particle that physicists had been pursuing for half a century.

Instead, they produced death and destruction on a staggering scale.

Gaston Béranger, Director-General of CERN, was a compact, hairy man with a sharp, high-bridged nose. He had been sitting in his office when the phenomenon occurred. It was the largest office on the CERN campus, with a long real-wood conference table directly in front of his desk, and a large, mirror-backed, well-stocked bar. Béranger didn't drink himself—not anymore; there was nothing harder than being an alcoholic in France, where wine flowed with every meal; Gaston had lived in Paris until his appointment at CERN. But when ambassadors came to see what their millions were being spent on, he needed to be able to pour them a glass without ever once showing how desperately he would have liked to have joined them.

Of course, Lloyd Simcoe and his sidekick Theo Procopides

were trying their big experiment in the LHC this afternoon; he could have cleared his schedule to have gone and watched that—but there was always something major going, and if he went to watch every run of the accelerators he'd never get any work done. Besides, he needed to prepare for his meeting tomorrow morning with the team from Gec Alsthom, and—

"You pick that up!"

Gaston Béranger had no doubt where he was: it was his house, on Geneva's Right Bank. The Ikea Billy bookcases were the same, as were the couch and the easy chair. But the Sony TV, and its stand, were gone. Instead, what must have been a flat-panel monitor was mounted on the wall above where the TV used to be. It was showing an international lacrosse game. One team was clearly Spain's, but he didn't recognize the other team, clad in green-and-purple jerseys.

A young man had come into the room. Gaston didn't recognize him, either. He had been wearing what appeared to be a black leather jacket, and had thrown it over the end of the couch, where it had slipped down to the carpeted floor. A small robot, not much bigger than a shoebox, rolled out from under an end table and started toward the fallen coat. Gaston pointed a finger at the robot and barked, *"Arrêt!"* The machine froze, then, after a moment, retreated back under the table.

The young man turned around. He looked to be maybe nineteen or twenty. On his right cheek there was what seemed to be an animated tattoo of a lightning bolt; it zigzagged its way across the young man's face in five discrete jumps, then repeated the cycle over and over again.

As he turned the left side of his face became visible—and it was horrifying, all the muscles and blood vessels clearly visible, as if, somehow, he'd treated his skin with a chemical that had turned it transparent. The young man's right hand was covered over with an exoskeletal glove, extending his fingers into long, mechanical digits terminating in glistening surgically sharp silver points.

"I said pick that up!" snapped Gaston in French—or, at least it was his voice; he had no sense of willing the words out. "As long as I'm paying for your clothes, you'll take good care of them."

The young man glared at Gaston. He was positive he didn't know him, but he did bear a resemblance to . . . whom? It was hard to tell with that ghastly half-transparent face, but the high forehead, the thin lips, those cool gray eyes, that aquiline nose . . .

The pointed tips of the finger extensions retracted with a whir, and the boy picked up the jacket between mechanical thumb and forefinger, holding it now as if it were something distasteful. Gaston's gaze tracked with him as he moved across the living room. As it did so, Gaston couldn't help noticing that a lot of other details were wrong, too: the familiar pattern of books on the shelves had changed completely, as if someone had reorganized everything at some point. And, indeed, there seemed to be far fewer volumes than there should have been, as though a purge had been done of the family library. Another robot, this one spiderlike and about the size of a splayed human hand, was working its way along the shelves, apparently dusting.

On one wall, where they used to have a framed print of Monet's *Le Moulin de la Galette*, there was now an alcove, displaying what looked like a Henry Moore sculpture—but, no, no, there could be no alcove there; that wall was shared with the house next door. It must have really been a flat piece, a hologram or something similar, hanging on the wall and giving the illusion of depth; if so, the illusion was absolutely perfect.

The closet doors had changed, too; they slid open of their own volition as the boy approached. He reached in, pulled out a hanger, and put the jacket on it. He then replaced the hanger inside the closet . . . and the jacket slipped from it to the closet floor.

Gaston's voice lashing out again: "Damn it, Marc, can't you be more careful?"

Marc . . .

Marc!

Mon Dieu!

That's why he looked familiar.

A family resemblance.

Marc. The name Marie-Claire and he had chosen for the child she was carrying.

Marc Béranger.

Gaston hadn't even yet held the baby in his arms, hadn't burped it over his shoulder, hadn't changed its diaper, and yet here he was, grown up, a man—a frightening, hostile man.

Marc looked at the fallen jacket, his cheek still flashing, but then he walked away from the closet, letting the door hiss shut behind him.

"Damn you, Marc," said Gaston's voice. "I'm getting sick of your attitude. You're never going to get a job if you keep behaving like this."

"Screw you," said the boy, his voice deep, his tone a sneer.

Those were baby's first words—not "mama," not "papa," but "Screw you."

And, as if there could be any doubt remaining, Marie-Claire entered Gaston's field of view just then, emerging through another sliding door from the den. "Don't speak to your father that way," she said.

Gaston was taken aback; it *was* Marie-Claire, without question, but she looked more like her own mother than herself. Her hair was white, her face was lined, and she'd put on a good fifteen kilos.

"Screw you, too," said Marc.

Gaston rather suspected that his voice would protest, "Don't talk to your mother like that." It did not disappoint him.

Before Marc turned back around, Gaston caught sight of a shaved area at the back of the kid's head, and a metal socket surgically implanted there.

It had to be a hallucination. It *had* to. But what a terrible hallucination to have! Marie-Claire was due any day now.

They'd tried for years to get pregnant—Gaston ran a facility that could precisely unite an electron and a positron, but somehow he and Marie-Claire had been unable to get an egg and a sperm, each millions of times larger than those subatomic particles, to come together. But finally it had happened; finally God had smiled upon them, finally she was pregnant.

And now, at last, nine months later, they were soon to give birth. All those Lamaze classes, all that planning, all that fixing up of the nursery . . . it was soon going to come to fruition.

And now this dream; that's all it must be. Just a bad dream. Cold feet; he'd had the worst nightmare of his life just before he got married. Why should this be any different?

But it *was* different. This was much more realistic than any dream he'd ever had. He thought about the plug on the back of his son's head; thought about images being pumped directly into a brain—the drug of the future?

"Get off my back," said Marc. "I've had a hard day."

"Oh, really?" said Gaston's voice, dripping with sarcasm. "You've had a hard day, eh? A hard day terrorizing tourists in Old Town, was it? I should have let you rot in jail, you ungrateful punk—"

Gaston was shocked to find himself sounding so much like his own father—the things his father had said to him when he was Marc's age, the things he'd promised himself he'd never say to his own children.

"Now, Gaston . . ." said Marie-Claire.

"Well, if he doesn't appreciate what he's got here . . ."

"I don't need this shit," sneered Marc.

"Enough!" snapped Marie-Claire. "Enough."

"I hate you," said Marc. "I hate you both."

Gaston's mouth opened to reply, and then—

—and then, suddenly, he was back in his office at CERN.

After reporting the news of all the deaths, Michiko Komura had immediately gone back into the front office of the LHC control center. She kept trying to phone the school in Geneva that her eight-year-old daughter Tamiko attended; Michiko was divorced from her first husband, a Tokyo executive. But all she got was busy signal after busy signal, and the Swiss phone company, for some reason, wasn't offering to automatically notify her when the line became free.

Lloyd was standing behind her as she kept trying, but finally she looked up at him, her eyes desperate. "I can't get through," she said. "I've got to go there."

"I'll come with you," said Lloyd at once. They ran out of the building, into the warm April air, the ruddy sun already kissing the horizon, the mountains looming in the distance.

Michiko's car—a Toyota—was parked here, too, but they took Lloyd's leased Fiat, with Lloyd driving. They made their way out of the CERN campus, passing by the towering cylindrical liquid helium tanks, and got onto Route de Meyrin, which took them through Meyrin, the town just east of CERN. Although they saw some cars at the sides of the road, things looked no worse than they did after one of the rare winter storms, except, of course, that there was no snow on the ground.

They passed quickly through the town. A short distance outside it was Geneva's Cointrin Airport. Pillars of black smoke rose to the sky; a large Swissair jet had crashed on the one runway. "My God," said Michiko. She brought a knuckle to her mouth. "My God."

They continued on into Geneva proper, situated at the westernmost tip of Lac Léman. Geneva was a wealthy metropolis of 200,000, known for ultra-posh restaurants and wildly expensive shops.

Signs that would normally be lit up were out, and lots of cars—many of them Mercedes and other expensive makes—had veered off the roads and plowed into buildings. The plate-glass windows on several storefronts had shattered, but there didn't seem to be any looting going on. Even the tourists were apparently too stunned by what had happened to take advantage of the situation.

They did spot one ambulance, tending an old man at the

side of the road; they also heard the sirens of fire trucks or other emergency vehicles. And at one point, they saw a helicopter embedded in the glass side of a small office tower.

They drove across the Pont de l'Ile, passing over the river Rhône, gulls wheeling overhead, leaving the Right Bank with its patrician hotels, and entering the historic Left Bank. The route around *Vieille Ville*—Old Town—was blocked by a four-car traffic accident, so they had to try negotiating their way through its narrow, crooked, one-way streets. They drove down Rue de la Cité, which turned into Grand Rue. But it, too, was blocked, too, by a *Transports Publics Genevois* bus that had spun out of control and was now swung across both lanes. They tried an alternate route, Michiko fretting more and more with each passing minute, but it was also obstructed by damaged vehicles.

"How far is the school?" asked Lloyd.

"Less than a kilometer," said Michiko.

"Let's do it on foot." He drove back to Grand Rue, then pulled the car over at the side of road. It wasn't a legal parking spot, but Lloyd hardly thought anybody would be worrying about that at a time like this. They got out of the Fiat and began running up the steep, cobbled streets. Michiko stopped after a few paces to remove her high heels so she could run faster. They continued on up the streets, but had to stop again for her to replace her shoes as they came to a sidewalk covered with glass shards.

They hurried up Rue Jean-Calvin, passing the Musée Barbier-Mueller, switched to Rue du Puits St. Pierre, and hustled by the seven-hundred-year-old Maison Tavel, Geneva's oldest private home. They had slowed only slightly by the time they passed the austere Temple de l'Auditoire, where John Calvin and John Knox had once held forth.

Hearts pounding, breath ragged, they pushed onward. On their right were the Cathédrale St-Pierre and Christie's auction house. Michiko and Lloyd hurried through the sprawling square of Place du Bourg-de-Four, with its halo of open-air *cafés* and *patisseries* surrounding the central fountain. Many tourists and Genevois were still prone on the paving stones; others were sitting up on the ground, either tending to their own scrapes and bruises or being aided by other pedestrians.

Finally, they made it to the school grounds on Rue de Chaudronniers. The Ducommun School was a long-established facility catering to the children of foreigners working in or near Geneva. The core buildings were over two hundred years old, but several additional structures had been added in the last few decades. Although classes ended at 4:00 P.M., after-school activities were provided until 6:00 P.M., so that professional parents could leave kids there all day, and, although it was now getting on to 7:00 P.M., scores of kids were still here.

Michiko was hardly the only parent to have rushed here. The grounds were crisscrossed by the long shadows of diplomats, rich business people, and others whose kids attended Ducommun; dozens of them were hugging children and crying with relief.

The buildings all looked intact. Michiko and Lloyd were both huffing and puffing as they continued running across the immaculate lawn. By long tradition, the school flew the flags of the home countries of every student out front; Tamiko was the only Japanese currently enrolled, but the rising sun was indeed snapping in the spring breeze.

They made it into the lobby, which had beautiful marble floors and dark-wood paneling on the walls. The office was off to the right, and Michiko led the way to it. The door slid open, revealing a long wooden counter separating the secretaries from the public. Michiko made it over to the counter, and, between shuddering breaths, she began, "Hello, I'm—"

"Oh, Madame Komura," said a woman emerging from an office. "I've been trying to call you, but haven't been able to get through." She paused awkwardly. "Please, come in."

Michiko and Lloyd made their way behind the counter and into the office. A PC sat on the desk, with a datapad docked to it.

"Where's Tamiko?" said Michiko.

"Please," said the woman. "Have a seat." She looked at

Lloyd. "I'm Madame Severin; I'm the headmistress here."

"Lloyd Simcoe," said Lloyd. "I'm Michiko's fiancé."

"Where's Tamiko?" said Michiko again.

"Madame Komura, I'm so sorry. I'm—" She stopped, swallowed, started again. "Tamiko was outside. A car came plowing through the parking lot, and . . . I'm so very sorry."

"How is she?" asked Michiko.

"Tamiko is dead, Madame Komura. We all—I don't know what happened; we all blacked out or something. When we came to, we found her."

Tears were welling out of Michiko's eyes. Lloyd felt a horrible constriction in his chest. Michiko found a chair, collapsed into it, and put her face in her hands. Lloyd knelt down next to her and put an arm around her.

"I'm so sorry," said Severin.

Lloyd nodded. "It wasn't your fault."

Michiko sobbed a while longer, then looked up, her eyes red. "I want to see her."

"She's still in the parking lot. I'm sorry—we *did* call for the police, but they haven't come yet."

"Show me," said Michiko, her voice cracking.

Severin nodded, and led them out behind the building. Some other youngsters were standing, looking at the body, terrified of it and yet drawn to it, something beyond their ken. The staff were too busy dealing with kids who had been injured to be able to corral all the pupils back into the school.

Tamiko was lying there—just lying there. There was no blood, and her body seemed intact. The car that had presumably hit her had backed off several meters and was parked at an angle. Its bumper was dented.

Michiko got within five meters, and then collapsed completely, crying loudly. Lloyd drew her into his arms, and held her. Severin hovered nearby for a bit, but was soon called away to deal with another parent, and another crisis.

At last, because she wanted it, Lloyd led Michiko over to the body. He bent over, his vision blurring, his heart breaking, and gently smoothed Tamiko's hair away from her face.

Lloyd had no words; what could he possibly say that might bring comfort at a time like this? They stood there, Lloyd holding Michiko for perhaps half an hour, her body convulsing with tears the whole time.

3

◈

THEO PROCOPIDES STAGGERED DOWN THE mosaic-lined corridor to his tiny office, its walls covered with cartoon posters: Asterix le Gauloix here, Ren and Stimpy there, Bugs Bunny and Fred Flintstone and Gaga from Waga above the desk.

Theo felt woozy, shell-shocked. Although he hadn't had a vision, it seemed everyone else had. Still, even just having blacked out would have been enough to unnerve him. Added to that were the injuries to his friends and coworkers, and the news of the deaths in Geneva and the surrounding towns. He was utterly devastated.

Theo was aware that people thought of him as cocky, arrogant—but he wasn't. Not really, not down deep. He just knew he was good at what he did, and he knew that while others were talking about their dreams, he was working hard day in and day out to make his a reality. But this—this left him confused and disoriented.

Reports were still coming in. One hundred and eleven people had died when a Swissair 797 crashed at Geneva Airport. Under normal circumstances, some might have survived the actual crash—but no one moved to evacuate before the plane caught fire.

Theo collapsed in his black leather swivel chair. He could see smoke rising in the distance; his window faced the airport—you needed a lot more seniority to get one that faced the Jura mountains.

He and Lloyd had intended no harm. Hell, Theo couldn't even begin to fathom what had caused everyone to black out. A giant electromagnetic pulse? But surely that would have done more damage to computers than to people, and all of CERN's delicate instruments seemed to be running normally.

Theo had swiveled the chair around as he'd sat down in it; his back was now to the open door. He wasn't aware that someone else had arrived until he heard a masculine throat-clearing. He rotated the chair and looked at Jacob Horowitz, a young grad student who worked with Theo and Lloyd. He had a shock of red hair and swarms of freckles.

"It's not your fault," Jake said, emphatically.

"Of course it is," said Theo, as if it were plainly obvious. "We clearly didn't take some important factor into consideration, and—"

"No," said Jake, strongly. "No, really. It's not your fault. It had nothing to do with CERN."

"What?" Theo said it as if he hadn't understood Jake's words.

"Come down to the staff lounge."

"I don't want to face anyone just now, and—"

"No, come on. They've got CNN on down there, and—"

"It's made CNN already?"

"You'll see. Come."

Theo rose slowly from his chair and started walking. Jake motioned for him to move more quickly, and at last Theo began to jog alongside Jake. When they arrived, there were maybe twenty people in the lounge.

"—Helen Michaels reporting from New York City. Back to you, Bernie."

Bernard Shaw's stern, lined face filled the high-definition

TV screen. "Thanks, Helen. As you can see," he said to the camera, "the phenomenon seems to be worldwide—which suggests that the initial analyses that it must have been some sort of foreign weapon are unlikely to be correct, although of course the possibility that it was a terrorist act remains. No credible party, as yet, has stepped forward to claim responsibility, and—ah, we now have that Australian report we promised you a moment ago."

The view changed to show Sydney with the white sails of the Opera House in the background, lit up against a dark sky. A male reporter was standing in the center of the shot. "Bernie, it's just after four A.M. here in Sydney. There's no one image I can show you to convey what's happened down here. Reports are only slowly coming in as people realize that what they experienced was not an isolated phenomenon. The tragedies are many: we have word from a downtown hospital of a woman who died during emergency surgery when everyone in the operating theater simply stopped working for several minutes. But we also had a story of an all-night convenience-store robbery thwarted when all parties—including the robber—collapsed simultaneously at 2:00 A.M. local time. The robber was knocked unconscious, apparently, as he struck the floor, and a patron who woke up before he did was able to get his gun. We still have no good idea what the death count is here in Sydney, let alone the rest of Australia."

"Paul, what about the hallucinations? Are those being reported down under, as well?"

A pause while Shaw's question bounced off satellites from Atlanta to Australia. "Bernie, people are buzzing about that, yes. We don't know what percentage of the population experienced hallucinations, but it seems to be a lot. I myself had quite a vivid one."

"Thanks, Paul." The graphic behind Shaw changed to the American Presidential seal. "President Boulton will address the nation in fifteen minutes, we're told. Of course, CNN will bring you live coverage of his remarks. Meanwhile, we have a report now from Islamabad, Pakistan. Yusef, are you there—?"

"See," said Jake, *sotto voce.* "It had nothing to do with CERN."

Theo felt simultaneously shocked and relieved. Something had affected the entire planet; surely their experiment couldn't have done that.

And yet—

And yet, if it hadn't been related to the LHC experiment, then what could have caused it? Was Shaw right—was it some sort of terrorist weapon? It had only been a little over two hours since the phenomenon. The CNN team was showing amazing professionalism; Theo was still struggling to get his own equilibrium back.

Shut off the consciousness of the entire human race for two minutes, and what would the death toll be?

How many cars had collided?

How many planes had crashed? How many hang-gliders? How many parachutists had blacked out, failing to pull their ripcords?

How many operations had gone bad? How many *births* had gone bad?

How many people had fallen from ladders, fallen down stairs?

Of course, most airplanes would fly just fine for a minute or two without pilot intervention, as long as they actually weren't taking off or landing. On uncrowded roads, cars might even manage just to roll safely to a stop.

But still . . . still . . .

"The surprising thing," said Bernard Shaw, on the TV, "is that as near as we can tell, the consciousness of the human race shut off at precisely noon Eastern Time. At first it seemed that the various times were not all exactly the same, but we've been checking the clocks of those who've reported in against our own clocks here at CNN Center in Atlanta, which, of course, are set against the time signal from the National Institute for Standards and Technology in Boulder, Colorado. Adjusting for slightly incorrect settings that other people had, we find that the phenomenon occurred to the second at 12:00 noon Eastern, and—"

To the second, thought Theo.

To the second.

Jesus Christ.

CERN, of course, used an atomic clock. And the experiment was programmed to begin at precisely 17h00 Geneva time, which is—

—is noon in Atlanta.

"As he has been for the last two hours, we have astronomer Donald Poort of Georgia Tech with us," said Shaw. "He was to be a guest on *CNN This Morning*, and we're fortunate that he was already here in the studio. Dr. Poort looks a little pale; please forgive that. We rushed him onto the air before he had a chance to go through makeup. Dr. Poort, thank you for agreeing to join us."

Poort was a man in his early fifties, with a thin, pinched face. He did indeed look pallid under the studio lights—as though he hadn't seen the sun since the Clinton administration. "Thanks, Bernie."

"Tell us again what happened, Dr. Poort."

"Well, as you observed, the phenomenon occurred precisely to the second at noon. Of course, there are thirty-six hundred seconds in every hour, so the chances of a random event occurring precisely at the top of the clock—to use a phrase you broadcasters like—are one in thirty-six hundred. In other words, vanishingly small. Which leads me to suspect that we *are* dealing with a human-caused event, something that was *scheduled* to occur. But as to what could have caused it, I have no idea . . ."

Damn it, thought Theo. God damn it. It *had* to be the LHC experiment; it couldn't be a coincidence that the highest-energy particle collision in the history of the planet happened at precisely the same moment as the onset of the phenomenon.

No. No, that wasn't being honest. It wasn't a phenomenon;

it was a *disaster*—possibly the biggest one in the history of the human race.

And he, Theo Procopides, had somehow caused it.

Gaston Béranger, CERN's Director-General, came into the lounge at that moment. "There you are!" he said, as if Theo had been missing for weeks.

Theo exchanged a nervous glance with Jake, then turned to the Director-General. "Hi, Dr. Béranger."

"What the hell have you done?" demanded Béranger in angry French. "And where's Simcoe?"

"Lloyd and Michiko went off to get Michiko's daughter— she's at the Ducommun School."

"What happened?" demanded Béranger again.

Theo spread his hands. "I have no idea. I can't imagine what could have caused it."

"The—the *whatever* it was occurred at precisely the scheduled time for your LHC experiment to begin," said Béranger.

Theo nodded, and jerked a thumb at the TV. "So Bernard Shaw was saying."

"It's on CNN!" wailed the French man, as if all were now lost. "How did they find out about your experiment?"

"Shaw didn't mention anything about CERN. He just—"

"Thank God! Look, you're not to say anything to anyone about what you were doing, understand?"

"But—"

"Not a word. The damage is doubtless in the billions, if not the trillions. Our insurance won't cover more than a tiny fraction of it."

Theo didn't know Béranger well, but all science administrators worldwide were doubtless cut from the same cloth. And hearing Béranger go on about culpability brought it all into perspective for the young Greek. "Dammit, there was no way we could have known this would happen. There's no expert anywhere who could claim that this was a foreseeable consequence of our experiment. But *something* has occurred that has never been experienced before, and we're the only ones who have even a clue as to what caused it. We've got to investigate this."

"Of course we'll investigate," said Béranger. "I've already got more than forty engineers down in the tunnel. But we've got to be careful, and not just for CERN's sake. You think there aren't going to be lawsuits launched individually and collectively against every single member of your project team? No matter how unpredictable this outcome was, there'll be those who will say it was a result of gross criminal negligence, and we should be personally held accountable."

"Personal lawsuits?'

"That's right." Béranger raised his voice. "Everyone! Everyone, your attention please."

Faces turned toward him.

"This is how we're going to handle this issue," he said to the group. "There will be no mention of CERN's possible involvement to anyone outside the facility. If anyone gets email or phone calls asking about the LHC experiment that was supposed to be performed today, reply that its scheduled running had been delayed until seventeen-thirty, because of a computer glitch, and that, in the aftermath of whatever it was that happened, it didn't get run at all today. Is that clear? Also, absolutely no communication with the press; it all goes through the media office, understand? And for God's sake, no one activates the LHC again without written authorization from me. Is that clear?"

There were nods.

"We'll get through this people," said Béranger. "I promise you that. But we're going to have to work together." He lowered his voice and turned back to Theo. "I want hourly reports on what you've learned." He turned to go.

"Wait," said Theo. "Can you assign one of the secretaries to watch CNN? Somebody should be monitoring this stuff in case anything important comes up."

"Give me a little credit," said Béranger. "I'll have people monitor not just CNN, but the BBC World Service, the French all-news channel, CBC Newsworld, and anything else we can pull off a satellite; we'll save it all on tape. I want an exact record of what's reported as it happens; I don't want anyone inflating damage claims later."

"I'm more interested in clues as to what caused the phenomenon," said Theo.

"We'll look for that, too, of course," said Béranger. "Remember, update me every hour, on the hour."

Theo nodded, and Béranger left. Theo took a second to rub his temples. Damn, but he wished Lloyd were here. "Well," he said at last, to Jake, "I guess we should start a complete diagnostic on every system here in the control center; we need to know if anything malfunctioned. And let's get a group together and see what we can make of the hallucinations."

"I can round some people up," said Jake.

Theo nodded. "Good. We'll use the big conference room on the second floor."

"Okay," said Jake. "I'll meet you there as soon as I can."

Theo nodded, and Jake left. He knew he should spring into action, too, but for a moment he just stood there, still stunned by it all.

Michiko managed to pull herself together enough to try to call Tamiko's father in Tokyo—even though it was not yet 4:00 A.M. there—but the phone lines were jammed. It wasn't the sort of message one wanted to send by email, but, well, if any international communications system was still up and running, it would be the Internet, that child of the Cold War designed to be completely decentralized so that no matter how many of its nodes had been taken out by enemy bombs, messages would still get through. She used one of the school's computers and dashed off a note in English—she had a *kanji* keyboard in her apartment, but none was available here. Lloyd had to actually issue the commands to send the message, though: Michiko broke down again as she was trying to click the appropriate button.

Lloyd didn't know what to say or do. Ordinarily, the death

of a child was the biggest crisis a parent could face, but, well, Michiko was surely not the only one going through such a tragedy today. There was so much death, so much injury, so much destruction. The background of horror didn't make the loss of Tamiko one whit easier to bear, of course, but—

—but there were things that had to be done. Perhaps Lloyd never should have left CERN; it was, after all, his and Theo's experiment that had likely caused all this. Doubtless he'd accompanied Michiko not just out of love for her and concern for Tamiko but also because, at least in part, he'd wanted to run away from whatever had gone wrong.

But now—

Now they had to return to CERN. If anyone was going to figure out what had happened—not just here but, as the radio reports and comments from other parents he'd overheard indicated, all over the world—it would be the people at CERN. They couldn't wait for an ambulance to come to take the body—it might be hours or days. Surely the law was that they couldn't move the body, either, until the police had looked at it, although it seemed highly unlikely that the driver could be held culpable.

At last, though, Madame Severin returned, and she volunteered that she and her staff would look after Tamiko's remains until the police came.

Michiko's face was puffy and red, and her eyes were bloodshot. She'd cried so much that there was nothing left, but every few minutes her body heaved as if she were still sobbing.

Lloyd loved little Tamiko, too—she would have been his stepdaughter. He'd spent so much time comforting Michiko that he hadn't really had a chance to cry himself yet; that would come, he knew—but for now, for *right* now, he had to be strong. He used his index finger to gently lift Michiko's chin. He was all set with the words—duty, responsibility, work to be done, we have to go—but Michiko was strong in her own way, too, and wise, and wonderful, and he loved her to her very soul, and the words didn't need to be said. She managed a small nod, her lips trembling. "I know," she said in English, in a tiny, raw voice. "I know we have to head back to CERN."

He helped her as she walked, one arm around her waist, the other propping her up by the elbow. The keening of sirens had never stopped—ambulances, fire trucks, police cars, warbling and wailing and Doppler shifting, a constant background since just after the phenomenon had occurred. They made their way back to Lloyd's car through the dim evening light— many of the streetlamps were out of commission—and drove along the debris-littered streets to CERN, Michiko hugging herself the whole time.

As they drove, Lloyd thought for a moment about an event his mother had once told him about. He'd been a toddler, too young to remember it himself: the night the lights went out, the great power failure in Eastern North American in 1965. The electricity had been off for hours. His mother had been home alone with him that night; she said everybody who had lived through that incredible blackout would remember for the rest of their lives exactly where they were when the power had failed.

This would be like that. Everyone would remember where they'd been when this blackout—a blackout of a different sort—had occurred.

Everyone who had lived through it, that is.

4

By THE TIME LLOYD AND MICHIKO RETURNED, Jake and Theo had gathered a group of LHC workers together in a conference room on the second floor of the control center.

Most of CERN's staff lived either in the Swiss town of Meyrin (which bordered the east end of the CERN campus), a dozen kilometers farther along in Geneva, or in the French towns of St. Genis or Thoiry, northwest of CERN. But they had come from all over Europe, as well as the rest of the world. The dozen faces now staring at Lloyd were widely varied. Michiko had joined the circle, too, but was detached, her eyes glazed. She simply sat in a chair, rocking slowly back and forth.

Lloyd, as project leader, led the debriefing. He looked from person to person. "Theo told me what CNN's been saying. I guess it's pretty clear that there were a variety of hallucinations worldwide." He took a deep breath. Focus, purpose—that's what he needed now. "Let's see if we can get a handle on exactly what happened. Can we go around the circle? Don't go into any detail; just give us a single sentence about what you saw. If you don't mind, I'll take notes, okay? Olaf, can we start with you?"

"Sure, I guess," said a muscular blond man. "I was at my parents' vacation home. They've got a chalet near Sundsvall."

"In other words," said Lloyd, "it was a place you're familiar with?"

"Oh, yes."

"And how accurate was the vision?"

"Very accurate. It was exactly as I remembered it."

"Was there anyone else beside yourself in the vision?"

"No—which was kind of strange. The only reason I go there is to visit my parents, and they weren't there."

Lloyd thought of the wizened version of himself he'd seen in the mirror. "Did you—did you see yourself?"

"In a mirror or something, you mean? No."

"Okay," said Lloyd. "Thanks."

The woman next to Olaf was middle-aged and black. Lloyd felt awkward; he knew he *should* know her name, but he didn't. Finally, he simply smiled and said, "Next."

"It was downtown Nairobi, I think," said the woman. "At night. It was a warm evening. I thought it was Dinesen Street, but it looked too built-up for that. And there was a McDonald's there."

"Don't they have McDonald's in Kenya?" asked Lloyd.

"Sure, but—I mean, the sign *said* it was McDonald's, but the logo was wrong. You know, instead of the golden arches they had this big M that was all straight lines—very modern looking."

"So Olaf's vision was of a place he'd often been to, but yours was of somewhere you'd never been before, or at least of something you'd never seen before?"

The woman nodded. "I guess that's right."

Michiko was four places away around the circle. Lloyd couldn't tell if she was absorbing any of this or not.

"What about you, Franco?" asked Lloyd.

Franco della Robbia shrugged. "It was Rome, at night.

But—I don't know—it must have been some video game, really. Some VR thing."

Lloyd leaned forward. "Why do you say that?"

"Well, it *was* Rome, all right. Right by the Coliseum. And I was driving a car—except I wasn't driving, not exactly. The car seemed to be working of its own volition. And I couldn't tell for sure about the one I was in, but a lot of the cars were *hovering* maybe twenty centimeters off the ground." He shrugged. "Like I said, a simulation of some sort."

Sven and Antonia, who had both spoken of flying cars earlier in the day, were nodding vigorously. "I saw the same thing," said Sven. "Well, not Rome—but I did see floating cars."

"Me, too," said Antonia.

"Fascinating," said Lloyd. He turned to his young grad student, Jacob Horowitz. "Jake, what did you see?"

Jake's voice was thin, reedy. He ran freckled fingers nervously through his red hair. "The room was pretty nondescript. A lab somewhere. Yellow walls. There was a periodic table on one of the walls, though, and it was labeled in English. And Carly Tompkins was there."

"Who?" said Lloyd.

"Carly Tompkins. At least, I think it was her. She looked a lot older than the last time I'd seen her."

"Who is Carly Tompkins?"

The answer came not from Jake but from Theo Procopides, sitting farther around the circle. "You should know her, Lloyd—she's a fellow Canuck. Carly's a meson researcher; last I heard, she was with TRIUMF."

Jake nodded. "That's right. I've only met her a couple of times, but I'm pretty sure it was her."

Antonia, whose turn would have been next, raised her eyebrows. "If Jake's vision was of Carly, I wonder whether Carly's vision was of Jake?"

Everyone looked at the Italian woman, intrigued. Lloyd shrugged a little. "There's one way to find out. We could phone her." He looked at Jake. "Do you have her number?"

Jake shook his head. "Like I said, I hardly know her. We went to some of the same seminars at the last APS meeting, and I sat in on her paper on chromodynamics."

"If she's in APS," said Antonia, "she'll be in the directory." She waddled across the room and rummaged on a shelf until she found a slim volume with a plain cardboard cover. She riffled through it. "Here she is," said Antonia. "Home and work numbers."

"I—ah, I don't want to call her," said Jake.

Lloyd was surprised by his reluctance, but didn't pursue the matter. "That's all right. You shouldn't speak to her anyway. I want to see if she spontaneously comes up with your name."

"You may not be able to get through," said Sven. "The phones have been jammed with people trying to check on family and friends—not to mention all the lines knocked down by motorists."

"It's worth a try," said Theo. He got up, walked across the room, and took the directory from Antonia. But then he looked at the phone, and looked back at the numbers in the directory. "How do you dial Canada from here?"

"It's the same as dialing the U.S.," said Lloyd. "The country code's the same: zero-one."

Theo's finger danced on the keypad, entering a long string of digits. Then, for the benefit of his audience, he held up fingers to indicate how many rings had occurred. One. Two. Three. Four—

"Oh, hello. Carly Tompkins, please. Hi, Dr. Tompkins. I'm calling from Geneva, from CERN. Look, there's a bunch of us here. Is it okay if I put you on the speakerphone?"

A sleepy voice: "—if you like. What's going on?"

"We want to know what your hallucination was when you blacked out."

"What? Is this some kind of prank?"

Theo looked at Lloyd. "She doesn't know."

Lloyd cleared his voice, then spoke up. "Dr. Tompkins, this is Lloyd Simcoe. I'm also a Canadian, although I was with the D-Zero Group at Fermilab until 2007, and for the last two years I've been here at CERN." He paused, not sure what to say next. Then: "What time is it there?"

"Just before noon." The sound of a stifled yawn. "Today is my day off; I was sleeping in. What's this all about?"

"So you haven't been up yet today?"

"No."

"Do you have a TV in the room you're in?" asked Lloyd.

"Yes."

"Turn it on. Look at the news."

She sounded irritated. "I can hardly get the Swiss news here in British Columbia."

"It doesn't have to be the Swiss news. Put on any news channel."

The whole room heard Tompkins sighing into the mouthpiece of her phone. "All right. Just a second."

They could hear what was presumably CBC Newsworld muffled in the background. After what seemed an eternity, Tompkins returned to the handset.

"Oh, my God," she said into the phone. "Oh, my God."

"But you slept through it all?" said Theo.

"I did, I'm afraid," said the voice from half a world away. She paused for a second. "Why did you call me?"

"Has the news program you've been watching mentioned the visions yet?"

"Joel Gotlib is going on about that now," she said, presumably referring to a Canadian newscaster. "It sounds crazy. Anyway, nothing like that happened to me."

"All right," said Lloyd. "We're sorry to have disturbed your sleep, Dr. Tompkins. We'll be—"

"Wait," said Theo.

Lloyd looked at the younger man.

"Dr. Tompkins, my name is Theo Procopides. We've met, I think, once or twice at conferences."

"If you say so," said Tompkins's voice.

"Dr. Tompkins," continued Theo. "I'm like you—I didn't see anything either. No vision, no dream, no nothing."

"Dream?" said Tompkins's voice. "Well, now that you mention it, I guess I did have a dream. Funny thing was it was in color—I never dream in color. But I remember the guy in it had red hair."

Theo looked disappointed—he'd clearly been pleased to find he wasn't alone. But everyone else's eyebrows flew up, and they turned to look at Jake.

"Not only that," said Carly, "he had red underwear, too."

Young Jake now turned the aforementioned color. "Red *underwear?*" repeated Lloyd.

"That's right."

"Did you know this man?" asked Lloyd.

"No, I don't think so."

"He didn't look like anyone you'd ever met before?"

"I don't think so."

Lloyd leaned closer to the speakerphone. "What about—what about the *father* of someone you'd met before? Did he look like somebody's father?"

"What are you getting at?" asked Tompkins.

Lloyd sighed then looked around the room, seeing if anyone was going to object to him going on. No one did. "Does the name Jacob Horowitz mean anything to you?"

"I don't—oh, wait. Oh, right. Sure, sure. *That's* who he reminded me of. Yeah, it was Jacob Horowitz, but, geez, he should take better care of himself. He looked like he'd aged decades since I last saw him."

Antonia made a small gasp. Lloyd felt his heart pounding.

"Look," said Carly. "I want to make sure my family members are okay. My parents are in Winnipeg—I've got to get going."

"Can we call you back in a bit?" asked Lloyd. "You see, we've got Jacob Horowitz here, and his vision seems to match yours—sort of, anyway. He said he was in a lab, but . . ."

"Yes, that's right. It was a lab."

Incredulity crept into Lloyd's voice. "And he was in his underwear?"

"Well, not by the end of the vision . . . Look, I've got to go."

"Thanks," said Lloyd. "Bye."

"Bye."

Swiss dial tone issued from the speaker. Theo reached over and shut it off.

Jacob Horowitz still looked decidedly embarrassed. Lloyd thought about telling him that probably half of all the physicists he knew had done it at one time or another in a lab, but the young man looked like he'd have a nervous breakdown if anyone said anything to him just now. Lloyd started to shift his gaze around the circle again. "All right," he said. "All right. I'm going to say it, because I know you're all thinking it. Whatever happened here caused some sort of time effect. The visions weren't hallucinations; they were actual insights into the future. The fact that Jacob Horowitz and Carly Tompkins both apparently saw the same thing strongly suggests that."

"But Raoul's vision was psychedelic, didn't someone say that?" said Theo.

"Yeah," said Raoul. "Like a dream, or something."

"Like a dream," repeated Michiko. Her eyes were still red, but she was reacting to the outside world.

That was all she said, though, but, after a moment Antonia caught her meaning and elaborated. "Michiko's right," said the Italian physicist. "No mystery there—at whatever point in the future the visions are of, Raoul will be asleep, and having an actual dream."

"But this is crazy," said Theo. "Look, I didn't have any vision."

"What *did* you experience?" asked Sven, who hadn't heard Theo describe it before.

"It was—I don't know, like a discontinuity, I guess. Suddenly, it was two minutes later; I had no sensation of passing time, and nothing at all like a vision." Theo folded his arms defiantly across his broad chest. "How do you explain that?"

There was quiet around the room. The pained expressions

on a lot of faces made clear to Lloyd that they'd gotten it, too, but no one wanted to voice it aloud. Finally, Lloyd shrugged a little. "Simple," he said, looking at his brilliant, arrogant, twenty-seven-year old associate, "in twenty years—or whatever time the visions are of . . ." He paused, then spread his hands. "I'm sorry, Theo, but in twenty years, you're dead."

5

❧

THE VISION LLOYD MOST WANTED TO HEAR about was Michiko's. But she was still—as she doubtless would be for a very long time—completely out of it. When it came to her turn in the circle, Lloyd skipped over her. He wished he could just take her home, but it was doubtless best for her to not be alone right now, and there was no way that Lloyd, or anyone else, could get away to be with her.

None of the other visions relayed by the little sampling of people in the conference room overlapped—there was no indication that they were of the same time or the same reality, although it did seem that almost everyone was enjoying a day off or a holiday. But there *was* the question of Jake Horowitz and Carly Tompkins—separated by almost half the planet and yet apparently seeing each other. Of course, it could be coincidence. Still, if the visions did match, not just in their broad strokes, but in precise details, that *would* be significant.

Lloyd and Michiko had retired to Lloyd's office. Michiko was curled up tightly in one of the chairs, and she had Lloyd's windbreaker pulled over her like a blanket. Lloyd picked up the handset on his desk phone and dialed. *"Bonjour,"* he said.

"La police de Genève? Je m'appelle Lloyd Simcoe; je suis avec CERN."

"Oui, Monsieur Simcoe," said a male voice. He switched to English; Swiss often did that in response to Lloyd's accent. "What can we do for you?"

"I know you're terribly busy—"

"An understatement, *monsieur*. We are, as you say, bogged."

Swamped, thought Lloyd. "But I'm hoping one of your witness examiners is free. We have a theory about the visions, and we need the help of someone proficient at taking testimony."

"I'll put you through to the right department," said the voice.

While he was on hold, Theo poked his head through the office door. "The BBC World Service is reporting that many people had matching visions," he said. "For instance, many married couples, even if they weren't in the same room at the time of the phenomenon, reported similar experiences."

Lloyd nodded at this bit of information. "Still, there's always a possibility, I guess, for whatever reason, of collusion, or, Carly and Jake notwithstanding, that synchronization of visions was a localized phenomenon. But . . ."

He left it unsaid—after all, it *was* Theo the visionless he was speaking to. But if Carly Tompkins and Jacob Horowitz— she in Vancouver, he near Geneva—really did see the exact same thing, then there would be little doubt that all the visions were of the same one future, mosaic pieces of tomorrow . . . a tomorrow that did not include Theo Procopides.

"Tell me about the room you were in," said the witness examiner, a middle aged Swiss woman. She had a datapad in front of her, and was wearing a loose polo shirt; last in fashion in the late 1980s, they were cycling back into popularity.

Jacob Horowitz closed his eyes, shutting out distractions, trying to recall every detail. "It's a lab of some sort. Yellow walls. Fluorescent lights. Formica counter tops. A periodic table on the wall."

"And is there anybody else in this lab?"

Jake nodded. God, why did the examiner have to be female? "Yes. There's a woman—a white woman, with dark hair. She looks to be about forty-five or so."

"And what is she wearing, this woman?"

Jake swallowed. "Nothing . . ."

The Swiss witness examiner had left, and Lloyd and Michiko were now comparing reports of Jacob's and Carly's visions; Carly had agreed to be similarly examined by the Vancouver police, and the report of that interview had been emailed to CERN.

In the intervening hours, Michiko had rallied a bit. She was clearly trying to focus, to go on, to help with the larger crisis, but every few minutes she would fade away and her eyes would go moist. Still, she managed to read through the two transcripts without getting the paper overly wet.

"There's no doubt," she said. "They match in every particular. They were in the same room."

Lloyd tried a small smile. "Kids," he said. He had only known Michiko for two years; they'd never made love in a lab—but in his grad-student days, Lloyd and his then girlfriend, Pamela Ridgley, had certainly heated up a few countertops at Harvard. But then he shook his head in wonder. "A glimpse of the future. Fascinating." He paused. "I imagine some people are going to get rich off this."

Michiko shrugged a bit. "Eventually, maybe. Those who happened to be looking at stock reports in the future might become wealthy—decades from now. That's a long time to wait for it to all pay off."

Lloyd was quiet for a moment, then: "You haven't told me what you saw yet—what your vision was."

Michiko looked away. "No," she said, "I haven't."

Lloyd touched her cheek gently, but said nothing.

"At the time—at the time I was having the vision, it seemed wonderful," she began. "I mean, I was disoriented and confused about what was going on. But the vision itself was joyous." She managed a wan smile. "Except now after what's happened . . ."

Again, Lloyd didn't push. He sat, outwardly patient.

"It was late at night," Michiko said at last. "I was in Japan; I'm sure it was a Japanese house. I was in a little girl's bedroom, sitting on the side of the bed. And this girl, maybe seven or eight, was sitting up in bed, and she was talking with me. She was a beautiful girl, but she wasn't—she wasn't—"

If the visions were of a time decades in the future, of course she wasn't Tamiko. Lloyd nodded gently, absolving her of having to finish the thought. Michiko sniffled. "But—but she *was* my daughter; she must have been. A daughter I haven't had yet. She was holding my hand, and she called me *okaasan;* that's Japanese for 'mommy.' It was like I was putting her to bed, wishing her good night."

"Your daughter . . ." said Lloyd.

"Well, *our* daughter, I'm sure," said Michiko. "Yours and mine."

"What were you doing in Japan?" asked Lloyd.

"I don't know; visiting family, I guess. My uncle Masayuki lives in Kyoto. Except for the fact that we had a daughter, I didn't really get any sense that it was in the future."

"This child, did she—"

Lloyd cut himself off. What he'd wanted to ask was boorish, crude. "Did she have slanted eyes?" Or maybe he would have caught himself in time and phrased it more elegantly: "Did she have epicanthic folds?" But Michiko wouldn't have understood. She'd have thought some prejudice underlay Lloyd's question, some silly misgivings about miscegenation. But that wasn't it. Lloyd didn't care if their eventual children were occidental or oriental in appearance. They could as easily be one as the other, or, of course, a mixture of the two, and he'd love them just the same, assuming—

Assuming, of course, that they were *his* children.

The visions seemed to be of a time perhaps two decades in the future. And in his vision, which he hadn't yet shared with Michiko, he was somewhere, maybe New England, with another woman. A white woman. And Michiko was in Kyoto, Japan, with a daughter who might be Asian or might be Caucasian or might be something in between, all depending on who her father was.

This child, did she—

"Did she what?" asked Michiko.

"Nothing," said Lloyd, looking away.

"What about your vision?" asked Michiko. "What did you see?"

Lloyd took a deep breath. He'd have to tell her sometime, he supposed, and—

"Lloyd, Michiko—you guys should come on down to the lounge." It was Theo's voice; he had just stuck his head in the door again. "We just recorded something off CNN that you'll want to see."

Lloyd, Michiko, and Theo entered the lounge. Four other people were already there. White-haired Lou Waters was jerking up and down on screen; the lounge VCR was an old unit—some staff member's hand-me-down—and didn't have a great pause function.

"Ah, good," said Raoul, as they entered. "Look at this." He touched the pause key on the remote, and Waters sprang into action.

"—David Houseman has more on this story. David?"

The picture changed to show CNN's David Houseman, standing in front of a wall of antique clocks—even with a breaking story, CNN still strove for interesting visuals.

"Thanks, Lou," said Houseman. "Most people's visions of course had no time reference in them, but enough people were in rooms with clocks or calendars on the wall, or reading electronic newspapers—there didn't seem to be any paper ones left—that we've been able to conjecture a date. It seems that the visions were of a time twenty-one years, six months, two days, and two hours ahead of the moment at which the visions occurred: the visions portray the period from 2:21 to 2:23 P.M. Eastern Time on Wednesday, October 23, 2030. That assumes the occasional aberrations are explicable: some people seemed to be reading newspapers dated October 22, 2030, or even earlier—presumably they were reading old editions. And the time references, of course, depend a great deal on what time zone the person happens to be in. We're assuming that the majority of people will still live in the same time zone two decades from now that they happen to live in today, and those that report times off by a whole number of hours from what we'd expect were in some other time zone—"

Raoul hit the pause key again.

"There it is," said Raoul. "A concrete number. Whatever we did here somehow caused the consciousness of the human race to jump ahead twenty-one years for a period of two minutes."

Theo returned to his office, the darkness of night visible through his window. All this talk of visions was disturbing—especially since he himself hadn't had one. Could Lloyd be right? Could Theo be dead a mere twenty-one years from now? He was only twenty-seven, for God's sake; in two decades, he'd still be well shy of fifty. He didn't smoke—not much of a statement for any of the North Americans to make, but still an achievement among Greeks. He worked out regularly. Why on earth should he be dead so soon? There had to be another explanation for him having no vision.

His phone bleeped. Theo picked up the handset. "Hello?"

"Hello," said a female voice, in English. "Is this, ah, Theodosios Procopides?" She stumbled over the name.

"Yes."

"My name is Kathleen DeVries," said the woman. "I've been mulling over whether to phone you. I'm calling from Johannesburg."

"Johannesburg? You mean in South Africa?"

"For the time being, anyway," she said. "If the visions are to be believed, it's going to be officially renamed Azania sometime in the next twenty-one years."

Theo waited silently for her to go on. After a moment, she did. "And it's the visions that I'm calling about. You see, mine involved you."

Theo felt his heart racing. What wonderful news! Maybe he hadn't had a vision of his own for whatever reason, but this woman had seen him twenty-one years hence. Of course he had to be alive then; of course, Lloyd was wrong when he said Theo would be dead.

"Yes?" Theo said breathlessly.

"Umm, I'm sorry to have bothered you," said DeVries. "Can I—may I ask what your own vision showed?"

Theo let out air. "I didn't have one," he said.

"Oh. Oh, I am sorry to hear that. But—well, then, I guess it wasn't a mistake."

"What wasn't a mistake?"

"My own vision. I was here, in my home, in Johannesburg, reading the newspaper over dinner—except it wasn't on newsprint. It was on this thing that looked like a flat plastic sheet; some sort of computerized reader screen, I think. Anyway, the article I was reading happened to be—well, I'm sorry there's no other way to say it. It was about your death."

Theo had once read a Lord Dunsany story about a man who fervently wished to see tomorrow's newspaper today, and when he finally got his wish, was stunned to discover it contained his own obituary. The shock of seeing that was enough to kill him, news which would of course be reported in the next day's edition. That was it; that was all—a zinger, a punch line. But this . . . this wasn't tomorrow's paper; it was a paper two decades hence.

"My death," repeated Theo, as though those two words had somehow been missed in his English classes.

"Yes, that's right."

Theo rallied a bit. "Look, how do I know this isn't some scam or prank?"

"I'm sorry; I knew I shouldn't have called. I'll be—"

"No, no, no. Don't hang up. In fact, please let me get your name and number. The damned call display is just showing 'Out of Area.' You should let me phone you back; this call must be costing you a fortune."

"My name, as I said, is Kathleen DeVries. I'm a nurse at a senior citizens' home here." She told him her phone number. "But, really, I'm glad to pay for the call. Honestly, I don't want anything from you, and I'm not trying to trick you. But, well—look, I see people die all the time. We lose about one a week here at the home, but they're mostly in their eighties or nineties or even their hundreds. But you—you're going to be just forty-eight when you die, and that's way too young. I thought by calling you up, by letting you know, maybe you could somehow prevent your own death."

Theo was quiet for several seconds, then, "So, does the—the obituary say what I died of?" For one bizarre moment, Theo was kind of pleased that his passing had been worthy of note in international newspapers. He almost asked if the first two words in the article happened to be "Nobel laureate." "I know I should cut down on my cholesterol; was it a heart attack?"

There was silence for several seconds. "Umm, Dr. Procopides, I'm sorry, I guess I should have been more clear. It's not an obituary I was reading; it's a news story." He could hear her swallow. "A news story about your murder."

Theo fell silent. He could have repeated the word back to her incredulously. But there was no point.

He was twenty-seven; he was in good health. As he'd been thinking a few moments ago, of course he wouldn't be dead of natural causes in a mere twenty-one years. But—murder?

"Dr. Procopides? Are you still there?"

"Yes." For the time being.

"I'm—I'm sorry, Dr. Procopides. I know this must come as quite a shock."

Theo was quiet for a few moments longer, then: "The article you were reading—does it say who kills me?"

"I'm afraid not. It's an unsolved crime, apparently."

"Well, what *does* the article say?"

"I've written down as much of it as I remember; I can email you it, but, well, here, let me read it to you. Remember, this is a reconstruction; I think it's pretty accurate, but I can't guarantee every word." She paused, cleared her throat, then went on. "The headline was, 'Physicist Shot Dead.'"

Shot, thought Theo. God.

DeVries went on. "The dateline was Geneva. It said, 'Theodosios Procopides, a Greek physicist working at CERN, the European center for particle physics, was found shot to death today. Procopides, who received his Ph.D. from Oxford, was director of the Tachyon-Tardyon Collider at—"

"Say that again," said Theo.

"The Tachyon-Tardyon Collider," said DeVries. She was mispronouncing "tachyon," saying it with a CH blend instead of a K sound. "I'd never heard those words before."

"There's no such collider," said Theo. "At least, not yet. Please, go on."

"'. . . director of the Tachyon-Tardyon Collider at CERN. Dr. Procopides had been with CERN for twenty-three years. No motive has been suggested for the killing, but robbery has been ruled out, as Dr. Procopides's wallet was found on him. The physicist was apparently shot sometime between noon and 1:00 P.M. local time yesterday. The investigation is continuing. Dr. Procopides is survived by his . . .'"

"Yes? Yes?"

"I'm sorry, that's all it said."

"You mean your vision ended before you finished reading the article?"

There was a small silence. "Well, not exactly. The rest of the article was off-screen, and instead of touching the pagedown button—I could clearly see such a button on the side of the reading device—I went on to select another article." She paused. "I'm sorry, Dr. Procopides. *I*—the 2009 me—was interested in what the rest of the story said, but the 2030 version didn't seem to care. I did try to will her—to will *me*—to touch the page-down control, but it didn't work."

"So you don't know who killed me, or why?"

"I *am* sorry."

"And the paper you were reading—you're sure that it was the then-current one? You know, the October 23, 2030, one."

"Actually, no. There was a—what would you call it? A status line? There was a status line at the top of the reader that said the date and the name of the paper quite prominently: *The Johannesburg Star*, Tuesday, October 22, 2030. So I guess it was yesterday's paper, so to speak." She paused. "I'm sorry to be the bearer of bad news."

Theo was quiet for a time, trying to digest all this. It was hard enough dealing with the fact that he might be dead in a mere twenty years, but the idea that someone might *kill* him was almost too much to bear.

"Ms. DeVries, thank you," he said. "If you recall any other details—anything at all—please, please let me know. And please do fax me the transcript you mentioned." He gave her his fax number.

"I will," she said. "I—I'm sorry; you sound like a nice young man. I hope you can figure out who did it—who's *going* to do it—and find a way to prevent it."

6

⬡

IT WAS NOW ALMOST MIDNIGHT. LLOYD AND Michiko were walking down the corridor toward his office when they heard Jake Horowitz's voice calling out from an open door. "Hey, Lloyd, have a look at this."

They entered the room. Young Jake was standing next to a TV set. Its screen was filled with snow.

"Snow," said Lloyd, helpfully, as he crossed over to stand beside Jake.

"Indeed."

"What channel are you trying to get?"

"No channel. I'm playing back a tape."

"Of what?"

"This happens to be the security camera at the main gate-house to the CERN campus." He hit the eject button; the VHS tape popped out. He replaced it with another cassette. "And this is the security camera at the Microcosm." He hit play; the screen again filled with snow.

"Are you sure this is the right kind of VCR?" Switzerland used the PAL recording format, and, although multistandard machines were common, there were a few NTSC-only VCRs at CERN.

Jake nodded. "I'm sure. Took me a while to find one that would show what was actually on the tape, too—most VCRs just go to solid blue if there's no picture signal."

"Well, if it's the right kind of VCR, then there must be something wrong with the tapes." Lloyd frowned. "Maybe there *was* an electromagnetic pulse associated with the—the whatever it was; it could have wiped the tapes."

"That was my first thought, too," said Jake. "But watch this." He hit the remote's reverse button. The snow speeded up its dancing on screen, and the letters REV—the abbreviation was the same in many European languages—appeared in the upper right corner. After about half a minute, a picture suddenly appeared, showing the Microcosm Exhibit, CERN's gallery devoted to explaining particle physics to tourists. Jake rewound the tape some more then took his finger off the button.

"See?" he said. "That's earlier on the tape—look at the time stamp." In the center of the screen near the bottom, a digital readout was superimposed on the image, with the time incrementing: "16h58m22s," "16h58m23s," "16h58m24s" . . .

"About a minute and a half before the phenomenon began," said Jake. "If there'd been something like an EMP, it would have wiped what was already on the tape, too."

"So what are you saying?" asked Lloyd. "The tape goes all snowy right at the beginning of the phenomenon?" He liked Jake's word for what had happened.

"Yes—and it picks up again exactly one minute and forty-three seconds later. It's the same on all the tapes I've checked: one minute and forty-three seconds of static."

"Lloyd, Jake—come quick!" It was Michiko's voice; the two men turned around to see her beckoning to them from the doorway. They ran after her into the room next door—the lounge, which had its own TV set, still showing CNN.

"—and of course there were hundreds of thousands of videos made during the period when people's minds were elsewhere," said anchor Petra Davies. "Security-camera footage, home-video cameras left running, tapes from TV studios—including our own archival tapes made right here at CNN, which the FCC requires us to produce—and more. We'd assumed they would clearly show everyone in them blacking out, and bodies collapsing to the ground—"

Lloyd and Jake exchanged a glance. "But," continued Davies, "none of them show anything. Or, more precisely, they show nothing but snow—black and white flecks, roiling on the screen. As far as we can tell, every video made anywhere in the world during the Flashforward shows snow for precisely one minute and forty-three seconds. Likewise, our other recording devices, such as those hooked up to the weather instruments we use in making forecasts, recorded no data during the period in which everyone blacked out. If anyone watching this *does* have a tape or recording made during that time that shows a picture, we'd like to hear about it. You can phone us toll-free at . . ."

"Incredible," said Lloyd. "It *does* make you wonder just exactly what was going on during all that time."

Jake nodded. "That it does."

" 'Flashforward,' eh?" said Lloyd, savoring the term the newscaster had used. "That's not a bad name for it."

Jake nodded. "It certainly beats 'the CERN disaster,' or anything like that."

Lloyd frowned. "That it does."

Theo leaned back in his office chair, hands behind his head, staring at the constellations of holes in the acoustic ceiling tiles, thinking about what that DeVries woman had said.

It wasn't like knowing you were going to die in an accident. If you were forewarned that you'd be hit by a car on such-and-such a street at such-and-such a time, well, then you simply had to avoid being at that place at that moment, and—*voilà!*—crisis averted. But if someone was hell-bent on murdering you, it would happen sooner or later. Just not being here—or wherever the murder was going to take place; the story from the *Johannesburg Star* didn't actually mention the precise location—on October 21, 2030, wouldn't necessarily be enough to save Theo.

Dr. Procopides is survived by his . . .

Survived by his what? His parents? Poppa would be eighty-two then, and Momma would be seventy-nine. Theo's father had suffered a heart attack a few years ago, but had been scrupulous ever since about his cholesterol, giving up his *saganaki* and the feta-cheese salads that he so loved. Sure, they could still be alive then.

How would Poppa take it? A father isn't supposed to out-live his son. Would Poppa think he'd already lived a good, long time? Would he give up on life, passing on within a few more months, leaving Momma to go on all alone? Theo certainly hoped his parents would be alive in twenty-one years, but . . .

Dr. Procopides is survived by his . . .

. . . by his wife and children?

That's what they usually say in obituaries. By his wife—his wife *Anthoula*, perhaps, a nice Greek girl. That would make Poppa happy.

Except . . .

Except Theo didn't know any nice Greek girls—or any nice girls of any nationality. At least—a thought came up, but he fought it down—at least, not any who were free.

He had devoted himself to his work. First to getting grades good enough to go to Oxford. Next to getting his doctorate. Then to getting assigned here. Oh, there'd been women, of course—American schoolgirls back in Athens, one-night stands with other students, and even once, when in Denmark, a hooker. But he'd always thought there would be time later for love, a wife, children.

But when would that time come?

He had indeed wondered if the article would start "Nobel laureate." It didn't, but he *had* wondered—and, if he were hon-est with himself, it was a serious bit of wondering. A Nobel meant immortality; it meant being remembered forever.

The LHC experiment that he and Lloyd had spent years crafting should have produced the Higgs; if they had produced that, the Nobel surely would have followed. But they hadn't made the breakthrough.

The breakthrough—as if he'd have been content with only one.

Dead in twenty-one years. Who would remember him?

It was all so crazy. So unbelievable.

He was Theodosios Procopides, for God's sake. He was immortal.

Of course he was. Of course he was. What twenty-seven-year-old was not?

A wife. Children. Surely the obituary had mentioned those. Surely if Ms. DeVries had only paged down, she would have seen their names, and maybe their ages.

But wait—wait!

How many pages in a typical big-city newspaper? Two hundred, say. How many readers? Typical circulation of a big daily might be half-a-million copies. Of course, DeVries had said she was reading *yesterday's* newspaper. Still, she couldn't have been the only one looking at that article during the two-minute glimpse of the future.

And besides, Theo would apparently be killed here in Switzerland—the article had listed a Geneva dateline—and yet the story had made a South African newspaper. Which meant it must have made other newspapers and newsgroups all over the world, possibly with different accounts of the events. Certainly the *Tribune de Genève* would have a more-detailed article. There had to be hundreds—maybe thousands—of people who had read reports of his death.

He could advertise for them, on the Internet and in major newspapers. Find out more—and find out, for sure, whether there was any truth to what this DeVries woman had said.

•　　　•　　　•

"Look at this," said Jake Horowitz. He plunked his datapad down on Lloyd's desk; it was showing a web page.

"What is it?"

"Stuff from the United States Geological Survey. Seismograph readings."

"Yeah?"

"Look at the readings for earlier today," said Jake.

"Oh, my."

"Exactly. For almost two minutes, starting at seventeen hundred hours our time, the recorders detected nothing at all. Either they registered zero disturbances—which is impossible, the Earth is always trembling slightly, even if just from tidal interactions with the moon—or they registered no data at all. It's just like the video cameras: no record of what was actually happening during those two minutes. And I've checked with various national weather services. Their weather instruments— wind speed, temperature, air pressure, and so on—recorded nothing during the Flashforward. And NASA and the ESA report dead periods in their satellite telemetry during that two-minute period, too."

"How could that be?" asked Lloyd.

"I don't know," said Jake, running a hand through his red hair. "But somehow every camera, every sensor, every recording instrument anywhere in the world simply stopped registering while the Flashforward was occurring."

Theo sat at his desk in his office, a plastic Donald Duck peering down at him from atop the monitor, thinking of how to phrase what he wanted to say. He decided to be simple and direct. After all, he'd need to place the information in the form of a classified ad in hundreds of newspapers worldwide; it would cost a fortune if he wasn't concise. He had three keyboards—a French AZERTY, an English QWERTY, and a Greek one. He was using the English one:

> Theodosios Procopides, a native of Athens, working at
> CERN, will be murdered Monday, October 21, 2030. If

your vision related to this crime, please contact procopi-des@cern.ch.

He thought about leaving it at that, but then added a final line: "I am hoping to prevent my own death."

Theo could translate it into Greek and French himself; in theory, his computer could translate it into other languages for him, but if there was one thing that his time at CERN had taught him it was that computer translations were often in-accurate—he still remembered the horrible Christmas-banquet incident. No, he would enlist the aid of various people at CERN to help him—and also to advise him which newspapers were significant in which countries.

But one thing he could do immediately: post his note to various newsgroups. He did that before going home to bed.

Finally, at one in the morning, Lloyd and Michiko left CERN. Again, they abandoned her Toyota in the parking lot—it was hardly unusual for people at CERN to pull all-nighters.

Michiko worked for Sumitomo Electric; she was an engineer specializing in superconducting-accelerator technology, on long-term assignment to CERN, which had bought several components for the LHC from Sumitomo. Her employer had provided her, and Tamiko, with a wonderful apartment on Geneva's Right Bank. Lloyd was less well paid, and didn't have a housing allowance; his apartment was in the town of St. Genis. He liked living in France while working mostly in Switzerland; CERN had its own special border crossing that allowed its staff to pass between the two countries without worrying about showing passports.

Lloyd rented the apartment furnished; although he'd been at CERN two years, he didn't think of it as being his home, and the idea of buying furniture, which would be a bear to import back to North America, didn't make sense to him. The provided furnishings were a bit old-fashioned and ornate for his tastes, but at least everything coordinated well: the dark wood, the burnt-orange carpet, the dark-red walls. It had a cozy, warm feel, at the expense of making the place look smaller than it really was. But he had no emotional attachment to this apartment—he'd never been married or lived with anyone of the opposite sex, and, in the twenty-five years since he'd moved out on his own, he'd had eleven different addresses. Still, tonight there was no question that they should go to his place, not hers. There would be too much of Tamiko at the flat in Geneva, too much to face so soon.

Lloyd's apartment was in a forty-year-old building, heated by electric radiators. They sat on the couch. He had an arm around her shoulder, and he was trying to comfort her. "I'm sorry," said Lloyd.

Michiko's face was still puffy. She had periods of calm, but the tears would suddenly start again and they seemed to go on forever. She nodded slightly.

"There was no way to foresee this," said Lloyd. "No way to prevent it."

But Michiko shook her head. "What kind of mother am I?" she said. "I took my daughter half a world away from her grandparents, from her home."

Lloyd said nothing. What could he say? That it had seemed like a wonderful thing to do? Getting to study in Europe, even if only at age eight, would have been a terrific experience for any child. Surely bringing Tamiko to Switzerland had been the right idea.

"I should try to call Hiroshi," said Michiko. Hiroshi was her ex-husband. "Make sure he got the e-mail."

Lloyd thought about observing that Hiroshi probably wouldn't evince any more interest in his daughter now that she was dead than he had when she was alive. Even though he'd never met him, Lloyd hated Hiroshi, on many different levels. He hated that Hiroshi had made his Michiko sad—not just once or twice, but for years on end. It pained Lloyd to think of her trudging through life without a smile on her face, with no joy in her heart. He also, if he were brutally honest with himself, hated Hiroshi because he had had her first. But

Lloyd didn't say anything. He simply stroked Michiko's lustrous black hair.

"He didn't want me to bring her here," said Michiko, sniffling. "He wanted her to stay in Tokyo, go to a Japanese school." She wiped her eyes. " 'A proper school,' he said." A pause. "If only I'd listened to him."

"The phenomenon *was* worldwide," said Lloyd gently. "She would have been no safer in Tokyo than in Geneva. You can't blame yourself."

"I don't," said Michiko. "I—"

But she stopped herself. Lloyd couldn't help wondering if she was going to say, "I blame you."

Michiko hadn't come to CERN to be with Lloyd, but there was no doubt in either of their minds that he was the reason she'd decided to stay. She'd asked Sumitomo to keep her on here, after the equipment she was responsible for was installed. For the first two months, Tamiko had been back in Japan, but Michiko, once she'd decided to extend her stay, had arranged to have her daughter brought to Europe.

Lloyd had loved Tamiko, too. He knew the lot of stepfather was always a difficult one, but the two of them had hit it off. Not all youngsters are pleased when a divorced parent finds a new partner; Lloyd's own sister had broken up with her boyfriend because her two young sons didn't care for the new man in her life. But Tamiko had once told Lloyd that she liked him because he made her mother smile.

Lloyd looked at his fiancée. She was so sad, he wondered if he'd ever see her smile again. He felt like crying himself, but there was something stupid and masculine that wouldn't let him do that while she was also crying. He held it in.

Lloyd wondered what impact this was going to have on their upcoming marriage. He had brought no other agenda to his proposal than simply that he loved Michiko, totally and completely. And he did not doubt Michiko's love for him, but, nonetheless, to some degree, there had to have been a secondary reason for Michiko to want to marry him. No matter how modern and liberated a woman she was, and, by Japanese standards at least, Michiko was *very* modern, she still had, in some measure, to have been looking for a father for her child, someone who would have helped her to bring up Tamiko, who would have provided a male presence in her life.

Had Michiko really been in the market for a husband? Oh, yes, she and Lloyd were terrific together—but many couples were terrific together without marriage or any long-term commitment. Would she still wish to marry him now?

And, of course, there was that other woman, the one in his vision, the proof, vivid and full-blown . . .

The proof that, just as his own parents' marriage had ended in divorce, so, too, would the one he was supposed to enter with Michiko.

7

❖

Day Two: Wednesday, April 22, 2009

NEWS DIGEST

The death count keeps rising after yesterday's Flashforward phenomenon. In Caracas, Venezuela, Guillermo Garmendia, 36, apparently disconsolate over the death of his wife, Maria, 34, shot and killed his two sons, Ramon, 7, and Salvador, 5, then turned the gun on himself.

•

The government of Queensland, Australia, has declared a formal state of emergency, following the Flashforward.

•

Bondplus Corporation of San Rafael, California, is in a great state of turmoil. The chief executive officer, chief financial officer, and entire board of directors perished when their corporate jet crashed on take-off during the Flashforward. Bondplus was in the middle of defending itself from a hostile takeover bid from arch-rival Jasmine Adhesives.

•

A one-billion-dollar (Canadian) class-action suit has been launched against the Toronto Transit Commission, on behalf of transit riders injured or killed during the Flashforward. The suit claims that the Commission was negligent in not providing padded flooring at the bottom of staircases and escalators to protect people in the event of a fall.

•

A massive sell-off of Japanese yen has precipitated yet another crisis in the Japanese economy, following indications from the Flashforward that the yen will be worth only half its current value against the U.S. dollar in 2030.

The race was on.

Theo had his head bent down, poring over the computer logs strewn across his desk. There had to be an answer—a rational explanation for what had happened. Throughout the CERN campus, physicists were investigating, exploring, and debating possible explanations.

The door to Theo's office opened and Michiko Komura came in, some pieces of paper held in her hand. "I hear you're looking for information about your own murder," she said.

Theo felt his heart rate increasing. "Do you know something?"

"Me?" Michiko frowned. "No. No, sorry."

"Oh." A beat. "Then why bring it up?"

"Well, I was thinking, that's all. You can't be the only one desperate to know more about his or her future."

"I guess."

"And, well, it seems to me there should be a central method for coordinating that. I mean, I saw your newsgroup posting this morning—and it was hardly the only one like that.''

"Oh?"

"Their are tons of people looking for information about their futures. Not everyone is looking for facts about their own deaths, of course, but—well, here, let me read some of them to you."

She sat down and began to read from the pieces of paper. " 'Anyone with information about the future whereabouts of Marcus Whyte, please contact . . .' 'University student seeking career advice: if your vision indicated anything about which jobs are in demand in 2030, please let me know.' 'Information sought about the future of the International Committee of the Red Cross . . .' "

"Fascinating," said Theo. He knew what Michiko was doing: burying herself in something—anything—rather than thinking about the loss of Tamiko.

"Isn't it, though?" she said. "And there are also a bunch of display ads on the Web already—come-ons from big corporations, looking for information that might help them. I didn't know you could get a banner ad placed so quickly, but I guess almost anything's possible if you're willing to pay for it." She paused and looked away; doubtless a thought of Tamiko had come to the front of her mind—some things, unfortunately, were impossible at any price. After a moment, she went on. "In fact, you know, you probably shouldn't go public with the info about your upcoming murder. I was saying to Lloyd this morning that life-insurance companies are probably already gathering details about anyone who is dead in the next twenty years so that they can turn down policy applications."

Theo felt his stomach fluttering. He hadn't thought of that. "So you think someone should coordinate all this?" he said.

"Well, not the corporate stuff—I wouldn't let my bosses at Sumitomo hear me say this, but I don't care about which companies get rich. But the personal stuff—people trying to figure out what their own futures hold, trying to make sense of their visions. I think we should help them."

"You and me?"

"Well, not just us. All of CERN."

"Béranger will never go for that," said Theo, shaking his head. "He doesn't want us to admit any involvement."

"We don't have to. We can just volunteer to coordinate a database. We've certainly got the computing and, after all, CERN's got a history of altruistic computing. The World Wide Web was created here, after all."

"So what do you propose?" asked Theo.

Michiko lifted her shoulders a bit. "A central repository. A Web site with a form: describe your vision in, I don't know, maybe two hundred words. We could index all the descriptions so that people could search them via keywords and Boolean operators. You know, all visions that mention Aberdeen but not sporting events. Stuff like that. Of course, the indexing program would automatically cross reference hockey, *baseboru*, and so on, to general terms like 'sporting events.' Not only would it help you, it would help a lot of other people."

Theo found himself nodding. "That makes sense. But why limit the length of the entries? I mean, storage space is cheap. I'd encourage people to be as detailed in their accounts as possible. After all, what's seemingly irrelevant to the person having the vision might be vitally important to somebody else."

"Good point," said Michiko. "As long as Béranger's moratorium on using the LHC is in effect, I've really got nothing much to do, so I'm willing to work on this. But I'll need some help. Lloyd is useless when it comes to programming; I thought maybe you could give me a hand." Lloyd and Theo's partnership had begun because Lloyd needed someone with much more programming expertise than he had to encode his physics ideas into experiments that could be run using ALICE.

Theo was already thinking of an angle. They could announce it with a press release—that woman in public relations who had knocked herself out during her vision could send it out to wherever such things went. But in the press release, they could use Theo's own case as an example—it would be the perfect way of making sure his problem got worldwide attention. "Sure," said Theo. "Sure thing."

After Michiko left, Theo turned back to his computer and checked his e-mail. There were the usual things, including spam from some company in Mauritania. The Mauritanian government had pulled off a remarkable coup: by being one of the few nations not to ban spamming by domestic companies, they'd brought thousands of businesses to their shores.

Theo clicked through the other messages. A note from a friend in Sorrento. A request for a copy of a paper Theo had coauthored; for some researcher at MIT, at least, it was back to business as usual. And—

Yes! More information about his murder.

It was from a woman in Montréal. She was French, but had been born in France, not Canada, and so followed news from her homeland. CERN, of course, straddled the Switzerland/France border, and although Geneva was the closest city, a murder at the facility was as much a French story as a Swiss one.

Her vision had been of reading the write-up in *Le Monde* about Theo's murder. The facts all matched what Kathleen DeVries had related—the first confirmation Theo had actually had that the South African woman wasn't perpetrating a hoax. But the words of the news report, as she relayed them, were quite different. It wasn't just a translation of the one DeVries had seen; rather, it was a completely different article. And it contained one salient fact that had been absent from the Johannesburg account. According to this French woman, the name of the detective who would be investigating Theo's murder was Helmut Drescher of the Geneva police.

The woman concluded her e-mail with, *"Bonne chance!"*

Bonne chance. Good luck. Yes, he'd certainly need a lot of that.

Theo knew the emergency number for the Geneva police off by heart: 1-1-7; indeed, it was printed on a sticker attached to all of CERN's phones. But he had no idea what the general-inquiry number was. He used the telephone keyboard on his phone, found the number, and dialed it.

"*Allo*," said Theo. "*Détective Helmut Drescher, s'il vous plaît.*"

"We don't have a detective by that name," said the male cop at the other end of the phone.

"He might have some other position. Something more junior."

"There's no one here by that name at all," said the voice.

Theo considered. "Do you have a directory of other police departments in Switzerland? Is there any way to check?"

"I don't have anything like that here; we'd have to dig around a bit."

"Could you do that?"

"What's this all about?"

Theo decided that honesty—or, at least, semi-honesty—was the best policy. "He's investigating a murder, and I've got some information."

"All right; I'll look into it. How can I reach you?"

Theo left his name and number, thanked the officer, then hung up. He decided to try a more direct approach, tapping out Drescher's name on the telephone keyboard.

Pay dirt. There was only one Helmut Drescher in Geneva; he lived on Rue Jean-Dassier.

Theo dialed the number.

8

NEWS DIGEST

Striking hospital workers in Poland voted unanimously to return to work today. "Our cause is just, and we will take labor action again—but for now, our duty to humanity must come first," said Union leader Stefan Wyszynski.

•

Cineplex/Odeon, a large movie-theater chain, has announced free tickets for all patrons who were attending movies during the Flashforward. Although apparently the movies played on during the event, the audience lost consciousness, missing about two minutes of the action. Other theater chains are expected to follow suit.

•

After a record number of applications were filed in the last 24 hours, the United States Patent Office has closed until further notice, pending a decision from Congress on the patenting of inventions gleaned from the visions.

•

The Committee for Scientific Investigation of Claims of the
Paranormal has issued a press release, pointing out that
although we don't yet have an explanation for the Flashforward, there is no reason to invoke supernatural causes.

•

European Mutual, the largest insurance company in the
European Union, has declared bankruptcy.

It was time, sooner than they'd thought. The shock of yesterday had pushed Marie-Claire Béranger into labor. Gaston took
his wife to the hospital in Thoiry; the Bérangers lived in Geneva, but it was important emotionally to them both that their
son be born on French soil.

As CERN's Director-General, Gaston was well rewarded,
and Marie-Claire, a lawyer, made a good income, too. Still, it
was reassuring to know that regardless of their means, Marie-
Claire would have gotten all the medical care she needed
while she was expecting. Gaston had heard that in the United
States many women see a doctor for the first time during their
pregnancy on the day they give birth. It was no wonder that
the U.S. had an infant-mortality rate many times higher than
did Switzerland or France. No, they were going to give their
son the best of everything. He knew it was a boy, and not just
because of the vision. Marie-Claire was forty-two, and their
doctor had recommended a series of sonograms during the
pregnancy; they had quite clearly seen the little feller's little
feller.

Of course there had been no way to conceal his vision from
Marie-Claire; Gaston wasn't one for keeping secrets from his
wife, anyway, but in this case, it was impossible. She'd had a
corresponding vision—the same fight with Marc, but from her
point of view. Gaston was glad that Lloyd Simcoe had managed to prove that the visions were synchronized by talking

to his grad student and that woman in Canada; Marie-Claire and Gaston had vowed to keep their vision private.

Still, there had been issues, even though they'd both been part of the same scene. Marie-Claire had asked Gaston to describe what she looked like twenty years hence. Gaston had glossed over some details, her weight gain among them; she'd complained for months about how huge she was because of the pregnancy, and how she was determined to get her figure back quickly.

For his part, Gaston had been surprised to learn from her that he would have a beard in 2030; he'd never grown one in his youth, and now that his whiskers were already coming in gray, he'd assumed he'd never have one in the future, either. She told him he would keep his hair, though—but whether that was the truth, just a kindness on her part, or an indication that by the end of the third decade of this century that there would be easy and common cures for baldness, he didn't know.

The hospital was jammed with patients, many on gurneys out in corridors; they'd apparently been there since yesterday's event. Still, most of the injuries had either been instantly fatal, requiring no hospital visit, or broken bones and burns; comparatively few patients had actually been admitted. And, thankfully, the obstetrics ward was only slightly busier than usual. Marie-Claire was conveyed there in a wheelchair pushed by a nurse; Gaston walked alongside, holding his wife's hand.

Gaston was a physicist, of course—or, at least, had been one once; his various administrative portfolios had kept him from personally doing any real science for more than a dozen years. He had no idea what had caused the visions. Oh, certainly, they were likely related to the LHC experiment; the timing coincidence was too much to ignore. But whatever caused them, and however unpleasant his own one was, Gaston didn't regret his vision. It had been a warning, a wake-up call, a portent. And he would heed it—he wouldn't let things turn that way. He'd be a good father; he'd make lots of time for his son.

He squeezed his wife's hand.

And they headed into the delivery room.

The house was large and attractive—and, with its proximity to the lake, doubtless expensive. Its exterior lines suggested a chalet, but that was obviously an affectation: housing in cosmopolitan Geneva was as far-removed from Swiss chalets as that in Manhattan was from farmhouses. Theo rang the doorbell and waited, hands in his pockets, until it was opened.

"You must be the gentleman from CERN," said the woman. Although Geneva was located in the French-speaking part of Switzerland, the woman's accent was German. As headquarters of numerous international organizations, Geneva attracted people from all over the world.

"That's right," said Theo, then, guessing at the appropriate honorific, "Frau Drescher." She was perhaps forty-five, slim, very pretty, with hair that Theo guessed was naturally blonde. "My name is Theo Procopides. Thank you for letting me come."

Frau Drescher lifted her narrow shoulders once. "I wouldn't normally, of course—a stranger who calls on the phone. But it's been such a strange couple of days."

"It has indeed," said Theo. "Is Herr Drescher home?"

"Not yet. Sometimes his business keeps him late."

Theo smiled indulgently. "I can imagine. Police work must be very demanding."

The woman frowned. "Police work? What exactly is it you think my husband does?"

"He's a police officer, no?"

"Helmut? He sells shoes; he has a shop on rue du Rhône."

People could change careers in twenty years, of course—but from salesperson to detective? Not quite a Horatio Alger story, but still pretty darned improbable. And, besides, the glitzy stores on rue du Rhône were pricey as hell; Theo himself could afford to do nothing but window-shop there. A person might have to take a substantial cut in pay to become a cop after working in that part of town.

"I'm sorry. I'd just assumed—your husband is the only Helmut Drescher in the Geneva directory. Do you know anyone else who has the same name?"

"Not unless you mean my son."

"Your son?"

"We call him Moot, but he's really Helmut, Jr."

Of course—the old man worked in a shoe store, and the son was a cop. And naturally a cop would have an unlisted phone number.

"Ah, my mistake. It must be him. Can you tell me how to get in touch with your son?"

"He's up in his room."

"You mean he still lives here?"

"Of course. He's only seven years old."

Theo mentally kicked himself; he was still struggling with the reality of the glimpses of the future—and perhaps the fact that he had not had one himself excused him from not really realizing the timeframe involved but, still, he felt like an idiot.

If young Moot was seven now, he'd be twenty-eight at the time of Theo's death—a year older than Theo himself was now. And no point asking if he wants to be a police officer when he grows up—*every* seven-year-old boy does.

"I hate to impose," said Theo, "but if you don't mind, I would like to see him."

"I don't know. Perhaps I should wait until my husband gets home."

"If you like," said Theo.

She looked as though she'd expected him to push; his willingness to wait seemed to dispel her fears. "All right," she said, "come inside. But I have to warn you: Moot's been very reserved since that—that thing that happened yesterday, whatever it was. And he didn't sleep at all well last night, so he's a bit fussy."

Theo nodded. "I understand."

She led him inside. It was a bright, airy home, with a stunning view of Lac Léman; Helmut Senior apparently sold a *lot* of shoes.

The staircase consisted of horizontal wooden steps with no vertical pieces. Frau Drescher stood at the base of it and called out, "Moot! Moot! There's someone here to see you!" She then turned to look at Theo. "Won't you have a seat?"

She was gesturing at a low-slung wooden chair with white cushions; a nearby couch matched it. He sat down. The woman moved to the foot of the stairs again, behind Theo now, and called out. "Moot! Come here! There's someone to see you." She moved back to where Theo could see her and lifted her shoulders apologetically in what's-a-mother-to-do shrug.

Finally, there was the sound of light feet on the wooden steps. The boy descended quickly; he might have been reluctant to heed his mother's call but, like most kids, he apparently habitually rushed down staircases.

"Ah, Moot," said his mother, "this is Herr Proco—"

Theo had turned to look over his shoulder at the boy. The moment Moot saw Theo, he screamed and immediately ran up the stairs so fast that the open-construction staircase visibly shook.

"What's wrong?" called his mother to his departing back.

When he reached the upper floor, the boy slammed a door shut behind him.

"I'm so sorry," said Frau Drescher, turning to Theo. "I don't know what's gotten into him."

Theo closed his eyes. "I do, I think," he said. "I didn't tell you everything, Frau Drescher. I—twenty-one years from now, I'm dead. And your son, Helmut Drescher, is a detective with the Geneva Police. He's investigating my murder."

Frau Drescher went as white as the snow cap on Mont Blanc. *"Mein Gott,"* she said. *"Mein Gott."*

"You have to let me talk to Moot," Theo said. "He recognized me—which means his vision must have had something to do with me."

"He's just a little boy."

"I know that—but he's got information about my murder. I need to know whatever he knows."

"A child can't understand any of this."

"Please, Frau Drescher. Please—it's my *life* we're talking about."

"He wouldn't say anything about his—his vision," said the woman. "It had obviously frightened him, but he wouldn't talk about it."

"Please, I must know what he saw."

She thought about it for a few moments, then, as if it were against her better judgment, said: "Come with me."

She started up the staircase. Theo followed a few steps behind. There were four rooms on the upper floor: a washroom, its door open; two bedrooms, also with opened doors; and a fourth room, with a poster for the original *Rocky* movie taped to the outside of its closed door. Frau Drescher motioned for Theo to move back down the corridor a bit. He did so, and she rapped her knuckles on the door.

"Moot! Moot, it's momma. Can I come in?"

There was no reply.

She reached down to the brass-colored handle and turned it slowly, then tentatively opened the door part way. "Moot?"

A muffled voice, as if the boy was lying face down on a pillow. "Is that man still here?"

"He won't come in. I promise." A pause. "You know him from somewhere?"

"I saw that face. That chin."

"Where?"

"In a room. He was lying on a bed." A pause. "Except it wasn't a bed, it was made of metal. And it had a thing in it, like that plate you serve roasts on."

"A trough?" said Frau Drescher.

"His eyes were closed, but it was him, and . . ."

"And what?"

Silence.

"It's okay to say, Moot. It's okay to tell me."

"He didn't have any shirt or pants on. And there was this guy in a white smock, like we wear in art class. But he had a knife, and he was . . ."

Theo, standing in the corridor, held his breath.

"He had a knife, like, and he was . . . he was . . ."

Carving me open, Theo thought. An autopsy, the detective watching as the medical examiner performed it.

"It was *so* gross," said the boy.

Theo stepped quietly forward, standing now in the doorway behind Frau Drescher. The youngster was indeed lying on his stomach.

"Moot . . ." Theo said very softly. "Moot, I'm sorry you saw that, but—but I have to know. I have to know what the man was saying to you."

"I don't want to talk about it," said the boy.

"I know . . . I know. But it's very important to me. Please, Moot. Please. That man in the white smock, he was a doctor. Please tell me what he was saying."

"Do I have to?" said the boy to his mom.

Theo could see emotions warring across her face. On the one hand, she wanted to protect her son from an unpleasant situation; on the other, something bigger than that was clearly at stake. At last she said, "No, you don't have to—but it *would* be helpful." She moved across the room, sat on the edge of the bed, and stroked the boy's crewcut blond head. "You see, Herr Procopides here, he's in a lot of trouble. Somebody is going to try to kill him. But maybe you can help prevent that. You'd like to do that, wouldn't you, Moot?"

It was the boy's turn to wrestle with his thoughts. "I guess," he said at last. He lifted his head a bit, looked back at Theo, then immediately looked away.

"Moot?" said his mother, gently prodding.

"He dyes his hair," said the boy, as if it were a heinous thing to do. "It's really gray."

Theo nodded. Young Helmut didn't understand. How could he? Seven years old, suddenly transported from wherever he'd been—the playground, perhaps, or a classroom, or even the safety of this, his own bedroom. Transported from there to a morgue, watching a body being sliced open, watching thick, dark blood ooze down the channel in the pallet.

"Please," said Theo. "I—ah, I promise not to dye my hair anymore."

The boy was quiet for a while longer, then he spoke, tentatively, haltingly.

"They used a lot of fancy words. I didn't understand most of it."

"Were they speaking French?"

"No, German. The other guy, he had didn't have an accent, just like I don't."

Theo smiled a bit; Moot's accent was actually pretty thick, he thought. Still, two-thirds of Switzerland's population usually spoke German, while only eighteen percent regularly spoke French. Granted, Geneva was in the French-speaking part of the country, but it wouldn't be at all unusual for two native-German speakers to use that language if no one else was around.

"Did they say anything about an entrance wound?" asked Theo.

"A what?"

"An entrance wound." At the moment, Moot and Theo were speaking French; Theo hoped he had the right phrasing for that language. "You know, where the bullet went in."

"Bullets," said the boy.

"Pardon?"

"Bullets. There were three of them." He looked at his mother. "That's what the man in the smock said."

Three bullets, thought Theo. *Somebody wanted me* very *dead.*

"And the entrance wounds?" said Theo. "Did they say where the bullets went in?"

"In the chest."

So I would have seen the killer, thought Theo. "Is there anything else you can tell me?"

"I said something," said the boy.

"What?"

"I mean, it seemed like I was saying it. But it wasn't my voice. It was all deep, you know?"

Grown up. Of course it was deep. "What did you say?"

"That you'd been shot at close range."

"How did you know that?"

"I don't know it—I don't know why I said it. The words just sort of came out."

"Did the medical examiner—the man in the smock—did he say anything when you said that?"

The boy was now sitting up in bed, facing them. "No, he just nodded, sort of. Like he agreed with me."

"Well, then, did he say something that prompted you to observe it had been at close range?"

"I don't understand," said the boy. "Momma, do I have to do this?"

"Please," said Frau Drescher. "We'll have ice cream for dessert. Please just help the nice man for a few more minutes."

The boy frowned, as if weighing how much appeal the ice cream might have. Then: "He said you were killed in a boxing match."

Theo was startled. He might be arrogant, he might be pushy, but never in his adult life had he hit another human being. Indeed, he rather considered himself a pacifist, and had turned down several lucrative offers from defense companies after graduation. He'd never been to a boxing match in his life; he thought of it not as a sport but rather as an animalistic display.

"Are you sure he said that?" said Theo. He looked at the *Rocky* poster on the door again, then at the wall above Moot's bed, which sported a poster of heavyweight champ Evander Holyfield. Maybe the kid was conflating his dreams with his vision?

"Uh-huh," said Moot.

"But why would I be shot in a boxing match?"

The boy shrugged.

"Do you remember anything else?"

"He said something was really small."

"Something was small?'

"Yeah. Just nine millimeters."

Theo looked at the mother. "That's a gun size. I think it refers to the diameter of the bore."

"I hate guns," said Frau Drescher.

"Me, too," said Theo. He looked at the boy again. "What else did they say?"

" 'Glock.' The man kept saying 'Glock.' "

"That's a kind of gun. Did they say anything else?"

"Stuff about dallisics . . ."

"Dal—? You mean ballistics?"

"I guess. They were going to send the bullets to dallisics. Is that a city?"

Theo shook his head. "Did they say anything else about the bullets?"

"They were American. The man said it said 'Remington' on the shell casings, and I said, like I knew what I was talking about, 'American,' and he nodded."

"Did they say anything else? Anything while they were looking in my chest?"

The boy's face was pale. "There was so much blood. So much guts. I . . ."

Frau Drescher drew her son closer to her. "I'm sorry, Herr Procopides, but I think that's enough."

"But—"

"No. You'll have to go now."

Theo exhaled. He reached into his pocket, pulled out one of his cards, and crossed over to the boy's bed. "Moot, this is how you can reach me. Please keep this card. Any time—I mean any time, even years from now—if something occurs to you that you think I should know, I beg you to give me a call. It's very important to me."

The boy looked at the little rectangle; he'd probably never been handed a business card before in his life.

"Take it. Take the card. It's yours to keep."

Moot took it tentatively from Theo's hand.

Theo gave another card to the mother, thanked both Dreschers, and left.

9

NEWS DIGEST

Darren Sunday, star of the NBC television series *Dale Rice*, died today of injuries sustained in a fall during the phenomenon. Production on the series, which had been shooting around Sunday's absence, has halted.

•

The New York State Thruway Commission reports that the seventy-two-car pileup near Exit 44 (Canandaigua) has still not been cleared; the westbound Thruway is still blocked at that point. Drivers are advised to choose alternate routes.

•

A group of ten thousand Muslims in London, England, whose private prayers were interrupted by the Flashforward, came together today in Piccadilly Circus to face Mecca and pray *en masse*.

•

Pope Benedict XVI has announced a grueling schedule of international visits. He invites Catholics and non-Catholics to attend his masses, designed to give comfort to those who lost loved ones during the Flashforward. When questioned about whether the Flashforward constituted a miracle, the pontiff reserved judgment.

•

The United Nations Children's Fund has stepped in to help overburdened national adoption agencies in finding homes for children orphaned during the Flashforward.

Although CERN was jumping—every researcher had a pet theory about what had happened—Lloyd and Michiko went home early; nobody could blame them after what had happened to Michiko's daughter. "Home," again without discussion—none was necessary—was Lloyd's apartment in St. Genis.

Michiko was still crying every few hours, and Lloyd had finally found time at work to close his office door, put his head down on his desk, and cry his heart out, too. Sometimes, crying helped make the pain go away; it didn't in this case.

They had an early dinner; Lloyd cooked up chops, which he'd had in the fridge. Michiko, clearly wanting to do something—anything—to keep her mind busy, worked on straightening up Lloyd's apartment.

And, as they finished their dinner, and Michiko drank her tea and Lloyd his coffee, the question Lloyd had been dreading was finally asked again.

"What did you see?" asked Michiko.

Lloyd opened his mouth to reply, but then closed it.

"Oh, come on," said Michiko, evidently reading his face. "It couldn't have been that bad."

"It was," said Lloyd.

"What did you see?" she asked again.

"I—" He closed his eyes. "I was with another woman."

Michiko blinked several times. Finally, her voice frosty, she said, "You were cheating on me?"

"No—no."

"Then what?"

"I was—God, honey, I am *so* sorry—I was married to another woman."

"How do you know you were married?"

"We were both in bed together; we were wearing matching wedding bands. And we were in a cottage in New England."

"Maybe it was her place."

"No. I recognized some of the furniture."

"You were married to someone else," said Michiko, as if trying to digest the concept. She had such a shock recently that perhaps anything else would have been too much to absorb.

Lloyd nodded. "We—you and I—we must have been divorced. Or . . ."

"Or?"

He shrugged. "Or maybe we never went through with the marriage in the first place."

"Don't you still love me?" asked Michiko.

"Of course I do. Of course I do. But—look, I didn't want to have that vision. I didn't enjoy it at all. Remember when we were talking about our vows? Remember when we discussed whether to leave 'till death do us part' in there? You said it was old fashioned; you said nobody says that anymore. And, well, you *have* been married once before. But I said we should leave it in. That's what I wanted. I wanted a marriage that would last forever. Not like my parents—and not like your first marriage."

"You were in New England," said Michiko, still trying to deal with it. "And I—I was in Kyoto."

"With a little girl," said Lloyd. He paused, unsure whether he should give voice to the nagging question. But then he did, not quite meeting her eyes as he spoke. "What did the girl look like?"

"She had long black hair," said Michiko.

"And . . . ?"

Michiko looked away. "And Asian features. She looked Japanese." She paused. "But that doesn't mean anything; lots of kids of mixed couples look more like one parent than the other."

Lloyd felt his heart move in his chest. "I thought we were meant for each other," he said softly. "I thought . . ." He trailed off, unable to say, "I thought you were my soulmate." His eyes were stinging; so, apparently, were hers. She rubbed them with the backs of her hands.

"I love you, Lloyd," she said.

"I love you too, but . . ."

"Yes," she said. "But . . ."

He reached across and touched her hand, which was now sitting on the tabletop. She gripped his fingers. They sat silently together for a very long time.

Theo sat for a while in his car on the street outside the Dreschers' home, his mind racing. He'd been shot by a Glock 9mm; he was pretty sure from cop shows he'd watched that the Glock was a semiautomatic pistol, popular with police forces worldwide. But the ammunition had been American; maybe it had been an American who had pulled the trigger. Of course, Theo had probably not yet met whoever it was who would one day want him dead. Surely there would be almost no overlap between his current circle of friends, acquaintances, and colleagues and those who would comprise those groups two decades hence.

Still, Theo already knew a lot of Americans.

But none well. None, except Lloyd Simcoe.

Of course, Lloyd wasn't really an American. He was born in Canada. And Canadians didn't like guns, either—they had no Second Amendment, or whatever damned thing it was that made Americans think they could go around armed.

But Lloyd had lived in the U.S. for seventeen years before coming to CERN, first at Harvard, then as an experimenter with the Tevatron at Fermilab near Chicago. And, by Lloyd's own admission, he'd be living in the U.S. again by the time of the visions. He could have gotten a gun easily enough.

But no—Lloyd had an alibi. He was in New England when Theo was—what was it the Americans say? When Theo was *wasted.*

Except . . .

Except that Theo was/would be killed October 21—and Lloyd's vision, like everyone else's, was of October 23.

Lloyd had told Theo his vision—he'd said he hadn't told Michiko yet, but Theo had insisted, and Lloyd had relented, although he did swear the young Greek to secrecy. Lloyd had said his vision had him making love to an old woman, presumably his then-wife.

Old people surely didn't make love that often, thought Theo. Indeed, they probably only did it on special occasions. Like when one of them had returned from a long absence. It's only a six-hour flight from New England to Switzerland . . . and that's today. Twenty years hence, it might be much less.

No, Lloyd could easily have been at CERN on Monday and back home in New Hampshire, or wherever the hell it was, on Wednesday. Not that Theo could think of any reason that Lloyd would want to kill him.

Except that, of course, by 2030, Theo, not Lloyd, was apparently director of what sounded like an incredibly advanced particle accelerator at CERN: the Tachyon-Tardyon Collider. Academic and professional jealousy had led to more than one murder over the years.

And, of course, there was the fact that Lloyd and Michiko were no longer together. If he were honest with himself, Theo fancied Michiko, too. What man wouldn't? She was gorgeous and brilliant and warm and funny. And, well, she *was* closer to his age than to Lloyd's. Could he have had a role in their breakup?

Just as he had pushed Lloyd to share his vision, so, too, had he pushed Michiko to share hers: Theo was hungry for insight, vicariously trying to experience what everyone else had been lucky enough to see. In Michiko's vision, she was in Kyoto, perhaps, as she had said, taking her daughter to visit Michiko's uncle. Could Lloyd have waited until she was temporarily away from Geneva to come over to settle an old score with Theo?

Theo hated himself for even considering such possibilities. Lloyd had been his mentor, his partner. They'd always talked about sharing a Nobel Prize. But—

But there was no mention of a Nobel in the two articles he'd found now about his own death. Of course, that didn't mean Lloyd wouldn't get one, but . . .

Theo's mother was diabetic; Theo had researched the history of diabetes when she'd been diagnosed. The names Banting and Best kept coming up—the two Canadian researchers who had discovered insulin. Indeed, they were another pair people sometimes likened Lloyd and Theo to: like Crick and Watson, Banting and Best were of different ages—Banting was clearly the senior researcher. But although Crick and Watson had been jointly awarded the Nobel, Banting had shared his not with his true research partner, young Best, but rather with J. R. R. Macleod, Banting's boss. Perhaps Lloyd *would* get a Nobel—not for the Higgs discovery, which had failed to materialize, but rather for an explanation of the time-displacement effect. And perhaps he would share it not with his young partner but rather with his boss—with Béranger, or someone else in the CERN hierarchy. What would that do to their friendship, their partnership? What jealousies and hatreds would fester between now and the year 2030?

Madness. Paranoia. And yet—

And yet, if he were killed on the CERN grounds—Moot Drescher's suggestion of a shoot-out in a sports arena still seemed a dubious proposition—then he would be killed by someone who had managed to gain access to the campus. CERN wasn't a maximum-security facility by any means, but neither did it allow just anyone to enter its gates.

No, someone who could get into CERN had likely killed him. Someone whom Theo would meet with face-to-face. And someone who wanted him not just dead, but who had clearly vented pent up anger, pumping shot after shot into Theo's body.

Lloyd and Michiko had moved to the couch in the living room; the dishes could wait for later.

Dammit, thought Lloyd, why did this have to happen? Everything had been going so well, and now—

And now, it looked like it all was going to fall apart.

Lloyd wasn't a young man. He'd never intended to wait this long to get married, but . . .

But work had gotten in the way, and—

No. No, that wasn't it. Let's be honest. Let's face it.

He thought of himself as a good man, kind and gentle, but—

But, truth be told, he wasn't polished, he wasn't slick; it had been easy for Michiko to improve his wardrobe, because, of course, almost any change would have been for the better.

Oh, sure, women—and men, for that matter—said he was a good listener, but Lloyd knew that it wasn't so much that he was sage but rather that he simply didn't know what to say. And so he sat, taking it in, taking in the peaks and valleys of other people's lives, the highs and lows, the trials and travails of those whose existence had more variation, more excitement, more angst than his own.

Lloyd Simcoe wasn't a lady's man; he wasn't a raconteur; he didn't have a reputation as an after-dinner speaker. He was just a scientist, a specialist in quark-gluon plasma, a typical nerd who'd started out as a kid who couldn't throw a baseball, who spent his adolescence with his nose buried in books when others his age were out honing interpersonal skills in a thousand and one different situations.

And the years had slipped by—his twenties, his thirties,

and now, here, most of his forties. Oh, he'd had success at his work, and he'd dated now and again, and there had been Pam, all those years ago, but nothing that looked as though it was going to be permanent, no relationship that seemed destined to stand the test of time.

Until this one, with Michiko.

It had felt so right. The way she laughed at his jokes; the way he laughed at hers. The way, even though they'd grown up in vastly different societies—him in conservative, rural Nova Scotia; her in cosmopolitan, overwhelming Tokyo—that they shared the same politics and morals and beliefs and opinions, as if—the term came again, unbidden—as if they *were* soul mates, always meant to be together. Yes, she'd been married and divorced, yes, she is—was—a parent, but, still, they had seemed absolutely in sync, so very right for each other.

But now—

Now, it seemed as though that, too, was an illusion. The world might still be struggling to decide what, if any, reality the visions reflected, but Lloyd had already accepted them as fact, true depictions of tomorrow, the one unalterable space-time continuum in which he had always known he dwelled.

And yet he had to explain to her what he was feeling—him, Lloyd Simcoe, the man whom words always failed, the good listener, the brick, the one others turned to when they had doubts. He had to explain to her what was going through his mind, why a vision of a dissolved marriage twenty-one years—twenty-one years!—down the road so paralyzed him right now, so poisoned for him what he'd thought they had.

He looked at Michiko, dropped his gaze, tried again to meet her eyes, then focussed on a blank spot on the apartment's dark, wine-colored walls.

He'd never spoken of this to anyone—not even to his sister Dolly, at least not since they were kids. He took a deep breath, then began, his eyes still locked on the wall. "When I was eight years old, my parents called me and my sister down to the living room." He swallowed. "It was a Saturday afternoon. Tensions had been high for weeks in our house. That's an adult way of expressing it—'tensions were high.' As a kid, all I knew was that mom and dad weren't talking. Oh, they spoke when they had to, but it was always with sharp voices. And it often ended in choked-off phrases. *'If that's the way—!' 'I'm not—!' 'Don't you—!'* Like that. They tried to keep it civil when they knew we could hear them, but we heard a lot more than they thought."

He looked briefly at Michiko, then shifted his gaze to the wall again. "Anyway, they called us down to the living room. 'Lloyd, Dolly—come here!' It was my father. And, you know, when he yelled for us to come, it usually meant we were in trouble. We hadn't put away our toys; one of the neighbors had complained about something we'd done; whatever. Well, I came out of my room, and Dolly came out of hers, and we kind of looked at each other, you know, just a glance, just a shared moment of apprehension." He now looked at Michiko, just as he had at his sister all those years ago.

Lloyd continued. "We went down the stairs, and there they were: Mom and Dad. And they were both standing, and we stood, too. The whole time, we stood around, like we were waiting for the fucking bus. They were both quiet for a bit, like they didn't know what to say. And then, finally, my mother spoke up. She said, 'Your father is moving out.' Just like that. No preamble, no softening the blow: 'Your father is moving out.'

"And then he spoke. 'I'll get a place nearby. You'll be able to see me on weekends.'

"And my mother added, as if it needed to be said, 'Your father and I haven't been getting along.' "

Lloyd fell quiet.

Michiko made a sympathetic face. "Did you see him much, after he moved out?" she asked at last.

"He didn't move out."

"But your parents *are* divorced."

"Yes—six years later. But after the great announcement, he didn't move out. He didn't leave."

"So your parents made up?"

Lloyd shrugged a little. "No. No, the fighting continued. But they never mentioned him moving out again. We—Dolly and I—we kept waiting for the other shoe to fall, for him to move out. For months—really, all of the six years their marriage lasted after that—we thought he might leave at any moment. There was never a timeframe mentioned, after all—they never said *when* he was going to go. When they did finally split up, it was almost a relief. I love my dad, and my mom, too, but having that hanging over our heads for so long was just too much to bear." He paused. "And a marriage like that, one gone bad—I'm sorry, Michiko, but I don't think I could ever go through anything like that again."

10

Day Three: Thursday, April 23, 2009

<u>NEWS DIGEST</u>

The Los Angeles District Attorney's office has dropped all
pending misdemeanor cases to free up staff to deal with
the flood of new charges being laid related to looting in
the aftermath of the Flashforward.

•

The Department of Philosophy at the University of Wit-
watersrand, South Africa, reports record numbers of requests for course calendars.

•

Amtrak in the U.S., Via Rail in Canada, and British Rail
have reported huge increases in passenger volume. No
trains operated by those companies crashed during the
Flashforward.

•

The Church of the Holy Visions, begun yesterday in Stockholm, Sweden, now claims 12,000 adherents world-wide, making it the fastest-growing religion on the planet.

•

The American Bar Association reports a huge increase in requests for new wills to be drawn up, or existing wills to be revised.

The next day, Theo and Michiko were working on setting up their Web site for people to report their visions. They'd decided to call it the Mosaic Project, both in honor of the first popular (but now long abandoned) Web browser, and in acknowledgement of the now clearly established fact, thanks to the efforts of researchers and reporters worldwide, that each person's vision did indeed represent one small stone in a vast mosaic portrait of the year 2030.

Theo had a mug of coffee. He took a sip, then, "Can I ask you a question about your vision?"

Michiko looked out the window at the mountains. "Sure."

"That little girl you were with. Is she your daughter, do you think?" He'd almost said "your new daughter" but fortunately had censored the thought before it was free.

Michiko lifted her narrow shoulders slightly. "Apparently."

"And—and Lloyd's daughter, too?"

Michiko looked surprised by the question. "Of course," she said, but there was hesitation in her voice.

"Because Lloyd—"

Michiko stiffened. "He told you his vision, did he?"

Theo realized he'd put his foot in it. "No, not exactly. Just that he was in New England—"

"With a woman who wasn't me. Yes, I know."

"I'm sure it doesn't mean anything. I'm sure the visions aren't going to turn out to be true."

Michiko looked out at the mountains again; Theo found himself doing that a lot, too. There was something about them—something solid, permanent, unchanging. He found it calming to look at them, to know that there were things that endured not just for decades but for millennia.

"Look," she said, "I've been divorced once already. I'm not naïve enough to think that all marriages will last forever. Maybe Lloyd and I *will* break up at some point. Who knows?"

Theo looked away, unable to meet her eyes, unsure how she'd react to the words he felt bubbling up within him. "He'd be a fool to let you go," he said.

His hand had been lying on the tabletop. Suddenly he felt Michiko's hand touching his, patting its back affectionately. "Why, thank you," she said. He did look at her and she was smiling. "That's the nicest thing anyone ever said to me."

She took back her hand . . . but not for a few more delicious seconds.

Lloyd Simcoe walked from the LHC control center to the main administration building. It normally took fifteen minutes to make the journey, but it ended up lasting half an hour because he was stopped three times by physicists going the other way who wanted to ask Lloyd questions about the LHC experiment that might have caused the time displacement, or to suggest theoretical models to explain the Flashforward. It was a beautiful spring day—cool, but with great mountains of cumulonimbus in the bright blue sky rivaling the peaks to the east of the campus.

At last he entered the admin building and made his way down to Béranger's office. Of course, he'd made an appointment (for which he was now fifteen minutes late); CERN was a huge operation, and there was no way in which you could just drop in on its Director-General.

Béranger's secretary told Lloyd to head right in, and Lloyd did just that. The office's third-floor window looked out over the CERN campus. Béranger rose from behind his desk and took a seat at the long conference table, much of which was covered with experimental logs related to the Flashforward. Lloyd sat down on the opposite side.

"*Oui?*" said Béranger. Yes? What is it?

"I want to go public," said Lloyd. "I want to tell the world about our role in what happened."

"*Absolument pas,*" said Béranger. No way.

"Dammit, Gaston, we have to come clean at some point."

"You don't know that we're at fault, Lloyd. You can't prove it—and nobody else can, either. The phones have been ringing off the hook, of course: I imagine every scientist in the world is getting calls from the media asking for opinions about what happened. But nobody has connected it to us yet—and hopefully nobody will."

"Oh, come on! Theo says you came storming over to the LHC control center right after the Flashforward—you knew it was us from the very first moment."

"That's when I thought it was a localized phenomenon. But once I learned it was worldwide, I reconsidered. You think we were the only facility doing something interesting at that time? I've checked. KEK was running an experiment that had started just five minutes before the Flashforward; SLAC was doing a set of particle collisions, too. The Sudbury Neutrino Observatory picked up a burst at just before 17h00; there was also, just before 17h00, an earthquake in Italy measuring three-point-four on the Richter scale. A new fusion reactor came online in Indonesia at precisely 17h00 our time. And there was a series of rocket-motor tests going on at Boeing."

"Neither KEK nor SLAC can produce energy levels close to what we were doing with the LHC," said Lloyd. "And the rest are hardly unusual events. You're grasping at straws."

"No," said Béranger. "I'm conducting a proper investigation. You're not sure—not to a moral certainty—that it was us, and until you are, you're not saying a word."

Lloyd shook his head. "I know you spend your days pushing paper around, but I thought in your heart you were still a scientist."

"I *am* a scientist," said Béranger. "This *is* about science—

good science, the way it's supposed to be done. You're ready to make an announcement before all the facts are in. I'm not." He paused, took a breath. "Look," he said, "people's faith in science has already been shaken enough over the years. Way too many science stories have turned out to be frauds or hype."

Lloyd looked at him.

"Percival Lowell—who just needed better lenses and a less-active imagination—claimed to see canals on Mars. But there were no canals there.

"We're still dealing with the aftermath of one idiot in Roswell who decided to declare that what he was looking at was the remains of an alien spaceship, instead of just a weather balloon.

"Do you remember the Tasaday? The stone-age tribe discovered in New Guinea in the 1970s that had no word for war? Anthropologists were falling all over themselves to study them. Only one problem—they were a hoax. But scientists were too quick to want to get on talk shows and didn't bother to look at the evidence."

"I'm not trying to get on a talk show," said Lloyd.

"Then we announced cold fusion to the world," said Gaston, ignoring him. "Remember that? The end of the energy crisis, the end of poverty! More power than humanity would ever need. Except it wasn't real—it was just Fleischmann and Pons jumping the gun.

"Then we started talking about life on Mars—the antarctic meteorite with supposed microfossils, proof that evolution had begun on another planet besides Earth. Except that it turned out the scientists had spoken too soon again, and the fossils weren't fossils at all, but just natural rock formations."

Gaston took a breath. "We've got to be careful here, Lloyd. You ever listened to anybody from the Institute for Creation Research? They spout absolute gibberish about the origin of life, but you can see people in the audience nodding their heads and agreeing with them—the creationists say the scientists don't know what they're talking about, and they're right, half the time we don't. We open our mouths too early, all in some desperate bid for primacy, for credit. But every time we're wrong—every time we say we've made a breakthrough in the fight for a cure for cancer or we've solved a fundamental mystery of the universe and then have to turn around a week or a year or a decade later and say, oops!, we were wrong, we didn't check our facts, we didn't know what we were talking about—every time that happens we give a boost to the astrologers and creationists and New Agers and all the other ripoff artists and charlatans and just plain nut cases. We *are* scientists, Lloyd—we're supposed to be the last bastion of rational thought, of verifiable, reproducible, irrefutable proof, and yet we're our own worst enemies. You want to go public—you want to say CERN did it, we displaced human consciousness through time, we can see the future, we can give you the gift of tomorrow. But I'm not convinced, Lloyd. You think I'm just an administrator who is trying to cover his ass, indeed, the collective ass of all of us, and of our insurers. But that's not it—or, to be honest, that's not *entirely* it. Dammit, Lloyd—I'm sorry, more sorry than you can possibly imagine, about what happened to Michiko's daughter. Marie-Claire gave birth yesterday; I shouldn't even be here—thank God her sister is staying with us—but there's so much to be done. I've got a son now, and even though I've only had him for a matter of hours, I could never stand losing him. What Michiko has faced—what you're facing—is beyond imagining to me. But I want a better world for my son. I want a world in which science *is* respected, in which scientists speak from hard data not wild speculations, in which when someone reports a science story the people in the audience will sit up and take notice because something new and fundamental about the way the universe works is being revealed—rather than having them roll their eyes and say, geez, I wonder what they're claiming *this* week. You don't know for a fact—for an honest-to-God fact—that CERN had *anything* to do with what happened . . . and until you—until *I* know that, no one is giving a press conference. Is that clear?''

Lloyd opened his mouth to protest, closed it, then opened it again. "And if I can prove that CERN had something to do with it?"

"You're not to reactivate the LHC—not at 1150-TeV levels. I'm reshuffling the experimental queue. Anyone who wants to use the LHC for proton-proton collisions may do so, once we finish all the diagnostics, but no one is firing up that accelerator for nuclear collisions until I say so."

"But—"

"No buts, Lloyd," said Béranger. "Now, look, I've got a ton of work to do. If there's nothing else . . . ?"

Lloyd shook his head, and left the office, left the administration building, and headed back.

More people stopped Lloyd on his way back; it seemed there was a new theory being put forth every few minutes and old ones being shot down just as frequently. At last Lloyd returned to his office. Waiting on his desk was the initial report of the engineering team that had been scouring the entire twenty-seven kilometers of the LHC tunnel, looking for any abnormality in the equipment that might have accounted for the time displacement; so far, nothing unusual had cropped up. And the ALICE and CMS detectors had also received clean bills of health, passing every diagnostic test run on them to date.

There was also a copy of the front page of the *Tribune de Genève* waiting; someone had placed it there and had circled a particular story:

Man Who Had Vision Dies
Future Not Fixed, Professor Says

MOBILE, ALABAMA (AP): James Punter, 47, was killed in an automobile accident today on the I-65. Punter had previously recounted a precognition vision to his brother Dennis Punter, 44.

"Jim had told me all about his vision," said

Dennis. "He was at home—the same house he lived in today—in the future. He was shaving, and had the fright of his life when he saw himself in the mirror, all old and wrinkled."

Punter's death has wide-ranging implications, says Jasmine Rose, a philosophy professor at the State University of New York at Brockport.

"Ever since the visions occurred, we've been arguing about whether they portrayed the real future or only one possible future, or, indeed, whether they might simply be hallucinations," she said.

"Punter's death clearly indicates that the future is not fixed; he had a vision and yet is no longer around to see that vision come true."

Lloyd was still steamed from his encounter with Béranger, and he found himself crumpling up the newspaper page and throwing it across his office.

A philosophy professor!

Punter's death didn't prove a thing, of course. His account was entirely anecdotal. There was no supporting evidence for it—no newspaper or TV show glimpsed that could be compared with others' accounts of the same things, and no one else had apparently seen him in their visions. A forty-seven-year-old could easily be dead in twenty-one years. He could have made up the vision—and a very unimaginative one it was, too—rather than revealing that he hadn't had one. As Michiko had said, Theo had probably ruined his chances of ever getting life insurance by revealing his own lack of a vision; Punter might have decided it was better to pretend to have a vision than admit that he was going to be dead.

Lloyd sighed. Couldn't they have gotten a scientist to address this issue? Someone who understands what really constitutes evidence?

A philosophy professor. Give me a fucking break.

•   •   •

Michiko was doing most of the work related to setting up the Web site; Theo was running computer simulations of the LHC collision on a separate PC in the same room, making himself available as needed to help Michiko. Of course, CERN had all the latest authoring tools, but there still was much to be done by hand, including writing up descriptions of various lengths to submit to the hundreds of different search engines available worldwide. She figured they would have everything ready to go in another day.

A window popped up on Theo's monitor announcing that he had new mail. Normally, he would have ignored it until a more convenient time, but the subject line demanded immediate attention: *"Betreff: Ihre Ermordung,"* German for "Re: Your Murder."

Theo told the computer to display the message. The whole thing was in German, but Theo had no trouble reading it. Michiko, looking over his shoulder, didn't read any German, though, and so he translated it for her.

"It's from a woman in Berlin," said Theo. "It says something like, 'I saw your posting forwarded to a newsgroup I read. You're looking for people who might know something about your murder. Well, a person who lives in the same apartment building I do knows something about it. We all'—it's congregated, gathered, something like that—'we all gathered in the lobby after whatever it was happened, and shared our visions. A fellow—I don't know him that well, but he lives one floor above me—had a vision of watching a television newscast about the murder of a physicist at, I thought he said, Lucerne but when I read your posting I realized he'd actually said CERN, which, I confess, I'd never heard of. Anyway, I've forwarded a blind copy of your message to him, but I don't know if he'll get in touch with you or not. His name is Wolfgang Rusch, and you can reach him at . . .' That's what it says."

"What are you going to do?" asked Michiko.

"What else? Contact this guy." He picked up the phone, dialed his billing code for personal long-distance calls, then tapped out the number that was still glowing on his screen.

11

◈◈

NEWS DIGEST

A national day of mourning has been declared in the Philippines, to honor President Maurice Maung and all the other Filipinos who died during the Flashforward.

•

A group calling itself the April 21 Coalition is already lobbying Congress to approve a memorial on the Washington, D.C., mall in honor of the Americans killed during the Flashforward. They propose a giant mosaic, depicting a view of Times Square in New York City, as it will apparently be in 2030, based on accounts of thousand of people whose visions depicted that locale. There would be one tile in the mosaic for each individual who perished in the event, with each tile laser inscribed with an individual's name.

•

Castle Rock Entertainment has announced a delay in the release of its much-anticipated summer blockbuster *Catastrophe* "until a more appropriate time."

•

Separatist sentiment in Quebec is at an all-time low, according to a *Maclean's* opinion poll: "The apparently certain knowledge that Quebec will still be part of Canada twenty-one years hence has caused even many diehard separatists to throw in the towel," observed a *Maclean's* editorial.

•

As an emergency measure to free up doctors to deal with those physically injured during the Flashforward, the United States Food and Drug Administration has approved eleven formerly prescription antidepressants for over-the-counter sales for a one-year period.

That night, Lloyd and Michiko sat again on the couch in Lloyd's apartment, a five-centimeter-thick stack of printouts and reports Lloyd had brought home sitting on the coffee table. Michiko hadn't cried once since they got home, but Lloyd knew that she would doubtless cry herself to sleep again tonight, as she had the last two nights. He was trying to do the right thing: he didn't want to avoid the topic of Tamiko—that, he knew, was tantamount to denying that she had ever existed—but he would only pursue it if Michiko herself mentioned her.

And, of course, he wanted to avoid the topic of their wedding and their visions, and all the doubts that were swirling through his minds. And so they sat, and he held her when she needed holding, and they talked about other things.

"Gaston Béranger was going on about the role of science today," said Lloyd. "And, dammit all, he got me to thinking maybe he was right. We've been saying outrageous things, we scientists. We've been deliberately using loaded words, making the public think we're doing things that we aren't."

"I admit we haven't always done a good job of presenting scientific truths to the public," said Michiko. "But—but if CERN *is* responsible . . . if you—"

If you are responsible . . .

That's doubtless what she'd started to say before she'd caught herself. If *you* are responsible . . .

Yes, if he was responsible—if his experiment, his and Theo's, had somehow been responsible for all that death, all that destruction, for the death of Tamiko . . .

He'd sworn to himself that he'd never make Michiko sad, that he'd never do to her what Hiroshi had done. But if his experiment had been what had led, however inadvertently, however indirectly, to Tamiko's death, then he'd harmed Michiko far more than all Hiroshi's indifference and neglect ever had.

Wolfgang Rusch had seemed reluctant to talk on the phone, and Theo had finally declared outright that he was coming to Germany to see him. Berlin was only eight hundred and seventy kilometers from Geneva. He could drive it in a day, but he decided to first call a travel agent, on the off-chance that there might be a cheap seat available.

It turned out that there were *a lot* of seats available.

Yes, there had been a slight reduction in the world's fleet of airplanes—some had crashed, although most of the thirty-five hundred planes that had been aloft during the Flashforward had flown on merrily without pilot intervention. And, yes, there was an influx of people who had no choice but to travel in order to deal with family emergencies.

But, according to the travel agent, everyone else was staying home. Hundreds of thousands of people worldwide were refusing to get on planes—and who could blame them? If the blackout effect happened again, more aircraft would smash into runways. Swissair was waiving all the usual travel restrictions—no advanced booking required, no minimum stay needed—and was giving quadruple frequent-flyer points, plus granting First Class seating on a first-come, first-served no-extra-cost basis; other airlines were offering similar deals. Theo booked a flight, and was in Germany less than ninety minutes later. He'd put the flight time to good use, running some more lead-nuclei collision simulations on his notebook computer.

When he arrived at Rusch's apartment, it was a little after 8:00 P.M. "Thank you for agreeing to see me," said Theo.

Rusch was in his mid-thirties, thin, with blond hair and eyes the color of graphite. He stood aside to let Theo into the small apartment, but didn't seem at all happy to have a visitor. "I have to tell you," he said in English, "I wish you hadn't come. This is a very difficult time for me."

"Oh?"

"I lost my wife during the—whatever you call it. The German press has been referring to it as *Der Zwischenfall*—'the incident.'" He shook his head. "Seems a wholly inadequate name to me."

"I'm sorry."

"I'd been here at home when it happened. I don't teach on Tuesdays."

"Teach?"

"I'm an associate professor of chemistry. But my wife—she was killed on her way home from work."

"I am so sorry," said Theo, sincerely.

Rusch shrugged. "That doesn't bring her back."

Theo nodded, conceding the point. He was glad, though, that Béranger had so far vetoed Lloyd going public with CERN's involvement in the accident—he doubted Rusch would be talking to him at all if he knew of the relationship.

"How did you find me?"

"A tip—I've been getting a bunch of them. People seem intrigued by my . . . my quest. Someone emailed me saying you had told them that your vision involved watching a television news report about my death."

"Who?"

"One of your neighbors. I don't think it matters which one." Theo hadn't actually been sworn to secrecy, but it didn't seem prudent to name his source, either. "Please," he said, "I've come a long way, at considerable expense, to speak with you. There must be more that you can tell me than what you said on the phone."

Rusch seemed to soften a bit. "I guess. Look, I'm sorry. You have no idea how much I loved my wife."

Theo cast his eyes about the room. There was a photo on a low bookcase: Rusch, looking about ten years younger than his current mid-thirties, and a beautiful dark-haired woman. "Is that her?" Theo asked.

Rusch looked as though his heart had skipped a beat—as though he thought Theo was pointing to his wife, in the flesh, miraculously made whole again. But then his eyes lighted on the picture. "Yes," he said.

"She's very pretty."

"Thank you," mumbled Rusch.

Theo waited a few moments, then simply went on. "I've spoken to a few people who were reading newspaper or online articles about my—my murder, but you are the first I've found who actually saw something on TV. Please, what can you tell me about it?"

Rusch finally indicated that Theo should sit down, which he did, near the picture of the late Frau Rusch. On the coffee table, there was bowl full of grapes—probably one of the new genetically engineered varieties that stayed succulent even without refrigeration.

"There isn't much to tell," said Rusch. "Although there was one strange thing, now that I think about it. The news report wasn't in German. Rather, it was in French. Not many French newscasts here in Germany."

"Were there call letters or a network logo?"

"Oh, probably—but I didn't pay any attention to them."

"The newscaster—did you recognize him?"

"Her. No. She was efficient, though. Very crisp. But it's no surprise I didn't recognize her; she was certainly under thirty, meaning she'd be less than ten years old today."

"Did they superimpose her name? If I can find her today, her vision, of course, would be of her giving that newscast, and maybe she remembered something that you didn't."

"I wasn't watching the newscast live; it was recorded. My vision started with me fast-forwarding; I wasn't using a remote, though. Rather, the player was responding to my voice. But it was skipping ahead. It wasn't videotape; the sped-up image was absolutely smooth, with no snow or jerkiness." He paused. "Anyway, as soon as a graphic came up behind her showing a picture of—well, it was of you, I guess, although you were older, of course—I stopped fast-forwarding, and began to watch. The words under the graphic said '*Un Savant tué*'—'death of a scientist.' I guess that title intrigued me, you know, being a scientist myself."

"And you watched the whole report?"

"Yes."

A thought crossed Theo's mind. If Rusch had watched the whole report, then it must have lasted less than two minutes. Of course, three minutes was an eternity on TV, but . . .

But his whole life, dismissed in under one minute and forty-three seconds . . .

"What did the reporter say?" asked Theo. "Anything you can remember will be a help."

"I honestly don't recall much. My future self may have been intrigued, but, well, I guess I was panicking. I mean— what the hell was going on? I'd been sitting at the kitchen table, over there, drinking some coffee and reading some student papers, then suddenly everything changed. The last thing I was interested in was paying attention to the details of some news story about somebody I didn't know."

"I understand that it must have been very disorienting," said Theo, but having not had a vision himself he suspected he really didn't understand. "Still, as I said, any details you could remember would be helpful."

"Well, the woman said you were a scientist—a physicist, I think. Is that right?"

"Yes."

"And she said you were—you will be—forty-eight years old."

Theo nodded.

"And she said you were shot."

"Did she say where?"

"Ah, in the chest, I think."

"No, no. Where I was shot—what place?"

"I'm afraid not."

"Was it at CERN?"

"She said you worked at CERN, but—but I don't recall her saying that was where you were killed. I'm sorry."

"Did she mention a sports arena? A boxing match?"

Rusch looked surprised by the question. "No."

"Do you remember anything else?"

"I'm sorry, no."

"What was the story that came on after the one about me?" He didn't know why he asked that—maybe to see where he had fitted into the pecking order.

"I'm sorry, I don't know. I didn't watch the rest of the newscast. When the piece on you was finished, a commercial came on—for a company that lets you create designer babies. That *did* fascinate me—the 2009 me—but my 2030 self seemed to have no interest in it. He just turned off the—well, it wasn't really a TV, of course; it was a hanging flatscreen thing. But he just turned it off—he said the word 'Off' to it, and it went dark, just like that; no fading out. And then he—me—we turned around and—I guess I was in a hotel room; there were two large beds in it. I went and lay down on one of the beds, fully clothed. And I spent the rest of the time just staring at the ceiling, until my vision ended and I was back at the kitchen table." He paused. "I had a nasty bump on my forehead, of course; I'd smashed it into the tabletop when the vision began. And I'd spilled hot coffee on my hand, too; I must have knocked over my mug when I pitched forward. I was lucky that I wasn't seriously burnt. It took me a while to collect my wits, and then I found out that everyone in the building had also had some sort of hallucination. And then I tried to call my wife, only to find out that . . . that . . ." He swallowed hard. "It took them a while to find her, or, at least, to contact me. She'd been walking up a steep flight of stairs, coming out of the subway. She'd almost made it to the top, according to others who saw her, and then she'd blacked out, and fallen backwards, down sixty or seventy steps. The fall broke her neck."

"My God," said Theo. "I'm sorry."

Rusch nodded this time, simply accepting the comment.

There was nothing else to be said between them, and, besides, Theo had to get back to the airport; he didn't want to run up the cost of a hotel room in Berlin.

"Many thanks for your time," said Theo. He reached into his pocket and pulled out his business-card case. "If you recall anything else that you think might be helpful, I'd really appreciate it if you'd give me a call or drop me an email." He handed Rusch a card.

The man took it, but didn't look at it. Theo left.

Lloyd went back to Gaston Béranger's office the next day. This time the journey took even longer: he was waylaid by a unified-field-theory group on their way over to the Computer Center. When he at last made it to Béranger's office, Lloyd began, "I'm sorry, Gaston, you can try to oust me if you want, but I'm going to go public."

"I thought I was clear—"

"We *have* to go public. Look, I just got through speaking to Theo. Did you know he went to Germany yesterday?"

"I can't keep track of the comings and goings of three thousand employees."

"He went to Germany—on a moment's notice, and he got a cheap fare. Why? *Because people are afraid to fly.* The whole world is still paralyzed, Gaston. Everyone is afraid that the time displacement is going to happen again. Check the newspapers or the TV, if you don't believe me; I just did myself. They're avoiding sports, driving when only absolutely necessary, and not flying. It's as if—it's as if they're waiting for the other shoe to drop." Lloyd thought again about the announcement that his father was leaving. "But it isn't going to happen, isn't it? So long as we don't replicate what we were doing here, there's no way in which the time-displacement will repeat. We can't leave the world hanging. We've done enough damage already. We can't let people be afraid to get on with their lives, to go back—as much as possible—to the way things were before."

Béranger seemed to be considering this.

"Come on, Gaston. Someone is going to leak it soon enough anyway."

Béranger exhaled. "I know that. You think I don't know that? I don't want to be obstructionist here. But we do need to think about the consequences—the legal ramifications."

"Surely it's better if we come forward of our own volition, rather than waiting for someone to blow the whistle on us."

Béranger looked at the ceiling for a time. "I know you don't like me," he said, without meeting Lloyd's eyes. Lloyd opened his mouth to protest, but Béranger raised a hand. "Don't bother denying it. We've never gotten along; we've never been friends. Part of that is natural, of course—you see it in every lab in the world. Scientists who think the administrators exist to stymie their work. Administrators who act as though the scientists are an inconvenience instead of the heart and soul of the place. But it goes beyond that, doesn't it? No matter what our jobs were, you wouldn't like me. I'd never stopped to think about stuff like that before. I always knew some people didn't like me and never would, but I never figured it might be my fault." He paused, then shrugged a little. "But maybe it is. I never told you what my vision showed . . . and I'm not about to tell you now. But it got me thinking. Maybe I *have* been fighting you too much. You think we should go public? Christ, I don't know if that's the right thing to do or not. I don't know that *not* going public is the right thing, either."

He paused. "We've come up with a parallel, by the way— something to toss the press if it does leak out, an analogy to demonstrate why we aren't culpable."

Lloyd raised his eyebrows.

"The Tacoma Narrows Bridge collapse," said Béranger.

Lloyd nodded. Early on November 7, 1940, the pavement on the Tacoma Narrows suspension bridge in Washington state began to ripple. Soon the whole bridge was oscillating up and down, massively heaving, until, at last, it collapsed. Every high-school physics student in the world had seen film of this, and for decades they were given the best-guess explanation: that perhaps the wind had generated a natural resonance with the bridge, causing it to undulate in waves.

Surely the bridge-builders should have foreseen that, people had said at the time; after all, resonance was as old as tuning forks. But the resonance explanation was wrong; resonance requires great precision—if it didn't, every singer could shatter a wine glass—and random winds almost certainly couldn't produce it. No, it was shown in 1990 that the Tacoma Narrows Bridge had collapsed due to the fundamental nonlinearity of suspension bridges, an outgrowth of chaos theory— a branch of science that hadn't even existed when the bridge was built. The engineers who had designed it hadn't been culpable; there was no way with the knowledge then available that they could have predicted or prevented the collapse.

"If it had just been visions," said Béranger, "you know, we wouldn't need to cover our asses; I suspect most people would thank you. But there were all those car accidents and people falling off ladders, and so on. Are you prepared to take the blame? Because it won't be me that takes the fall, and it won't be CERN. When it comes right down to it, no matter how much we talk about Tacoma Narrows and unforeseen consequences, people will still want a specific human scapegoat, and you know that's going to be you, Lloyd. It was your experiment."

The Director-General stopped talking. Lloyd considered all this for a time, then said, "I can handle it."

Béranger nodded once. *"Bien.* We'll call a press conference." He looked out his window. "I guess it *is* time we came clean."

BOOK II

SPRING 2009

Free will is an illusion.
It is synonymous with incomplete perception.

—Walter Kubilius

BOOK II.

SPRING 1944

12

Day Five: Saturday, April 25, 2009

THE ADMINISTRATIVE BUILDING AT CERN had all sorts of seminar halls and meeting spaces. For the press conference, they were using a lecture hall with two hundred seats—every one of which was filled. All the PR people had needed to do was tell the media that CERN was about to make a major announcement about the cause of the time displacement, and reporters arrived from all over Europe, plus one from Japan, one from Canada, and six from the United States.

Béranger was being true to his word: he was letting Lloyd take center stage; if there were to be a scapegoat, it was going to be him. Lloyd walked up to the lectern and cleared his throat. "Hello, everyone," he said. "My name is Lloyd Simcoe." He'd been coached by one of CERN's PR people to spell it out, and so he did just that: "That's S-I-M-C-O-E, and 'Lloyd' begins with a double-L." The reporters would all receive DVDs with Lloyd's comments and bio on them, but many would be filing stories immediately, without a chance to consult the press kits. Lloyd went on. "My specialty is quark-gluon plasma studies. I'm a Canadian citizen, but I worked for many years in the United States at the Fermi National Accelerator Laboratory. And for the last two years, I've been here at CERN, developing a major experiment for the Large Hadron Collider."

He paused; he was buying time, trying to get his stomach to calm down. It wasn't that he had a fear of public speaking; he'd spent too long as a university professor for any of that to remain. But he had no way of knowing what the reaction would be to what he was about to say.

"This is my associate, Dr. Theodosios Procopides," continued Lloyd.

Theo half-rose from his chair, next to the lectern. "Theo," he said, with a little smile at the crowd. "Call me Theo."

One big happy family, thought Lloyd. He spelled Theo's first and last names slowly for the reporters, then took a deep breath and pressed on. "We were conducting an experiment here on April 21, at precisely 1600 hours Greenwich Mean Time."

He paused again and looked from face to face. It didn't take long for it to sink in. Journalists immediately started shouting questions, and Lloyd's eyes were assaulted by camera flashes. He raised his hands, palms out, waiting for the reporters to be quiet.

"Yes," he said, "yes, I suspect you're right. We have reason to believe that the time-displacement phenomenon had to do with the work we were doing here with the Large Hadron Collider."

"How can that be?" asked Klee, a stringer for CNN.

"Are you sure?" called out Jonas, a correspondent for the BBC.

"Why didn't you come forward before this?" called the Reuters reporter.

"I'll take that last question first," said Lloyd. "Or, more precisely, I'll let Dr. Procopides take it."

"Thanks," said Theo, standing now and moving to the mike. "The, ah, reason we did not come forward earlier is that we didn't have a theoretical model to explain what happened." He paused. "Frankly, we still don't; it has, after all, only been four days since the Flashforward. But the fact is we engineered the highest-energy particle collision in the history of this planet, and it occurred precisely—to the very second— at the moment the phenomenon began. We can't ignore that a causal relationship might exist."

"How sure are you that the two things are linked?" asked a woman from the *Tribune de Genève.*

Theo shrugged. "We can't think of anything in our experiment that could have caused the Flashforward. Then again, we can't think of anything else *other* than our experiment that could have caused it, either. It just seems that our work is the most likely candidate."

Lloyd looked over at Dr. Béranger, whose hawklike face was impassive. When they'd rehearsed this press conference, Theo had originally said "the most likely culprit," and Béranger had sworn a blue streak at the word choice. But it turned out to make no difference. "So are you admitting responsibility?" asked Klee. "Admitting all the deaths were your fault?"

Lloyd felt his stomach knot, and he could see Béranger's face crease into a frown. The Director-General looked like he was ready to step in and take over the press conference.

"We admit that our experiment seems the most likely cause," said Lloyd, moving over to stand next to Theo. "But we contend that there was no way—absolutely none—to predict anything remotely like what happened as a consequence of what we did. This was utterly unforeseen—and unforeseeable. It was, quite simply, what the insurance industry calls an act of God."

"But all the deaths—" shouted one reporter.

"All the property damage—" shouted another.

Lloyd raised his hands again. "Yes, we know. Believe me, our hearts go out to every person who was hurt or who lost someone they cared about. A little girl very dear to me died when a car spun out of control; I would give anything to have her back. But it could not have been prevented—"

"Of course it could have," shouted Jonas. "If you hadn't done the experiment, it never would have happened."

"Politely, sir, that's irrational," said Lloyd. "Scientists do experiments all the time, and we take every reasonable precaution. CERN, as you know, has an enviable safety record. But people can't simply stop doing things—science can't stop marching forward. We didn't know that this would happen; we *couldn't* know it. But we're coming clean; we're telling the world. I know people are afraid that it's going to happen again, that at any moment their consciousness might be transported once more into the future. But it won't; we were the cause, and we can assure you—assure everyone—that there's no danger of something similar happening again."

There were, of course, cries of outrage in the press—editorials about scientists messing with things humans were not meant to know about. But, try as they might, even the sleaziest tabloid wasn't able to come up with a credible physicist willing to claim that there was any reason to have suspected that the CERN experiment would cause the displacement of consciousness through time. Of course, that engendered some half-hearted comments about physicists protecting one another. But polls rapidly switched from blaming the team at CERN to accepting that this was something that had been utterly unpredictable, something totally new.

It was still a difficult time personally for Lloyd and Michiko. Michiko had flown back to Tokyo with Tamiko's body. Lloyd, had, of course, offered to go with her, but he spoke no Japanese. Normally, those who spoke English would have politely tried to accommodate Lloyd, but under such dire circumstances it seemed clear that he would be left out of almost every conversation. There was also the awkwardness of it all: Lloyd wasn't Tamiko's stepfather; he wasn't Michiko's husband. This was a time for Michiko and Hiroshi, regardless of whatever differences they'd had in the past, to mourn and lay to rest their daughter. As much as he, too, was crushed by what had happened to Tamiko, Lloyd had to admit that there was little he could do to aid Michiko in Japan.

And so, while she flew east to her homeland, Lloyd stayed at CERN, trying to make a baffled world understand the physics of what had occurred.

"Dr. Simcoe," said Bernard Shaw, "perhaps you can explain to us what happened?"

"Of course," said Lloyd, making himself comfortable. He was in CERN's teleconferencing room, a camera no bigger than a thimble facing him from atop an emaciated tripod. Shaw, naturally, was at CNN Center in Atlanta. Lloyd had five other similar interviews lined up for later in the day, including one in French. "Most of us have heard the term 'spacetime' or 'the space-time continuum.' It refers to the combination of the three dimensions of length, width, and height, and the fourth dimension of time."

Lloyd nodded at a female technician standing off camera, and a still image of a dark-haired white man appeared on the monitor behind him. "That's Hermann Minkowski," said Lloyd. "He's the fellow who first proposed the concept of the space-time continuum." A pause. "It's hard to illustrate the concept of four dimensions directly, but if we simplify it by removing one spatial dimension, it's easy."

He nodded again and the picture changed.

"This is a map of Europe. Of course, Europe is three dimensional, but we're all used to using two-dimensional maps. And Hermann Minkowski was born here in Kaunas, in what is now Lithuania, in 1864."

A light lit up inside Lithuania.

"There it is. Actually, though, let's pretend that the light isn't the city of Kaunas, but rather Minkowski himself, being born in 1864."

The legend "A.D. 1864" appeared at the lower-right of the map.

"If we go back a few years, we can see there's no Minkowski before that point."

The map date changed to A.D. 1863, then A.D. 1862, then

A.D. 1861, and, sure enough, it was Minkowskiless throughout.

"Now, let's go back to 1864."

The map obliged, with Minkowski's light glowing brightly at the latitude and longitude of Kaunas.

"In 1878," said Lloyd, "Minkowski moved to Berlin to go to university."

The 1864 map fell away as if it were one leaf on a calendar pad; the map beneath was labeled 1865. In rapid succession, other maps dropped off, labeled 1866 through 1877, each with the Minkowski light at or near Kaunas, but when the 1878 one appeared, the light had moved 400 kilometers west to Berlin.

"Minkowski didn't stay in Berlin," said Lloyd. "In 1881, he transferred to Königsberg, near the modern Polish border."

Three more maps fell away, and when the one labeled 1881 was exposed, the Minkowski light had relocated again.

"For the next nineteen years, our Hermann bopped about from university to university, coming back to Königsberg in 1894, then going to Zurich here in Switzerland in 1896, and at last to the University of Göttingen, in central Germany, in 1902."

The changing maps reflected his movements.

"And he stayed in Göttingen until his death on January 12, 1909."

More maps fell away, but the light remained stationary.

"And, of course, after 1909, he was no more."

Maps labeled "1910," "1911" and "1912" fell away, but none of them had lights.

"Now," said Lloyd, "what happens if we take our maps and stack them back up in chronological order, and tip them a bit, so that we view them obliquely?"

The computer-generated graphics on the screen behind him obligingly did just that.

"As you can see, the light made by Minkowski's movements forms a trail through time. He starts down here near the bottom in Lithuania, moves about Germany and Switzerland, and finally dies up here in Göttingen."

The maps were stacked one atop another, forming a cube,

and the path of Minkowski's life, weaving through the cube, was visible through it, like a glowing gopher's burrow climbing up toward the top.

"This kind of cube, which shows someone's life path through spacetime, is called a Minkowski cube: good old Hermann himself was the first to draw such a thing. Of course, you can draw one for anybody. Here's one for me."

The map changed to show the entire world.

"I was born in Nova Scotia, Canada, in 1964, moved to Toronto then Harvard for university, worked for years at Fermilab in Illinois, and then ended up here, on the Swiss/French border, at CERN."

The maps stacked up, forming a cube with a weaving light-path within.

"And, of course, you can map other people's path onto the same cube."

Five other light paths, each one a different color, wended their ways up the cube. Some started earlier than Lloyd's, and some ended before the top was reached.

"The top of the cube, here," said Lloyd, "represents today, April 25, 2009. And, of course, we all agree that today *is* today. That is, we all remember yesterday, but acknowledge that it has passed; and we all are ignorant of tomorrow. We're all collectively looking at this particular slice through the cube." The cube's top face lit up.

"You can imagine the collective mind's eye of humanity regarding that slice." A drawing of a human eye, complete with lashes, floated outside the cube, parallel to its top. "But what happened during the Flashforward was this: the mind's eye moved up the cube into the future, and instead of regarding the slice representing 2009, it found itself looking at 2030."

The cube extended upward into a block, and most of the color-coded life paths continued on up farther into it. The floating eye jumped up, and the highlighted plane was now very near the top of the elongated block. "For two minutes, we were looking in on another point along our life paths."

Bernard Shaw shifted in his chair. "So you're saying spacetime is like a bunch of motion-picture frames stacked up, and 'now' is the currently illuminated frame?"

"That's a good analogy," said Lloyd. "In fact, it helps me make my next point, which is this: Say you're watching *Casablanca*, which happens to be my favorite movie. And say this particular moment is what's on screen right now."

Behind Lloyd, Humphrey Bogart was saying, "You played it for her, you can play it for me. If she can stand it, I can stand it."

Dooley Wilson didn't meet Bogey's eyes. "I don't remember the words."

Bogart, through clenched teeth: "Play it!"

Wilson turned his gaze up at the ceiling and began to sing "As Time Goes By" while his fingers danced on the piano keys.

"Now," said Lloyd, sitting in front of the screen, "just because *this* frame is the one you're currently looking at"—as he said "this," the image froze on Dooley Wilson—"it doesn't mean that *this* other part is any less fixed or real."

Suddenly the image changed. A plane was disappearing into the fog. A dapper Claude Rains looked at Bogart. "It might be a good idea for you to disappear from Casablanca for a while," he said. "There's a Free French garrison over at Brazzaville. I could be induced to arrange a passage."

Bogey smiled a bit. "My letter of transit? I could use a trip. But it doesn't make any difference about our bet. You still owe me ten thousand francs."

Rains raised his eyebrows. "And that ten thousand francs should pay our expenses."

"*Our* expenses?" said Bogart, surprised.

Rains nodded. "Uh-huh."

Lloyd watched their backs as they walked off together into the night. "Louis," says Bogart—in a voiceover Lloyd knew had been recorded in post-production—"this could be the beginning of a beautiful friendship."

"You see?" said Lloyd, turning back to look at the camera, at Shaw. "You might have been watching Sam play 'As Time

Goes By' for Rick, but the ending *is already fixed*. The first time you see *Casablanca*, you're on the edge of your seat wondering if Ilsa is going to go with Victor Laszlo or stay with Rick Blaine. But the answer always was, and always will be, the same: the problems of two little people really don't amount to a hill of beans in this crazy world.''

"You're saying the future is as immutable as the past?" said Shaw, looking more dubious than he usually did.

"Precisely."

"But, Dr. Simcoe, with all due respect, that doesn't seem to make sense. I mean, what about free will?"

Lloyd folded his arms in front of his chest. "There's no such thing as free will."

"Of course there is," said Shaw.

Lloyd smiled. "I knew you were going to say that. Or, more precisely, anyone looking at our Minkowski cubes from outside knew you were going to say that—because it was already written in stone."

"But how can that be? We make a million decisions a day; each of them shapes our future."

"You made a million decisions yesterday, but they are immutable—there's no way to change them, no matter how much we might regret some of them. And you'll make a million decisions tomorrow. There's no difference. You *think* you have free will, but you don't."

"So, let me see if I understand you, Dr. Simcoe. You're contending that the visions aren't of just one possible future. Rather, they are of *the* future—the only one that exists."

"Absolutely. We really do live in a Minkowski block universe, and the concept of 'now' really is an illusion. The future, the present, and the past are each just as real and just as immutable."

13

It was early evening; Lloyd had finally finished his last interview for the day, and although he had a stack of reports to read before going to bed, he was now walking down one of the drab streets of St. Genis. He headed over to a bakery and a cheese store to get some bread and a hunk of Appenzeller for tomorrow's breakfast.

A compact man of about thirty-five approached him. He was wearing glasses—reasonably unusual in the developed world now that laser keratotomy had been perfected—and a dark-blue sweatshirt. His hair, like Lloyd's own, was cropped fashionably short.

Lloyd felt a twinge of panic. He was probably crazy to be out alone in public after half the world had seen his face on TV. He looked left and right, sizing up his escape routes. There were none. "Yes?" he said, tentatively.

"Dr. Lloyd Simcoe?" He was speaking English, but with a French accent.

Lloyd swallowed "That's me." Tomorrow, he'd talk to Béranger about arranging a security escort.

Suddenly the man's hand found Simcoe's own and began pumping it furiously. "Dr. Simcoe, I want to thank you!" The man held up his left hand, as if to forestall an objection. "Yes, yes, I know you didn't intend what happened, and I guess some people were hurt by it. But I've got to tell you, that vision was the best thing that ever happened to me. It turned my life around."

"Ah," said Lloyd, retrieving his hand. "That's nice."

"Yes, sir, before that vision I was a different man. I never believed in God—not ever, not even as a little kid. But my vision—my vision showed me in a church, praying with a whole congregation of people."

"Praying on a Wednesday evening?"

"That's just what I said, Dr. Simcoe! I mean, not at the time I was having the vision, but later, after they announced on the news what time the visions were of. Praying on a Wednesday evening! Me! Me, of all people. Well, I couldn't deny that it was happening, that sometime between now and then I will find my way. And so I picked up a Bible—went to a bookstore and bought one. I never knew there were so many different kinds! So many different translations! Anyway, I got myself one of the ones that's got Jesus' actual words printed in red, and I began reading it. I figured, okay, sooner or later I was going to come to this, I might as well find out what it's all about. And I just kept reading—I even read all those begats, those wonderful names, like music: Obadiah, Jebediah—what great names! Oh, sure, Dr. Simcoe, if I hadn't had the vision, twenty-one years down the road I would have found all this anyway, but you got me going on it now, in 2009. I've never felt more at peace, more loved. You really did me a great favor."

Lloyd didn't know what to say. "Thank you."

"No, sir—thank you!" And he pumped Lloyd's hand again, then dashed upon his way.

•   •   •

Lloyd got home around 21h00. He missed Michiko a lot, and thought about calling her, but it was just 05h00 in Tokyo—too early to phone. He put his cheese and bread away, and sat down to watch some television—unwind for a few moments before he tackled the latest stack of reports.

He flipped channels until something on a Swiss news program caught his eye: a discussion of the Flashforward. A female journalist was doing a satellite hookup with the United States. Lloyd recognized the man being interviewed by his great mane of reddish-brown hair: the Astounding Alexander, master illusionist and debunker of supposed psychic powers. Lloyd had seen the guy on TV often over the years, including on *The Tonight Show*. His full name was Raymond Alexander, and he was a professor at Duke.

The interview had obviously had some post-production done on it: the journalist was speaking in French, but Alexander was answering in English, and an interpreter's voice was speaking over his own, giving a French version of what the American was saying. Alexander's actual words were barely audible in the background.

"You've no doubt heard," said the interviewer, "that man from CERN claiming that the visions showed the one and only real future."

Lloyd sat up.

"*Oui*," said the translator's voice. "But that's patently absurd. You can easily demonstrate that the future is malleable." Alexander shifted in his chair. "In my own vision, I was at my apartment. And on my desk, then as now, was this." There was a table in front of him in the studio. He reached forward and picked up a paperweight. The camera zoomed in: it was a malachite block with a small gold *Triceratops* on it.

"Now, it may be chintzy," said Alexander, "but I'm actually rather fond of this little item; it's a souvenir of a trip I quite enjoyed to Dinosaur National Monument. But I'm not as fond of it as I am of rationality."

He reached below the table, and pulled out a piece of burlap. He set it down, then placed the paperweight on top of it. Next, he pulled a hammer from under the table, and, as the camera watched, he proceeded to smash the souvenir to bits, the malachite fracturing and crumbling, and the small dinosaur—which couldn't have been solid metal—crushing into an unrecognizable lump.

Alexander smiled triumphantly at the camera: reason once more held sway. "That paperweight was in my vision; that paperweight no longer exists. Therefore, whatever it was that the visions showed was in no way a view of an immutable future."

"We have, of course," said the interviewer, "only your word that the paperweight was in your vision."

Alexander looked annoyed, irritated that his integrity was being questioned. But then he nodded. "You're right to be skeptical—the world would be a better place if we were all a little less credulous. The fact is that anyone can do this experiment themselves. If in your vision you saw a piece of furniture you currently own, destroy—or sell—that piece. If you could see your own hand in your vision, get a tattoo on your hand. If others saw you, and you had a beard, get facial electrolysis so that you'll never be able to grow one."

"Facial electrolysis!" said the interviewer. "That seems an extreme length to go to."

"If your vision disturbed you, and you want to be reassured that it never will come true, that would be one way to do it. Of course the most effective way to disprove the visions on a large scale would be to find some landmark that thousands of people had seen—the Statue of Liberty, say— and tear it down. But I don't suppose the National Park Service is going to let us do that."

Lloyd leaned back into his couch. Such bullshit. None of the things Alexander had suggested were real proof—and all of them were subjective; they depended on people's own recountings of their visions. And, well, what a great way to get on TV—not just for Alexander, but for anyone who wanted to be interviewed. Just claim that you've disproved the immutability of the future.

Lloyd looked at the clock sitting on one of the shelves mounted against the dark red walls of his apartment. It was 21h30—meaning it'd only be 1:30 in the afternoon at the Colorado/Utah border, where Dinosaur National Monument was located; Lloyd had been there himself once. He thought for a few minutes more, then picked up the phone, spoke to a directory-assistance operator, and finally to a woman who worked in the gift shop at Dinosaur Monument.

"Hello," he said. "I'm looking for a particular item—a paperweight made out of malachite."

"Malachite?"

"It's a green mineral—you know, an ornamental stone."

"Oh, yes, sure. The ones we've got have little dinos on them. We've got one with a *T. rex*, one with a *Stegosaurus*, and one with a *Triceratops*."

"How much is the *Triceratops?*"

"Fourteen ninety-five."

"Do you do mail order?"

"Sure."

"I'd like to buy one of those and send it to . . ." He stopped to think; where the heck *was* Duke? "To North Carolina."

"Okay. What's the full address?"

"I'm not sure. Just put 'Professor Raymond Alexander, Duke University, Durham, North Carolina.' I'm sure it'll get there."

"UPS?"

"That would be fine."

Keyclicks. "The shipping is eight-fifty. How'd you like to pay for it?"

"On my Visa."

"Number, please?"

He pulled out his wallet, and read the string of digits to her; he also gave her the expiration date and his name. And then he hung up the phone, settled back into the couch, and folded his arms across his chest, feeling quite satisfied.

Dear Dr. Simcoe:

Forgive me for bothering you with an unsolicited email; I hope this makes it through your spam filter. I know you must be inundated with letters ever since you went on TV, but I just had to write and let you know the impact my vision had on me.

I'm eighteen years old, and I'm pregnant. I'm not very far along—only about two months. I hadn't told my boyfriend yet, or my parents. I thought getting pregnant was the worst thing that could have possibly happened: I'm still in high school, and my boyfriend will start university in the fall. We both still live with our parents, and we have no money. There was no way, I thought, that we could bring a child into the world . . . and so I was going to have an abortion. I'd already made the appointment.

And then I had my vision—and it was incredible! It was me, and Brad (that's my boyfriend) and our daughter, and we were all together, living in a nice house, twenty-one years down the road. My daughter was all grown up—even a little older than I am now—and she was so beautiful and she was telling us about how she was seeing this guy at school, and could she bring him over for dinner one night, and she knew we'd just love him, and of course we said yes, because she was our daughter and it was important to her, and . . .

Well, I'm babbling. The point is that my vision let me see that things *were* going to work out. I canceled the abortion, and Brad and I are looking for a small place to live together, and, to my surprise, my parents didn't freak and they're even going to help us a bit with expenses.

I know a lot of people will be telling you how their visions ruined their lives. I just wanted you to know that it improved mine enormously, and that it actually saved the life of the little girl I'm carrying inside me now.

Thank you . . . for everything.

Jean Alcott

Dr. Simcoe,

You hear on the news about people who had fascinating visions. Not me. My vision had myself in the exact same house I live in today. I was all alone, which isn't unusual—my kids are grown and my wife is often busy with her work. Indeed, although a few things looked different—furniture slightly rearranged, a new painting on one wall— there was nothing to give any real indication that this was the future.

And you know what? I like that. I'm a happy man; I've got a good life. That I'm going to have another couple of decades of precisely the same life is a very soothing thought. This whole vision thing has turned a lot of people's lives upside down, apparently—but not mine. I just wanted you to know that.

Best wishes,
Tony DiCiccio

POSTINGS TO THE
MOSAIC PROJECT WEB SITE

Brooklyn, New York: Okay, there was this American flag in my dream, right? And it had, I think, 52 stars: a row of 7, then a row of 6, then 7, then 6, like that, for a total of 52. Now, I'm figuring that the 51st star, that must be Puerto Rico, right? But it's driving me crazy trying to guess what the 52nd might be. If you know, please e-mail . . .

•

Edmonton, Alberta: I am not smart. I have Down's Syndrome, but I am a good person. In my vision, I was talking and using big words, so I must have been smart. I want to be smart again.

•

Indianapolis, Indiana: Please stop sending me email saying that I will be the President of the United States in 2030; it's flooding my mailbox. I know I'll be President—and when I come to power, I will have the IRS audit anyone who tells me again . . .

•

Islamabad, Pakistan (autotranslated from the original Arabic): In my vision, I have two arms—but today, I have only one (I am a veteran of the India-Pakistan ground war). It didn't feel like a prosthesis in the vision. I'd be interested in hearing from anyone who has any information on artificial limbs or possibly even limb regeneration twenty-one years hence.

•

Changzhou, China (autotranslated from the original Mandarin): I am apparently dead in twenty-one years, which does not surprise me for I am mightily old now. But I would be interested in any news of the success of my children, grandchildren, or great grandchildren. Their names are . . .

•

Buenos Aires, Argentina: Almost everybody I've spoken to is celebrating a holiday or is off work during the Flashforward. Well, the third Wednesday in October isn't a holiday anywhere I know of in South America, so I'm thinking maybe we've gone to a four-day workweek, with Wednesdays off. Me, I'd prefer a three-day weekend. Anybody know for sure?

•

Auckland, New Zealand: I know four of the winning numbers in the New Zealand Super Eight draw of October 19, 2030—in my vision, I was cashing a ticket that earned a $200 prize for matching those four numbers. If you know other winning numbers in the same lottery, I would like to pool my information with yours.

•

Geneva, Switzerland (posted in fourteen languages): Anybody with information about the murder of Theodosios ("Theo") Procopides, please contact me at . . .

14

Day Six: Sunday, April 26, 2009

LLOYD AND THEO WERE EATING LUNCH TO-
gether in the large cafeteria at the LHC control center. Around
them, other physicists were arguing theories and interpreta-
tions to account for the Flashforward—a promising lead related to a supposed failure of one of the quadrapole magnets
had been torpedoed in the last hour. The magnet, it turned
out, was operating just fine; it was the testing equipment that
was faulty.

Lloyd was having a salad; Theo a kebab he'd made the
night before and had reheated in the microwave. "People seem
to be dealing with things better than I would have thought,"
said Lloyd. The windows looked out on the nucleus courtyard,
where the spring flowers were in bloom. "All that death, all
the destruction. But people are dusting themselves off, getting
back to work, and getting on with their lives."

Theo nodded. "I heard a guy on the radio this morning.
He was saying that there had turned out to be far less call for
counseling services than people had predicted. In fact, a lot of
people have been apparently canceling their previously scheduled therapy sessions since the Flashforward."

Lloyd lifted his eyebrows. "Why?"

"He said it's because of the catharsis." Theo smiled. "I tell you, good old Aristotle knew exactly what he was talking about: you give people a chance to purge their emotions, and they actually end up more healthy after it. So many people lost someone they cared about during the Flashforward; the outpouring of grief has been very good psychologically. The guy on the radio said something similar happened a dozen years ago when Princess Diana died; there was a huge reduction worldwide in the use of therapists for months following that. Naturally, the biggest catharsis was in England, but just after Di was killed, even twenty-seven percent of Americans felt as though they had lost someone they knew personally." A pause.

"Of course, you don't get over the loss of a spouse or a child easily, but an uncle? A distant cousin? An actor you liked? One of your coworkers? It's a big release."

"But if everyone's going through it . . ."

"That was his whole point," said Theo. "See, normally, if you lose someone in an accident, you go to pieces, and it goes on for months or years . . . with everyone around you reinforcing your right to be sad. 'Take some time,' they say. Everyone provides emotional support for you. But if everyone else is dealing with a loss, too, there isn't that crutch effect; there's no one to say soothing words. You've got no choice but to get a grip and go back to work. It's like those who live through a war—any war is much more devastating in gross terms than any isolated personal tragedy, but after a war is over, most people just go on with their lives. Everybody suffered the same; you have to just wall it off, forget about it, and go on. That's what's happening here, apparently."

"I don't think Michiko will ever get over the loss of Tamiko." Michiko would come home from Japan that evening.

"No, no, of course not. Not in the sense that it'll ever stop hurting. But she *is* going on with her life; what else can she do? There really is no other choice."

At that moment, Franco della Robbia, a middle-aged,

bearded physicist, appeared at their table, holding a tray. "Mind if I join you?"

Lloyd looked up. "Hi, Franco. Not at all."

Theo shuffled his chair to the right, and della Robbia sat down.

"You're wrong about Minkowski, you know," said della Robbia, looking at Lloyd. "The visions can't be of an actual future."

Lloyd took a forkful of salad. "Why not?"

"Well, look: let's take your premise. Twenty-one years from now, I will have a connection between my future self and my past self. That is, my past self will see exactly what my future self is doing. Now, my future self may not have any overt indication that the connection has begun, but that doesn't matter; I'll know to the second when the connection will start and end. I don't know what your vision showed, Lloyd, but mine had me in what I think was Sorrento, sitting on a balcony, overlooking the Bay of Naples. Very nice, very pleasant—but not at all what I'd be doing on October 23, 2030, if I knew I was in contact with myself in the past. Rather, I'd be somewhere utterly free of anything that might divert my past self's attention—an empty room, say, or simply staring at a blank wall. And at precisely 19h21 Greenwich Mean Time that day, I would start reciting out loud facts that I wanted my past self to know: 'On March eleven, 2012, be careful crossing Via Colombo, lest you trip and break your leg;' 'In your time, stock in Bertelsmann is selling for forty-two euros a share, but by 2030, it'll be six hundred and ninety euros a share, so buy lots now to pay for your retirement;' 'Here are the winners of the World Cup for every year between your time and mine.' Like that; I would have it all written out on a piece of paper, and would just recite it, cramming as much useful information as possible into that one-minute-and-forty-three-second window." The Italian physicist paused. "The fact that no one has reported a vision of doing anything like that means that what we saw couldn't be the actual future of the timeline we're currently in."

Lloyd frowned. "Maybe some people *did* do that. Really, the public only knows the content of a tiny percentage of the billions of visions that must have occurred. If I was going to give myself a stock tip, and I didn't know that the future was immutable, the first thing I'd say to my past self was, 'Don't share this with anyone.' Maybe those who did what you're suggesting are simply keeping quiet about it."

"If a few dozen people had visions," said della Robbia, "that might be possible. But with billions? Someone would have said that that was what they were doing. In fact, I firmly believe almost everyone would be trying to communicate with their past selves."

Lloyd looked at Theo, then back at della Robbia. "Not if they knew it was futile; not if they knew that nothing they said could change things that were already carved in stone."

"Or maybe everyone forgot," said Theo. "Maybe, between now and 2030, the memory of the visions will fade. The memories of dreams fade, after all. You can recall one when you first wake up, but hours later, it's gone completely. Maybe the visions will erase themselves over the next twenty-one years."

Della Robbia shook his head emphatically. "Even if that were the case—and there's no reason at all to think it might be—all the media reporting about the visions would still survive until the year 2030. All the news reports, all the TV coverage, all the things people wrote about themselves in their own diaries and in letters to friends. Psychology isn't my field; I won't debate the fallible nature of memory. But people *would* know what's happening on October 23, 2030, and many would be attempting to communicate with the past."

"Wait a minute," said Theo. His eyebrows were high. "Wait a minute!" Lloyd and della Robbia turned to look at him. "Don't you see? It's Niven's Law."

"What is?" said Lloyd.

"Who's Niven?" said della Robbia.

"An American science-fiction writer. He said that in any universe in which time travel is a possibility, no time machine will ever be invented. He even wrote a little story to dramatize it: a scientist is building a time machine and just as he gets it finished, he looks up and sees the sun going nova—the universe is going to snuff him out, rather than allow the paradoxes inherent in time travel."

"So?" said Lloyd.

"So communicating with yourself in the past is a form of time travel—it's sending information back in time. And for those people who tried to do it, the universe might block the attempt—not by anything as grandiose as blowing up the sun, but simply by preventing the communication from working." He shifted his gaze from Lloyd to della Robbia and back again. "Don't you see? That must have been what I was trying to do in 2030—I'd been attempting to communicate with myself in the past, and so, instead, I simply ended up having no vision at all."

Lloyd tried to make his voice sound gentle. "There seems to be a lot of supporting evidence from other people's visions that you really are dead in 2030, Theo."

Theo opened his mouth, as if to protest, but then he closed it. A moment later, he spoke again. "You're right. You're right. Sorry."

Lloyd nodded; he hadn't really realized before just how hard all of this must be on Theo. He turned and looked at della Robbia. "Well, Franco, if the visions weren't of our future, then what did they portray?"

"An alternative timeline, of course. That's completely reasonable, given MWI." The many-worlds interpretation of quantum physics says that every time an event can go two ways, instead of one or the other way happening, both happen, each in a separate universe. "Specifically, the visions portray the universe that split from this universe at the moment of your LHC experiment; they show the future as it is in a universe in which the time-displacement effect did *not* occur."

But Lloyd was shaking his head. "You don't still believe in MWI, do you? TI demolishes that."

A standard argument in favor of the many-worlds interpretation is the thought experiment of Schrödinger's cat: put a cat in a sealed box with a vial of poison that has a fifty-fifty chance of being triggered during a one-hour period. At the end of the hour, open the box and see if the cat is still alive. Under the Copenhagen interpretation—the standard version of quantum mechanics—until someone looks in, the cat is supposedly neither alive nor dead, but rather a superposition of both possible states; the act of looking in—of observing—collapses the wave function, forcing the cat to resolve itself into one of two possible outcomes. Except that, since the observation could go two ways, what MWI proponents say really happens is that the universe splits at the point at which the observation is made. One universe continues on with a dead cat; the other, with a living one.

John G. Cramer, a physicist who had often done work at CERN, but was normally with the University of Washington, Seattle, disliked the Copenhagen interpretation's emphasis on the observer. In the 1980s, he proposed an alternative explanation: TI, the transactional interpretation. During the nineties and aughts, TI had become increasingly popular amongst physicists.

Consider Schrödinger's hapless cat at the moment it is sealed in the box, and the observer's eye, at the moment, an hour later, that it looks upon the cat. In TI, the cat sends out an actual, physical "offer" wave, which travels forward into the future *and* backward into the past. When the offer wave reaches the eye, the eye sends out a "confirmation" wave, which travels backward into the past and forward into the future. The offer wave and the confirmation wave cancel each other out everywhere in the universe except in the direct line between the cat and the eye, where they reinforce each other, producing a transaction. Since the cat and the eye have communicated across time, there is no ambiguity, and no need for collapsing wave fronts: the cat exists inside the box exactly as it will eventually be observed. There's also no splitting of the universe into two; since the transaction covers the entire relevant period, there's no need for branching: the eye sees the cat as it always was, either dead or alive.

"You *would* like TI," said della Robbia. "It demolishes free will. Every emitted photon knows what will eventually absorb it."

"Sure," said Lloyd, "I admit that TI reinforces the block-universe concept—but it's your many-worlds interpretation that really demolishes free will."

"How can you possibly say that?" said della Robbia, with expressive Italian exasperation.

"There's no hierarchy among the many worlds," said Lloyd. "Say I'm walking along and come to a fork in the road. I could go left, or I could go right. Which one do I choose?"

"Whichever one you want!" crowed della Robbia. "Free will!"

"Nonsense," said Lloyd. "Under MWI, I choose whichever one the other version of me *didn't* choose. If he goes right, I have to go left; if I go right, he has to go left. And only arrogance would lead one to think that it was always my choice in this universe that was considered, and that it was always the other choice that was simply the alternative that had to be expressed in another universe. The many-worlds interpretation gives the *illusion* of choice, but it's actually completely deterministic."

Della Robbia turned to Theo, spreading his arms in an appeal for common sense. "But TI depends on waves that travel backward in time!"

Theo's voice was gentle. "I think we've now abundantly demonstrated the reality of information traveling backward in time, Franco," he said. "Besides, what Cramer actually said was the transaction occurs atemporally—outside of time."

"And," said Lloyd, warming to the fight now that he had an ally, "your version of what happened is the one that demands time travel."

Della Robbia looked stunned. "What? How? The visions simply portray a parallel universe."

"Any parallel MWI universes that might exist would surely be moving in temporal lockstep with ours: if you could see into a parallel universe, you'd still see today, April 26,

2009; indeed, the whole concept of quantum computing depends on parallel universes being precisely in lockstep with ours. So, yes, if you could see into a parallel universe, you might see a world in which you'd gone over to sit down with Michael Burr, over there, instead of with me and Theo, but it'd still be *now*. What you're suggesting is adding contact with parallel universes *on top of* seeing into the future; it's hard enough to accept one of those ideas without also having to accept the other, and—"

Jake Horowitz had appeared at their table. "Sorry to interrupt," he said, "but there's a call for you, Theo. Says it's about your posting on the Mosaic web site."

Theo hurried away from the table, abandoning his half-eaten kebab. "Line three," said Jacob, trailing behind him. There was an empty office just outside the lunch room; Theo ducked in. The phone's caller ID simply said "Out of Area." He picked up the handset.

"Hello," he said. "Theo Procopides here."

"My God," said the male voice, in English, at the other end of the phone. "This is weird—talking to somebody you know is going to be dead."

Theo didn't have any response for that, so he simply said, "You have some information about my murder?"

"Yes, I think so. I was reading something about it in my vision."

"What did it say?"

The man recounted the gist of what he'd read. There were no new facts.

"Was there anything about survivors?" asked Theo.

"How do you mean? It wasn't a plane crash."

"No, no, no. I mean, did it say anything about who survived me—you know, about whether I had a wife or kids."

"Oh, yeah. Let's see if I can remember . . ."

See if I can remember. His future was all incidental; nobody really cared. It wasn't important, wasn't real. Just some guy they'd read about.

"Yeah," said the voice. "Yeah, you'll be survived by a son and by your wife."

"Did the paper give their names?"

The person blew air into the mouthpiece of his phone as he thought. "The son was—Constantin, I think."

Constantin. His father's name; yes, Theo had always thought he might name a son that.

"And the boy's mother? My wife?"

"I'm sorry. I don't remember."

"Please try."

"No, I'm sorry. I just don't remember."

"You could undergo hypnosis—"

"Are you crazy? I'm not going to do that. Look, I called you up to help you out; I figured I'd do you a good turn, you know? I just thought it'd be a nice thing to do. But I'm not going to be hypnotized, or pumped full of drugs, or anything like that."

"But my wife—my widow . . . I need to know who she is."

"Why? I don't know who I'll be married to in twenty-one years; why should you know?"

"She might have a clue as to why I was killed."

"Well, I guess. Maybe. But I've done all I can for you."

"But you saw the name! You know the name!"

"Like I said, I don't remember it. I'm sorry."

"Please—I'll pay you."

"Seriously, man, I don't remember. But, look, if it comes to me, I'll get back in touch. But that's all I can do."

Theo forced himself not to protest again. He pursed his lips, then nodded solemnly. "All right. Thank you. Thanks for your time. Can I just get your name, though, for my records?"

"Sorry, man. Like I said, if anything else occurs to me, I'll call you."

And the phone went dead.

15

MICHIKO RETURNED THAT NIGHT FROM TO-
kyo. She seemed if not at peace at least no longer about to go
to pieces.

Lloyd, who had spent the afternoon going over a new
round of computer simulations, picked Michiko up at Geneva
airport, and drove the dozen kilometers to his apartment in
St. Genis, and then—

And then they made love, for the first time in the five days
since the Flashforward. It was early evening; the lights in the
room were off, but there was plenty of illumination seeping
in around the blinds from outside. Lloyd had always been
more adventurous than her, although she was coming up to
speed nicely. Perhaps his tastes had been a little too wild, a
little too Western, for her liking initially, but she had warmed
to his suggestions as time went by, and he always tried to be
an attentive lover. But today it had been perfunctory; the mis-
sionary position, nothing more. The sheets were usually damp
with sweat when they were done, but this time they were
mostly dry. They were even still tucked in along one side.

Lloyd lay on his back, looking up at the dark ceiling. Michiko lay next to him, a pale arm draped across his naked, hairy chest. They were quiet for a long time, each alone with their thoughts.

At last, Michiko said, "I saw you on CNN when I was in Tokyo. You really believe we have no free will?"

Lloyd was surprised. "Well," he said at last, "we think we have it, which amounts to the same thing, I guess. But inevitability is a constant in lots of belief systems. Look at the Last Supper. Jesus told Peter—Peter, mind you, the rock he'd said he would build his church on—Jesus told Peter that Peter would renounce him three times. Peter protested that there was no way that would ever happen, but, of course, he did it. And Judas Iscariot—a tragic figure, I always thought—was fated to turn Christ in to the authorities, whether he wanted to or not. The concept of having a role to play, a destiny to fulfill, is much older than the concept of free will." A pause. "Yes, I really believe the future is as fixed as the past. And surely the Flashforward bears that out; if the future wasn't fixed, how could everyone be having visions of a coherent tomorrow? Wouldn't everyone's vision be different—or, indeed, wouldn't it be impossible for anyone to have any visions at all?"

Michiko frowned. "I don't know. I'm not sure. I mean, what's the point of going on if it's all already fixed?"

"What's the point of reading a novel whose ending has already been written?"

She chewed her lower lip.

"The block universe concept is the only thing that makes sense in a relativistic universe," said Lloyd. "Indeed, it's really just relativity writ large: relativity says no point in space is more important than any other; there is no fixed frame of reference against which to measure other positions. Well, the block universe says no time is more important than any other—'now' is utterly and completely an illusion, and if there's no such thing as a universal now, if the future is already written, then free will is obviously an illusion, too."

"I'm not as certain as you are," said Michiko. "It seems as if I've got free will."

"Even after this?" said Lloyd. His voice was growing a little sharp. "Even after the Flashforward?"

"There are other explanations for the coherent version of the future," said Michiko.

"Oh? Like what?"

"Like it's only *one* possible future, one roll of the dice. If the Flashforward were to be reproduced, we might see a completely different future."

Lloyd shook his head, his hair rustling against the pillow. "No," he said. "No, there's only one future, just as there's only one past. No other interpretation makes sense."

"But to live without free will . . ."

"That's the way it is, all right?" snapped Lloyd. "No free will. No choices."

"But—"

"*No buts.*"

Michiko fell silent. Lloyd's chest was rising and falling rapidly, and doubtless she could feel his heart pounding. There was quiet between them for a long time, and then, at last, Michiko said, "Ah."

Lloyd raised his eyebrows even though Michiko couldn't see his expression. But she must have registered somehow that his facial muscles were moving.

"I get it," she said.

Lloyd was irritated, and he let his voice show it. "What?"

"I get why you're adamant about the immutable future. Why you believe there's no such thing as free will."

"And why is that?"

"Because of what happened. Because of all the people who died, and all the other people who were hurt." She paused, as if waiting for him to fill in the rest. When he didn't, she went on. "If we have free will, you'd have to blame yourself for what happened; you'd have to take responsibility. All that blood would be on your hands. But if we don't—if we don't, then it's not your fault. *Que sera est.* Whatever will be already is. You pushed the button that started the experiment because you always had and always will push that button; it's as frozen in time as any other moment."

Lloyd said nothing. There was nothing to say. She was right, of course. He felt his cheeks growing flush.

Was he that shallow? That desperate?

There was nothing in any physical theory that could possibly have predicted the Flashforward. He wasn't some M.D. who had failed to keep up to date on side effects; this wasn't physics malpractice. No one—not Newton, not Einstein, not Hawking—could have predicted the outcome of the LHC experiment.

He'd done nothing wrong.

Nothing.

And yet—

And yet he'd give anything to change what had happened. Anything.

And he knew that if he allowed for even one second the possibility that it *could* have been changed, that it could have gone down differently, that he could have avoided all those car crashes and plane crashes and botched operations and falls down stairs, that he could have prevented little Tamiko from losing her life, then he'd spend the rest of his life being crushed by guilt over what had happened. Minkowski absolved him of that.

And he needed that absolution. He needed it if he were to go on, if he were to follow his light path up through the cube without being tortured.

Those who wished to believe that the visions didn't portray the actual future had hoped that, taken collectively, they would be inconsistent: that in one person's vision, a Democrat would be president of the United States, while in another's a Republican would be in the Oval Office. In one, flying cars would be everywhere; in another, all personal vehicles would have been banned in favor of public transit. In one, perhaps aliens had come to visit Earth; in another, we'd found that we really are alone.

But Michiko's Mosaic Project was a huge success, with over a hundred thousand postings a day, and it all combined together to portray a consistent, coherent, plausible 2030, each reported vision a tile in the greater whole.

In 2017, at the age of ninety-one, Elizabeth II, Queen of England, Scotland, Northern Ireland, Canada, the Bahamas, and countless other places, died. Charles, her son, at that time sixty-nine, was mad as a loon, and, with some prodding from his advisors, chose not to ascend to the throne. William, Charles's eldest son, next in line, shocked the world by renouncing the throne, leading Parliament to declare the Monarchy dissolved.

Quebec was still part of Canada; the secessionists were now a tiny but ever-vocal minority.

In 2019, South Africa completed, at long last, its post-Apartheid crimes-against-humanity trials, with over five thousand people convicted. President Desmond Tutu, eighty-eight, pardoned them all, an act, he said, not just of Christian forgiveness but of closure.

No one had yet set foot upon Mars—the early visions that suggested the contrary turned out to be virtual-reality simulations at Disney World.

The President of the United States was African-American and male; there had apparently yet to be a female American president in the interim. But the Catholic Church did indeed now ordain women.

Cuba was no longer Communist; China was the last remaining Communist country, and its grip on its people seemed as firm twenty-one years hence as it was today. China's population was now almost two billion.

Ozone depletion was substantial; people wore hats and sunglasses, even on cloudy days.

Cars couldn't fly—but they could levitate up to about two meters off the ground. On the one hand, road work was being curtailed in most countries. Cars no longer required a smooth, hard surface; some places were even dismantling roads and putting in greenbelts instead. On the other hand, roads were getting so much less wear and tear that those left intact required little maintenance.

Christ had not come again.

The dream of artificial intelligence was still unfulfilled. Though computers that could talk existed in abundance, none exhibited any measure of consciousness.

Male sperm counts continued their precipitous drop worldwide; in the developed world, artificial insemination was now common, and was covered by the socialized medical programs in Canada, the European Union, and even the United States. In the Third World, birth rates were falling for the first time ever.

On August 6, 2030—the eighty-fifth anniversary of the dropping of the atomic bomb on Hiroshima—a ceremony occurred in that city announcing a worldwide ban on the development of nuclear weapons.

Despite bans on their hunting, sperm whales were extinct by 2030. Over one hundred committed suicide in 2022 by beaching themselves at locales all over the world; no one knows why.

In a victory for common sense worldwide, fourteen of North America's largest newspapers simultaneously agreed to stop running horoscopes, declaring that printing such nonsense was at odds with their fundamental purpose of disseminating the truth.

A cure for AIDS was found in 2014 or 2015. Total worldwide death count from that plague was estimated at seventy-five million, the same figure the Black Death had killed seven hundred years previously. A cure for cancer still remained elusive, but most forms of diabetes could be diagnosed and corrected in the womb prior to birth.

Nanotechnology still didn't work.

George Lucas still hadn't finished his nine-part *Star Wars* epic.

Smoking was now illegal in all public areas, including out-

door ones, in the United States and Canada. A coalition of
Third World countries was now suing the United States at the
World Court in the Hague for willfully promoting tobacco use
in developing nations.

Bill Gates lost his fortune: Microsoft stock tumbled badly
in 2027, in response to a new version of the Year-2000 crisis.
Older Microsoft software stored dates as thirty-two-bit strings
representing the number of seconds that had passed since January 1, 1970; they ran out of storage space in 2027. Attempts
by key Microsoft employees to divest themselves of their stock
drove the price even lower. The company finally filed for
Chapter Eleven in 2029.

The average income in the United States seemed to be
$157,000 per year. A loaf of bread cost four dollars.

The top-grossing film of all time was the 2026 remake of
War of the Worlds.

Learning Japanese was now mandatory for all M.B.A. students at the Harvard Business School.

The fashion colors for 2030 would be pale yellow and
burnt orange. Women were wearing their hair long again.

Rhinoceroses were now bred on farms specifically for their
horns, still highly prized in the East. They were no longer in
danger of extinction.

It was now a capital crime to kill a gorilla in Zaire.

Donald Trump was building a pyramid in the Nevada des-
ert to house his eventual remains. When done, it will be ten
meters taller than the Great Pyramid at Giza.

The 2029 World Series will be won by the Honolulu Vol-
canoes.

The Turks and Caicos Islands joined Canada in 2023 or
2024.

After DNA tests conclusively proved one hundred previous cases of wrongful execution, the United States abolished
the death penalty.

Pepsi won the cola wars.

There will be another huge stock market crash; those who

know what year it will take place are apparently keeping that information to themselves.

The United States will finally go metric.

India established the first permanent base on the Moon.

A war is under way between Guatemala and Ecuador.

The world's population in 2030 will be eleven billion; four billion of those were born after 2009, and so could never have had a vision.

Michiko and Lloyd were eating a late dinner in his apartment. Lloyd had made raclette—cheese melted and served over boiled potatoes—a traditional Swiss dish he'd grown fond of. They had a bottle of *Blauburgunder* with it; Lloyd was never much of a drinker, but wine flowed so freely in Europe, and he was at the age at which a glass or two a day was beneficial for his heart.

"We'll never know for sure, will we?" said Michiko, after eating a small piece of potato. "We'll never know who that woman you were with was, or who the father of my child was."

"Oh, yes, we will," said Lloyd. "You'll presumably know who the father is sometime in the next thirteen or fourteen years—before the child is born. And I'll know who that woman is whenever I do finally meet her—I'd certainly recognize her, even if she were years younger than she was in my vision."

Michiko nodded, as if this were obvious. "But I mean we won't know in time for our own wedding," she said, her voice small.

"No," said Lloyd. "We won't."

She sighed. "What do you want to do?"

Lloyd lifted his eyes from the table and looked at Michiko. Her lips were pressed tightly together; perhaps she was trying to keep them from trembling. On her hand was the engagement ring—so much less than he'd wanted to get her, so much more than he could really afford. "It's not fair," he said. "I mean, Christ, even Elizabeth Taylor probably thought it was 'till death do us part' each time she got married; nobody should have to go into a marriage knowing it's bound to fail."

He could tell Michiko was looking at him, tell that she was trying to seek out his eyes. "So that's you're decision?" she said. "You want to call off the engagement?"

"I do love you," said Lloyd, finally. "You know that."

"Then what's the problem?" asked Michiko.

What *was* the problem? Was it divorce that so terrified him—or just a *messy* divorce, like the one his parents had gone through? Who would have thought that such a simple thing as dividing up community property could have escalated into out-and-out warfare, with vicious accusations on both sides? Who would have thought that two people who had scrimped and saved and sacrificed year after year to buy each other lavish Christmas presents as tokens of their love would end up using legal claws to pry those presents back from the only person in the world to whom they meant anything? Who would have thought that a couple who had oh-so-cutely given their children names that were anagrams—Lloyd and Dolly— would turn around and use those same children as pawns, as weapons?

"I'm sorry, honey," said Lloyd. "It's tearing me apart but, I just don't know what I want to do."

"Your parents long ago booked flights to come to Geneva, and so did my mother," said Michiko. "If we're not going to go through with the wedding, we have to tell people. You've got to make a decision."

She didn't understand, thought Lloyd. She didn't understand that his decision was already made; that whatever he would do/had done was described for all time in the block universe. It wasn't that he *had* to make a decision; rather, the decision that had always been made simply had to be revealed.

And so—

16

IT WAS TIME FOR THEO TO GO HOME. NOT TO
the apartment in Geneva that he'd called home for the last two
years, but home to Athens. Home to his roots.

It also, frankly, would be wise for him to not be around
Michiko for a while. Crazy thoughts about her kept running
through his head.

Theo didn't suspect that anyone in his family had anything
to do with his death—although, as he'd begun reading up on
such things, it became apparent that it *was* usually the case,
ever since Cain slew Abel, ever since Livia poisoned Augustus,
ever since O. J. killed his wife, ever since that astronaut aboard
the international space station had been arrested, despite the
seemingly perfect alibi, for having killed her own sister.

But, no, Theo suspected none of his family members. And
yet, if any visions were likely to shed light on his own death,
surely it would be those of his close relatives? Surely some of
them would have been doing investigations of their own
twenty-one years hence, trying to figure out who had killed
their dear Theo?

Theo took an Olympic Airlines flight to Athens. The seat

sales were over; people were flying again as before, assured that the consciousness-displacement would not recur. He spent the flight time poking holes in a model for the Flashforward that had been emailed to him by a team at DESY, the Deutsches Elektronen-Synchrotron, Europe's other major particle-accelerator facility.

Theo hadn't been home for four years now, and he regretted it. Christ, he might be dead in twenty-one years—and he'd let a span of one-fifth that length slip by without hugging his mother or tasting her cooking, without seeing his brother, without enjoying the incredible beauty of his homeland. Yes, the Alps were breathtaking, but there was a sterile, barren quality about them. In Athens, you could always look up, always see the Acropolis looming above the city, the midday sun flaring off the restored, polished marble of the Parthenon. Thousands of years of human habitation; millennia of thought, of culture, of art.

Of course, as a youth, he had visited many of the famous archeological sites. He remembered being seventeen: a school bus had taken his class to Delphi, home of the ancient oracle. It had been pouring rain, and he hadn't wanted to get off the bus. But his teacher, Mrs. Megas, had insisted. They had clambered over slippery dark rocks through lush forest, until they came to where the oracle had once supposedly sat, dispensing cryptic visions of the future.

That kind of oracle had been better, thought Theo: futures that were subject to interpretation and debate, instead of the cold, harsh realities the world had recently seen.

They'd also gone to Epidaurus, a great bowl out of the landscape, with concentric rings of seats. They'd seen *Oedipus Tyrannos* performed there—Theo refused to join the tourists in calling it *Oedipus Rex*; "Rex" was a Latin word, not Greek, and represented an irritating bastardization of the play's title.

The play was performed in ancient Greek; it might as well have been in Chinese for all the sense Theo could make of the dialog. But they'd studied the story in class; he knew what was happening. Oedipus's future had been spelled out for

him, too: you will marry your mother and murder your father.
And Oedipus, like Theo, had thought he could circumvent
destiny. Forearmed with the knowledge of what he was supposed to do, why, he'd simply avoid the issue altogether, and
live a long, happy life with his queen, Iocasta.

Except . . .

Except that, as it turned out, Iocasta *was* his mother, and
the man Oedipus had slain years before during a quarrel on
the road to Thebes had indeed been his father.

Sophocles had written his version of the Oedipus story
twenty-four hundred years ago, but students still studied it as
the greatest example of dramatic irony in western literature.
And what could be more ironic than a modern Greek man
faced with the dilemmas of the ancients—a future prophesied,
a tragic end foretold, a fate inevitable? Of course, the heroes
of ancient Greek tragedies each had a *hamartia*—a fatal flaw—
that made their downfall unavoidable. For some, the *hamartia*
was obvious: greed, or lust, or an inability to follow the law.

But what had been Oedipus's fatal flaw? What in his character had brought him to ruin?

They'd discussed it at length in class; the narrative form
employed by the ancient Greek tragedians was inviolate—
there was *always* a *hamartia*.

And Oedipus's was—what?

Not greed, not stupidity, not cowardice.

No, no, if it were anything, it was his arrogance, his belief
that he could defeat the will of the gods.

But, Theo had protested, that's a circular argument; Theo
was always the logician, never much for the humanities. Oedipus's arrogance, he said, was only evidenced in his trying to
avoid his fate; had his fate been less severe, he'd never have
rebelled against it, and therefore never would have been seen
as arrogant.

No, his teacher had said, it was there, in a thousand little
things he does in the play. Indeed, she quipped, although Oedipus meant "Swollen Foot"—an allusion to the injury sustained when his royal father had bound his feet as a child and

left him to die—he could just as easily be called "Swollen Head."

But Theo couldn't see it—couldn't see the arrogance, couldn't see the condescension. To him, Oedipus, who solved the vexing riddle of the Sphinx, was a towering intellect, a great thinker—exactly what Theo felt himself to be.

The riddle of the Sphinx: what walks on four legs in the morning, two at noon, and three in the evening? Why, a man, of course, who crawls at the beginning of life, walks erect in adulthood, and requires a cane in old age. What an incisive bit of reasoning on Oedipus's part!

But now Theo would never live to need that third leg, would never see the natural sunset of his span. Instead, he'd be murdered in middle-age . . . just as Oedipus's real father, King Laius, was left dead at the side of a well-worn road.

Unless, of course, he could change the future; unless he could outwit the gods and avoid his destiny.

Arrogance? thought Theo. Arrogance? It is to laugh.

The plane started its descent into nighttime Athens.

"Your parents long ago booked flights to come to Geneva, and so did my mother," Michiko had said. "If we're not going to go through with the wedding, we have to tell people. You've got to make a decision."

"What do you want to do?" asked Lloyd, buying time.

"What do I want to do?" repeated Michiko, sounding stunned by the question. "I want to get married; I don't believe in a fixed future. The visions will only come true if you make them do so—if you turn them into self-fulfilling prophecies."

The ball was back in his court. Lloyd lifted his shoulders. "I'm so sorry, honey. Really, I am, but—"

"Look," she said, cutting off words she didn't want to hear. "I know your parents made a mistake. But we aren't."

"The visions—"

"We *aren't*," said Michiko firmly. "We're right for each other. We're *meant* for each other."

Lloyd was silent for a time. Finally, gently, he went on. "You said before that maybe I was embracing the idea that the future was immutable too readily. But I'm not. I'm not just looking for a way to avoid guilt—and I'm certainly not looking for a way to avoid marrying you, darling. But that the visions are real is the only conclusion possible based on the physics I know. The math is abstruse, I'll grant you, but there's an excellent theoretical basis for supporting the Minkowski interpretation."

"Physics can change in twenty-one years," said Michiko. "There was a lot of stuff they believed in 1988 that we know isn't true today. A new paradigm, a new model, might displace Minkowski or Einstein."

Lloyd didn't know what to say.

"It could happen," said Michiko earnestly.

Lloyd tried to make his tone soft. "I need—I need something more than just your fervent wish. I need a rational explanation; I need a solid theory that could explain why the visions are anything but the one true fixed future." He stopped himself before he added, "A future in which we aren't meant to be together."

Michiko's voice was growing desperate. "Well, okay, all right, maybe the visions are of an actual, real future—but not of 2030."

Lloyd knew he shouldn't push it; knew that Michiko was vulnerable—hell, knew that *he* was vulnerable. But she had to face reality. "The evidence from newspapers seems pretty conclusive," he said softly.

"No—no, it's not." Michiko sounded increasingly adamant. "It isn't really. The visions could be of a time much farther in the future."

"What do you mean?"

"Do you know who Frank Tipler is?"

Lloyd frowned. "A candid drunk?"

"What? Oh, I get it—but it's Tipler with one P. He wrote *The Physics of Immortality*."

"The Physics of *what*?" said Lloyd, eyebrows rising.

"Immortality. Living forever. It's what you always wanted, isn't it? All the time in the world; all the time to do all the things you want to do. Well, Tipler says that at the Omega Point—the end of time—we will all be resurrected and live forever."

"What kind of gibberish is that?"

"I admit it's a whopper," said Michiko. "But he made a good case."

"Oh?" said Lloyd, the syllable pregnant with skepticism.

"He says that computer-based life will eventually supplant biological life, and that information-processing capabilities will continue to expand year after year, until at some point, in the far future, no conceivable computing problem will be impossible. There will be nothing that the future machine life won't have the power and resources to calculate."

"I suppose."

"Now, consider an exact, specific description of every atom in a human body: what type it is, where it is located, and how it relates to the other atoms in the body. If you knew that, you could resurrect a person in his entirety: an exact duplicate, right down to the unique memories stored in the brain and the exact sequence of nucleotides making up his DNA. Tipler says that a sufficiently advanced computer far enough in the future could easily recreate you, just by building up a simulacrum that reflects the same information—the same atoms, in the same places."

"But there's no record of me. You can't reconstruct me without—I don't know—some kind of *scan* of me . . . something like that."

"It doesn't matter. You could be reproduced without any *specific* info about you."

"What *are* you talking about?"

"Tipler says there are about 110,000 active genes that make up a human being. That means that all the possible permutations of those genes—all the possible biologically distinct human beings that could conceivably exist—amount to about ten to the tenth to the sixth different people. So if you were to simulate all those permutations—"

"Simulate ten to the tenth to the sixth human beings?" said Lloyd. "Come on!"

"It all follows from saying that you have essentially infinite information-processing capabilities," said Michiko. "There may be oodles of possible humans, but it *is* a finite number."

"Just *barely* finite."

"There are also a finite number of possible memory states. With enough storage capacity, not only could you reproduce every possible human being, but also every possible set of memories each of them could have."

"But you'd need one simulated human for every memory state," said Lloyd. "One in which I ate pizza last night—or at least had memories of doing that. Another in which I ate a hamburger. *Et cetera, et cetera, ad nauseam.*"

"Exactly. But Tipler says you could reproduce all possible humans that could ever exist, and all possible memories that they could ever have, in ten to the tenth to the twenty-third bits."

"Ten to the tenth to the . . ."

"Ten to the tenth to the twenty-third."

"That's crazy," said Lloyd.

"It's a finite quantity. And it could all be reproduced on a sufficiently advanced computer."

"But why would anyone do that?"

"Well, Tipler says the Omega Point loves us, and—"

"*Loves* us?"

"You really should read the book; he makes it sound much more reasonable than I do."

"He'd pretty much have to," said Lloyd, deadpan.

"And remember that the passage of time will slow down as the universe comes to an end, if it eventually is going to collapse down into a Big Crunch—"

"Most studies indicate that's not going to happen, you know; there isn't enough mass, even taking into account dark matter, to close the universe."

Michiko pressed on. "But if it does collapse, time will be protracted so that it will seem to take forever to do so. And that means the resurrected humans will seem to live forever: they'll be immortal."

"Oh, come on. Someday, if I'm lucky, maybe I'll get a Nobel. But that's about as much immortality as anyone could ever hope for."

"Not according to Tipler," said Michiko.

"And you buy this?"

"Wellll, no, not entirely. But even if you set aside Tipler's religious overtones, couldn't you envision a far, far future in which—I don't know, in which some bored high-school student decides to simulate every possible human and every possible memory state?"

"I guess. Maybe."

"In fact, he doesn't have to simulate all the possible states—he could simulate just one random one."

"Oh, I see. And you're saying that what we saw—the visions—they're not of the actual future twenty-one years from now, but rather are from this far-future science experiment. A simulation, one possible take. Just one of the infinite—excuse me, *almost* infinite possible futures."

"Exactly!"

Lloyd shook his head. "That's pretty hard to swallow."

"Is it? Is it really? Is it any harder to swallow than the idea that we have seen the future, and that future is immutable, and even foreknowledge of it won't be enough to allow us to prevent that future from coming true? I mean, come on: if you have a vision that says you'll be in Mongolia in twenty-one years, all you have to do to defeat the vision is *not* go to Mongolia. Surely you're not predicting that you're going to be forced to go there, against your will? Surely we have volition."

Lloyd tried to keep his voice soft. He was used to arguing science with other people, but not with Michiko. Even an intellectual debate had a personal edge. "If the vision has you in Mongolia, you'll end up being there. Oh, you may have every intention of never going there, but it'll happen, and it'll seem quite natural at the time. You know as well as I do that humans are lousy at realizing their desires. You can make a promise today that you're going to go on a diet, and have every intention of still being on it a month from now, but, somehow, without it seeming like you have no free will at all, you might very well be off your diet by then."

Michiko looked concerned. "You think I need to go on a diet?" But then she smiled. "Just kidding."

"But you see my point. There's no evidence even in the short term that we can avoid things through a simple act of will; why should we think that over a span of decades we'll have self-determination?"

"Because we *have* to," said Michiko, earnest again. "Because if we don't, then there's no way out." She sought out his eyes. "Don't you see? Tipler *has* to be right. Or if he's not, there has to be some other explanation. That *can't* be the future." She paused. "It can't be *our* future."

Lloyd sighed. He did love her, but—damn it, damn it, damn it. He found his head shaking back and forth in negation. "I don't want that to be the future anymore than you do," he said softly.

"Then don't let it," said Michiko, taking his hand, intertwining her fingers with his. "Don't let it."

17

◈

"HELLO?" A PLEASANT FEMALE VOICE.

"Ah, hello, is that—is that Dr. Tompkins?"

"Speaking."

"Ah, hi. This is—this is Jake Horowitz. You know, from CERN?"

Jake didn't know what he'd expected to hear over the phone. Affection? Relief that he'd made the first contact? Surprise? But none of those emotions were conveyed by Carly's voice. "Yes?" she said, her tone even. That was all; just "yes."

Jacob felt his heart sinking. Maybe he should just hang up, get the hell off the phone. It wouldn't hurt anything; if Lloyd was right, they were *bound* to be together eventually. But he couldn't bring himself to do that.

"I—I'm sorry to bother you," he stammered. He'd never been good at phoning women. And, indeed, he hadn't phoned one—not like this—since high school, since that time he'd worked up enough courage to call Julie Cohan and ask her for a date. It had taken him days to prepare, and he still remembered how his finger was shaking as he stabbed out her number on the phone in his parents' basement. He could hear his older brother walking around upstairs, the wooden floor creaking with each of his ponderous footsteps, an Ahab on deck. He'd been terrified that David would try to come down while he was on the phone.

Julie's father had answered the phone, and then had called out to her to pick up on an extension—he hadn't covered the mouthpiece, and he spoke to her roughly. Nothing like the way he'd have treated Julie. And then she picked up the phone, and her father had let the handset tumble back onto the cradle, and she said, in that wonderful voice of hers, "Hello?"

"Ah, hello, Julie. This is Jake—you know, Jake Horowitz." Silence, nothing. "From your American History class."

A tone of perplexity, as if he'd just asked her to calculate the last digit of *pi*. "Yes?"

"I was wondering," he'd said, trying to sound nonchalant, trying to sound as if his whole life didn't depend on this, trying to sound as though his heart weren't about to burst, "I was wondering if you—if you'd like, you know, to go out with me, maybe Saturday . . . if you're free that is." More silence; he remembered when he was a kid the phone lines used to crackle with faint static. He missed that now.

"Maybe a movie," he'd said, filling the void.

Heartbeats more, and then: "What makes you think I'd possibly want to go out with you?"

He'd felt his vision blur, felt his stomach churn, felt the wind being kicked out of him. He couldn't remember what he'd said after that, but somehow he'd gotten off the phone, somehow he'd kept from crying, somehow he'd just sat there in the basement, listening to his older brother pacing above.

That was the last time he'd called a woman and asked for a date. Oh, he wasn't a virgin—of course not, of course not. Fifty dollars rectified that particular handicap one night in New York City. He'd felt terrible after that, cheap and unclean. but someday he would be with a woman he wanted to be with, and he owed it to her, whomever she might be, to be— well, if not skilled, certainly not flailing about without a clue.

And now, now it looked like he *would* be with a woman—with Carly Tompkins. He remembered her as being beautiful, remembered her as having chestnut hair and eyes that were green or gray. He'd liked looking at her, liked listening to her, when she gave her presentation at the APS conference. But the exact details of her appearance were elusive. He recalled freckles—yes, surely she'd had freckles, although not as many as he himself had, but a gentle dusting along the bridge of her small nose and her full cheeks. Surely he wasn't imagining that—

Carly's perplexed "yes?" still rang in his ears. She *must* know why he was calling. She must—

"We're going to be together," he said, stupidly blurting it out, wishing the moment the words were free that he could recant them. "In twenty years, we're going to be together."

She was silent for a moment, then: "I guess."

Jake was relieved; he'd been afraid that she was going to deny the vision. "So I was thinking," Jake said, "I was thinking maybe we should get to know each other. You know, maybe go for coffee." His heart was pounding; his stomach was churning. He was seventeen again.

"Jacob," she said. Jacob, saying his name—no one ever started good news by saying your name. Jacob, reminding him of who he really was. Jacob, what makes you think I'd possibly—

"Jacob," she continued, "I'm seeing someone."

Of course, he thought. Of course she's seeing someone. A dark-haired beauty with those freckles. Of course.

"I'm sorry," he said. He meant for her to take that to mean he was sorry he'd disturbed her, but he felt it both ways. He *was* sorry she was seeing someone.

"Besides," said Carly, "I'm here in Vancouver; you're in Switzerland."

"I have to be in Seattle later this week; I'm a grad student here, but my field is computer modeling of HEP reactions, and CERN is flying me in to Microsoft for a seminar. I could—we'll, I'd thought about, you know, coming to North America a day or two early, maybe by way of Vancouver. I've got tons of frequent-flyer points; it won't cost me anything."

"When?" asked Carly.

"I—I could be there as early as the day after tomorrow." He tried to make his tone light. "My seminar starts Thursday; the world may be in crisis, but Microsoft soldiers on." At least for the time being, he thought.

"All right," said Carly.

"All right?"

"All right. Come up to TRIUMF, if you want to. I'd be glad to meet you."

"What about your boyfriend?"

"Who said it was a boy?"

"Oh." A pause. *"Oh."*

But then Carly laughed. "No, just kidding. Yes, it's a guy— his name's Bob. But it's not that serious, and . . ."

"Yes?"

"And, well, I guess we *should* get to know each other better."

Jacob was glad that the act of grinning from ear to ear didn't make a sound. They firmed up a time, and then they said their goodbyes.

His heart was pounding. He'd always known the right woman would come along eventually; he'd never given up hope. He wouldn't bring her flowers—he would never get them through customs. No, he'd bring her something decadent from Chocolats Micheli; Switzerland, was, after all, the land of chocolate.

With his luck, though, she'd turn out to be a diabetic.

Theo's younger brother, Dimitrios, lived with three other young men in suburban Athens, but when Theo came calling, late in the evening, Dimitrios was home alone.

Dim was studying European literature at the National Capodistrian University of Athens; ever since childhood, Dim had wanted to be a writer. He'd mastered his alpha-betagammas before he'd entered school, and was constantly typing up stories on the family computer. Theo had promised years ago to transfer all of Dim's stories from three-and-a-half-inch diskettes onto optical wafers; no home computers came with diskette readers anymore, but CERN's computing facility had some legacy systems that still used them. He thought about making the offer again, but didn't know whether it was better that Dim think he'd simply forgotten, or that he realize that years—years!—had gone by without his big brother having managed three minutes to request that simple favor from someone in the computing department.

Dim had answered the door wearing blue jeans—how retro!—and a yellow T-shirt imprinted with the logo of *Anaheim*, a popular American TV series; even a European Literature major apparently couldn't help falling under the thrall of American pop culture.

"Hello, Dim," said Theo. He had never hugged his younger brother before, but had an urge to do so now; facing the fact of one's own mortality fostered such feelings. But Dim would doubtless not know what to make of such an embrace; their father, Constantin, was not an affectionate man. Even when the ouzo was flowing more than it should have, he might pinch a waitress's behind but he'd never even tousled the hair of his boys.

"Hey, Theo," said Dimitrios, as if he had seen him just yesterday. He stepped aside to let his brother enter.

The house looked like you'd expect the home of four guys in their early twenties to look—a pig sty, with items of clothing draped over furniture, take-out food boxes piled on the dining-room table, and all sorts of gadgets, including high-end stereo and virtual-reality decks.

It felt good to be speaking Greek again; he'd gotten sick of French and English, the former with its excess verbiage and the latter with its harsh, unpleasant sounds. "How are you doing?" Theo asked. "How's school?"

"How's university, you mean," said Dim.

Theo nodded. He'd always referred to his own post-secondary studies as university, but his brother, pursuing the arts, was just in school. Perhaps the slight *had* been intended; there were eight years between them, a long time, but still not enough of a buffer to insure the absence of sibling rivalry. "Sorry. How's university?"

"It's okay." He met Theo's eyes. "One of my professors died during the Flashforward, and one of my best friends had to leave to look after his family after his parents were injured."

There was nothing to say. "Sorry," said Theo. "It was unforeseen."

Dim nodded and looked away. "Have you seen Mama and Poppa yet?"

"Not yet. Later."

"It's been hard on them, you know. All their neighbors know you work at CERN—'my son the scientist,' Poppa used to say. 'My boy, the new Einstein.'" Dimitrios paused. "He doesn't say that anymore. They've had to take a lot of heat from those who lost people."

"Sorry," said Theo again. He looked around the messy room, trying to find anything on to which he could shift the conversation.

"You want a drink?" asked Dimitrios. "Beer? Mineral water?"

"No, thanks."

Dimitrios was quiet for a few moments. He walked into the living room; Theo followed. Dim sat on the couch, pushing some papers and clothes onto the floor to make room. Theo found a chair that was reasonably free of clutter and sat on it.

"You've ruined my life," said Dimitrios, his eyes meeting then avoiding his brother's. "I want you to know that."

Theo felt his heart jump. "How?"

"These—these visions. Dammit, Theo, don't you know how hard it is to face the keyboard each day? Don't you know how easy it is to become discouraged?"

"But you're a terrific writer, Dim. I've read your work. The way you handle the language is beautiful. That piece you did about the summer you spent on Crete—you captured Knossos perfectly."

"It doesn't matter; none of that matters. Don't you see? Twenty-one years hence, I won't be famous. I won't have made it. Twenty-one years hence, I'll be working in a restaurant, serving *souvlaki* and *tzatziki* to tourists."

"Maybe it was a dream—maybe you're dreaming in the year 2030."

Dim shook his head. "I found the restaurant; it's over by the Tower of the Winds. I met the manager; he's the same guy who'll be running it twenty-one years from now. He recognized me from his vision and I recognized him from mine."

Theo tried to be gentle. "Many writers don't make their living writing. You know that."

"But how many would go on, year after year, if they didn't think that someday—maybe not today, maybe not next year, but eventually—that they would break out? That they'd make it?"

"I don't know. I've never thought about it."

"It's the dream that makes artists go on. How many struggling actors are giving up today—right now—because their visions proved to them that they'll never make it? How many painters on the streets of Paris threw away their palettes this week because they know that even decades hence they'll never be recognized? How many rock bands, practicing in their parents' garages, have broken up? You've taken away the dream from millions of us. Some people were lucky—they were sleeping in the future. Because they were dreaming then, their real dreams haven't been shattered."

"I—I hadn't thought about it that way."

"Of course you hadn't. You're so obsessed with finding out who killed you that you can't see straight. But I've got news for you, Theo. You're not the only one who's dead in the year 2030. I'm dead, too—a waiter in an overpriced tourist joint! I'm dead, and so, I'm sure, are millions of others. And you killed them: you killed their hopes, their dreams, their futures."

18

❧

Day Eight: Tuesday, April 28, 2009

JAKE AND CARLY TOMPKINS COULD HAVE MET
at TRIUMF, but they decided not to. Instead, they met at the
Chapters superstore in the Vancouver suburb of Burnaby. This
one still devoted about half its space to actual pre-printed
books that were for sale: guaranteed bestsellers by Stephen
King, John Grisham, and Coyote Rolf. But the rest of the facility was taken up by individual display copies of titles that
could be printed on demand. It took only fifteen minutes to
produce a single copy of any book, either in mass-market pa-
perback or as an octavo hardcover. Large-print editions could
be had, as well, and computer-translated editions in any one
of twenty-four languages could be produced in only an additional few minutes. And, of course, no title was ever out of
stock.

In a brilliant bit of preadaptive evolution, book superstores
had been building coffee shops into their facilities for twenty
years now—giving people the perfect place to spend some
pleasant time while their custom books were printed. Jake got
to Chapters early, entered the attached Starbucks, ordered
himself a tall decaffeinated Sumatra, and found a seat.

Carly arrived about ten minutes after the appointed time. She was wearing a London Fog trench coat, the sash pulled smartly about her waist; blue slacks; and low heels. Jake rose to greet her. As he approached, he was surprised to see that she wasn't as pretty as he'd remembered.

But it was definitely her. They looked at each other for a moment, he wondering, as he expected she was, how you should greet someone whom you know for a fact you will one day have sex with. They were acquaintances, already; Jake had encountered people he'd known less well at various times and had either bestowed or received a kiss on the cheek—especially, of course, in France. But Carly decided the matter, extending her right hand. He managed a smile and shook it; her grip was firm, and her skin cool to the touch.

A Chapters employee came around to ask Carly what she wanted to drink; Jake remembered when Starbucks used to have only counter service, but of course someone had to deliver your books to you when they were printed. She ordered a grande Ethiopia Sidamo.

Carly opened her purse and reached in to fish out her wallet. Jake let his gaze fall inside her purse. The entire coffee shop was non-smoking of course; all restaurants throughout North America were these days; even in Paris, such rules were coming into effect. But he was relieved to see no pack of cigarettes hiding in the purse; he didn't know what he would have done if she'd been a smoker.

"Well," she said.

Jake forced a smile. It *was* an awkward situation. He knew what she looked like naked. Of course—of course that was twenty years hence. She was about his age now, twenty-two, twenty-three. She'd be in her early forties two decades from now; hardly run down, hardly a hag. And yet—

She had been lovely twenty years hence; surely, though, she was even lovelier now. Surely—

Yes, yes, there was still anticipation, still wonder, still tension.

Of course, she'd seen him naked, too, twenty years further

down the road. He knew what she looked like—her chestnut hair color was natural, or at least dyed in both places; wine-colored nipples; those same enchanting freckles painting constellations across her chest. But him? What did he look like twenty years hence? He was no athlete even now. What if he'd put on weight? What if his chest hair had gone gray?

Maybe her present reluctance was based on what she'd seen of the future him. He couldn't promise he'd work out, couldn't promise he'd keep trim, couldn't promise anything— she *knew* what he'd be like in 2030, even if he himself did not.

"It's good to see you again," said Jake, trying to sound calm, trying to sound warm.

"You, too," said Carly.

And then she smiled.

"What?"

"Nothing."

"No, come on. Tell me."

She smiled again, then lowered her eyes. "I was just picturing us naked," she said.

He felt his features stretching into a grin. "Me, too."

"This is strange," she said. And then: "Look, I never go to bed with anyone on the first date. I mean—"

Jake lifted his hands off the tabletop. "Me neither," he said.

She smiled at that. Maybe she was as beautiful as he remembered after all.

The Mosaic Project didn't just reveal the futures of individual human beings. It also had a lot to say about the future of governments, companies, and organizations—including CERN itself.

It seemed that in 2022, a team at CERN—Theo and Lloyd were on it—would developed a whole new kind of physics tool: the Tachyon-Tardyon Collider. Tachyons were particles that traveled faster than the speed of light; the more energy they carried, the closer to light-speed they traveled. As their energy went down, their speed went up—to almost infinite velocities.

Tardyons, on the other hand, were ordinary matter: they traveled at speeds below that of light. The more energy you pumped into a tardyon, the faster it would go. But, as old Einstein had said, the faster it goes, the more massive a tardyon gets. Particle accelerators, such as CERN's Large Hadron Collider, worked by imparting great energies to tardyons, thereby boosting them to high speeds, and hurtling them together, releasing all that energy when the particles collide. Such machines were huge.

But imagine taking a stationary tardyon—a proton, say, held in place by a magnetic field—and getting a tachyon to collide with it. You wouldn't need huge accelerator rings to get the tachyon up to speed—it was naturally whipping along at superluminal velocities. All you needed to do was make sure that it hit the tardyon.

And so the TT Collider was born.

It did not require a tunnel twenty-seven kilometers in circumference, as the LHC did.

It did not cost billions of dollars to build.

It did not demand thousands of people to maintain and operate it.

A TTC was about the size of a large microwave oven. The early models—the ones available in 2030—cost about forty million American dollars, and there were only nine in the world. But it was predicted that they'd eventually be cheap enough that every university would have its own.

The effect on CERN was devastating; more than twenty-eight hundred people were laid off. The impact on the towns of St. Genis and Thoiry was also great—suddenly over a thousand homes and apartments became available as people moved away. The LHC would apparently be left operational, but would rarely be used; it was so much easier to do, and redo, experiments using a TTC.

•   •   •

"You know this is crazy," said Carly Tompkins, after taking a sip of her Ethiopian coffee.

Jake Horowitz looked at her, eyebrows raised.

"What happened in that vision," said Carly, lowering her eyes, "that was *passionate*. It wasn't two people who had been together for twenty years."

Jake lifted his shoulders. "I never want it to get stale, to get old. People can have a good love life for decades on end."

"Not like that. Not ripping each other's clothes off in the workplace."

Jake frowned. "You never know."

Carly was quiet for a moment, then: "You want to come back to my place? You know, just for coffee . . ."

They were sitting in a coffee shop, of course, so the offer made little sense. Jake's heart was pounding. "Sure," he said. "That would be nice."

19

❖

ANOTHER NIGHT AT LLOYD'S APARTMENT, Lloyd and Michiko sitting on the couch, no words passing between them.

Lloyd pursed his lips, thinking. Why couldn't he just go ahead and commit to this woman? He *did* love her. Why couldn't he just ignore what he'd seen? Millions of people were doing just that, after all—for most of the world, the idea of a fixed future was ridiculous. They'd seen it a hundred times in TV shows and movies: Jimmy Stewart realizes that it's a wonderful life after watching the world unfold without him. Superman, incensed at the death of Lois Lane, flies around the Earth so quickly that it spins backwards, letting him return to a time before her demise, saving her. Caesar, son of the chimpanzee scientists Zira and Cornelius, sets the world on a path of interspecies brotherhood, hoping to avoid Earth's destruction by nuclear holocaust.

Even scientists spoke in terms of contingent evolution. Stephen Jay Gould, taking a metaphor from the Jimmy Stewart movie, told the world that if you could rewind the skein of time, it would doubtless play out differently, with something other than human beings emerging at the end.

But Gould wasn't a physicist; what he proposed as a thought experiment was impossible. The best you could do was a riff on what had happened during the Flashforward—move the marker for "now" to another instant. Time *was* fixed; in the can, each frame exposed. The future wasn't a work in progress; it was a done deal, and no matter how many times Stephen Jay Gould watches *It's A Wonderful Life*, Clarence will always get his wings . . .

Lloyd stroked Michiko's hair, wondering what was written above this slice in the spacetime block.

Jake was lying on his back, one arm bent behind his head. Carly was snuggling against him, playing with his chest hair. They were both naked.

"You know," said Carly, "we've got a chance for something really wonderful here."

Jake lifted his eyebrows. "Oh?"

"How many couples have this, in this day and age? A guarantee that they'll be together twenty years from now! And not just together, but still passionately in . . ." She trailed off; it was one thing to discuss the future, it was quite another, apparently, to give premature voice to the L-word.

They were quiet for a time. "There isn't somebody else, is there?" asked Carly, finally, her voice small. "Back in Geneva?"

Jake shook his head, his red hair rustling against the pillow. "No." And then he swallowed, working up his courage. "But there's someone else here, isn't there? Your boyfriend—Bob."

Carly exhaled. "I'm sorry," she said. "I know a lie is a terrible way to begin a relationship. I—look, I didn't know anything about you. And male physicists are such hound dogs, really they are. I've even got an old wedding band I sometimes wear to conferences. There is no Bob; I just said there was so I'd have a convenient out, you know, if things didn't seem to be going well."

Jake didn't know whether to be offended or not. Once, when he'd been sixteen or seventeen, he was chatting to his cousin Howie's girlfriend on a July night, out front of Howie's house. There were a bunch of people around; they'd been having a barbecue around back. It was dark, and it was clear, and she had struck up a conversation with him, after noting that he was looking up at the stars. She didn't know any of their names, and was stunned that he could point out Polaris, plus the three corners of the Summer Triangle, Vega, Deneb, and Altair. He started to show her Cassiopeia, but it was hard to see, half obscured by the trees rising up behind the house. And yet he wanted her to see it—the great W in the sky, one of the easiest constellations to spot once you've been introduced to it. And so he said, here, cross the street with me, you'll be able to see it from the other side. It was a nice suburban street, devoid of traffic at that time of night, with lit-up houses behind neatly trimmed lawns.

She looked at him and said, "No."

He didn't get it—not for half a second. She thought he might try to throw her behind a bush, try to rape her. Emotions ran through him: offense at the suggestion—he was Howie's cousin, after all! And a sadness, too: a regret for what it must be to be a woman, constantly on the lookout, always afraid, always checking for escape routes.

Jake had shrugged a little, and had walked away, so stunned that he couldn't think of anything else to say. Clouds had rolled in shortly after that, obscuring the stars.

"Oh," Jake said, to Carly; he could think of no other response to her lie about Bob.

Carly moved her shoulders. "Sorry. A woman has to be careful."

He hadn't been thinking about settling down—but . . . but . . . what a gift! Here she was, a beautiful, intelligent woman, working in the same field he was in, and the certain knowledge that they'd still be together, and still be happy, two decades hence.

"What time do you have to be at work tomorrow?" asked Jake.

"I think I'll call in sick," Carly said.

He rearranged himself on the bed, facing her.

Dimitrios Procopides sat on the mess-covered couch, and stared at the wall. He'd been thinking about this ever since his brother Theo's visit two days ago. That thousands—maybe even millions—were contemplating the same thing didn't make it easier for him.

It would be such a simple thing to do: he'd bought the sleeping pills over the counter, and he'd had no trouble finding information on the World Wide Web about how big a dose of this particular brand would be required to insure fatality. For someone who weighed seventy-five kilos, as Dimitrios did, seventeen pills might be enough, and twenty-two would surely do the trick, but thirty would likely induce vomiting, defeating the purpose.

Yes, he could make it happen. And it would be painless— just falling into a deep sleep that would last forever.

But there was a Catch-22—one of the few American novels he'd read had introduced him to that concept. By committing suicide—he wasn't afraid to think the word—he could prove that his future wasn't predestined; after all, in not just his own vision, but in that of the restaurant manager, he was alive twenty years hence. So, if he killed himself today—if he swallowed the pills right *now*—he'd demonstrate conclusively that the future wasn't fixed. But it would be like Pyrrhus's defeats of the Romans at Heraclea and Asculum, the kind of victory that still bears his name, a victory at a horrible cost. For if he *could* commit suicide, then the future that had so depressed him was not inevitable—but, of course, he'd no longer be around to pursue his dream.

There were lesser ways, perhaps, to test the reality of the future. He could pluck out an eye, cut off an arm, get a tattoo on his face—anything that would make his appearance permanently different from what others had seen of him in their visions.

But no. That wouldn't work.

It wouldn't work because none of those things *were* permanent. A tattoo could be removed; an arm could be replaced with a prosthetic; a glass eye could be fitted in the vacated socket.

No: he couldn't have a glass eye; in his own vision of that damnable restaurant he'd had normal stereoscopic sight. So, plucking out an eye *would* be a convincing test of whether the future was immutable.

Except . . .

Except they were making advances in prosthetics and genetics all the time. Who was to say that two decades down the road they wouldn't be able to clone him a new eye, or a new arm? And who was to say that he would refuse such a thing, a chance to overcome the damage caused by an impetuous act in his youth?

His brother Theo desperately wanted to believe that the future was not fixed. But Theo's partner—that tall guy, the Canadian—what's his name? Simcoe, that was it. Simcoe said the exact opposite—Dim had seen him on TV, making his case for the future being carved in stone.

And if the future *was* carved in stone—if Dim was never going to make it as a writer—then he really did not want to go on. Words were his only love, his only passion—and, if he were honest, his only talent. He was lousy at math (how hard it had been to follow Theo through the same schools, with teachers expecting him to share his older brother's talent!), he couldn't play sports, he couldn't sing, he couldn't draw, computers defeated him.

Of course, if he really was going to be miserable in the future, he could kill himself then.

But apparently he had not.

Of course not. Days and weeks slip by easily enough; one doesn't necessarily notice that one's life isn't moving forward, isn't progressing, isn't becoming what you'd always dreamed it would be.

No, it would be easy to end up living like *that*—the empty life he saw in his vision—if you let it sneak up on you, day after dreary day.

But he'd been given a gift, an insight. That Simcoe fellow had spoken of life as an already exposed film—but the projectionist had put the wrong reel on the projector, and it had been two minutes before he'd realized his mistake. There'd been a jump cut, a sharp transition from today to a distant tomorrow, and then back again. That perspective *was* different from life just unrolling one frame after another. He could see now, with clarity, that the life ahead of him wasn't one that he wanted—that, in a very real sense, as he served up moussaka and set saganaki ablaze, he was already dead.

Dim looked at the bottle of pills again. Yes, countless others, all over the world, were doubtless contemplating their futures, wondering if, now that they knew what tomorrow held, it was worth going on.

If even one of them actually did it—actually took his or her own life—surely that would prove the future was mutable. Doubtless this thought had occurred to others, as well. Doubtless many were waiting for someone else to do it first—waiting for the reports that would surely flood the nets: "Man seen by others in 2030 found dead." "Suicide proves future is fluid."

Dim picked up the amber-colored plastic bottle again, rolling it back and forth, hearing the pills clatter over one another inside it.

It would be so easy to take off the lid, pressing it into his palm—he did that now—and twisting, defeating the safety mechanism, letting the pills spill out.

What color were they? he wondered. Crazy, that: he was thinking of taking his own life, and yet had no idea what color the potential instrument of his demise was. He removed the lid. There was some cotton, but not enough to hold the pills immobile. He pulled the batting out.

Well, I'll be—

The pills were green. Who would have thought that? Green pills; a green death.

He tipped the bottle, tapped its base until a pill fell out into his hand. It had a crease down its middle, where the pressure of a thumbnail could presumably cleave it in two for a smaller dose.

But he didn't want a small dose.

There was bottled water at hand; he'd gotten it without fizz—in contrast to his usual preference—lest the carbonation interfere with the action of the pills. He popped the pill in his mouth. He'd half-expected a lime or mint flavor, but it had no flavor at all. A thin coating covered the tablet—the kind you got on premium aspirin. He lifted the water bottle and took a swig. The film did its job; the pill slid smoothly down his throat.

He tipped the pill bottle again, tapped out three more of the green tablets, popped all three into his mouth, and chased them with a large gulp of mineral water.

That was four; the maximum adult dose, marked on the bottle, was two tablets, and there was a warning about avoiding use on consecutive nights.

Three had gone down easily enough at a single gulp. He put a new trio in his palm, dropped them into his mouth, and took another swig of water.

Seven. A lucky number, that. That's what they said.

Did he really want to do this? There was still time to stop. He could call the emergency number; he could stick a finger into the back of his throat.

Or—

Or he think about it some more. Give himself a few additional minutes to reflect.

Seven pills probably wasn't enough to do any real harm.

Surely not. Surely that kind of minor overdose happened all the time. Why, the Web site had said he'd need at least another ten . . .

He spilled some more pills into his palm, and stared at them, a pile of little green stones.

20

❧

Day Nine: Wednesday, April 29, 2009

"I WANT TO SHOW YOU SOMETHING," SAID
Carly.

Jake smiled and indicated with a hand gesture for her to
proceed. They were at TRIUMF now, the Tri-University Meson
Facility, Canada's leading particle-physics laboratory.

She began walking down a corridor; Jake followed. They
passed doors with science-related cartoons taped to them.
They also passed a few other people, each wearing cylindrical
dosimeters that served the same purpose but looked nothing
like the film badges everyone sported at CERN.

Finally, Carly came to a stop. She was standing in front of
a door. On one side of it was a coiled-up fire hose behind a
glass cover; on the other, a drinking fountain. Carly rapped
her knuckles on the door. There was no response, so she
turned the knob and opened it up. She went in and beckoned
with a crooked finger and smile for Jake to follow. He did so,
and once he was inside, Carly closed the door behind him.

"Well?" she said.

Jake lifted his shoulders, helpless.

"Don't you recognize it?" asked Carly.

Jake looked around. It was a good-sized lab, with beige walls, and—

—oh, my God!—

Yes, the walls were beige now, but sometime in the next twenty years they'd be repainted yellow.

It was the room in the vision. There was the chart of the periodic table, just as he'd seen it. And that workbench right there—that's the bench they'd been doing it on.

Jake felt his face grow flush.

"Pretty neat, huh?" said Carly.

"That it is," said Jake.

Of course they couldn't inaugurate the room just now; it was the middle of the work day . . .

But his vision . . . well, if the time estimates were correct, then it was of 7:21 P.M. Geneva time, which was—what?— 2:21 P.M. in New York, and—let's see—11:21 A.M. here in Vancouver. Eleven twenty-one in the morning . . . on a *Wednesday*. Surely TRIUMF would have been busy then, too. How could they possibly have been making love here at that time on a weekday? Oh, doubtless sexual mores would continue to loosen up over the next twenty years just as they had over the last fifty, but surely even in the far-off year of A.D. 2030 you didn't run off with your sweetie for a boink-break while at work. But maybe October 23 was a holiday; maybe everyone else was off work. Jake had a vague recollection that Canadian Thanksgiving was sometime in October.

He walked around the room, comparing its present reality to what he'd seen in his vision. There was an emergency shower, common enough in labs where chemicals are used, and some equipment lockers, and a small computer workstation. There'd been a personal computer on the same spot in the vision, but it had been quite a different model, of course. And next to it . . .

Next to it, there'd been a device, cubic in shape, about a half-meter on a side, with two flat sheets rising up out of its top, facing each other.

"That thing that was there," said Jake. "I mean, that thing that *will* be there. Any idea what it is?"

"Maybe a Tachyon-Tardyon Collider?"

Jake lifted his eyebrows. "That could—"

The door to the lab swung open, and a large Native Canadian man walked in. "Oh, excuse me," he said. "Didn't mean to interrupt."

"Not at all," said Carly. She smiled at Jake. "We'll come back later."

"You want proof?" said Michiko. "You want to know for sure whether we should get married? There's one way to do that."

Lloyd had been alone in his office at CERN, examining a series of printouts of the last year's worth of 14-TeV LHC runs looking for any indication of instability prior to the first 1,150-TeV run—the one that produced the time-displacement. Michiko had just come in, and those were her first words.

Lloyd raised his eyebrows at her. "A way to get proof? How?"

"Repeat the experiment. See if you get the same results."

"We can't do that," said Lloyd, stunned. He was thinking of all the people who had died the last time. Lloyd had never believed in the 'there are some things humanity is not meant to know' philosophy, but if there ever was a test that shouldn't be done again, doubtless this was it.

"You'd have to announce the new attempt in advance, of course," said Michiko. "Warn everybody, make sure no one is flying, no one is driving, no one is swimming, no one is on a ladder. Make sure the whole human race is sitting down or lying down when it happens."

"There's no way to do that."

"Sure there is," she said. "CNN. NHK. The BBC. The CBC."

"There are places in the world that still don't get TV, or even radio, for that matter. We couldn't warn everyone."

"We couldn't *easily* warn everyone," said Michiko, "but it

could be done, certainly with a ninety-nine-percent success rate."

Lloyd frowned. "Ninety-nine percent, eh? There are seven billion people. If we missed just one percent, that's still seventy million who wouldn't be warned."

"We could do better than that. I'm positive we could. We could get it down to a few hundred thousand who didn't get word—and, let's face it, those few hundred thousand would be in nontechnological areas, anyway. There's no chance they'd be driving cars or flying planes."

"They could be eaten by animals."

Michiko stopped short. "Could they? Interesting thought. I guess animals didn't lose consciousness during the Flashforward, did they?"

Lloyd scratched his head. "We certainly didn't see the ground littered with dead birds that had fallen out of the sky. And, according to the news reports, no one found giraffes that had broken their legs by falling. The phenomenon seemed to be one of consciousness; I read in the *Tribune* that chimpanzees and gorillas who've been questioned by sign language reported some sort of effect—many said they were in different places—but they lacked the vocabulary and the psychological frame of reference to confirm or deny that they'd actually seen their own futures."

"It doesn't matter. Most wild animals won't eat unconscious prey anyway; they'll think it's dead, and natural selection long ago bred out carrion feeding from most life forms. No, I'm sure we could reach almost everyone, and the few that we don't reach are unlikely to be in any sort of hazardous position anyway."

"All well and good," said Lloyd, "but we can't just announce that we're going to repeat the experiment. The French or Swiss authorities would stop us, if no one else did."

"Not if we got their permission. Not if we got everyone's permission."

"Oh, come on! Scientists might be curious as to whether it's a reproducible result, but why would anyone else care?

Why would the world give its permission—unless, of course, they needed to reproduce the results in order to find me, or CERN, culpable."

Michiko blinked. "You're not thinking, Lloyd. *Everyone* wants another glimpse of the future. We're hardly the only ones with loose ends left by the first set of visions. People want to know more about what tomorrow holds. If you tell them that you can let them see the future again, no one is going to stand in your way. On the contrary, they'll move heaven and earth to make it possible."

Lloyd was quiet, digesting this. "You think so?" he said at last. "I'd imagine there would be a lot of resistance."

"No, everyone's curious. Don't *you* want to know who that woman was?" A pause. "Don't you want to know for sure who was the father of the child I was with? Besides, if you're wrong about the future being immutable, then maybe we'll all see a completely different tomorrow, one in which Theo doesn't die. Or maybe we'll get a glimpse at a different time: five years down the road, or fifty. But the point is that there's not a person on the planet who wouldn't want another vision."

"I don't know," said Lloyd.

"Well, then, look at it this way: you're torturing yourself with guilt. If you try to reproduce the Flashforward and fail to do so, then the LHC had nothing to do with it, after all. And that means you can relax."

"Maybe you're right," said Lloyd. "But how do we get permission to reproduce the experiment? Who could give that permission?"

Michiko shrugged. "The nearest city is Geneva," she said. "What's it most famous for?"

Lloyd frowned, running down the litany of possibly appropriate answers. And it came to him: the League of Nations, forerunner of the UN, had been founded there in 1920. "You're suggesting we take this to the United Nations?"

"Sure. You could go to New York and present your case."

"The UN can never agree on anything," said Lloyd.

"They'll agree on this," said Michiko. "It's too seductive to turn down."

Theo had talked to his parents and his family's neighbors, but none of them seemed to have meaningful insights into his future death. And so he caught an Olympic Airlines 7117 back to the Geneva International Airport at Cointrin. Franco della Robbia had dropped him off for his outgoing flight, but Theo now took a cab—pricey at thirty Swiss francs—back to the campus. Since they hadn't fed him on the plane, he decided to go straight to the cafeteria in the LHC control center for a bite to eat. When he entered, to his surprise he spotted Michiko Komura sitting alone at a table near the back. Theo got himself a small bottle of orange juice and a serving of *longeole* sausage, and headed toward her, passing several knots of physicists eating and arguing about possible theories to explain the Flashforward. Now he understood why Michiko was alone; the last thing she wanted to be thinking about was the event that had caused her daughter's death.

"Hi, Michiko," said Theo.

She looked up. "Oh, hi, Theo. Welcome back."

"Thanks. Mind if I join you?"

She indicated the vacant seat opposite her with a hand gesture. "How was your trip?" she asked.

"I didn't learn much." He thought about not saying anything further, but, well, she *did* ask. "My brother Dimitrios—he says the visions ruined his dream. He wants to be a great writer, but it doesn't look like he's ever going to make it."

"That's sad," said Michiko.

"How are you doing?" asked Theo. "How are you holding up?"

Michiko spread her arms a bit, as if there were no easy answer. "I'm surviving. I go literally whole minutes where I don't think about what happened to Tamiko."

"I'm so sorry," said Theo, for the hundredth time. A long pause. "How's it going otherwise?"

"Okay."

"Just okay?"

Michiko was eating a tart-sized cheese quiche *au bleu de Gex*. She also had a half-drunk cup of tea; she took a sip, gathering her thoughts. "I don't know. Lloyd—he's not sure he wants to go through with the wedding."

"Really? My God."

She looked around, gauging how alone they were; the nearest person was four tables away, apparently absorbed in reading something on a datapad. She sighed, then shrugged a little. "I love Lloyd—and I know he loves me. But he can't get over this possibility that our marriage won't last."

Theo lifted his eyebrows. "Well, he does come from a broken home. The break-up was quite nasty, apparently."

Michiko nodded. "I know; I'm trying to understand. Really, I am." A pause. "How was your parents' marriage?"

Theo was surprised by the question. He frowned as he considered it. "Fine, I guess; they still seem to be happy. Dad was never very demonstrative, but Mom never seemed to mind."

"My father is dead," said Michiko. "But I suppose he was a typical Japanese of his generation. Kept everything inside, and his work was his whole life." She paused. "Heart attack; forty-seven years old. When I was twenty-two."

Theo searched for the right words. "I'm sure he'd be very proud of you if he'd lived to see what you've become."

Michiko seemed to consider this sincerely, instead of just dismissing it as a platitude. "Maybe. In his traditional view, women did not pursue careers in engineering."

Theo frowned. He didn't really know much about Japanese culture. There were conferences in Japan he could have arranged to attend, but although he'd been all over Europe, to America once, and to Hong Kong when he was a teenager, he'd never had an urge to travel to Japan. But Michiko was so fascinating—her every gesture, her every expression, her way of speaking, her smile and the way it crinkled her little nose, her laugh with its perfect high notes. How could he be fascinated by her and not by her culture? Shouldn't he want to know what her people were like, what her country was like, every facet of the crucible that had formed her?

Or should he just be honest? Should he face the truth that his interest was purely sexual? Michiko was certainly beautiful . . . but there were three thousand people working at CERN, and half of them were women; Michiko was hardly the only beautiful one.

And yet there *was* something about her—something exotic. And, well, she obviously liked white guys . . .

No, that wasn't it. That wasn't what made her fascinating. Not when he got right down to it; not when he looked at it head on, without making excuses. What was most fascinating about Michiko was that she had selected Lloyd Simcoe, Theo's partner. They'd both been single, both available. Lloyd was a decade older than Michiko; Theo eight years younger than her.

It wasn't that Theo was some sort of a workaholic, and that Lloyd had stopped to smell the roses. Theo frequently took rented sail boats out into Lac Léman; Theo played croquet and badminton in the CERN leagues; Theo made time to listen to jazz at Geneva's Au Chat Noir and to take in alternative theater at L'Usine; he even occasionally visited the Grand Casino.

But this fascinating, beautiful, intelligent woman had chosen the staid, quiet Lloyd.

And now, it seemed, Lloyd wasn't prepared to commit to her.

Surely that was no good reason to want her himself. But the heart was separate from physics; its reactions could not be predicted. He *did* want her, and, well, if Lloyd was going to let her slip through his fingers . . .

"Still," said Theo, finally replying to Michiko's comment that her father wouldn't approve of her having gone into engineering, "surely he must have admired your intelligence."

Michiko shrugged. "Inasmuch as it reflected well on him, I suppose he did." She paused. "But he wouldn't have approved of me marrying a white man."

Theo's heart skipped a beat—but whether it was for Lloyd's sake or his own, he couldn't say. "Oh."

"He distrusted the West. I don't know if you know this, but it's popular in Japan for young people to wear clothes with English phrases on them. It doesn't really matter what they say—what matters is that they're being seen to embrace American culture. Actually, the slogans are quite amusing for those of us who are fluent in English. 'This End Up.' 'Best Before Date on Bottom.' 'In order to form a more perfect onion.' " She smiled that beautiful, nose-crinkling smile of hers. " 'Onion.' I couldn't stop laughing the first time I saw that one. But one day I came home with a shirt that had English words on it—just words, not even a phrase, words in different colors on a black background: 'puppy', 'ketchup', 'hockey rink', 'very', and 'purpose.' My dad punished me for wearing such a shirt."

Theo tried to look sympathetic while at the same time wondering what form such a punishment would take. No allowance—or did Japanese parents not give their kids allowances? Being sent to her room? He decided not to ask.

"Lloyd's a good man," he said. The words came out without him thinking about them first; perhaps they sprang from some inner sense of fair play that he was glad to know he possessed.

Michiko considered this, too; she had a way of taking every comment and searching for the truth behind it.

"Oh, yes," she said. "He's a very good man. He worries because of that stupid vision that our marriage might not last forever—but there are so many things that, being with him, I know *I* will never have to worry about. He will never hit me, of that I'm sure. He'll never humiliate me or embarrass me. And he has a great mind for remembering details. I told him my nieces' names once, in passing, months ago. They came up again in conversation last week, and he knew their names instantly. So I can be sure he'll never forget our anniversary or my birthday. I've been involved with men before—both Japanese and foreign—but there's never been one about whom

I've felt so sure, so confident, that he would always be kind and gentle."

Theo felt uncomfortable. He thought of himself as a good man, too, and certainly would never raise his hand to a woman. But, well, he *did* have his father's temper; in an argument, yes, if the truth be told, he might say things that were designed to wound. And, indeed, someone someday would hate him enough to want to kill him. Would Lloyd—Lloyd the good—ever arouse such feelings in another human being?

He shook his head slightly, dispelling those thoughts. "You chose well," he said.

Michiko dipped her head, accepting the compliment. And then she added, "So did Lloyd." Theo was surprised; it wasn't like Michiko to be immodest. But then her next words made plain what she'd meant. "He couldn't have picked a better person to be his best man."

I'm not so sure about that, thought Theo, but he didn't give the words voice.

He couldn't pursue Michiko, of course. She was Lloyd's fiancée.

And besides . . .

Besides, it wasn't her lovely, captivating Japanese eyes.

It wasn't even a jealousy or fascination born of her choice of Lloyd instead of him.

Down deep, he knew the real reason for his sudden interest in her. Of course he knew it. He figured if he embarked on some crazy new life, if he took some wild left turn, made a totally unpredictable move—such as running off and marrying his partner's fiancée—that somehow he'd be giving the finger to fate, changing his own future so radically that he'd never end up staring down the barrel of a loaded gun.

Michiko was devastatingly intelligent, and she was very beautiful. But he would not pursue her; it would be craziness to do so.

Theo was surprised when a chuckle emanated from his throat—but it *was* amusing, in a way. Maybe Lloyd was right—maybe the whole universe was a solid block, with time immutable. Oh, Theo had thought about doing something wild and crazy, but then, after what seemed careful consideration, weighing the options and reflecting on his own motives, he had ended up doing exactly what he would have been doing had the issue never been raised.

The movie of his life continued to unfold, frame after already exposed frame.

21

MICHIKO AND LLOYD HAD PLANNED NOT TO
move in together until after the wedding, but, except for the
time she'd spent in Tokyo, Michiko had ended up staying at
Lloyd's every night since Tamiko's death. Indeed, she'd only
been home a couple of times, briefly, since the Flashforward,
eight days ago. Everything she saw there reduced her to tears:
Tamiko's tiny shoes on the mat by the door; her Barbie doll,
perched on one of the living-room chairs (Tamiko always left
Barbie sitting up comfortably); her finger paintings, held to the
fridge door by magnets; even the spot on the wall where Tamiko had written her name in Magic Marker, and Michiko had
never quite been able to get it clean.

So, they stayed at Lloyd's place, avoiding the memories.

But, still, Michiko often drifted off, staring into space.
Lloyd couldn't stand seeing her so sad, but knew that there
was nothing he could do. She would grieve—well, probably
forever.

And, of course, he wasn't an ignoramus: he had read
plenty of articles on psychology and relationships, and he'd
even seen his share of *Oprah* and *Giselle* programs. He knew

he shouldn't have said it, but sometimes words just came out, tumbling forth, spoken without thought. All he'd been trying to do was fill the silence between himself and Michiko.

"You know," he said, "you're going to have another daughter. Your vision—"

But she silenced him with a look.

She didn't say a word, but he could read it in her eyes. You can't replace one child with another. Every child is special.

Lloyd knew that; even though he'd never—yet—been a parent, he knew it. Years ago, he'd seen an old Mickey Rooney film called *The Human Comedy,* but it wasn't funny at all, and, in the end, Lloyd thought it wasn't very human, either. Rooney played an American soldier in World War II who had gone overseas. He had no family of his own, but enjoyed vicarious contact with the people they were all fighting for back home through the letters his bunkmate received from his family. Rooney got to know them all—the man's brother, his mother, his sweetheart in the States—through the letters the man shared with Rooney. But then that man was killed in battle, and Rooney returned to the man's hometown, bringing back his personal effects. He ran into the man's younger brother outside the family homestead, and it was as if Rooney had known him all his life. The younger brother ended up going into the house, calling out, "Mom—the soldier's home!"

And then the credits rolled.

And the audience was supposed to believe that Rooney somehow would take the place of this woman's late son, shot dead in France.

It had been a cheat; even as a teenager—he'd been maybe sixteen when he saw the film on TV—he knew it was a cheat, knew that one person could never replace another.

And now, foolishly, for one brief moment, he'd implied that Michiko's future daughter might somehow take the place in her heart of poor dead Tamiko.

"I'm sorry," he said.

Michiko didn't smile, but she did nod, almost imperceptibly.

Lloyd did not know if it was the right time—his whole life, he'd been plagued by his inability to sense when the right moment was: the right moment to make his move with a girl in high school, the right moment to ask for a raise, the right moment to interrupt two other people at a party so that he could introduce himself, the right moment to excuse himself when other people obviously wanted to be alone. Some people had an innate sense of such things, but not Lloyd.

And yet—

And yet the matter *did* have to be resolved.

The world had dusted itself off; people were getting on with their lives. Yes, many were walking with crutches; yes, some insurance companies had already filed for bankruptcy; yes, there was a still-untold number of dead. But life had to go on, and people were going to work, going home, eating out, watching movies, and trying with varying degrees of success to push ahead.

"About the wedding . . ." he said, trailing off, letting the words float between them.

"Yes?"

Lloyd exhaled. "I don't know who that woman is—the woman in my vision. I have no idea who she is."

"And so you think she might be better than me, is that it?"

"No, no, no. Of course not. It's just . . ."

He fell silent. But Michiko knew him too well. "You're thinking that there are seven billion people on the planet, aren't you? And that it's blind luck that we met at all."

Lloyd nodded; guilty as charged.

"Perhaps," said Michiko. "But when you consider the odds *against* you and I meeting, I think it's more than that. It's not like you got stuck with me, or me with you. You were living in Chicago; I was living in Tokyo—and we ended up together, here, on the Swiss-French border. Is that random chance, or destiny?"

"I'm not sure you can believe in destiny while at the same time believing in free will," Lloyd said gently.

"I suppose not." She lowered her eyes. "And, well, maybe you're not really ready for marriage. So many of my friends over the years have gotten married because they thought it was their last chance. You know: they'd reached a certain age, and they figured if they didn't get married soon, they never would. If there's one thing your vision has demonstrated, it's that I'm *not* your last chance. I guess that takes the pressure off, doesn't it? No need to move quickly anymore."

"It's not that," said Lloyd, but his voice was shaky.

"Isn't it?" said Michiko. "Then make up your mind, right now. Make a commitment. Are we going to get married?"

Michiko was right, Lloyd knew. His belief in an immutable future did help ease his guilt over what had happened—but, still, it *was* the position he'd always taken as a physicist: space-time is an immutable Minkowski cube. What he was about to do he had already done; the future was as indelible as the past.

No one, as far as they knew, had reported any vision that corroborated that Michiko Komura and Lloyd Simcoe were ever married; no one had reported being in a room that had contained a wedding photo in an expensive frame, showing a tall Caucasian man with blue eyes and a beautiful, shorter, younger Asian woman.

Yes, whatever he said now had always been said—and would always be said. But he had no insight whatsoever into what answer spacetime had recorded in it. His decision, right now, at this moment, at this slice, on this page, in this frame of the film, was unrevealed, unknown. It was no easier giving voice to it—whatever it was that was about to come out of his mouth—even knowing that it was inevitable that he would say it / had said it.

"Well?" demanded Michiko. "What's it going to be?"

●   ●   ●

Theo was still at work, late in the evening, running another simulation of his and Lloyd's LHC experiment, when he got the phone call.

Dimitrios was dead.

His little brother. Dead. Suicided.

He fought back tears, fought back anger.

Memories of Dim ran through Theo's mind. The times he'd been good to him when he was a kid, and the times he'd been mean. And how everyone in the family was terrified all those years ago when they went to Hong Kong and Dim got lost. Theo had never been happier to see anyone than he was to see little Dim, hoisted up on that policeman's shoulder, coming through the crowded street toward them.

But, now, now he was dead. Theo would have to make another trip to Athens for the funeral.

He didn't know how to feel.

Part of him—a very large—was incredibly saddened by his brother's death.

And part—

Part was elated.

Not because Dim was dead, of course.

But the fact that he *was* dead altered everything.

For Dimitrios had experienced a vision, a vision verified with another person—and to have a vision he needed to be alive twenty-one years hence.

But if he were dead here, now, in 2009, there was no way he could be alive in 2030.

So the block universe had shattered. What people had seen might indeed make up a coherent picture of tomorrow . . . but it was only one possible tomorrow, and, indeed, since that tomorrow had included Dimitrios Procopides, it was no longer even that—no longer even possible.

Chaos theory said that small changes in initial conditions must have big effects over time. Surely the world of 2030 could not possibly now turn out as it had been portrayed in the billions of brief glimpses people had already had of it.

Theo paced the halls of the LHC control center: past the

big mosaic, past the plaque that gave the institution's original full name, past offices, and laboratories, and washrooms.

If the future was now uncertain—indeed, was now surely *not* going to turn out exactly as the visions portrayed—then perhaps Theo could give up his search. Yes, in one once-possible future, someone had seen fit to kill him. But so much would change over the next two decades that surely that same outcome wouldn't happen again. Indeed, he might never meet the person who had killed him, never have any encounter with whomever that man might be. Or, in fact, that man might himself now die before 2030. Either way, Theo's murder was hardly inevitable.

And yet—

And yet it might still happen. Surely some things would turn out as the visions had indicated. Those who weren't going to die unnatural deaths would live the same spans; those who had secure jobs now might well still hold them then; those marriages that were good and solid and true had no reason not to endure.

No.

Enough doubt, enough wasted time.

Theo resolved to get on with his life, to give up this foolish quest, to face tomorrow, whatever it might bring, head on. Of course, he would be careful—he certainly didn't want one of the points of convergence between the 2030 of the visions and the 2030 yet to come to be his own death. But he would continue on, trying to make the most out of whatever time he had.

If only Dimitrios had been willing to do the same.

His walk had taken him back to his office. There was someone he should call; someone who needed to hear it from a friend first, before it blew up in his face in media all over the world.

Michiko's words hung between them: "What's it going to be?"

It *was* time, Lloyd knew. Time for the appropriate frame

to be illuminated; the moment of truth, the instant at which the decision spacetime had already recorded in it would be revealed. He looked into Michiko's eyes, opened his mouth, and—

Brrrring! Brrrring!

Lloyd cursed, glanced at the phone. The caller ID said "CERN LHC." No one would call from the office this late if it wasn't an emergency. He picked up the handset. *"Hello?"*

"Lloyd, it's Theo."

He wanted to tell him this wasn't a good time, tell him to call back later, but before he could, Theo pressed on.

"Lloyd, I just got a call. My brother Dimitrios is dead."

"Oh, my God," said Lloyd. "Oh, my God."

"What is it?" said Michiko, eyes wide with concern.

Lloyd covered the mouthpiece. "Theo's brother is dead." Michiko brought a hand to her mouth.

"He killed himself," said Theo, through the phone. "An overdose of sleeping pills."

"I am so sorry, Theo," said Lloyd. "Can I—is there anything I can do?"

"No. No. Nothing. But I thought I should let you know right away."

Lloyd didn't understand what Theo was getting at. "Ah, thank you," he said, his voice tinged with confusion.

"Lloyd, Dimitrios had a vision."

"What? Oh." And then a long pause. *"Oh."*

"He told me about it himself."

"He must have made it up."

"Lloyd, this is my *brother;* he didn't make it up."

"But there's no way—"

"You know he's not the only one; there've been other reports, too. But this one—this one is corroborated. He was working in a restaurant in Greece; the guy who runs the restaurant in 2030 also does it here in 2009. He saw Dim in his vision, and Dim saw the guy. When they put that on TV . . ."

"I—ah, shit," said Lloyd. His heart was pounding. "Shit."

"I'm sorry," said Theo. "The press will have a field day."

A pause. "Like I said, I thought you should know."

Lloyd tried to calm himself. How could he have been so wrong? "Thanks," he said, at last. And then, "Look, look, that's not important. How are you? Are you okay?"

"I'll be all right."

" 'Cause if you don't want to be alone, Michiko and I can come over."

"No, that's okay. Franco della Robbia is still here at CERN; I'll spend some time with him."

"Okay," said Lloyd. "Okay." Another pause. "Look, I've got to—"

"I know," said Theo. "Bye."

"Bye."

Lloyd replaced the handset in its cradle.

He'd never met Dimitrios Procopides; indeed, Theo didn't speak of him very often. No surprise there; Lloyd rarely mentioned his sister Dolly at work, either. When it all came down to it, it was just one more death in a week of countless deaths, but . . .

"Poor Theo," said Michiko. She shook her head gently back and forth. "And his brother—poor guy."

He looked at her. She'd lost her own daughter, but for now, at this instant, she found room in her heart to grieve for a man she'd never met.

Lloyd's heart was still racing. The words he'd been about to say before the phone rang still echoed in his head. What was he thinking now? That he wanted to continue to play the field? That he wasn't ready to settle down? That he had to know that white woman, find her, meet her, and make a sensible, balanced choice between her and Michiko?

No.

No, that wasn't it. That couldn't be it.

What he was thinking was: I am an idiot.

And what he was thinking was: She's been incredibly patient.

And what he was thinking was: Maybe the warning that the marriage might not automatically last was the best damned thing that could have happened. Like every couple, they'd assumed it would be till death did they part. But now he knew, from day one, in a way that no one else ever had, not even those others like him who were children of broken homes, that it wasn't *necessarily* forever. That it was only permanent if he fought and struggled and worked to make it permanent every waking moment of his life. Knew that if he was going to get married, it would have to be his first priority. Not his career, not the damned elusive Nobel, not peer-review, not fellowships.

Her.

Michiko.

Michiko Komura.

Or—or Michiko Simcoe.

When he'd been a teenager, in the 1970s, it looked like women would forever dispense with the silliness of taking someone else's name. Still, to this day, most *did* adopt their husbands' last names; they'd already discussed this, and Michiko had said that it was indeed her intention to take on his name. Of course, Simcoe wasn't nearly as musical as Komura, but that was a small sacrifice.

But no.

No, she shouldn't take his name. How many divorced women carried not their birth names but the cognomen of someone decades in their past, a daily reminder of youthful mistakes, of love gone bad, of painful times? Indeed, Komura wasn't Michiko's maiden name—that was Okawa; Komura was Hiroshi's last name.

Still, she *should* retain that. She should remain a Komura so that Lloyd would be reminded, day in and day out, that she wasn't his; that he had to work at their marriage; that tomorrow was in his hands.

He looked at her—her flawless complexion, her beguiling eyes, her oh-so-dark hair.

All those things would change with time, of course. But he wanted to be around for that, to savor every moment, to enjoy the seasons of life with her.

Yes, with *her*.

Lloyd Simcoe did something he hadn't done the first time—oh, he'd thought about it then, but had rejected it as silly, old-fashioned, unnecessary.

But it *was* what he wanted to do, what he needed to do.

He lowered himself onto one knee.

And he took Michiko's hand in his.

And he looked up into her patient, lovely face.

And he said, "Will you marry me?"

And the moment held, Michiko clearly startled.

And then a smile grew slowly across her face.

And she said, almost in a whisper, "Yes."

Lloyd blinked rapidly, his eyes misting over.

The future was going to be glorious.

22

Ten Days Later: Wednesday, May 6, 2009

GASTON BÉRANGER HAD BEEN SURPRISINGLY easy to convince that CERN should try to replicate the LHC experiment. But, of course, he felt they had nothing to lose and everything to gain if the attempt failed: it would be very hard to prove CERN's liability for any damage done the first time if the second attempt produced no time displacement.

And now it was the moment of truth.

Lloyd made his way to the polished wooden podium. The great globe-and-laurel-leaf seal of the United Nations spread out behind him. The air was dry; Lloyd got a shock as he touched the podium's metal trim. He took a deep breath, calming himself. And then he leaned into the mike. "I'd like to thank—"

He was surprised that his voice was cracking. But, dammit all, he was speaking to some of the most powerful politicians in the world. He swallowed, then tried again. "I'd like to thank Secretary-General Stephen Lewis for allowing me to speak to you today." At least half the delegates were listening to translations provided through wireless earpieces. "Ladies and gentlemen, my name is Dr. Lloyd Simcoe. I'm a Canadian currently living in France and working at CERN, the European center for particle physics." He paused, swallowed. "As you've no doubt heard by now, it was, apparently, an experiment at CERN that caused the consciousness-displacement phenomenon. And, ladies and gentlemen, I know at first blush this will sound crazy, but I've come here to ask you, as the representatives of your respective governments, for permission to repeat the experiment."

There was an eruption of chatter—a cacophony of languages even more varied than what one hears at CERN's various cafeterias. Of course, all the delegates had known in advance roughly what Lloyd was going to say—one didn't get to speak in front of the UN without going through a lot of preliminary discussions. The General Assembly hall was cavernous; his eyesight really wasn't good enough to make out many individual faces. Nonetheless, he could see anger on the face of one of the Russian delegates and what looked like terror on the faces of the German and Japanese delegates. Lloyd looked over at the Secretary-General, a handsome white man of seventy-two. Lewis gave him an encouraging smile, and Simcoe went on.

"Perhaps there is no reason to do this," said Lloyd. "We seem to have clear evidence now that the future portrayed in the first set of visions is not going to come true—at least not exactly. Nevertheless, there's no doubt that a great many people found real personal insight through the glimpses."

He paused.

"I'm reminded of the story *A Christmas Carol,* by the British writer Charles Dickens. His character Ebenezer Scrooge saw a vision of Christmas Yet to Come, in which the results of his actions had led to misery for many other people and himself being hated and despised in death. And, of course, seeing such a vision would have been a terrible thing—had the vision been of the one, true immutable future. But Scrooge was told that, no, the future he saw was only the logical extrapolation of his life, should he continue on the way he had been. He could change his life, and the lives of those around him, for the better; that glimpse of the future turned out to be a wonderful thing."

He took a sip of water, then continued.

"But Scrooge's vision was of a very specific time—Christmas day. Not all of us had visions of significant events; many of us saw things that were quite banal, frustratingly ambiguous, or, indeed, for almost a third of us, we saw either dreams or just darkness—we were asleep during that two-minute span twenty-one years from now." He paused and shrugged his shoulders, as if he himself did not know what the right thing to do was. "We believe we can replicate the experience of having visions; we can offer all of humanity another glimpse of the future." He raised a hand. "I know some governments have been leery of these insights, disliking some of the things revealed, but now that we know the future is *not* fixed, I'm hoping that you will allow us to simply give this gift, and the benefit of the Ebenezer Effect, to the peoples of the world once more. With the cooperation of you men and women, and your governments, we believe we can do this safely. It's up to you."

Lloyd came through the tall glass doors of the General Assembly building. The New York air stung his eyes—damn, but they were going to have to do something about that one of these days; the visions said it would be even worse by 2030. The sky overhead was gray, crisscrossed by airplane contrails. A crowd of reporters—perhaps fifty in all—rushed over to meet him, camcorders and microphones thrust out.

"Doctor Simcoe!" shouted one, a middle-aged white man. "Doctor Simcoe! What happens if consciousness doesn't drop back to the present day? What happens if we're all stuck twenty-one years in the future?"

Lloyd was tired. He hadn't been as nervous speaking in front of people since his Ph.D. oral defense. He really just wanted to go back to his hotel room, pour himself a nice Scotch, and crawl into bed.

"We have no reason to think that such a thing could happen," he said. "It seemed to be a completely temporary phenomenon that began the moment we started the particle collisions and ceased the moment we ended them."

"What about the families of any people who might die this time? Will you take personal responsibility for them?"

"How about the ones who are already dead? Don't you feel you owe them something?"

"Isn't this all just some cheap quest for glory on your part?"

Lloyd took a deep breath. He *was* tired, and he had a pounding headache. "Gentlemen and ladies—and I use those terms loosely—you are apparently used to interviewing politicians who can't be seen to lose their temper, and so you can get away with asking them questions in haranguing tones. Well, I am *not* a politician; I am, among other things, a university professor, and I am used to civilized discourse. If you can't ask polite questions, I will terminate this exchange."

"But, Dr. Simcoe—isn't it true that all the death and destruction was your fault? Didn't you in fact design the experiment that went awry?"

Lloyd kept his tone even. "I'm not kidding, people. I have had quite my fill of media exposure already; one more bullshit question like that, and I'm walking away."

There was stunned silence. Reporters looked at each other, then back at Lloyd.

"But all those deaths . . ." began one.

"That's it," snapped Lloyd. "I'm out of here." He began walking away.

"Wait!" cried one reporter, and "Stop!" shouted another.

Lloyd turned around. "Only if you can manage intelligent, civilized questions."

After a moment's hesitation, a melanic-American woman raised her hand, almost meekly.

"Yes?" said Lloyd, lifting his eyebrows.

"Dr. Simcoe, what decision do you think the UN will make?"

Lloyd nodded at her, acknowledging that this was an

acceptable interrogative. "I'm honestly not sure. My gut feeling is that we should indeed try to replicate the results—but I'm a scientist, and replication is my stock-in-trade. I do think the people of Earth want this, but whether their leaders will be willing to do what the people desire I have no way of knowing."

Theo had come to New York, as well, and he and Lloyd that night enjoyed the extravagant seafood buffet at the Ambassador Grill in the UN Plaza-Park Hyatt.

"Michiko's birthday is coming up," said Theo, cracking a lobster's claw.

Lloyd nodded. "I know."

"Are you going to throw a surprise party for her?"

Lloyd paused. After a moment, he said, "No."

Theo gave him a "if you really loved her, you'd do it" look. Lloyd didn't feel like explaining. He'd never really thought about it before, but it came to him full blown, as if he'd always known it. Surprise parties were a cheat. You let someone you were supposed to care about think you'd forgotten their birthday. You deliberately bring them down, make them feel neglected, uncared for, unremembered, unappreciated. And then you lie—lie!—to them for weeks on end leading up to the event. All this, so that in the moment when people yell "Surprise!" the person will feel loved.

In the marriage he and Michiko were going to have, Lloyd wouldn't have to manufacture situations in order to make Michiko feel that way. She'd know of his love every day—every minute; her confidence in that would never be shaken. It would be her constant companion, his love, until the day she died.

And, of course, he'd never lie to her—not even when it was supposedly for her own good.

"You sure?" said Theo. "I'd be glad to help you organize it."

"No," said Lloyd, shaking his head a little. Theo was so young, so naïve. "No, thank you."

23

THE UNITED NATIONS DEBATES CONTINUED. While he was in New York, Theo got another reply to his ads looking for information about his own death. He was about to simply issue a short, polite response—he was going to give up the quest, really he was—but, damn it all, the message was just too enticing. "I did not contact you initially," it said, "because I had been led to believe that the future is fixed, and that what was going to happen, including my role in it, was inevitable. But now I read otherwise, and so I must elicit your help."

The message was from Toronto—just a one-hour flight from the Big Apple. Theo decided to head on up and meet face to face with the man who'd sent the letter. It was Theo's first time visiting Canada, and he wasn't quite prepared for how hot it was in the summer. Oh, it wasn't hot by Mediterranean standards—rarely did the temperature rise above thirty-five degrees Celsius. But it did surprise him.

To get a cheaper airfare, Theo had to stay overnight, rather than fly in and out on the same day. And so he found himself with an evening to kill in Toronto. His travel agent had suggested he might enjoy a hotel out along the Danforth—part of Toronto's major east-west axis; Toronto's large Greek community was centered there. Theo agreed, and, to his delight, he found the street signs in that part of town were in both the English and Greek alphabets.

His appointment, though, wasn't on the Danforth. Rather, it was up in North York, an area that apparently had once been a city in its own right but had been subsumed into Toronto, which now had a population of three million. Toronto's subway took him there the next day. He was amused to discover that the public transit system was referred to as the TTC (for Toronto Transit Commission); the same abbreviation would doubtless be applied to the Tachyon-Tardyon Collider he would supposedly someday helm.

The subway cars were spacious and clean, although he'd heard they were severely overcrowded during rush hour. One thing that had impressed him greatly was riding the subway—poorly named at this particular point—over the Don Valley Parkway; here the train ran what must be a hundred meters above the ground in a special set of tracks hanging below the Danforth. The view was spectacular—but what was most impressive was that the bridge over the Don Valley had been built decades before Toronto got its first subway line, and yet it had been constructed so as to eventually accommodate two sets of tracks. One didn't often see evidence of cities planning that far into the future.

He changed trains at Yonge Station, and rode up to North York Centre. He was surprised to find that he didn't have to go outside to enter the condominium tower he'd been told to come to; it had direct access from the station. The same complex also contained a book superstore (part of a chain called Indigo), a movie-theater complex, and a large food store called Loblaws, which seemed to specialize in a line of products called President's Choice. That surprised Theo; he would have expected it to be Prime Minister's Choice in this country.

He presented himself to the concierge, who directed him through the marble lobby to the elevators, and he rode up to the thirty-fifth floor. From there, he easily found the apartment he was looking for and knocked on the door.

The door opened, revealing an elderly Asian man. "Hello," he said, in perfect English.

"Hello, Mr. Cheung," said Theo. "Thank you for agreeing to see me."

"Won't you come in?"

The man, who must have been in his mid-sixties, moved aside to let Theo pass. Theo slipped off his shoes, and stepped into the splendid apartment. Cheung led Theo into the living room. The view faced south. Far away, Theo could see downtown Toronto, with its skyscrapers, the slender needle of the CN Tower and, beyond, Lake Ontario stretching to the horizon.

"I appreciated you emailing me," said Theo. "As you can imagine, this has been very difficult for me."

"I am sure it has," said Cheung. "Would you care for tea? Coffee?"

"No, nothing, thank you."

"Well, then," said the man. "Do have a seat."

Theo sat down on a couch upholstered in orange leather. On the end table sat a painted porcelain vase. "It's beautiful," said Theo.

Cheung nodded agreement. "From the Ming Dynasty, of course; almost five hundred years old. Sculpture is the greatest of the arts. A written text is meaningless once the language has fallen out of use, but a physical object that endures for centuries or millennia—that is something to cherish. Anyone today can appreciate the beauty of ancient Chinese or Egyptian or Aztec artifacts; I collect all three. The individual artisans who made them live on through their work."

Theo made a noncommittal sound, and settled back in the couch. On the opposite wall was an oil painting of Kowloon harbor. Theo nodded at it. "Hong Kong," he said.

"Yes. You know it?"

"In 1996, when I was fourteen, my parents took us there on vacation. They wanted us—me and my brother—to see it before it changed hands back to Communist China."

"Yes, those last couple of years were exceptional for tourism," said Cheung. "But they were also great times for leaving the country; I myself left Hong Kong and came to Canada then. Over two hundred thousand Hong Kong natives moved to Canada before the British handed our country back to the Chinese."

"I imagine I would have gotten out, too," said Theo sympathetically.

"Those of us who could afford it did so. And, according to the visions people have had, things get no better in China during the next twenty-one years, so I am indeed glad I left; I could not stand the idea of losing my freedom." The old man paused. "But you, my young friend, stand to lose even more, do you not? For my part, I would have fully expected to be dead twenty-one years from now; I was delighted to learn that the fact that I had a vision implies that I will still be alive then. Indeed, since I felt reasonably spry, I begin to suspect that I might in fact have much more than twenty-one years left. Still, your time may be cut short—in my vision, as I told you by email, your name was mentioned. I had never heard of you before—forgive me for saying so. But the name was sufficiently musical—Theodosios Procopides—that it stuck in my mind."

"You said that in your vision someone had spoken to you about plans to kill me."

"Ominous, to be sure. But as I also said, I know little more than that."

"I don't doubt you, Mr. Cheung. But if I could locate the person you were speaking to in your vision, obviously that person knows more."

"But, as I said, I do not know who he was."

"If you could describe him?"

"Of course. He was white. White, like a northern European, not olive-skinned like yourself. He was no older than fifty in my vision, meaning he'd be about your age today. We were speaking English, and his accent was American."

"There are many American accents," said Theo.

"Yes, yes," said Cheung. "I mean he spoke like a New Englander—someone from Boston, perhaps."

Lloyd's vision apparently placed him in New England as well; of course, it couldn't be Lloyd that Cheung had been speaking to—at that moment, Lloyd was off boinking that crone . . .

"What else can you tell me about the man's speech? Did he sound well-educated?"

"Yes, now that you mention it, I suppose he did. He used the word 'apprehensive'—not an overly fancy term, but not one likely to be employed by an illiterate."

"What exactly did he say? Can you recount the conversation?"

"I will try. We were indoors somewhere. It was North America. That much was apparent by the shape of the electrical outlets; I always think they look like surprised babies here. Anyway, this man said to me, 'He killed Theo.' "

"The man you were speaking with killed me?"

"No. No, I was quoting him. He said, 'he'—some other he—'killed Theo.' "

"You're sure he said 'he'?"

"Yes."

Well, that was something, anyway; in one fell swoop, four billion potential suspects had been eliminated.

Cheung continued. "He said, 'He killed Theo,' and I said, 'Theo who?' And the man replied, 'You know, Theodosios Procopides.' And I said, 'Oh, yeah.' That is precisely how I said it—'Oh, yeah.' I fear my spontaneous English speech has not yet attained that degree of informality, but, apparently given another twenty-one years, it will. In any event, it was clear I will know you—or at least know of you—in the year 2030."

"Go on."

"Well, then my interlocutor said to me, 'He beat us to him.' "

"I—I beg your pardon?"

"He said, 'He beat us to him.'" Cheung lowered his head. "Yes, I know how that sounds—it sounds as though my associate and I had designs on your life as well." The old man spread his arms. "Dr. Procopides, I am a wealthy man—indeed, a very wealthy man. I will not say to you that people do not reach my level without being ruthless, for we both know that that is untrue. I have dealt very harshly with rivals over the years, and I have perhaps even skirted the edges of the law. But I am not just a businessman; I am also a Christian." He lifted a hand. "Please, do not be alarmed; I will not lecture you—I know that in some Western circles to boldly declare one's faith engenders discomfort, as if one had brought up a topic best never discussed in polite company. I mention it only to establish a salient fact: I may be a hard man, but I am also a God-fearing man—and I would never countenance murder. At my current advanced age, you can well imagine that I am set in my ways; I cannot believe that in the final years of my life, I will break a moral code I have lived by since childhood. I know what you are thinking—the obvious interpretation of the words 'he beat us to him' is that that somebody else killed you before my associates could have done the deed. But I say again that I am no murderer. Besides, you are, I know, a physicist, and I do little business in that realm—my principal area of investment, besides real estate, which, of course, everyone should invest in, is biological research: pharmaceuticals, genetic engineering, and so on. I am not a scientist myself, you understand—just a capitalist. But I think you would agree that a physicist would not possibly be an obstacle to the sorts of things I pursue, and, as I say, I am no killer. Still, there are those words, which I report to you verbatim: 'He beat us to him.'"

Theo looked at the man, considering. "If that's the case," he said at last, measuring his words carefully, "why are you telling me this?"

Cheung nodded, as if he'd expected the question. "Naturally, one does not normally discuss plans to commit murder with the intended victim. But, as I said, Dr. Procopides, I am a Christian; I believe, therefore, that not only is your life at stake, but so too is my soul. I have no interest in becoming involved, even peripherally, in such a sinful business as homicide. And since the future *can* be changed, I wish it to be so. You are on the trail of whomever it was who will kill you; if you do manage to prevent your death at the hands of that person, whomever it might be, well, then, my associates will not be beaten to it. I take you into my confidence in hopes that you will not only avoid being shot—it was death by gunshot, was it not?—by this other person, but also by anyone involved with me. I do not want your—or anyone's—blood on my hands."

Theo exhaled noisily. It was staggering enough to think that one person would someday want him dead—but to hear now that multiple parties would wish him that way was shocking.

Perhaps the old man was crazy—although he didn't seem that way. Still, twenty-one years hence he would be . . . would be . . . well, exactly how old? "Forgive my impertinence," said Theo, "but may I ask when you were born?"

"Certainly: February 29, 1932. That makes me all of nineteen years old."

Theo felt his eyes go wide. He *was* dealing with a loon . . .

But Cheung smiled. "Because I was born February 29, you see—which comes but once every four years. Seriously, I am seventy-seven years old."

Which made him a good deal older than Theo had guessed, and—my God!—would mean he'd be ninety-eight in the year 2030.

A thought occurred to Theo: he had talked to enough people who were dreaming in 2030; it was usually not hard to distinguish a dream from reality. But if Cheung was ninety-eight, could he perhaps have Alzheimer's in the future? What would the thoughts of such a brain be like?

"I'll save you from asking," said Cheung. "I do not have the gene for Alzheimer's. I'm as surprised as you are to think that I will be alive twenty-one years hence, and as shocked as you are that I, already having lived a full life, will apparently outlive a young man such as yourself."

"Were you really born February 29?" asked Theo.

"Yes. It's hardly a unique attribute; there are about five million people alive who have that birthday."

Theo considered this, then: "So this man said to you, 'He beat us to him.' What did you say after that?"

"I said, and, again, I ask you to forgive my words, 'It's just as well.' "

Theo frowned.

"And then," continued Cheung, "I added, 'Who's next?' To which my associate replied, 'Korolov.' Korolov—which I guess would be K-O-R-O-L-O-V. A Russian name, no? Does it mean anything to you?"

Theo shook his head. "No." A pause. "So you were—are—going to eliminate this Korolov, too?"

"That's an obvious interpretation, yes. But I have no idea who he or she might be."

"He."

"I thought you said you didn't know this person?"

"I don't—but Korolov is a male last name. Female Russian last names end in -ova; male ones in -ov."

"Ah," said Cheung. "In any event, after the man I was speaking to said 'Korolov,' I replied, 'Well, I can't imagine anyone else is after him.' And my associate replied, 'No need to be apprehensive, Ubu—' Ubu being a nickname I allow only close friends to use, although, as I said, I have, as of yet, not met this man. 'No need to be apprehensive, Ubu,' he said. 'The guy who got Procopides can't have any possible interest in Korolov.' And then I said, 'Very well. See to it, Darryl'— which, I presume was the name of the man I was speaking to. He opened his mouth to speak again, but then I was suddenly back here, in 2009."

"And so that's all you know? That you and a man named Darryl will be out to get several people, including myself and someone named Korolov, but that someone else, a man, who will have no designs against this Korolov, will kill me first?"

Cheung shrugged apologetically, but whether with regret over the frustrating holes in the information or over the fact that he would one day apparently want to see Theo dead, Theo couldn't say. "That's it."

"This Darryl—did he look like a boxer? You know, a prize-fighter?"

"No. I would say he was too paunchy to be any sort of athlete."

Theo leaned back in the couch, dumbfounded. "Thank you for letting me know," he said at last.

"It was the least I could do," said Cheung. He paused, as if assessing the prudence of saying more, then: "Souls are about life immortal, Dr. Procopides, and religion is about just rewards. I rather suspect that great things await you, and that you *will* appropriately be rewarded—but only, of course, if you manage to stay alive long enough. Do yourself a favor—do us *both* a favor—and do not give up your quest."

24

THEO RETURNED TO NEW YORK, TELLING Lloyd all about his encounter with Cheung. Lloyd was as perplexed as Theo was about what the old man had said. Theo and Lloyd stayed in New York for another eight days, while the United Nations continued to heatedly debate their proposal.

China spoke in favor of the motion to authorize replication of the experiments. Even though it was now clear that the future was *not* fixed, the fact that during the first set of visions China's totalitarian government still clearly reigned with an iron hand had done an enormous amount to quell dissidents in that country. For China, that was the key issue. There were only two possible versions of the future: either Communist dictatorship continued, or it did not. The first visions had shown that it had indeed continued. If the second visions showed the same thing—that, even with foreknowledge of a malleable future, Communism would not be brought down—then the dissident spirit would be crushed: a perfect example of what, in an English pun in questionable taste, *The New York Times* had called "taking a Dim view of the future," in honor of Dimitrios Procopides, who, having had his spirit broken by what he saw of tomorrow, gave up on ever being able to change it.

And what if the second visions showed Communism having fallen? Then China would be no worse off than it was before the first Flashforward, with its future in question. It was a worthwhile gamble, in the view of Beijing government.

The European Union ambassadors also were clearly going to vote as a block in favor of replication, for two reasons. If replication failed, then the unending stream of lawsuits being filed against CERN and its member countries would possibly be stemmed. And if replication succeeded, well, this second glimpse of the future would be free, but subsequent glimpses could be sold to humanity for billions of euros apiece. True, other nations might try to build atom smashers capable of producing the same sorts of energies unleashed by the LHC, but the first set of visions had shown a world of plentiful Tachyon-Tardyon Colliders, and still, it seemed, visions couldn't be invoked easily. If CERN was responsible, it was apparently *uniquely* responsible—some specific combination of parameters, unlikely to be reproduced at another accelerator, had made the Flashforward possible.

Objection to replication was most vehement in the western hemisphere—those countries in which people had mostly been awake when consciousness departed for A.D. 2030 and, therefore, in which large numbers of people had been injured or killed. The objections were based mostly on outrage over the damage done the last time, and fears that similar carnage and destruction would accompany a second set of visions.

In the eastern hemisphere, comparatively little damage had been done; in many nations, more than ninety percent of the population had been asleep—or at least safely recumbent in bed—when the Flashforward had occurred; very few casualties had occurred, and only negligible property damage had been sustained. Clearly, they argued, an organized, announced-in-advance replication wouldn't put many people at risk. They denounced the arguments against replication as more emotional than rational. Indeed, surveys worldwide showed that those who had visions were overwhelmingly pleased that they had had them, even though they had now been shown to not reveal a fixed future. Indeed, now that the world was sure the future could be changed, those who had seen what they regarded as a negative personal future were on average even more pleased to have had the insight than those who saw what they described as a positive future.

Although he had no formal voice in the UN debate, Pope Benedict XVI weighed into the fray, announcing that the visions were fully consistent with Catholic doctrine. That attendance at masses had swollen enormously since the Flashforward was doubtless a factor in the pontiff's stance.

The prime minister of Canada likewise endorsed the visions, since they showed Quebec still a part of her country. The President of the United States was less enthused: although America clearly continued to be the world's leading power two decades hence, there was substantial concern among the President's advisors that the first glimpse had already done much to damage national security, with people—children, even—who were not yet bound by oaths of secrecy having access to all sorts of back-room information. And, of course, it rankled the Democrat incumbent that the Republican Franklin Hapgood, currently a political-science professor at Purdue, was apparently destined to hold the office in 2030.

So the American delegation continued to argue against replication: "We're still burying our dead," said one ambassador. But the Japanese delegation countered by claiming that even if the visions hadn't portrayed the actual future, they clearly represented a *working* future. The U.S.—a country in which a very high percentage of people had had meaningful, daytime visions—was trying to hoard to itself the technological benefits to be gleaned from those visions. The first Flashforward had been to 11:21 A.M. in Los Angeles, and 2:21 P.M. in New York, it had been to 3:21 A.M. in Tokyo; most Japanese had had visions of nothing more exciting than themselves dreaming in the future. America was capitalizing on new technologies and new inventions portrayed in its citizens' visions; Japan and the rest of the Eastern hemisphere was being unfairly left behind.

That set off the Chinese delegation again; they had apparently been waiting for someone to raise this very issue. The Flashforward had been to 2:21 A.M. Beijing time; most Chinese likewise had simply had visions of themselves asleep in the future. If another Flashforward was to be invoked, surely, they argued, it should begin at a time offset twelve hours from the last attempt. That way, if consciousness jumps ahead the same fixed twenty-one years, six months, two days, and two hours, then those in the Eastern hemisphere would reap the most benefits this time, balancing things out.

The Japanese government immediately supported the Chinese on this point. India, Pakistan, and both Koreas chimed in that this was only fair.

The east was perhaps right about America trying to gain the technological upper hand: if there was going to be replication, the U.S. argued strongly that it should be at the same time of day. They couched their argument in scientific terms: replication was, in fact, replication, so as much as humanly possible, every experimental parameter must be the same.

Lloyd Simcoe was called back to address the General Assembly on this point. "I would caution strongly against changing any factor needlessly," he said, "but, since we don't yet have a full working model for the phenomenon, I cannot say categorically that doing the experiment at night instead of during the day would make any difference. The LHC tunnel is, after all, heavily shielded against radiation leakage—and that shielding has the effect of keeping solar and other external radiation out as well. Still, I would argue against changing the time of day."

A delegate from Ethiopia pointed out that Simcoe was an American, and therefore likely to be trying to protect American interests. Lloyd countered that he was, in fact, a Canadian, but that didn't impress the African; Canada, too, had benefited disproportionately from the glimpses its citizens had had of the future.

Meanwhile, the Islamic world had mostly embraced the visions as *ilham* (divine guidance directly exerted upon the human mind and soul), rather than *wahy* (divine revelation of the actual future), since, by definition, only prophets were capable of the latter. That the visions turned out to indeed be of a malleable future apparently confirmed the Islamic view, and, although Islamic leaders did not invoke the Scrooge metaphor, the concept of receiving insight that would allow one to improve oneself along religious and spiritual lines was interpreted by most as being fully congruent with the Qur'an.

Some Muslims held the dissenting view that the visions were demonic, part of the unfolding destruction of the world, rather than divine. But either way, the Islamic spiritual leaders rejected wholeheartedly the notion that a physics experiment had been the cause: that was a misguided secular, Western interpretation. The visions clearly were of spiritual origin, and hardware was irrelevant to such experiences.

Lloyd had feared that the Islamic nations would oppose replication of the LHC experiment on that basis. But first the Wilayat al-Faqih in Iran, then the Shayk al-Azhar in Egypt, and then *shaykh* after *shaykh* and *iman* after *iman* across the Muslim world came to favor attempted replication, precisely so that when the attempt failed, the infidels would have it proven to them that the original occurrence had indeed been spiritual, not secular, in nature.

Of course, governments in Islamic nations were often at odds with the faithful in their lands. For those governments that kowtowed to the west, supporting replication, so long as it was offset, as the Asians were insisting, by twelve hours from the first occurrence, was a win-win scenario: if replication failed, the Western scientists would end up with egg on their faces, and the secular worldview would take a drubbing; if it succeeded, the economies of Muslim nations would get a boost, by having their citizens attain the same sort of insights into future technologies that Americans had already received.

Lloyd had expected those who had had no vision—those who were apparently dead in the future—to be against replication, too, but, in fact, most of them turned out to favor it. Younger people who were visionless—dubbed "The Ungrateful Dead" by *Newsweek*—often cited a desire to prove that some other explanation besides their own deaths explained their lack of visions the first time. The older visionless, mostly already resigned to the fact that they would be dead twenty-one years hence, were simply curious to learn more, through others' accounts, about the future they would never otherwise live to see.

Some nations—Portugal and Poland among them—argued for delaying replication for at least a year. Three compelling counterarguments were presented. First, as Lloyd pointed out, the more time that elapsed, the more likely some external factor would change sufficiently to prevent replication. Second, the need for absolute safety during a replication was clear in the public's mind right now; the more the severity of the accidents that occurred last time faded into memory, the more likely that people would be cavalier in their preparations. Third, people wanted new visions that confirmed or denied the events portrayed in their first visions, letting those with disturbing insights see if they were indeed now on track to avoiding those futures. If the new visions would also be of a time twenty-one years, six months, two days, and two hours ahead of the moment at which the replicated experiment began, each passing day diminished the chances that the second vision would be sufficiently related to the first to make a comparison between the two possible.

There was also a good economic argument in favor of rapid replication, if replication were to happen at all. Many businesses were currently operating at reduced capacity, because of damage to equipment or personnel that had occurred during the first Flashforward. A work stoppage in the near future to accommodate a second Flashforward would result in less lost productivity than would one months or years down the road when all businesses and factories were back to full operation.

The debates ranged over countless topics: economics, national security (what if one nation launched a nuclear attack against another just prior to the departure of consciousness?), philosophy, religion, science, and democratic principles. Should a decision that affects everyone on the planet really be made on a one-vote-per-nation basis? Should votes be weighted according to each nation's population, in which the Chinese voice should be heard the loudest? Or should the decision be differed to a global referendum?

Finally, after much acrimony and argument, the UN made its decision: the LHC experiment would indeed be repeated, offset, as many had insisted, by twelve hours from the first occurrence.

The European Union ambassadors all insisted on one proviso, before agreeing to allow CERN to attempt to replicate the experiment: there would be no government-level lawsuits against CERN, the countries that owned it, or any of its staff members. A UN resolution was passed, preventing any such lawsuits from ever being brought at the World Court. Of course, nothing could prevent civil suits, although the Swiss and French governments had both declared that their courts would not hear such cases, and it was difficult to establish that any other courts had jurisdiction.

The Third World represented the biggest logistical problem: undeveloped or underdeveloped regions where news arrived slowly, if at all. It was decided that the experiment wouldn't be replicated for another six weeks: that should be enough time to get the word to everyone who could possibly be reached.

And so, preparations began for humanity to take another peek at tomorrow.

Michiko dubbed it Operation Klaatu. In the movie *The Day the Earth Stood Still*, Klaatu, an alien, neutralized all electricity worldwide for thirty minutes precisely at noon Washington time, in order to demonstrate the need for world peace, but he did it with remarkable care, so that no one was hurt. Planes stayed aloft, operating theaters still had power. This time, they were going to try to be as careful as Klaatu, even though, as Lloyd pointed out, in the movie Klaatu was shot dead for his efforts. Of course, being an alien, he managed to come back to life . . .

Lloyd was frustrated. The first time, for whatever reason, the experiment had failed to produce the Higgs boson; he wanted to tweak the parameters slightly, in hopes of producing that elusive particle. But he knew he had to reproduce everything exactly as before. He'd probably never get a chance to refine his technique; never get a chance to generate the Higgs. And that, of course, meant he'd likely never get his Nobel Prize.

Unless—

Unless he could come up with an explanation for the physics of what had happened. But even though it was his experiment that had apparently caused the twenty-one-year jump ahead, and even though he, and everyone at CERN, had been racking their brains trying to determine the cause, he had no special insights into why it had occurred. It was just as likely that someone else—indeed, possibly even someone other than a particle physicist—would figure out exactly what had happened.

25

All over the planet, people were lying down in bed, on

D-DAY.

Almost everything was the same. Of course, it was now the ungodly hour of five A.M., instead of five P.M., but since there were no windows in the LHC control room, there was no real way to tell. There were also more people present. It was hard to get a decent crowd of journalists for most particle-physics experiments, but for this one, the CERN Media Service actually had to draw lots to determine which dozen reporters could have access. Cameras were broadcasting the scene worldwide.

All over the planet, people were lying down in bed, on couches, on the floor, on the grass, on bare ground. No one was drinking hot beverages. No commercial, military, or private planes were flying. All traffic in all cities had come to a halt—indeed, had been at a halt for hours now, to make sure there would be virtually no need for emergency-room operations or air ambulances during the replication. Thruways and highways were either vacant or giant parking lots.

Two space shuttles—one American, one Japanese—were currently in orbit, but there was no reason to think they were in danger; the astronauts would simply enter their sleeping bags for the duration. The nine people aboard the International Space Station would do the same thing.

No surgery was under way; no pizzas were being tossed in the air; no machinery was being operated. At any given moment, a third of humanity is normally asleep—but right now almost all of Earth's seven billion people were wide awake. Ironically, though, less activity was going on than at any other point in history.

As with the first time, the collision was being controlled by computer. Lloyd really had nothing much to do. The reporters had their cameras on tripods, but they were lying on the floor or on tabletops. Theo was already lying down, too, and so was Michiko—a bit too close to Theo, for Lloyd's taste. There was an area of floor left in front of the main console. Lloyd lay down on it. He could see one of the clocks from there, and he counted down with it: "Forty seconds."

Would he be transported back to New England? Surely the vision wouldn't pick up where it had left off months ago. Surely he wouldn't be back in bed with—God, he didn't even know her name. She hadn't said a word; she could have been American, of course, or from Canada, Australia, the United Kingdom, Scandinavia, France—it was so hard to tell.

"Thirty seconds," Lloyd said.

Where had they met? How long had they been married? Did they have kids?

"Twenty seconds."

Was it a happy marriage? It had certainly seemed to be, during that one brief glimpse. But, then, he'd even seen his own parents be tender toward each other upon occasion.

"Ten seconds."

Maybe the woman wouldn't even be in his next vision.

"Nine seconds."

Indeed, it was likely he'd be sleeping—and not necessarily even dreaming—twenty-one years from now.

"Eight seconds."

The chances were almost zero that he'd see himself again—

that he'd be anywhere near a mirror, or be watching himself on closed-circuit TV.

"Seven."

But surely he'd see *something* revelatory, something significant.

"Six."

Something that would answer at least a few of his burning questions.

"Five."

Something that would bring closure to what he'd seen before.

"Four."

He did love Michiko, of course.

"Three."

And he and she would be married, regardless of what the first vision, or this one, might portray.

"Two."

But, still, it would be nice to know that other woman's name . . .

"One."

He closed his eyes, as if that would better summon a vision.

"Zero."

Nothing. Darkness. Dammit, he was asleep in the future! It wasn't fair; it was *his* experiment after all. If anyone deserved a second vision, it was him, and—

He opened his eyes; he was still flat on his back. Over his head, high above, was the ceiling of the LHC control center.

Oh, Christ—oh, Christ.

Twenty-one years from now he would be sixty-six years old.

And twenty-one years from this vision, a few months later—

He'd be dead.

Just like Theo.

God damn it. God damn it.

He rolled his head to the side, and happened to see the clock.

The blue digits were silently metamorphosing: 22:00:11; 22:00:12, 22:00:13 . . .

He hadn't blacked out—

Nothing had happened.

The attempt at replicating the Flashforward had failed, and—

Green lights.

Green lights on the ALICE console!

Lloyd rose to his feet. Theo was getting up as well.

"What happened?" asked one of the reporters.

"A big fat nothing," said another.

"Please," said Michiko. "Please, everyone stay on the floor—we don't know that it's safe yet."

Theo thumped the flat of his hand against Lloyd's back. Lloyd was grinning from ear to ear. He turned and embraced Theo.

"Guys," said Michiko, propping herself up on her elbow. "Nothing happened."

Lloyd and Theo disengaged, and Lloyd surged across the room. He reached out and took Michiko's hands and pulled her to her feet, then hugged her.

"Honey," said Michiko, "what is it?"

Lloyd gestured at the console. Michiko's eyes went wide. *"Sinjirarenai!"* she exclaimed. "You got it!"

Lloyd grinned even more. "We got it!"

"Got what?" asked one of the reporters. "Nothing happened, damn it!"

"Oh, yes it did," said Lloyd.

Theo was grinning, too. "Yes, indeed!"

"What?" demanded the same reporter.

"The Higgs!" said Lloyd.

"The what?"

"The Higgs boson!" said Lloyd, his arm around Michiko's waist. "We got the Higgs!"

Another reporter stifled a yawn. "Big fucking deal," he said.

Lloyd was being interviewed by one of the journalists. "What happened?" asked the man, a gruff, middle-aged correspondent for the London *Times*. "Or, more precisely, why didn't anything happen?"

"How can you say nothing happened? We got the Higgs boson!"

"Nobody cares about that. We want—"

"You're wrong," said Lloyd emphatically. "This is major; this is as big as it gets. Under any other circumstances, this would have been a front-page story in every newspaper in the world."

"But the visions—"

"I have no explanation for why they weren't reproduced. But today's event was hardly a failure. Scientists have been hoping to find the Higgs boson ever since Glashow, Salam, and Weinberg predicted its existence half a century ago—"

"But people were expecting another glimpse of the future, and—"

"I understand that," said Lloyd. "But finding the Higgs—not some damn-fool quest for precognition—was why the Large Hadron Collider was built in the first place. We knew we'd need to get up over ten trillion electron volts to produce the Higgs. That's why the nineteen countries that own CERN came together to build the LHC. That's why the United States, Canada, Japan, Israel, and other countries donated billions to the project as well. This *was* good science, important science—"

"Even so," said the reporter, "the *Wall Street Journal* estimated the aggregate total cost for your labor stoppage amounted to over fourteen *billion* dollars. That makes Project Klaatu the most expensive undertaking in human history."

"But we got the Higgs! Don't you see? Not only does this confirm the electroweak theory, it proves the existence of the

Higgs field. We now know what causes objects—you, me, this table, this planet—to have mass. The Higgs boson carries a fundamental field that endows elementary particles with mass—*and we've confirmed its existence!*"

"No one cares about a boson," said the reporter. "People can't even say the word without snickering."

"Call it the Higgs particle, then; lots of physicists do. But whatever you call it, it's the most important physics discovery so far in the twenty-first century. Sure, we're not even a decade into the century yet, but I'll bet that at the end of this century, people will look back and say this was *still* the most important physics discovery of the century."

"That doesn't explain why we didn't get anything—"

"We *did*," said Lloyd, exasperated.

"I mean why we didn't get any visions."

Lloyd puffed his cheeks and blew out air. "Look, we tried the best we could. Maybe the original phenomenon was a one-time fluke. Maybe it had a high degree of dependence on initial conditions that have subtly changed. Maybe—"

"You took a dive," said the reporter.

Lloyd was taken aback. "Pardon?"

"You took a dive. You deliberately muffed the experiment."

"We did *not* take—"

"You wanted to torpedo all the lawsuits; even after that song-and-dance at the UN, you still wanted to be sure that no one could ever successfully sue you, and, well, if you showed that CERN had nothing to do with the Flashforward the first time—"

"We didn't fake this. We didn't fake the Higgs. We made a *breakthrough*, for God's sake."

"You cheated us," said the man from the *Times*. "You cheated the entire planet."

"Don't be ridiculous," said Lloyd.

"Oh, come on. If you didn't take a dive, then why weren't you able to give us all another glimpse of the future?"

"I—I don't know. We tried. Really, we tried."

"There'll be an inquest, you know."

Lloyd rolled his eyes, but the reporter was probably right. "Look," said Lloyd. "We did everything we could. The computer logs will prove that; they'll show that every single experimental parameter was exactly the same. Of course, there is the problem of chaos, and dependent sensitivity, but we really did the best we could, and the result was hardly a failure—not by a long shot." The reporter looked like he was about to object again—probably claim that the logs could have been tampered with. But Lloyd held up a hand. "Still, maybe you *are* right; maybe this does prove that CERN in actuality had nothing to do with what happened before. In which case . . ."

"In which case, you're off the hook," the reporter said bitterly.

Lloyd frowned, considering. Of course, he probably already was off the hook legally for what had happened the first time. But morally? Without the absolution provided by a block universe, he had indeed been haunted—ever since Dim's suicide—by all the death and destruction he had caused.

Lloyd felt his eyebrows rising. "I guess you're right," he said. "I guess I *am* off the hook."

26

LIKE EVERY PHYSICIST, THEO WAITED WITH
interest each year to see who would be honored with the Nobel Prize—who would join the ranks of Bohr, Einstein, Feyn-
man, Gell-Mann, and Pauli. CERN researchers had earned
more than twenty Nobels over the years. Of course, when he
saw the subject header in his email box, he didn't have to open
the letter to know that his name wasn't on this year's list of
honorees. Still, he did like to see which of his friends and
colleagues were getting the nod. He clicked the OPEN button.

The laureates were Perlmutter and Schmidt for their work,
mostly done a decade ago, that showed that the universe was
going to expand forever, rather than eventually collapsing
down in a big crunch. It was typical that the award was for
work completed years previously; there had to be time for
results to be replicated and for the ramifications of the research
to be considered.

Well, thought Theo, they were both good choices. There'd
doubtless be some bitterness here at CERN; rumor had it that
McRainey was already planning his celebratory party, although that was doubtless just scurrilous gossip. Still, Theo

wondered, as he did every year at this time, whether he'd someday see his own name on the list.

Theo and Lloyd spent the next few days working on their paper about the Higgs. Although the press had already (somewhat halfheartedly) announced the particle's production to the world, they still had to write up their results for publication in a peer-reviewed journal. Lloyd, as was his habit, doodled endlessly on his datapad; Theo paced back and forth.

"Why the difference?" asked Lloyd, for the dozenth time. "Why didn't we get the Higgs the first time, but did get it this time?"

"I don't know," said Theo. "We didn't change anything. Of course, we couldn't match everything exactly, either. It's been weeks since the first attempt, so the Earth has moved millions of kilometers in its orbit around the sun, and of course the sun has moved through space, as it always does, and . . ."

"The sun!" crowed Lloyd. Theo looked at him blankly. "Don't you see? Last time we did this, the sun was up, but this time it was down. Maybe the first time the solar wind was interfering with our equipment?"

"The LHC tunnel is a hundred meters below ground, and it's got the best radiation shielding money can buy. There's no way any appreciable quantity of ionized particles could have gotten through to it."

"Hmmm," said Lloyd. "But what about particles that we can't shield against? What about neutrinos?"

Theo frowned. "For them, it shouldn't make any difference if we're facing the sun or not." Only one out of every two hundred million neutrinos passing through the Earth actually hits anything; the rest just come on through the other side.

Lloyd pursed his lips, thinking. "Still, maybe the neutrino count was particularly high the day we did it the first time." Something tickled his mind; something Gaston Béranger had said, when he was enumerating all the other things that had been happening at 17h00 on April 21. "Béranger told me the

Sudbury Neutrino Observatory picked up a burst just before we ran our experiment."

"I know someone at SNO," said Theo. "Wendy Small. We were in grad school together." Opened in 1998, the Sudbury Neutrino Observatory, located beneath two kilometers of Precambrian rock, was the world's most sensitive neutrino detector.

Lloyd gestured at the phone. Theo walked over to it. "Do you know the area code?"

"For Sudbury? It's probably 705; that's the one for most of northern Ontario."

Theo dialed a number, spoke to an operator, hung up, then dialed again. "Hello," he said, in English. "Wendy Small, please." A pause. "Wendy, it's Theo Procopides. What? Oh, funny. Funny woman." Theo covered the mouthpiece and said to Lloyd, "She said, 'I thought you were dead.'" Lloyd made a show of suppressing a grin. "Wendy, I'm calling from CERN, and I've got someone else with me: Lloyd Simcoe. You mind if I put you on the speaker phone?"

"*The* Lloyd Simcoe?" said Wendy's voice, from the speaker. "Pleased to meet you."

"Hello," said Lloyd, weakly.

"Look," said Theo, "as you doubtless know, we tried to reproduce the time-displacement phenomenon yesterday, and it didn't work."

"So I noticed," said Wendy. "You know, in my original vision, I was watching TV—except it was three-dimensional. It was the climax of some detective show. I've been dying to find out who did it."

Me, too, thought Theo, but what he said was, "Sorry we weren't able to help."

"I understand," said Lloyd, "that the Sudbury Neutrino Observatory picked up an influx of neutrinos just before we did our original experiment on April 21. Were those neutrinos due to sunspots?"

"No, the sun was quiet that day; what we detected was an extrasolar burst."

"Extrasolar? You mean from outside the solar system?"

"That's right."

"What was the source?"

"You remember Supernova 1987A?" asked Wendy.

Theo shook his head.

Lloyd, grinning, said, "That was the sound of Theo shaking his head."

"I could hear the rattling," said Wendy. "Well, look: in 1987, the biggest supernova in three hundred and eighty-three years was detected. A type-B3 blue supergiant star called Sanduleak -69°202 blew up in the Large Magellanic Cloud."

"The Large Magellanic Cloud!" said Lloyd. "That's a hell of a long way away."

"A hundred and sixty-six thousand light-years, to be precise," said Wendy's voice. "Meaning, of course, that Sanduleak really blew up back in the Pleistocene, but we didn't see the explosion until twenty-two years ago. But neutrinos travel unimpeded almost forever. And, during the explosion in 1987, we detected a burst of neutrinos that lasted about ten seconds."

"Okay," said Lloyd.

"And," continued Wendy, "Sanduleak was a very strange star; you normally expect a red supergiant, not a blue one, to go supernova. Regardless, though, after exploding as a supernova, what normally happens is that the remnants of the star collapse either into a neutron star or a black hole. Well, if Sanduleak had collapsed into a black hole, we never should have detected the neutrinos; they shouldn't have been able to escape. But at twenty solar masses, Sanduleak was, we thought, too small to form a black hole, at least according to the then-accepted theory."

"Uh-huh," said Lloyd.

"Well," said Wendy, "back in 1993, Hans Bethe and Gerry Brown came up with a theory involving kaon condensates that would allow a smaller-massed star to collapse into a black hole; kaons don't obey Pauli's exclusion principle." The exclusion principle said that two particles of a given type could not simultaneously occupy the same energy state.

"For a star to collapse into a neutron star," continued Wendy, "all the electrons must combine with protons to form neutrons, but since electrons *do* adhere to the exclusion principle, as you try to push them together they instead just keep occupying higher and higher energy levels, providing resistance to the continued collapse—that's part of the reason why you need to start with a sufficiently massive star to make a black hole. But if the electrons were converted to kaons, they could all occupy the lowest energy level, putting up much less resistance, and making the collapse of a smaller star into a black hole theoretically possible. Well, Gerry and Hans said, look, suppose that's what happened at Sanduleak—suppose its electrons became kaons. Then it could have collapsed into a black hole. And how long would it take for the conversion of electrons into kaons? They mapped it out at ten seconds— meaning that neutrinos could escape for the first ten seconds of the supernova event but, after that, they'd be swallowed up by the newly formed black hole. And, of course, ten seconds is how long the neutrino burst lasted back in 1987."

"Fascinating," said Lloyd. "But what's this got to do with the burst that happened when we were running our experiment the first time?"

"Well, the object that forms out of a kaon condensate isn't really a black hole," said Wendy's voice. "Rather, it's an inherently unstable parasingularity. We call them 'brown holes' now, after Gerry Brown. It in fact should rebound at some point, with the kaons spontaneously reconverting to electrons. When that happens, the Pauli exclusion principle should kick in, causing a massive pressure against degeneracy, forcing the whole thing to almost instantaneously expand again. At that point, neutrinos should again be able to escape—at least until the process reverses, and the electrons turn back into kaons again. Sanduleak was due to rebound at some point, and, as it happens, fifty-three seconds before your original time-displacement event, our neutrino detector registered a burst coming from Sanduleak; of course, the detector—or its recording equipment—stopped working as soon as the time-displacement began, so I don't know how long the second burst lasted, but in theory it should have lasted longer than the first—maybe as long as two or three minutes." Her voice grew wistful. "In fact, I originally thought that the Sanduleak rebound burst was what caused the time displacement in the first place. I was all ready to book a ticket to Stockholm when you guys stepped forward and said it was your collider that did it."

"Well, maybe it *was* the burst," said Lloyd. "Maybe that's why we weren't able to replicate the effect."

"No, no," said Wendy, "it wasn't the rebound burst, at least not on its own; remember, the burst began fifty-three seconds *before* the time displacement, and the displacement coincided precisely with the start of the your collisions. Still, maybe the coincidence of the burst continuing to impact the Earth at the same time you were doing your experiment caused whatever bizarre conditions created the time displacement. And without such a burst when you tried to replicate your experiment, nothing happened."

"So," said Lloyd, "we basically created conditions here on Earth that hadn't existed since a fraction of a second after the Big Bang, and simultaneously we were hit by a whack of neutrinos spewing out of a rebounding brown hole."

"That's about the size of it," said Wendy's voice. "As you can imagine, the chances of that ever happening are incredibly remote—which is probably just as well."

"Will Sanduleak rebound again?" asked Lloyd. "Can we expect another neutrino burst?"

"Probably," said Wendy. "In theory, it will rebound several more times, sort of oscillating between being a brown hole and a neutron star until stability is reached and it settles down as a permanent, but non-rotating, neutron star."

"When will the next rebound occur?"

"I have no idea."

"But if we wait for the next burst," said Lloyd, "and then

do our experiment again at precisely that moment, maybe we could replicate the time-displacement effect."

"It'll never happen," said Wendy's voice.

"Why not?" asked Theo.

"Think about it, boys. You needed weeks to prepare for this attempt at replicating the experiment; everyone had to be safe before it began, after all. But neutrinos are almost massless. They travel through space at virtually the speed of light. There's no way to know in advance that they're going to arrive, and since the first rebound burst lasted no more than three minutes—it was over by the time my detector started recording again—you'd never have any advance warning that a burst was going to occur, and once the burst started, you'd have only three minutes or less to crank up your accelerator."

"Damn," said Theo. "God damn."

"Sorry I don't have better news," said Wendy. "Look, I've got a meeting in five minutes—I should get going."

"Okay," said Theo. "Bye."

"Bye."

Theo clicked off the speaker phone and looked at Lloyd. "Irreproducible," he said. "The world's not going to like that." He moved over to a chair and sat down.

"Damn," said Lloyd.

"You're telling me," said Theo. "You know, now that we know the future isn't fixed, I'm not that worried, I guess, about the murder, but, still, I would have liked to have seen *something*, you know. Anything. I feel—Christ, I feel left out, you know? Like everyone else on the planet saw the mothership, and I was off taking a whiz."

27

THE LHC WAS NOW DOING DAILY 1150-TEV lead-nuclei collisions. Some were long-planned experiments, now back on track; others were parts of the ongoing attempts to find a proper theoretical basis for the temporal displacement. Theo took a break from going over computer logs from ALICE and CMS to check his email. "Additional Nobel winners announced," said the subject line of the first message.

Of course, Nobels aren't just given in physics. Five other prizes are awarded each year, with the announcements staggered over a period of several days: chemistry, physiology or medicine, economics, literature, and the promotion of world peace. The only one Theo really cared about was the physics prize—although he had a mild curiosity about the chemistry award, too. He clicked on the message header to see what it said.

It wasn't the chemistry Nobel—rather, it was the literature one. He was about to click the message into oblivion when the laureate's name caught his eye.

Anatoly Korolov. A Russian novelist.

Of course, after that man Cheung in Toronto had recounted his vision to Theo, mentioning someone called Korolov, Theo had researched the name. It had turned out to be frustratingly common, and remarkably undistinguished. No one by that name seemed to be particularly famous or significant.

But now someone named Korolov had won a Nobel. Theo immediately logged onto *Britannica Online;* CERN had an unlimited-use account with them. The entry on Anatoly Korolov was brief:

> Korolov, Anatoly Sergeyevich. Russian novelist and polemicist, born 11 July 1965, in Moscow, then part of the USSR—

Theo frowned. Bloody guy was a year younger than Lloyd, for God's sakes. Of course no one had to replicate the experimental results outlined in a novel. Theo continued reading:

> Korolov's first novel *Pered voskhodom solntsa* ("Before Sunrise"), published in 1992, told of the early days after the collapse of the Soviet Union; his protagonist, young Sergei Dolonov, a disillusioned Communist Party supporter, goes through a series of serio-comic coming-of-age rituals, fighting to make sense of the changes in his country, ultimately becoming a successful businessperson in Moscow. Korolov's other novels include *Na kulichkakh* ("At the World's End"), 1995; *Obyknovennaya istoriya* ("A Common Story"), 1999; and *Moskvityanin* ("The Muscovite"), 2006. Of these, only *Na kulichkakh* has been published in English.

He'd doubtless get a bigger write-up in the next edition, thought Theo. He wondered if Dim had read this fellow during his studies of European literature.

Could this be the Korolov Cheung's vision had referred to? If so, what possible connection did he have to Theo? Or to Cheung, for that matter, whose interests seemed commercial rather than literary?

•   •   •

Michiko and Lloyd were walking down the streets of St. Genis, holding hands, enjoying the warm evening breeze. After a few hundred meters passed with nothing but silence between them, Michiko stopped walking. "I think I know what went wrong."

Lloyd looked at her, his face a question.

"Think about what happened," she said. "You designed an experiment that should have produced the Higgs boson. The first time you ran it, though, it didn't. And why not?"

"The neutrino influx from Sanduleak," said Lloyd.

"Oh? That might indeed have been part of what caused the time displacement—but how could it have possibly upset the boson production?"

Lloyd shrugged. "Well, it—it . . . hmm, that *is* a good question."

Michiko shook her head. They began walking again. "It couldn't have an effect. I don't doubt that there was an influx of neutrinos at the time the experiment was originally conducted, but it shouldn't have disrupted the production of the Higgs bosons. The bosons *should* have been produced."

"But they weren't."

"Exactly," said Michiko. "But there was no one to observe them. For almost three whole minutes there wasn't a single conscious mind on Earth—no one, anywhere, to actually observe the creation of the Higgs boson. Not only that, there was no one available to observe *anything*. That's why all the videotapes seem to be blank. They *look* blank—like they've got nothing but electronic snow on them. But suppose that's not snow—suppose instead that the cameras accurately recorded what they saw: an unresolved world. The whole enchilada, the entire planet Earth, unresolved. Without qualified observers— with *everyone's* consciousness elsewhere—there was no way to resolve the quantum mechanics of what was going on. No way to choose between all the possible realities. Those tapes show uncollapsed wave fronts, a kind of staticky limbo—the super-position of all possible states."

"I doubt that wave front superposition would look like snow."

"Well, maybe it's not an actual picture; but, regardless of whether it is or isn't, it's clear that all information about that three-minute span was censored, somehow; the physics of what was happening prevented any recording of data during that period. Without any conscious beings anywhere, reality breaks down."

Lloyd frowned. Could he have been that wrong? Cramer's transactional interpretation accounted for everything in quantum mechanics without recourse to qualified observers . . . but maybe such observers *did* have a role to play. "Perhaps," he said. "But—no, no, that can't be right. If everything was unresolved, then how did the accidents occur? A plane crashing—that *is* a resolution, one possibility made concrete."

"Of course," said Michiko. "It's not that three minutes passed during which planes and trains and cars and assembly lines operated without human intervention. Rather, three minutes passed during which nothing was resolved—all the possibilities existed, stacked into shimmering whiteness. But at the end of those three minutes, consciousness returned, and the world collapsed again into a single state. And, unfortunately but inevitably, it took the single state that made the most sense, given that there had been three minutes of no consciousness: it resolved itself into the world in which planes and cars had crashed. But the crashes didn't occur during those three minutes; they never occurred at all. We simply went in one jump from the way things were before to the way they were after."

"That's . . . that's crazy," said Lloyd. "It's wishful thinking."

They were passing a pub. Loud music, with French lyrics, spilled through the heavy closed door. "No, it's not. It's quantum physics. And the result is the same: those people are just as dead, or just as maimed, as if the accidents had actually taken place. I'm not suggesting there's any way around that—as much as I wish there were.''

Lloyd squeezed Michiko's hand, and they continued walking, up the road, into the future.

BOOK III

TWENTY-ONE YEARS LATER

AUTUMN 2030

Lost time is never found again.

—John H. Aughey

28

❖

Time passes; things change.

In 2017, a team of physicists and brain researchers mostly based at Stanford devised a full theoretical model for the time displacement. The quantum-mechanical model of the human mind, proposed by Roger Penrose thirty years earlier, had turned out to be generally true even if Penrose had gotten many of the details wrong; it was perhaps not surprising, then, that sufficiently powerful quantum physics experiments could have an effect on perception.

Still, the neutrinos were a key part of it, too. It had been known since the 1960s that Earth's sun was, for some reason, disgorging only half as many neutrinos as it should—the famous "solar-neutrino problem."

The sun is heated by hydrogen fusion: four hydrogen nuclei—each a single proton—come together to form a helium nucleus, consisting of two protons and two neutrons. In the process of converting two of the original hydrogen-provided protons into neutrons, two electron neutrinos should be ejected . . . but, somehow one out of every two electron neutrinos that should reach Earth disappears before it does so, almost as if they were somehow being censored, almost as if the universe knew that the quantum-mechanical processes underlying consciousness were unstable if too many neutrinos were present.

The discovery in 1998 that neutrinos had a trifling mass had made credible a long-standing possible solution to the solar-neutrino problem: if neutrinos have mass, theory suggested that they could perhaps change types as they traveled, making it only appear, to primitive detectors, that they had disappeared. But the Sudbury Neutrino Observatory, which was capable of detecting all types of neutrinos, still showed a marked shortfall between what should be produced and what was reaching Earth.

The strong anthropic principle said the universe needed to give rise to life, and the Copenhagen interpretation of quantum physics said it requires qualified observers; given what was now known about the interaction of neutrinos and consciousness, the solar-neutrino problem seemed to be evidence that the universe was indeed taking pains to foster the existence of such observers.

Of course, occasional extrasolar neutrino bursts happened, but under normal circumstances they could be tolerated. But when the circumstances were *not* normal—when a neutrino onslaught was combined with conditions that hadn't existed since just after the big bang—time displacement occurred.

In 2018, the European Space Agency launched the *Cassandra* probe toward Sanduleak -69°202. Of course, it would take millions of years to reach Sanduleak, but that didn't matter. All that mattered was that now, in 2030, *Cassandra* was 2.5 trillion kilometers from Earth—and 2.5 trillion kilometers closer to the remnant of Supernova 1987A—a distance that light, and neutrinos, would take three months to travel.

Aboard *Cassandra* were two instruments. One was a light detector, aimed directly at Sanduleak; the other was a recent invention—a tachyon emitter—aimed back at Earth. *Cassandra* couldn't detect neutrinos directly, but if Sanduleak oscillated out of brown-hole status, it would give off light as well as neutrinos, and the light would be easy to see.

In July 2030, light from Sanduleak was detected by *Cassandra*. The probe immediately launched an ultra-low-energy (and therefore ultra-high-speed) tachyon burst toward Earth. Forty-three hours later, the tachyons arrived there, setting off alarms.

Suddenly, twenty-one years after the first time-displacement event, the people of Earth were given three months' notice that if they wanted to try for another glimpse of the future, they could indeed do so with a reasonable chance of success. Of course, the next attempt would have to be made at the exact moment the Sanduleak neutrinos would start passing through Earth—and it couldn't be a coincidence that that would be 19h21 Greenwich Mean Time on Wednesday, October 23, 2030—the precise beginning of the two-minute span the last set of visions had portrayed.

The UN debated the matter with surprising speed. Some had thought that because the present had turned out to be different from what the first set of visions portrayed, people might decide that new visions would be irrelevant. But, in reality, the general response was quite the opposite—almost everybody wanted another peek at tomorrow. The Ebenezer Effect still was powerful. And, of course, there was now a whole generation of young people who had been born after 2009. They felt left out, and were demanding a chance to have what their parents had already experienced: a glimpse of their prospective futures.

As before, CERN was the key to unlocking tomorrow. But Lloyd Simcoe, now sixty-six, would not be part of the replication attempt. He had retired two years ago, and had declined to come back to CERN. Still, Lloyd and Theo had indeed shared a Nobel prize. It had been awarded in 2024, not, as it turned out, in honor of anything related to the time-displacement effect, or the Higg's boson, but rather due to their joint invention of the Tachyon-Tardyon Collider, the tabletop device that had put giant particle accelerators at places ranging from TRIUMF to Fermilab to CERN out of business. Most of CERN was abandoned now, although the original Tachyon-Tardyon Collider was housed on the CERN campus.

Maybe it was because Lloyd's marriage to Michiko had crumbled after ten years that Lloyd didn't want to be involved with this attempt to replicate the original experiment. Yes, Lloyd and Michiko had had a daughter together, but always, down deep, not even acknowledged by her at first, there was a feeling on Michiko's part that Lloyd *had* somehow been responsible for her first daughter's death. She'd surprised herself, no doubt, the first time that charge had come out during an argument between her and Lloyd. But there it was.

That Lloyd and Michiko loved each other there was no doubt, but they ultimately decided that they simply couldn't go on living together, not with that hanging, however diffusely, over everything. At least it hadn't been a painful divorce, like that of Lloyd's parents. Michiko moved back to Nippon, taking their daughter Joan with her; Lloyd got to visit with her only once a year, at Christmas.

Lloyd wasn't crucial to the replication of the original experiment, although his help would have been a real asset. But he was now happily remarried—and, yes, it was to Doreen, the woman he'd seen in his vision, and, yes, they did now own a cottage in Vermont.

Still, Jake Horowitz, who had long since left CERN to work at TRIUMF with his wife Carly Tompkins, did agree to come back for three months. Carly came as well, and she and Jake endured the gentle kidding of people asking them which labs at CERN they were going to baptize. They had been married for eighteen years now, and had three wonderful kids.

Theodosios Procopides and about three hundred other people still worked at CERN, running the TTC there. Theo, Jake, Carly, and a skeleton crew raced against time to get the Large Hadron Collider ready to run again, after five years of disuse, before the Sanduleak neutrinos hit.

29

THEO, NOW FORTY-EIGHT, WAS PERSONALLY delighted that the reality of 2030 had turned out to be different from what had been portrayed in the visions of 2009. For his own part, he'd grown a fine, full beard, covering his jutting jaw (and saving him from looking like he needed another shave by mid-afternoon). Young Helmut Drescher had said he could see Theo's chin in his vision; the beard was one of Theo's little ways of asserting his free will.

Still, as the replication date approached, Theo found himself growing more and more apprehensive. He tried to convince himself that it was nervousness about letting the whole world down again if something went wrong, but the LHC seemed to be operating perfectly, and so he had to admit that that wasn't really it.

No, what he was nervous about was the fact that the day on which the 2009 visions said he was going to die was rapidly approaching.

Theo found that he couldn't eat, couldn't sleep. If he had ever determined who it was who had originally wanted him dead, that would have perhaps made it easier—all he would have to do is avoid that person. But he had no idea who had/ would/might pull the trigger.

Finally, inevitably, it was Monday, October 21, 2030: the date that, in at least one version of reality, was laser-carved into Theo's tombstone. Theo woke that morning in a cold sweat.

There was still oodles of work to be done at CERN—it was only two days until the Sanduleak neutrinos would hit. He tried to put it all out of his mind, but even after he got to the office, he found himself unable to concentrate.

And, by a little after 10h00, he couldn't take it anymore. Theo left the LHC control center, putting on a forward-swept beige cap and mirrored sunglasses as he did so. It wasn't all that bright out; the temperature was cool, and about half the sky was covered by clouds. But no one went outside without head and eye protection anymore. Although the depleting of the ozone layer had finally been halted, nothing effective had been done yet about building it back up.

Sun glinted off the rocky pinnacles of the Jura mountains. There was a Globus Gateway bus in the parking lot; mostly deserted CERN wasn't a starred attraction in the *Guide Michelin*, of course, and, with the hubbub surrounding the replication attempt, no tourists were allowed on site, anyway. This bus had been chartered to bring a crowd of journalists from the airport; they had flown in to cover the work leading up to the replication.

Theo walked over to his car, a red Ford Octavia—good, serviceable transportation. He'd spent his youth playing with billion-dollar particle accelerators; he hardly needed a fancy car to establish his worth.

The car recognized him as he approached, and he nodded at it to indicate he really did want to enter. The driver-side door slid up into the roof. You could still buy cars with doors that hinged out to the side, but with parking spaces so tight in most urban centers doors that required no special clearance were more convenient.

Theo entered the car and told it where he wanted to go.

"At this time of day," said the car in a pleasant male voice, "it'll be fastest to take Rue Meynard."

"Fine," said Theo. "You drive."

The car began to do just that, lifting off the ground and starting on its way. "Music or news?" said the car.

"Music," said Theo.

The car filled with one of Theo's favorite bands, a popular Korean jag group. But the music did little to calm him. Dammit all, he knew he shouldn't even be here in Switzerland, but the Large Hadron Collider was still the biggest instrument of its type in the world; periodic attempts prior to the invention of the TTC to revive the Superconducting Supercollider project, killed by the U.S. Congress in 1993, had all failed. And running and repairing particle accelerators was a dying art. Most of those who had built the original LEP accelerator—the first one mounted in CERN's giant subterranean tunnel—were either dead or retired, and only a few of those involved with the LHC, which first went into service a quarter of a century ago, were still in that line of work. So: Theo's expertise was needed in Switzerland. But he was damned if he was going to be a sitting duck.

The car stopped outside the destination Theo had requested: Police Headquarters in Geneva. It was an old building—more than a century old, in fact, and although internal-combustion motors were illegal on any car manufactured after 2021, the building still showed the grime of decades of automobile exhausts; it would have to be sandblasted at some point.

"Open," said Theo. The door disappeared into the ceiling.

"There are no vacant parking spots within a five-hundred-meter radius," said the car.

"Keep driving around the block, then," said Theo. "I'll call you when I'm ready to be picked up."

The car chirped acknowledgment. Theo put on his cap and shades and stepped outside. He crossed the sidewalk, made his way up the steps, and entered the building.

"Bonjour," said a large blond man sitting behind a desk. *"Je peux vous aider?"*

"Oui," said Theo. *"Détective Helmut Drescher, s'il vous plaît."* Young Helmut Drescher was indeed a detective now; Theo, with then-idle curiosity, had checked on that several months before.

"Moot's not in," said the man, still speaking in French. "Can somebody else help you?"

Theo felt his heart sink. Drescher, at least, might understand, but to try to explain it to a complete stranger . . . "I was really hoping to see Detective Drescher," said Theo. "Do you expect him back soon?"

"I really don't—oh, say, this must be your lucky day. There's Moot now."

Theo turned around. Two men both about the right age were entering the building; Theo had no idea which one might be Drescher. "Detective Drescher?" he said tentatively.

"That's me," said the one on the right. Helmut had grown up to be a fine-looking man, with light brown hair, a strong, square jaw, and bright blue eyes.

"Like I said," said the desk officer from behind Theo. "Your lucky day."

Only if I live through it, thought Theo. "Detective Drescher," said Theo, "I need to talk to you."

Drescher turned to the other man he'd come in with. "I'll catch up with you later, Fritz," he said. Fritz nodded and headed deeper into the building.

Drescher showed no sign of recognizing Theo. Of course, it had been twenty-one years since they'd last seen each other, and, although there had been a lot of media coverage of the upcoming attempt to replicate the time displacement, Theo had been way too busy to be interviewed much on TV lately; he'd been leaving that mostly to Jake Horowitz.

Drescher led Theo toward the inner doors; he was dressed in plain clothes, but Theo couldn't help noticing that he had *very* nice shoes. Drescher laid his hand on a palmprint reader and the paired doors swung inward, letting them into the squad room. Flatsies—paper-thin computers—were piled high on some desks and spread out in overlapping patterns on others. One entire wall was a map showing Geneva's computer-controlled traffic, with every vehicle tracked by an individual transponder. Theo looked to see if he could spot his own car orbiting the building; it seemed his wasn't the only one doing that just now.

"Have a seat," said Drescher, indicating the chair that faced his desk. He took a flatsie from a pile and placed it between him and Theo. "You don't mind if I record this?" he said. The words—French—instantly appeared as text on the flatsie, with an attribution tag saying, "H. Drescher."

Theo shook his head. Drescher gestured at the flatsie. Theo realized he wanted a spoken reply. *"Non,"* he said. The flatsie duly recorded it, but simply put a glowing question mark where the speaker's name should be.

"And you are?"

"Theodosios Procopides," said Theo, expecting the name to ring a bell for Drescher.

The flatsie, at least, got it in one—indeed, Theo saw a little window appear on the sheet, showing the correct spelling of his name using the Hellenic alphabet and listing some basic facts about Theo. The attribution tags for the *"Non,"* and the stating of his name immediately changed to "T. Procopides."

"And what can I do for you?" asked Drescher, still oblivious.

"You don't know who I am, do you?" said Theo.

Drescher shook his head.

"The, ah, last time we saw each other, I didn't have the beard."

The detective peered at Theo's face. "Well, I—oh! Oh, God! Oh, it's you!"

Theo glanced down. The flatsie had done a commendable job of punctuating the detective's outburst. When he looked back up, he saw that all the color had drained from Drescher's face.

"Oui," said Theo. *"C'est moi."*

"Mon Dieu," said Drescher. "How that's haunted me over the years." He shook his head. "You know, I've seen a lot of autopsies since, and a lot of dead bodies. But yours—to see something like that when you're just a kid." He shuddered.

"I'm sorry," said Theo. He paused for a moment, then: "Do you remember me coming to visit you, shortly after you had that vision? Out at your parents' house—the one with that great staircase?"

Drescher nodded. "I remember. Scared the life out of me."

Theo lifted his shoulders slightly. "I'm sorry about that, too."

"I've tried to keep that vision out of my mind," said Drescher. "All these years, I've tried not to think about it. But it still comes back, you know. Even after all I've seen, that image still haunts me."

Theo smiled apologetically.

"Not your fault," said Drescher, gesturing dismissively with his hand. "What was your vision of?"

Theo was surprised by the question; Drescher was still having trouble connecting his own vision of that dead body with the reality of the human being sitting in front of him. "Nothing," said Theo.

"Oh, yeah, right," said Drescher, slightly embarrassed. "Sorry."

There was awkward silence between them for a few moments, then Drescher spoke again. "You know, it wasn't all bad—that vision, I mean. It got me interested in police work. I don't know that I would have signed up for the academy if I hadn't had that vision."

"How long have you been a cop?" asked Theo.

"Seven years—the last two as detective."

Theo had no idea if that was rapid advancement or not, but he found himself doing the math related to Drescher's age. He couldn't have a university degree. Theo spent far too much time with academics and scientists; he was always afraid he'd accidentally say something patronizing to those who hadn't gone any further than high school. "That's good," he offered.

Drescher shrugged, but then he frowned and shook his head. "You shouldn't be anywhere *near* here. You shouldn't be anywhere in Europe, for God's sake. You must have been killed in or near Geneva, or I wouldn't be the cop investigating it. If I'd had a vision that I was going to be killed here on this day, you can bet I'd be in Zhongua or Hawaii instead."

Theo's turn to shrug. "I didn't want to be here, but I have no choice. I told you, I'm with CERN. I was part of the team that led the Large Hadron Collider experiment twenty-one years ago. They need me to duplicate that the day after tomorrow. Believe me, if I had any choice in the matter, I *would* be somewhere else."

"You haven't taken up boxing, have you?"

"No."

"Because in my vision—"

"I know, I know. You said I was killed at a boxing match."

"My dad, he used to watch boxing all the time on TV," said Helmut. "Funny sport for a shoe salesman, I guess, but he liked it. I used to watch it with him, even when I was a little kid."

"Look," said Theo, "you know in a way that no one else does that I really *am* at risk. That's why I've come to see you." He swallowed. "I need your help, Helmut. I need police protection. Between now and when the experiment is replicated in—" He glanced at the wall clock, a flatsie held up with tape, fifteen centimeter digits glowing on its surface "—in fifty-nine hours."

Drescher gestured at all the other flatsies strewn across his desk. "I've got a lot of work to do."

"Please. You know what might happen. Most people have this coming Wednesday off work—you know, so they can be safe at home when the time-displacement is replicated. I hate to even ask, but you could use that time to catch up on any work you might miss today and tomorrow."

"I don't have Wednesday off." He gestured at the other people in the squad room. "None of us do—in case something goes wrong." A pause. "You have any idea who might shoot you?"

Theo shook his head, then, glancing at the recording flatsie, said, "No. None. I've wracked my brain for twenty-one years trying to figure it out—trying to determine who I might have pissed off so much that they'd want me dead, or who could profit from having me out of the way. But there's no one."

"No one?"

"Well, you know, you go crazy; you get paranoid. Something like this—it makes you suspect everybody. Sure, for a time, I thought maybe my old partner, Lloyd Simcoe, had done it. But I spoke to Lloyd just yesterday; he's in Vermont, and has no plans to come over to Europe anytime in the near future."

"It's only—what?—a three-hour flight, if he takes a supersonic," said Drescher.

"I know, I know—but, really, I'm sure it's not him. But there *is* somebody out there, some—what do you guys say? What's the phrase? Some person or persons unknown who may indeed make an attempt on my life today. And I'm asking you—I'm begging you, please—to keep that person or persons from getting at me."

"Where do you have to be today?"

"At CERN. Either in my office, in the LHC control center, or down in the tunnel."

"Tunnel?"

"Yeah. You must have heard of it: there's a tunnel at CERN twenty-seven kilometers in circumference buried a hundred meters down; a giant ring, you know? That's where the LHC is housed."

Drescher chewed on his lower lip for a moment. "Let me talk to my captain," he said. He got up, crossed the room, and rapped his knuckles against a door. The door slid aside, and Theo could see a stern, dark-haired woman within. Drescher entered, and the door closed behind him.

It seemed he was gone for an eternity. Theo looked about

nervously. On Drescher's desk was a hologram of a young woman who might be his wife or girlfriend, and an older man and woman. Theo recognized the older woman: Frau Drescher. Assuming it was a recent shot—and, really, it must be; holocameras had been priced out of reach of an honest cop until a couple of years ago—then the decades had been kind to her. She was still a very attractive woman, content to let her hair show its gray.

Finally, the door at the far end of the room opened again, and Detective Drescher emerged. He crossed the busy squad room and returned to his desk. "I'm sorry," he said, as he sat back down. "If someone had made a threat or something . . ."

"Let me speak to your captain."

Drescher snorted. "She won't see you; half the time she won't even see me." He softened his voice. "I *am* sorry, Mr. Procopides. Look—just be careful, that's all."

"I thought you—you, of all people—would understand."

"I'm just a cop," said Drescher. "I take orders." He paused, and a sly tone slipped into his voice. "Besides, maybe coming here was a big mistake. I mean, what if I'm the guy who shot you the first time out? Didn't Agatha Christie write a story like that once, in which the detective was the killer? It'd be kind of ironic, then, you coming to see me, no?"

Theo lifted his eyebrows. His heart was pounding, and he didn't know what to say. Jesus Christ, he *had* been shot with a Glock, a gun favored by police officers all over the world . . .

"Don't worry," said Drescher, grinning. "I'm just kidding. Figured I deserved to give you a fright after what you did to me all those years ago." But he did reach down and use a couple of swipes of his index finger to erase the last few lines of the transcript from the flatsie.

"Good luck, Mr. Procopides. Like I said, just be careful. For billions of people, the future turned out unlike what their visions portrayed. I shouldn't have to tell you this, you being a scientist and all, but there really is no good reason to think that your vision is going to be the one that actually comes true."

•   •   •

Theo used his cellular phone to call his car, and when it arrived, he got back in.

Drescher was doubtless right. Theo felt embarrassed about his panic attack; probably a bad dream the night before, coupled with anxiety about the upcoming replication, had brought it on. He tried to relax, looking out at the countryside as his car drove him back to the LHC control center. The tour bus was still there. It made him a bit nostalgic. Globus Gateway buses were seen all over Western Europe, of course. He'd never taken one of their tours himself, but as a horny teenager he and a couple of his friends had always watched for them in July and August. North American girls, looking for a summer of excitement, often traveled in such things; Theo had enjoyed more than one romantic evening with an American schoolgirl during his teenage years.

The pleasant memory faded to sadness, though; he was thinking of home, of Athens. He'd only been back twice since Dim's funeral. Why hadn't he made more time for his parents? Theo let his car find a vacant spot. He got out and headed into the LHC control center.

"Oh, Theo," said Jake Horowitz, coming at him from the other end of the mosaic-lined corridor. "I've been trying to get hold of you. I called your car but it said you'd been arrested or something."

"Funny car," said Theo. "Actually, I was just visiting—visiting someone I thought was an old friend."

"There's a problem with the LHC that Jiggs doesn't know how to fix."

"Oh?"

"Yeah, something with one of the cryostat clusters—number four-forty, in octant three."

Theo frowned. It had been years since the LHC had been cranked up to full power. Jiggs, all of thirty-four, was head of the maintenance division; he'd never actually seen the collider used at 14-TeV levels.

Theo nodded; cryostat controls were notoriously finicky. "I'll go have a look." In the old days, when CERN had a staff of three thousand, Theo never would have gone down into the LHC tunnel alone, but with his current skeleton crew, it seemed the best way to apportion his limited manpower, and, well, it was probably the safest place to be: sure, a crazy person might make it onto CERN's campus, looking to shoot Theo, but doubtless such an intruder would be stopped long before he could get down into the tunnel. Besides, no one but Jake and Jiggs—both of whom he trusted completely—would even know that he was down there.

Theo took the elevator to the minus-one-hundred-meter level. The air in the particle-accelerator tunnel was humid and warm, and smelled of machine oil and ozone. The light was dim—a bluish white from overhead fluorescents punctuated at regular intervals by yellow emergency lamps mounted on the walls. The throbbing of equipment, the hum of air pumps, and the clack of Theo's heels against the concrete floor all echoed loudly. In cross-section, the tunnel was circular, except for the flat floor, and its diameter varied between 3.8 and 5.5 meters.

As he'd often done before, Theo Procopides looked down the tunnel in one direction then turned and looked in the opposite direction. It wasn't *quite* straight. He could see along it for a great distance, but eventually the walls curved away.

Hanging from the tunnel roof was the I-beam track for the monorail, and, hanging from that, the monorail itself; Jiggs had left it parked here. The monorail consisted of a cab big enough to hold a single person, three small cars each designed for cargo rather than passengers, and a second cab, facing the opposite direction, capping the end. The cargo cars weren't much more than hanging baskets made of metal painted peacock-blue. Each cab was an open, orange frame with headlights mounted above its sloping windscreen and a wide rubber bumper mounted below. The windscreens sloped at a sharp angle.

The driver had to sit with his legs out in front of him; the cab wasn't tall enough to accommodate a normally seated person. The name ORNEX—the manufacturer of the monorail—was emblazoned across the cab's front. To either side of the name were small red reflectors, and below it was a wide strip with black-and-yellow safety markings; they wanted to be absolutely sure the cabs would be visible in the dim tunnel. The monorail had been upgraded in 2020; it could manage about sixty kilometers an hour now, meaning it could circumnavigate the tunnel in under thirty minutes.

Theo got a tool box from one of the supply lockers in the staging area, put on his yellow hard hat—even though he rarely went down into the tunnel, he was senior enough that he'd been given his own personal hat. He placed the tool box in one of the cargo cars, clambered into the cab that was facing in the direction he wanted to go—clockwise—and set the train in motion, whirring away into the darkness.

Detective Helmut Drescher tried to get on with his work; he had seven open case files to dig through, and Capitaine Lavoisier had been demanding he make some more progress. But Moot's mind kept turning back to the plight of Theo Procopides. The guy had seemed nice enough; he wished he could have helped him. He'd looked to be in good shape, too, for a man who must have been almost fifty. Moot found the flatsie that had recorded their earlier conversation; the biographical-data box about Theo was still displayed. Born 2 March 1982—so that would make him forty-eight. Pretty old to be a boxer—besides, he had the wrong build for it. Maybe in whatever alternative reality the visions had shown he'd been a coach or a referee, rather than an actual fighter. But no—that didn't seem right. Moot didn't have the business card with him that Theo had given him two decades ago, although he had saved it through all intervening years, and had looked at it occasionally: it had clearly said CERN on it. So, if he was already a physicist before the visions took place in 2009, it seemed unlikely that he'd switch to a career in sports. But

Moot remembered his own vision vividly: the man in the smock—the medical examiner, he knew now—had clearly said that Procopides was killed in the ring, and—

In the ring.

What was it Procopides had said earlier today? *You must have heard of it. There's a tunnel at CERN twenty-seven kilometers in circumference buried a hundred meters down; a giant ring, you know?*

He'd been a little kid—a little kid who watched boxing with his dad; a little kid who loved the movie *Rocky*. He'd just assumed back then that "in the ring" meant "in a boxing match," and he'd never given it any more thought since.

A giant ring, you know?

Shit. Maybe Procopides *was* in real danger. Moot got up from his desk and went back to see Capitaine Lavoisier.

The defective cryostat cluster was ten kilometers away; it would take the monorail about ten minutes to bring Theo there. The cab's headlight beams sliced into the darkness. There were fluorescent lighting fixtures throughout the whole tunnel, but it was pointless to illuminate all twenty-seven kilometers of it.

Finally, the monorail arrived at the location of the wonky cryostat cluster. Theo stopped the train, disembarked, found the panel for controlling the local lighting, and turned it on for fifty meters ahead and behind him. He then retrieved his tool kit and headed over to the defective unit.

This time Capitaine Lavoisier acquiesced, giving Moot permission to act as Theo's bodyguard until the end of the day. Moot took his usual unmarked car and drove to CERN. He suspected CERN was like most places: the transponder signal from a staff member's car would let it pass automatically through the gate, but Moot had to stop and show his badge to the guard computer before the barrier was lifted. He also asked the computer for direction; the CERN campus consisted of dozens of mostly empty buildings. It took him about five minutes to find the LHC control center. He let his car settle to the asphalt and hurried inside.

An attractive middle-aged woman with freckles was coming down a corridor lined with a series of mosaics. Moot showed her his badge. "I'm looking for Theo Procopides," he said.

The woman nodded. "He was here earlier today; let's see if we can find him."

The woman led the way deeper into the building; she tried a couple of rooms, but Theo was in neither of them. "Let's try my husband's office," she said. "He and Theo work together." They went down another corridor, and entered an office. "Jake, this man's a police officer. He's looking for Theo."

"He's down in the tunnel," said Jake. "That damned cryostat cluster in octant three."

"He may be in trouble," said Moot. "Can you take me to him?"

"In trouble?"

"In his vision, he is shot dead today—and I've got reason to believe it was down in the tunnel."

"My God," said Jake. "Um, sure, sure—I can take you to him, and—damn! God damn it, but he must have taken the monorail."

"The monorail?"

"There's a monorail that runs around the ring. But he'll have taken it ten kilometers from here."

"There's only one train?"

"We used to have three more, but we sold them off years ago. We've only got one left."

"You could fly over to the far access station," said the woman. "There's no road, but you could easily fly over the farmers' fields."

"Right—right!" said Jake. He smiled at his wife. "Beautiful and brilliant!" He turned to Moot. "Come on!"

Jake and Moot hurried down the corridors, through the

lobby, and out into the parking lot. "We'll take my car," said Moot. They got in, Moot hit the start button, and the car rose off the ground. He followed Jake's instructions for getting out of the campus. Then Jake pointed across an open farmer's field.

The car flew.

Theo looked at the cryostat cluster's housing. No wonder Jiggs had been having trouble fixing it: he'd been going in through the wrong access port. The panel he'd been working behind was still open but the potentiometers Jiggs used to fiddle with were hidden behind another panel.

Theo tried to open the access door that should have let him get at the right controls, but it wouldn't budge. After years of disuse in the dark, damp tunnel, the door had apparently corroded shut. Theo rummaged in his toolkit looking for something he could use to pry it open, but all he had were some screwdrivers that proved inadequate to the task. What he really needed was a crowbar or something similar. He swore in Greek. He could take the monorail back to the campus and get the appropriate tool, but that seemed like such a waste of time. Surely there was something down here in the tunnel that he could use. He looked back the way he'd come; he hadn't noted anything like what he needed during the last few hundred meters of his trip on the monorail but, of course, he wasn't really looking. Still, it seemed to make more sense to continue on clockwise around the tunnel, at least a short distance, and see if he could find something that would do the trick.

The far access station was an old concrete bunker in the middle of a farmer's colza field. Moot's car settled down on the small driveway—there was an access road leading out in the opposite direction—and he shut off its engine. He and Jake got out.

It was noon, and, since this was October, the sun didn't get very high in the sky. But at least the bees, which were a nuisance in summer, were gone. Up the mountainsides there were mostly conifers, of course, but down here there were lots of deciduous trees. The leaves on many of them had already changed color.

"Come on," said Jake.

Moot hesitated. "There's no chance of radiation, is there?"

"Not while the collider is turned off. It's perfectly safe."

As they came toward the blockhouse, a hedgehog scurried by, quickly hiding itself in the ninety-centimeter colza shoots. Jake stopped short at the door. It was an old-fashioned hinged door, with a deadbolt lock. But the door had been pried open; a crowbar lay in the grass next to the blockhouse.

Moot moved to the door. "No corrosion," he said, indicating the metal exposed where the lock had been broken. "This was done recently." He used the toe of his fancy shoes to nudge the crowbar slightly. "The grass underneath is still green; this must have happened today or yesterday." He looked at Jake. "Anything valuable kept down there?"

"Valuable yes," said Jake. "But salable? Not unless you know of a black-market for obsolete high-energy physics equipment."

"You say this collider hasn't been used recently?"

"Not for a few years."

"Might be squatters," said Moot. "Could someone live down there?"

"I—I suppose. It'd be cold and dark, but it is watertight."

Moot had a pouch at his hip; he pulled it open and removed a small electronic device, which he waved over the crowbar. "Lots of fingerprints," he said. Jake looked over; he could see the fingerprints fluorescing on the device's display screen. Moot pushed some buttons on his device. After about thirty seconds, some text scrolled across the screen. "No matches on file. Whoever did this has never been arrested anywhere in Switzerland or the E.U." A pause. "How far away is Procopides?"

Jake pointed. "About five kilometers that way. But there should be a couple of hovercarts parked here; we'll take one of those."

"Does he have a cellular? Can we phone him?"

"He's buried beneath a hundred meters of soil," said Jake. "Cell phones don't work."

They hurried into the blockhouse.

Theo had walked a couple of hundred meters down the tunnel without finding anything that would help him pry open the access door on the cryostat cluster. He glanced back; the cluster itself had disappeared around the gentle curve of the ring. He was about to give up in defeat and head back to the monorail when something caught his eye up ahead. It was somebody else, working next to one of the sextupole magnets. The person wasn't wearing a hardhat—a violation of regulations, that. Theo thought about calling out to him, but the acoustics were so bad in the tunnel he'd long ago learned not to bother trying to shout over any distance. Well, it didn't matter who it was, as long as he had a more complete toolkit than the one Theo had brought.

It took Theo another minute to get close to the man. He was working next to one of the air pumps; the racket it made must have masked the sound of Theo approaching. Sitting on the tunnel floor was a hovercart, a disk about a meter and a half in diameter with two single chairs under a canopy. Hovercarts had been developed for use on golf courses; they were much easier on the greens than old-fashioned motorized carts.

Back in the old days, there were thousands of CERN employees whom Theo didn't know on sight, but now, with just a few hundred, he was surprised to see somebody he didn't recognize.

"Hey, there," said Theo.

The man—a thin white fellow in his fifties with white hair and dark gray eyes—swung around, clearly startled. He did have a toolkit with him, but—

He'd opened a large access plate on the side of an air pump and had just finished inserting a device in there—

A device that looked like a small, aluminum suitcase with a string of glowing blue digits on its side.

Glowing digits that were counting down.

30

A SERIES OF LOCKERS LINED ONE WALL OF THE blockhouse. Jake helped himself to a yellow hard hat, and indicated that Moot should take one, too. There was an elevator inside, as well as a staircase leading down. Jake pushed the call button for the elevator; they waited an interminable time for the cab to appear.

"Whoever broke in must still be down there," he said. "Otherwise, the elevator would have been waiting at the top."

"Couldn't he have taken the stairs?" asked Moot.

"I suppose, but it's a hundred meters—that's the equivalent of thirty floors in an office building. Even going down, that's exhausting."

The elevator arrived and they got in. Jake pushed the button to activate it. The ride was frustratingly slow; it took a full minute to descend to the tunnel level. Jake and Moot disembarked. There was a hovercart parked here, and Jake started toward it. "Didn't you say there should be two hovercarts here?"

"That's what I'd have expected, yes," said Jake.

Jake got into the hovercart's driver seat, and Moot took the passenger seat. He turned on the cart's headlights and activated its ground-effect fans. The cart floated up, and they headed counterclockwise along the tunnel, going as fast as the little vehicle could manage.

Along the way, the tunnel straightened out for a distance; it did that near all four of the large detectors, to avoid synchrotron radiation. In the middle of the straight section, they saw the giant, twenty-meter-tall empty chamber that used to house the Compact Muon Solenoid detector with its 14,000-ton magnet. At the time it had been built, CMS had cost over a hundred million American dollars. After the development of the Tachyon-Tardyon Collider, CERN had put CMS, as well as ALICE, which used to reside in a similar chamber at another point in the tunnel ring, up for sale. The Nipponese government bought them both for use at their KEK accelerator in Tsukaba. Michiko Komura had supervised the dismantling of the massive machines here and their reassembly in her homeland. The sound of the hovercart's motors echoed in the vast chamber, big enough to house a small apartment building.

"How much longer?" asked Moot.

"Not long," said Jake.

They continued on.

Theo looked at the man, who was still crouching in the tunnel in front of the air pump. "*Mein Gott,*" said the man softly.

"You," said Theo, in French. "Who are you?"

"Hello, Dr. Procopides," said the man.

Theo relaxed. If the guy knew who he was, he couldn't be an intruder. Besides, he looked vaguely familiar.

The man looked back down the tunnel the way he'd come. And then he reached inside the dark leather jacket he was wearing and pulled out a gun.

Theo's heart jumped. Of course, years ago, after young Helmut had mentioned a Glock 9-mm, Theo had looked for a picture of one on the Web. The boxy semiautomatic weapon now facing him was just such a handgun; its clip could hold up to fifteen rounds.

The man looked down at the pistol, as if he himself was surprised to see it in his hand. Then he shrugged slightly. "A little something I picked up in the States—they're so much easier to come by over there." He paused. "And, yes, I know what you're thinking." He gestured at the aluminum suitcase with the blue LED timer. "You're thinking maybe that's a bomb. And that's precisely what it is. I could have planted it anywhere, I imagine, but I came a ways along the tunnel looking for a place to secrete it, lest someone find it. Inside this machine here seemed like a suitable spot."

"What—" Theo was surprised at how his voice sounded. He swallowed, trying to get it back under control. "What are you trying to accomplish?"

The man shrugged again. "It should be obvious. I'm trying to sabotage your particle accelerator."

"But why?"

He gestured at Theo with the gun. "You don't recognize me, do you?"

"You *do* look familiar, but . . ."

"You came to visit me in Deutschland. One of my neighbors had contacted you; my vision had shown me watching a newscast on videotape about your death."

"Right," said Theo. "I remember." He couldn't recall the man's name, but he did remember the meeting, twenty years ago.

"And why was I watching that newscast? Why was the story about your death the one story on that newscast that I'd fast-forwarded ahead to see? Because I was checking to see if they had any evidence pointing to me. I'd never meant to kill anyone, but I will kill you if I have to. It's only fair, after all. You killed my wife."

Theo began to protest that he'd done no such thing, but then it came to him. Yes, he recalled his visit with this man. His wife had fallen down the stairs at a subway station during the time-displacement event; she'd broken her neck.

"There was no way we could have known what would happen—no way we could have prevented it."

"*Of course* you could have prevented it," snapped the man—Rusch, that was his name. It came back to Theo: Wolfgang Rusch. "Of course you could have. You had no business doing what you were doing. Trying to reproduce conditions at the birth of the universe! Trying to force the handiwork of God out into the light of day. Curiosity, they say, killed the cat. But it was *your* curiosity—and it's my wife who's dead."

Theo didn't know what to say. How do you explain science—the need, the quest—to someone who is obviously a fanatic? "Look," said Theo, "where would the world be if we didn't—"

"You think I'm crazy?" said Rusch. "You think I'm nuts?" He shook his head. "I'm not nuts." He reached into his back pocket and pulled out his wallet. He fumbled with one hand to remove a yellow-and-blue laminated card from it and showed it to Theo.

Theo looked at it. It was a faculty ID card for The Humboldt University. "Tenured professor," said Rusch. "Department of Chemistry. Ph.D. from the Sorbonne." That's right—back in 2009, the man had said he taught chemistry. "If I had known your role in all this back then, I wouldn't have spoken to you. But you came to see me before CERN had gone public with its involvement."

"And now you want to kill me?" said Theo. His heart was pounding so hard he thought it was going to burst, and he could feel sweat breaking out all over his body. "That won't bring your wife back to life."

"Oh, yes it will," said Rusch.

He *was* mad. Dammit, why had Theo come down into the tunnel alone?

"Not your death, of course," said Rusch. "But what I'm doing. Yes, it will bring Helena back. It's all because of the Pauli exclusion principle."

Theo didn't know what to say; the man was raving. "What?"

"Wolfgang Pauli," said Rusch, nodding. "I like to tell my students I was named for him, but I wasn't—I was named for my father's uncle." A pause. "Pauli's exclusion principle originally just applied to electrons: no two electrons could simultaneously occupy the same energy state. Later, it was expanded to include other subatomic particles."

Theo knew all this. He tried to hide his mounting panic. "So?"

"So I believe that the exclusion principle also applies to the concept of *now*. All the evidence is there: there can only be one *now*—throughout all of human history, we have all agreed on what moment is the present. Never has there been a moment that some part of humanity thought was now, while another part thought it was the past, and still another considered it to be in the future."

Theo lifted his shoulders slightly, not following where this was going.

"Don't you get it?" asked Rusch. "Don't you see? When you shifted the consciousness of humanity ahead twenty-one years—when you moved 'now' from 2009 to 2030—the 'nowness' that should have been experienced by the people in 2030 had to shift somewhere else. The exclusion principle! Every moment exists as 'now' for those frozen in it—you can't superimpose the 'now' of 2009 on top of that of 2030; the two nows cannot exist simultaneously. When you shifted the 2009 now forward, the 2030 now had to vacate that time. When I heard that you were going to be replicating the experiment again at the exact time the original visions had portrayed, it all fell into place." He paused. "The Sanduleak supernova will oscillate for many decades or centuries to come—surely tomorrow's attempt won't be the last. Do you think humanity's taste for seeing the future will be sated with one more peek? Of course not. We are ravenous in our desire. Since ancient times, no dream has been more seductive than that of knowing the future. *Every* time it is possible to shift the sense of now, we will do it—assuming your experiment succeeds tomorrow."

Theo glanced at the bomb. If he was reading the display properly, it had over fifty-five hours before it would explode. He was trying to think clearly; he'd had no idea just how unnerving it could be to have a gun aimed at your heart. "So—so—what are you saying? That if there's no opening here in 2030 for the consciousness of 2009 to jump into, then that first jump will never happen?"

"Exactly!"

"But that's crazy. The first jump has *already* happened. We all lived through it twenty-one years ago."

"We didn't *all* live through it," said Rusch sharply.

"Well, no, but—"

"Yes, it happened. But I'm going to undo that. I'm going to retroactively rewrite the last two decades."

Theo didn't want to argue with the man, but: "That's not possible."

"Yes, it is. I know it is. Don't you see? I've already succeeded."

"What?"

"What did everybody's visions have in common the first time?" asked Rusch.

"I don't—"

"Leisure-time activities! The vast majority of the population seemed to be having a holiday, a day-off. And why? Because they'd all been told to stay home from work that day, to stay safe and secure, because CERN was going to attempt to replicate the time displacement. But something happened—something caused that replication to be called off, too late for people to go back to work. And so humanity got an unexpected holiday."

"It's more likely that what we saw the first time was simply a version of reality in which the precognition event had never occurred."

"Nonsense," said Rusch. "Sure, we saw some people at work—shopkeepers, street vendors, police, and so on. But most businesses were closed, weren't they? You've heard the speculation—that some great holiday would exist on Wednesday, October 23, in 2030, celebrated across the globe. A universal disarmament day, maybe, or a first-contact-with-aliens day. But now it *is* 2030, and you know as well as I do that no such holiday exists. Everyone was off work, preparing for a time displacement that didn't come. But they'd had *some* advance warning that it wasn't going to come—meaning the news story that Large Hadron Collider had been damaged must have broken sometime earlier that day. Well, I've got my bomb set to go off two hours before the Sanduleak neutrinos will arrive."

"But if something like that was in the news, surely someone would have seen it in their vision. Someone would have reported it."

"Who would be sitting home watching the news two hours into an unexpected holiday?" asked Rusch. "No, I'm sure the scenario I've described is correct. I will succeed in disabling CERN; the consciousness of 2030 Earth will stay put precisely where it belongs, and the change will propagate backwards from this point, back twenty-one years, rewriting history. My dear Helena, and all the other people who died because of your arrogance, will get to live again."

"You can't kill me," said Theo. "And you can't keep me here for two days. People will notice I'm missing, and they'll come down here to look for me, and they'll find your bomb and disarm it."

"A good point," said Rusch. Carefully keeping the Glock trained on Theo, he backed toward his bomb. He retrieved it from inside the air pump, lifting it up by its suitcase handle. He must have noted Theo's expression. "Don't worry," said Rusch. "It's not delicate." He placed the bomb on the tunnel floor and did something to the counter mechanism. Then he turned the case so that the long side was facing toward Theo. Theo looked down at the timer. It was still counting down, but now said 59 minutes, 56 seconds.

"The bomb will go off in one hour," said Rusch. "It's earlier than I planned, and with this much advanced notice, we're probably cheating people out of their holiday the day after tomorrow, but the gross effect will be the same. As long as the damage to the tunnel will take more than two days to repair, *Der Zwischenfall* will not be replicated.'' He paused. ''Now, let's you and I start walking. I'm not going to trust myself on a hovercart with you or—I imagine you took the monorail, no? Well, we won't. But in an hour, we can walk sufficiently far along the tunnel that neither of us will be hurt.'' He gestured with the gun. ''So let's get going.''

They began to walk counterclockwise—toward the monorail—but before they'd gotten more than a dozen meters, Theo became conscious of a faint whine behind them. He turned around, and so did Rusch. Just rounding the curve of the tunnel off in the distance was another hovercart.

''Damn it,'' said Rusch. ''Who's that?''

Jake Horowitz's red-and-gray hair was easy enough to make out, even at this distance, but the other person—

God! It looked like—

It was. Detective Helmut Drescher of Geneva's finest.

''I don't know,'' said Theo, pretending to squint.

The hovercart was rapidly approaching. Rusch looked left and right. There was so much equipment mounted on the sides of the tunnel wall that, with some advance warning, one could easily find crannies in which to hide. Rusch left the bomb at the side of the tunnel and started to retreat away from the approaching cart. But it was too late. Jake was clearly pointing at them. Rusch closed the distance between himself and Theo, and jabbed the pistol into Theo's ribs. Theo had never known his heart to beat so fast in his life.

Drescher had his own gun drawn as the hovercart settled to the tunnel floor about five meters away from Rusch and Theo.

''Who are you?'' said Jake to Rusch.

''Careful!'' blurted Theo. ''He's got a gun.''

Rusch looked panicked. A little bomb-planting was one thing, but hostage taking and potential murder was another. Still he jerked the Glock into Theo's side again. ''That's right,'' said Rusch. ''So back off.''

Moot was now standing with legs spread for maximum stability, holding his own gun in both hands aimed directly at Rusch's heart. "I'm a police officer," said Moot. "Drop your weapon."

"*Nein.*"

Moot's tone was absolutely even. "Drop your weapon or I will shoot."

Rusch's eyes darted left and right. "If you shoot, Dr. Procopides dies."

Theo's mind was racing. Had it gone down like this the first time? Rusch would have to shoot him not once, but three times, to match the vision. In a standoff like this, he might get one bullet into Theo's chest—not that it would take more—but surely as soon as he pulled the trigger the first time, Moot would blow Rusch away.

"Back off," said Rusch. "Back off!"

Jake looked as terrified as Theo felt, but Moot stood his ground. "Drop your weapon. You are under arrest."

Rusch's panic seemed to abate for a moment, as if he was simply stunned by the charge. If he really were just a university professor, he'd probably never been in trouble with the law his whole life. But then he brightened somewhat. "You can't arrest me."

"The hell I can't," said Moot.

"What police force are you with?"

"Geneva's."

Rusch actually managed a small, panicked laugh. He jabbed Theo with the gun again. "Tell him where we are."

Theo's insides were churning. He didn't understand the question. "In the Large Hadron—"

Rusch jabbed again. "The country."

Theo felt his heart sinking. "Oh." Damn. God damn it. "We're in France," he said. "The border goes right across the tunnel."

"So," said Rusch, looking at Moot, "you've got no jurisdiction here; Switzerland isn't an E.U. member. If you shoot me outside of your jurisdiction, that's murder."

Moot seemed to hesitate for a moment; the gun in his hand wavered. But then he brought it back to bear directly on Rusch's heart. "I will deal with whatever legalities there are after the fact," said Moot. "Drop your weapon now or I will shoot."

Rusch was standing so close to Theo that Theo could feel his breathing—rapid, shallow. The guy might hyperventilate.

"All right," said Rusch. "All right." He took a step away from Theo and—

Kablam!

The report echoing in the tunnel.

Theo's heart stopping—

—but only for a second.

Rusch's mouth had gone wide in horror, in terror, in fear—

—at the realization of what he'd done—

—as Moot Drescher staggered backward, tumbled and fell, landing on his back, dropping his gun, a growing pool of blood spreading across his shoulder.

"Oh my God!" shouted Jake, "Oh my God!" He surged forward, scrambling for Drescher's weapon.

Rusch looked absolutely dazed. Theo grabbed him from behind, putting his neck in a choke hold, and bringing his knee up into the small of Rusch's back. With his other hand, he tried to wrest the hot, smoking gun from Rusch.

Jake now had Drescher's gun. He tried to aim it at the combined form of Theo and Rusch, but his hands were shaking violently. Theo wrenched Rusch's arm and he dropped his gun. Theo dived out of the way, and Jake squeezed off a shot. But in his inexperienced, trembling hands, the bullet went wild, smashing into a fluorescent lighting tube overhead, which exploded in a shower of sparks and glass. Rusch was scrambling for his dropped gun, too. Neither he nor Theo seemed to be able to get a grip on it, and finally Theo kicked it from Rusch's grabbing hand. It skittered a dozen meters counterclockwise down the tunnel.

Theo had no weapon, and neither now did Rusch. Drescher was surrounded by a lake of blood, but seemed to be still alive; his chest was heaving. Jake tried another shot but it again missed its mark.

Rusch was only halfway to his feet before he started running after the Glock. Theo, realizing he'd never overtake him, decided to go the other way. "He's got a bomb," he shouted as he passed Jake. "Help Moot!"

Jake nodded. Rusch had now recovered his own gun, and had turned around and was running, weapon held in front of him, toward Jake, Moot, and the retreating Theo.

Theo was running for all he was worth, footfalls echoing loudly in the tunnel. Up ahead was the aluminum suitcase containing the bomb. He stole a glance over his shoulder. Jake, still holding Moot's gun, had gone to his knees next to the cop. Rusch passed them, keeping his own gun trained on Jake, preventing him from squeezing off another shot. Rusch turned around, running backward, keeping his weapon on Jake until he was out of Jake's shaky range. He then turned again and continued pursuing Theo.

Theo reached the bomb, scooping it up with one hand, and then—

He got onto Rusch's hovercart, and slammed his foot against the activator pedal. Theo looked back as the cart started to speed away clockwise.

Rusch doubled back. Jake, apparently assuming Rusch had gone, had set down Moot's gun and was pulling his own shirt off over his head, some buttons still done up—clearly, he wanted to use it as a pressure bandage to stanch the flow of blood out of Moot's body. Rusch had no trouble getting into the hovercart that had brought Jake and Moot to the scene, and he took off after Theo.

Theo had a good lead as he careened along the tunnel. But it was hardly straight-line flying—not only did the curve of the tunnel have to be negotiated, but so did all the giant pieces of equipment that jutted out willy-nilly along its length.

Theo glanced at the bomb's display: 41 minutes, 18 seconds. He hoped Rusch had been telling the truth when he said the explosives weren't fragile. There were a series of unlabeled buttons attached to the display—no way to tell which ones might reset the timer to a higher value, and which ones might cause the bomb to explode immediately. But if he could make it to the access station and get up to the surface, there would be plenty of time to abandon the bomb in the middle of one of the farmers' fields.

Theo's cart had a decided wobble—he was doubtless pushing it faster than its gyros could really deal with. He glanced behind himself again. At first, he began to breathe a sigh of relief—Rusch was nowhere to be seen—but after a second the pursuing cart appeared around the curving wall of the tunnel.

Darkness up ahead; Theo had only activated the roof lighting for a tiny arc of the tunnel's circumference. He hoped Jake had managed to stabilize Moot. Damn—he probably shouldn't have taken the hovercart; surely the need to get Moot to the surface was more important than protecting the equipment in the tunnel. He hoped Jake would realize that the monorail must be nearby.

Shit! Theo's cart touched the outer wall of the tunnel and started spinning around, its headlight beams cutting swaths through the darkness. He fought with the joystick that controlled the cart, trying to get it to keep from crashing into anything else. He got it going back in the right direction, but now Rusch's cart was about halfway down the visible part of the tunnel, instead of at its far end.

The hovercart wasn't going fast enough to make a real breeze, but it nonetheless felt like breakneck speed. Rusch still had the Glock, of course—but a hovercart wasn't like a car; you couldn't shoot out the tires in hopes of bringing it to a halt. The only sure way to stop such a vehicle was to shoot the driver; Theo had to keep pressure on the accelerator pedal for it to continue to move.

Theo kept rocking his cart left and right and raising and lowering it as much as he could in the cramped tunnel; if Rusch was trying to get a bead on him from the rear, he wanted to make himself a difficult target.

He checked the markers on the gently curving wall; the tunnel was divided into eight octants of about three and a half kilometers each, and each octant was subdivided into thirty-odd sections of a hundred meters apiece. According to the signage, he was in octant three, section twenty-two. The access station was at octant four, section thirty-three. He might just make it—

An impact!

A shower of sparks.

The sounds of metal ripping.

Dammit, he wasn't paying enough attention; the hovercart had banged against one of the cryogenics units. It had almost flipped over, which would have dropped Theo and the bomb down onto the floor. Theo fought again with the controls, desperately trying to stabilize the cart. A furtive glance back confirmed his fears: the collision had slowed him down enough that Rusch was now only about fifty meters back. He'd have to be a hell of a good shot to take Theo out at this distance in the dark, but if he got much closer . . .

The tunnel was constricted up ahead by more equipment; Theo had to drop the cart to only a few centimeters off the floor, but his control of the vehicle at its current speed was poor—the cart skittered across the flooring like a stone being skipped across a lake.

Another glance at the bomb's timing mechanism, the digits glowing bright blue in the dim light. Thirty-seven minutes.

Blam!

The bullet zipped past Theo; he instinctively ducked. It hit some metal fittings up ahead, illuminating the tunnel with sparks.

Theo hoped Jake and Moot had come down the elevator at the access station. If the car was up at the top, there was no way Theo could wait for it, and he'd have to try to make it up the numerous stairs before Rusch could get a bead on him.

Theo swerved again, this time to avoid a bracket supporting the beam pipe. He glanced back. Damn, but Rusch's cart must have had a fuller charge to its batteries; he was now quite close.

The curving tunnel wall continued to pass by, and—yes, by God, there it was! The access station staging area. But—

But Rusch was too close now—much too close. If Theo stopped his cart here, Rusch would blow him away. Dammit, dammit, dammit.

Theo felt his heart sink as he passed the access station. He turned around in his chair and watched it receding from view. Rusch, evidently deciding that he didn't want to chase Theo all the way around the tunnel, took another shot. This one did hit the hovercart, its metal body vibrating in response.

Theo urged the cart to go faster. He remembered the old golf carts CERN used to have for traveling short distances in the tunnel. He missed those; at least they weren't constantly in danger of flipping over at high speeds.

They continued on, farther and farther, swinging around the tunnel, and—

A great crashing sound from the rear. Theo looked back. Rusch's cart had smashed into the outside wall. It had come to a dead stop. Theo let out a small cheer.

He figured they'd gone about seventeen kilometers now—soon the staging area for the campus monorail station would be swinging into view. He might be able to get out there and take the elevator straight up into the LHC control center. He hoped he'd see the monorail parked back there, meaning Jake and Moot had made it to safety, and—

God damn it! His hovercart was dying, its battery exhausted. It had probably sounded an alarm earlier, but Theo had been unable to hear it over the noise the overtaxed engines were making. The cart dropped to the tunnel floor, skidding a distance along its concrete surface before coming to a dead halt. Theo grabbed the bomb and began to run. As a teenager, Theo had once participated in a re-creation of the run from Marathon to Athens made in 490 B.C. to announce a Hellenic victory over the Persians—but he'd been thirty years younger then. His heart was pounding now as he tried to go faster.

Kablam!

Another gunshot. Rusch must have gotten his cart going again. Theo kept running, his legs pounding, at least in his mind, like pistons. There, ahead, was the main campus staging area, a half dozen hovercarts parked along its wall. Only another twenty meters—

He glanced back. Rusch was closing rapidly. Christ, he couldn't stop here, either—Rusch would pick him off like a sitting duck.

Theo forced his body to make it the last few meters, and—

The chase continued.

He tumbled into another hovercart and sent himself careening once more down the tunnel, still heading clockwise. He looked back. Rusch dumped his own hovercart, presumably worried about its batteries, and transferred to a fresh one. He headed off in hot pursuit.

Theo glanced at the bomb's timer. Only twenty minutes left, but for once Theo seemed to have a decent lead. And, because of that, he actually stopped to think for a moment. Could Rusch possibly be right? Could there be a chance to undo all the damage, all the death that had occurred twenty-one years ago? If there had never been visions, Rusch's wife might still be alive; Michiko's daughter Tamiko might still be alive; Theo's brother Dimitrios might still be alive.

But, of course, no one conceived after the visions—no one born in the last twenty years—would be the same. Which sperm penetrated an egg was dependent on a thousand details; if the world unfolded differently, if women got pregnant on different days, or even different seconds, their children would be different. There were—what?—something like four billion people who had been born in the last two decades. Even if he could rewrite history, did he have any right to do so? Didn't those billions deserve the rest of their allotted three score and ten, rather than to be simply snuffed out, not even killed but completely expunged from the timeline?

Theo's cart continued its journey around the tunnel. He

glanced back; Rusch was emerging in the distance from behind the curve.

No. No, he wouldn't change the past even if he could. And besides, he didn't really believe Rusch. Yes, the future could be changed. But the past? No, that *had* to be fixed. Upon that much he'd always agreed with Lloyd Simcoe. What this Rusch was saying was crazy.

Another gunshot! The bullet missed him, impacting the tunnel wall up ahead. But there would doubtless be more, if Rusch realized where Theo was headed—

Another kilometer slipped by. The bomb's timer now read just eleven minutes. Theo looked at the wall markings, trying to make them out in the dim light of his headlights. It had to be just ahead, and—

There it was! Just where he'd left it!

The monorail, hanging from the ceiling. If he could make it there—

A new shot rang out. This one did hit the hovercart, and Theo almost lost control of the vehicle again. The monorail was still a hundred meters ahead. Theo fought with the joystick again, swearing at the cart, demanding it go faster, faster—

The monorail had five components—a cab at each end, and three cars in the middle. He had to make it to the far cab; the train would only move in the direction it thought of as forward.

Almost there—

He didn't slow the hovercart gently; instead, he just slammed the brake. The vehicle pitched forward, Theo being tossed with it. It smashed onto the tunnel floor, skidding along, sparks flying. Theo got out, grabbing the bomb, and—

Yet another shot and—

God!

A shower of Theo's own blood splashing against his face—

More pain than he'd ever felt in his life—

A bullet tearing into his right shoulder.

God—

He dropped the bomb, scrambled for it again with his left hand, and staggered into the monorail's cab.

The pain—incredible pain—

He hit the monorail's start button.

Its headlights, mounted above the angled windscreen, snapped on, illuminating the tunnel ahead. After the dimness of the last half hour, the light was painfully bright.

The monorail heaved into motion, whining as it did so. Theo pushed the speed control; the train moved faster and faster still.

Theo thought he was going to black out from the pain. He looked back. Rusch was negotiating his cart past Theo's abandoned one. The monorail used magnetic levitation; it was capable of very high speeds. Of course, no one had ever tested its maximum velocity in the tunnel—

Until now.

The bomb's display said eight minutes.

Another bullet rang out, but it missed its mark. Theo glanced back just in time to see Rusch's cart fall back around the curve of the tunnel.

Theo leaned his head out the side of the cab; there was wind in his face. "Come on," he said. "Come on . . ."

The tunnel's curving walls flashed by. The mag-lev generators hummed loudly.

There they were: Jake and Moot, the physicist attending to the cop, who was now sitting up, mercifully alive. Theo waved at them as the monorail zoomed past.

Kilometers passed, and then—

Sixty seconds.

He'd never make it to the far access station, never make it to the surface. Maybe he should just drop the bomb; yes, it would disable the LHC no matter where it exploded, but—

No.

No, he had come too far—and he had no fatal flaw; his downfall was not preordained.

If only—

He looked at the timer again, then at the wall markings.

Yes!

Yes! He might just make it!

He urged the train to go even faster.

And then—

The tunnel straightened out.

He hit the emergency brake.

Another shower of sparks.

Metal against metal.

His head whipping forward—

Agony in his shoulder—

He clambered out of the cramped cab and staggered away from the monorail.

Forty-five seconds—

Staggered a few meters farther along the tunnel—

To the entrance to the huge, empty, six-story-tall chamber that had once housed the CMS detector.

He forced himself to go on, into the chamber, placing the bomb in the center of the vast empty space.

Thirty seconds.

He turned around, ran as fast as he could, appalled to see the river of blood he'd left on his way in—

Back out to the monorail—

Fifteen seconds.

Clambering back into the cab, hitting the accelerator—

Ten seconds.

Zipping along the roof-mounted track—

Five seconds.

Around the curve of the tunnel—

Four seconds.

Almost unconscious from the pain—

Three seconds.

Urging the train to go faster.

Two seconds.

Covering his head with his hands, his shoulder protesting violently as he lifted his right arm—

One second.

Wondering briefly what the future held—

Zero!

Ka-boom!

The explosion echoing in the tunnel.

A flash of light from behind sending a huge shadow of the monorail's insectoid form onto the curving tunnel wall—

And then—

Glorious, healing darkness, the train speeding on as Theo collapsed against the tiny dashboard.

Two days later.

Theo was in the LHC control room. It was crowded, but not with scientists or engineers—almost everything was automated. Still, dozens of reporters were present, all of them were lying on the floor. Jake Horowitz was there, of course, as were Theo's own special guests, Detective Helmut Drescher, his shoulder in a sling, and Moot's young wife.

Theo started the countdown, then also lay down on the floor, waiting for it to happen.

31

LLOYD SIMCOE OFTEN THOUGHT OF HIS SEVEN-
year-old daughter, Joan, who now lived in Nippon. Of course,
they talked every couple of days by video phone, and Lloyd
tried to convince himself that seeing and hearing her was as
good as hugging her, and bouncing her on his knee, and holding her hand as they walked through parks, and wiping her
tears when she fell down and skinned her knee.

He loved her enormously and was proud of her beyond
words. True, despite her occidental name, she looked nothing
like him; her features were completely Asian. Indeed, more
than anything, she looked like poor Tamiko, the half-sister she
would never know. But externals didn't matter; half of what
Joan was had come from Lloyd. More than his Nobel Prize,
more than all the papers he had authored or co-authored, more
than anything else, *she* was his immortality.

And even though she came from a marriage that hadn't
lasted, Joan was doing just fine. Oh, Lloyd had no doubt that
sometimes she wished her mommy and daddy were still together. Still, Joan had attended Lloyd's wedding to Doreen,

capturing everyone's hearts as flower girl for the woman who would soon be her stepmother.

Stepmother. Half-sister. Ex-wife. Ex-husband. New wife. Permutations; the panoply of human interactions, of ways to constitute a family. Hardly anyone got married in a big ceremony anymore, but Lloyd had insisted. The laws in most states and provinces in North America said if two adults lived together for sufficient time, they were married, and if they ceased living together, they ceased to be married. Clean and simple, no muss, no fuss—and none of the pain that Lloyd's parents had gone through, none of the histrionics and suffering that he and Dolly had watched, wide-eyed, stunned by it all, their world crumbling around them.

But Lloyd had wanted the ceremony; he had forgone so much because of his fear of creating another broken home—a term, he'd noted, that his latest Merriam-Webster flagged as "archaic." He was determined never to be daunted by that—by the past—again. And so he and Doreen had tied one on as they tied the knot—a great party, everyone had said, a night to remember, full of dancing and singing and laughter and love.

Doreen had been past menopause by the time she and Lloyd got together. Of course there were procedures now, and techniques, and had she wanted a child she could still have had one. Lloyd was more than willing; he was a father already, but he surely wouldn't deny her the chance to be a mother. But Doreen had declined. She had been content with her life before meeting Lloyd, and enjoyed it even more now that they were together—but she didn't crave children, didn't seek immortality.

Now that Lloyd had retired, they spent a lot of time at the cottage in Vermont. Of course, both of their visions had placed them there on this day. They'd laughed as they furnished the bedroom, making it look exactly as it had when they'd first seen it, precisely positioning the old particle-board night table and knotty-pine wall mirror.

And now Lloyd and Doreen were lying side by side in their bed; she was even wearing a navy-blue Tilley work shirt. Through the window, trees dressed in glorious fall colors were visible. They had their fingers intertwined. The radio was on, counting down to the arrival of the Sanduleak neutrinos.

Lloyd smiled at Doreen. They'd been married now for five years. He supposed, being the child of divorce and now being himself once divorced, that he shouldn't be thinking naïve thoughts about being together with Doreen forever, but nonetheless he found himself constantly feeling that way. Lloyd and Michiko had been a good fit, but he and Doreen were a *perfect* one. Doreen had been married once before, but it had ended more than twenty years ago. She had assumed she'd never marry again, and had been getting on with a single life.

And then she and Lloyd had met, him a Nobel-Prize-winning physicist, and her a painter, two completely different worlds, more different in many ways than Michiko's Nippon was from Lloyd's North America, and yet they had hit it off beautifully, and love had blossomed between them, and now he divided his life into two parts, before Doreen and after.

The voice on the radio was counting down. "Ten seconds. Nine. Eight."

He looked at her and smiled, and she smiled back at him.

"Six. Five. Four."

Lloyd wondered what he would see in the future, but of one thing he had no doubt, no doubt whatsoever.

"Two! One!"

Whatever the future held, Doreen and he would be together, always.

Zero!

Lloyd saw a brief still frame of him and Doreen, much older, older than he would have thought it possible for them to be, and then—

Surely they didn't die. Surely he would be seeing nothing if his consciousness had ceased to be.

His body might have faded away but—a quick glimpse, a flash of an image . . .

A new body, all silver and gold, smooth and shiny . . .

An android body? A robot form for his human consciousness?

Or a virtual body, nothing more—or less—than a representation of what he was inside a computer?

Lloyd's perspective shifted.

He was now looking down on Earth, from hundreds of kilometers up. White clouds still swirled over it, and sunlight reflected off the vast oceans . . .

Except . . .

Except, in the one brief moment during which he was perceiving this, he thought perhaps that those weren't oceans, but rather the continent of North America, glinting, its surface covered over with a spiderwork of metal and machinery, the whole planet literally having become the World Wide Web.

And then his perspective changed again, but once more he glimpsed Earth, or what he'd thought might have been Earth. Yes, yes, surely it was, for there was the moon, rising over its limb. But the Pacific ocean was smaller, covering only a third of the face he was seeing, and the west coast of North America had changed radically.

Time was whipping by; the continents had had millennia enough to drift to new locations.

And still he skimmed ahead . . .

He saw the moon spiraling farther and farther away from the Earth, and then—

It seemed instantaneous, but perhaps it had taken thousands of years—

The moon crumbling to nothing.

Another shift . . .

And the Earth itself *reducing*, shrinking, being whittled away, growing smaller, a pebble, and then—

The sun again, but—

Incredible . . .

The sun was now half-encased in a metal sphere, capturing

every photon of energy that fell upon it. The Moon and Earth hadn't crumbled—they had been *dismantled*. Raw materials.

Lloyd continued his journey ahead. He saw—

Yes, it had been inevitable; yes, he'd read about it countless years ago, but he'd never thought he would live to see it.

The Milky Way galaxy, the pinwheel of stars that humanity called home, colliding with Andromeda, its larger neighbor, the two pinwheels intersecting, interstellar gas aglow.

And still he traveled on, ahead, into the future.

It was nothing like the first time—but then what in life ever is?

The first time the visions had occurred, the switch from the present to the future had seemed instantaneous. But if it took a hundred thousandth of a second, who would have noticed? And if that hundred thousandth of a second had been allotted as 0.00005 seconds per year jumped ahead, again, who would have been aware of that? But 0.00005 seconds times eight *billion* years added up to something over an hour—an hour spent skimming, gliding over vistas of time, never quite locking in, never quite materializing, never quite displacing the proper consciousness of the moment, and yet sensing, perceiving, seeing it all unfold, watching the universe grow and change, experiencing the evolution of humanity step by step from childhood into . . .

. . . into whatever it was destined to become.

Of course Lloyd wasn't really traveling at all. He was still firmly in New England, and he had no more control over what he was seeing or what his replacement body was doing than he'd had during his first vision. The perspective shifts were doubtless due to the repositioning of whatever he'd become as the millennia went by. There must have been some sort of persistence of memory, analogous to the persistence of vision that made watching movies possible. Surely he was touching each of these times for only the most fleeting moment; his consciousness looking to see if that slice through the cube was occupied, and, when it discovered that it was, something like the exclusion principle—Theo had emailed him all about Rusch and his apparent ravings—barring it from taking up residence there, speeding onward, forward, farther and farther into the future.

Lloyd was surprised that he still had individuality; he would have thought that if humanity were to survive at all for millions of years surely it would be as a linked, collective consciousness. But he heard no other voices in his mind; as far as he could tell, he was still a unique separate entity, even if the frail physical body that had once encapsulated him had long since ceased to exist.

He'd seen the Dyson sphere half-encasing the sun, meaning humanity would one day command fantastic technology, but, as yet, he'd seen no evidence of any intelligence beyond that of humans.

And then it hit him: a flash of insight. What was happening meant there was no other intelligent life anywhere—not on any of the planets of the two hundred billion stars that made up the Milky Way, or—he stopped to correct himself—the six hundred billion stars comprising the currently combined supergalaxy formed by the intersection of the smaller Milky Way with larger Andromeda. And not on any of the planets of any of the stars in the countless billion other galaxies that made up the universe.

Surely all consciousness everywhere had to agree on what constituted "now." If human consciousness was bouncing around, shifting, didn't that mean that there must be no other consciousness in existence, no other group vying for the right to assert which particular moment constituted the present?

In which case, humanity was staggeringly, overwhelmingly, unrelentingly alone in all the vast dark cosmos, the sole spark of sentience ever to arise. Life had proceeded on Earth very happily for four billion years before the first stirrings of self-awareness, and still, by 2030, no one had managed to duplicate that sentience in a machine. Being conscious, being aware that that was then and this is now and that tomorrow is another day, was an incredible fluke, a happenstance, a freak occurrence never before or since duplicated in the history of the universe.

And perhaps that explained the incredible failure of nerve that Lloyd had observed time and again. Even by 2030, humanity still hadn't ventured beyond the Moon; no one had gone on to Mars in the sixty-one years since Armstrong's small step, and there didn't seem to be any plans in the works to accomplish that. Mars, of course, could get as far from Earth as 377 million kilometers when the two worlds were on opposite sides of the sun. A human mind on Mars under those circumstances would be twenty-one light-minutes away from the other human minds on Earth. Even people standing right beside each other were separated somewhat in time—seeing each other not as they are but as they were a trillionth of a second earlier. Yes, some degree of desynchronization was clearly tolerable, but it must have an upper limit. Perhaps sixteen light-minutes was still acceptable—the separation between two people on the opposite sides of a Dyson sphere built at the radius of Earth's orbit—but twenty-one light minutes was too much. Or perhaps even sixteen exceeded what was allowable for conscious beings. Humanity had doubtless built the Dyson sphere Lloyd had observed—in so doing walling itself off from the empty, lonely vastness on the outside—but perhaps its entire inner surface was not populated. People might occupy only one portion of its surface. A Dyson sphere, after all, had a surface area millions of times that of planet Earth; even using a tenth of the territory it afforded would still give humanity orders of magnitude more land than it had ever known before. The sphere might harvest every photon put out by the central star, but humanity perhaps did not roam over its entire surface.

Lloyd—or whatever Lloyd had become—found himself pushing farther and farther ahead into the future. The images kept changing.

He thought about what Michiko had said: Frank Tipler and his theory that everyone who ever was, or ever could be, would be resurrected at the Omega Point to live again. The physics of immortality.

But Tipler's theory was based on an assumption that the universe was closed, that it had sufficient mass so that its own gravitational attraction would eventually cause everything to collapse back down into a singularity. As the eons sped by, it became clear that wasn't going to happen. Yes, the Milky Way and its nearest neighbor had collided, but even whole galaxies were minuscule on the scale of an ever-expanding universe. The expansion might slow to almost nothing, asymptotically approaching zero, but it would never stop. There would never be an omega point. And there would never be another universe. This was it, the one and only iteration of space and time.

Of course, by now, even the star enclosed by the Dyson sphere had doubtless given up the ghost; if twenty-first-century astronomers were correct, Earth's sun would have expanded into a red giant, engulfing the shell around it. Humanity had surely had billions of years of warning, though, and had doubtless moved—*en masse,* if that's what the physics of consciousness required—somewhere else.

At least, thought Lloyd, he hoped they had. He still felt disconnected from all that was playing out in individual illuminated frames. Maybe humanity had been snuffed out when its sun died.

But he—whatever he'd become—was somehow still alive, still thinking, still feeling.

There had to be someone else to share all this with.

Unless—

Unless this was the universe's way of sealing the unexpected rift caused by Sanduleak's neutrinos showering down on a re-creation of the first moments of existence.

Wipe out all extraneous life. Just leave one qualified observer—one omniscient form, looking down, on—

—on everything, deciding reality by its observations, locking in one steady *now*, moving forward at the inexorable rate of one second per second.

A god . . .

But of an empty, lifeless, unthinking universe.

Finally, the skimming through time came to an end. He'd arrived at his destination, at the opening up; the consciousness of this far distant year—if the word year had any meaning anymore, the planet whose orbit it measured having long since disappeared—having vacated for even more remote realms, leaving a hole here for him to occupy.

Of course the universe was open. Of course it went on forever. The only way consciousness from the past could keep leapfrogging ahead was if there was always some more-distant point for the present's consciousness to move into; if the universe was closed, the time displacement would never have occurred. It had to be an unending chain.

And before him now—

Before him now was the far, far future.

When he'd been young, Lloyd had read H. G. Wells's *The Time Machine*. And he'd been haunted by it for years. Not by the world of the Eloi and the Morlocks; even as a teenager, he'd recognized that as allegory, a morality play about the class structure of Victorian England. No, that world of A.D. 802,701 had made little impression on him. But Wells's time traveler had made another journey in the book, leaping millions of years ahead to the twilight of the world, when tidal forces had slowed the Earth's spin down so that it always kept the same face toward the sun, bloated and red, a baleful eye upon the horizon, while crab-like things moved slowly along a beach.

But what was before him now seemed even more bleak. The sky was dim—stars having receded so far from each other that only a few were visible. The only bit of loveliness was that these stars, rich in metals forged in the generations of suns that had come and gone before them, glowed with colors never seen in the young universe Lloyd had once known: emerald green stars, and purple stars, and turquoise stars, like gemstones across the velvet firmament.

And now that he was at his destination, Lloyd still had no control over his synthetic body; he was a passenger behind glass eyes.

Yes, he was still solid, still had physical form. He could now and again see what appeared to be his arm, perfect, unblemished, more like liquid metal than anything biological, moving in and out of his field of view. He was on a planetary surface, a vast plain of white powder that might have been snow and might have been pulverized rock and might have been something wholly unknown to the feeble science of billions of years past. There was no sign of buildings; if one had an indestructible body, perhaps one didn't need or desire shelter. The planet couldn't be Earth—it was long since gone—but the gravity felt no different. He wasn't conscious of any smell, but there were sounds—strange, ethereal sounds, something between a sighing zephyr and woodwind music.

He found his field of view shifting as he turned around. No, no, that wasn't it—he wasn't actually turning; rather, he was simply diverting his attention to another set of inputs, eyes in the back of his head. Well, why not? If you were going to manufacture a body, you'd certainly address the shortcomings of the original.

And in his new field of vision, there was another figure, another encapsulation of a human essence. To his surprise, the face was not stylized, not a simple ovoid. Rather it had intricate, delicately carved features, and if Lloyd's body seemed to be made of liquid metal, this other's was flowing green marble, veined and polished and beautiful, a statue incarnate.

There was nothing feminine—or masculine—about the form, but he knew in an instant who it must be. Doreen, of course—his wife, his beloved, the one he wanted to spend eternity with.

But then he studied the face, the carved features, the eyes—

The almond-shaped eyes . . .
And then—

Lloyd had been lying down in bed when the experiment was replicated, his wife by his side—no way they could hurt themselves or each other when they blacked out.

"That was incredible," said Lloyd, when it was over. "Absolutely incredible."

He turned his head, sought out Doreen's hand, and looked at her.

"What did you see?" he asked.

She used her other hand to shut off the radio. He saw that it was trembling. "Nothing," she said.

His heart sank. "Nothing? No vision at all?"

She shook her head.

"Oh, honey," he said, "I'm so sorry."

"How far ahead was your vision?" she asked. She must have been wondering how long she had left.

Lloyd didn't know how to put it in words. "I'm not sure," he said. It had been an amazing ride—but it was crushing to think that Doreen would not live to see it all, too.

She tried to sound brave. "I'm an old woman," she said. "I thought maybe I'd have another twenty or thirty years, but . . ." She trailed off.

"I'm sure you will," said Lloyd, trying to sound certain. "I'm sure you will."

"But you had a vision . . ." she said.

Lloyd nodded. "But it was—it was a long time from now."

"TV on," said Doreen into the air; her voice was anxious. "ABC."

One of the paintings on the wall became a TV screen. Doreen propped her head up to see it better.

"—great disappointment," said the newscaster, a white woman of about forty. "So far, no one has actually reported having a vision this time out. The replication of the experiment at CERN seemed to work, but no one here at ABC News, nor anyone else who has called in to us, has reported having a vision. Everyone seemed to just black out for—early estimates have it that perhaps as much as an hour passed while people were unconscious. As he has been throughout the day, Jacob Horowitz is joining us from CERN; Dr. Horowitz was part of the team that produced the first time-displacement phenomenon twenty years ago. Doctor, what does this mean?"

Jake lifted his shoulders. "Well, assuming a time displacement did occur—and we don't know that for sure yet, of course—it must have been to a time far enough in the future that everyone currently alive is—well, there's no nice way to put it, is there? Everyone currently alive must be dead at that point. If the displacement was, say, a hundred and fifty years, I suppose that's no surprise, but—"

"Mute," said Doreen, from the bed. "But you had a vision," she said to her husband. "Was it as much as a hundred and fifty years ahead?"

Lloyd shook his head. "More," he said softly. "Much more."

"How much?"

"Millions," he said. "Billions."

Doreen made a small laugh. "Oh, come on, dear! It must have been a dream—sure, you'll be alive in the future, but you'll be dreaming then."

Lloyd considered this. Could she be right? Could it have been nothing but a dream? But it had been so vivid—so realistic . . .

And he was sixty-six years old, for God's sake. No matter how many years they jumped ahead, if he had a vision surely younger people should have, as well. But Jake Horowitz was a quarter-century his junior, and doubtless ABC News had many employees in their twenties and thirties.

And none of them had reported visions.

"I don't know," he said, at last. "It didn't seem like a dream."

32

THE FUTURE *COULD* BE CHANGED; THEY'D DIS-
covered that when reality deviated from what had been seen
in the first set of visions. Surely, this future could be changed,
as well.

Sometime relatively soon a process for immortality—or
something damn near to it—would be developed, and Lloyd
Simcoe would undergo it. It wouldn't be anything as simple
as just capping telomeres, but whatever it was, it would work,
at least for hundreds of years. Later, his biological body would
be replaced with a more durable robotic one, and he would
live long enough to see the Milky Way and Andromeda kiss.

So, all he had to do was find a way to make sure Doreen
got the immortality treatment, too—whatever it cost, whatever
the selection criteria, he'd make sure his wife was included.

Doubtless there were other people besides himself already
alive who would become immortals. He couldn't have been
the only one to have a vision; after all, he hadn't been alone
at the end.

But, like himself, they were keeping quiet, still trying to
sort out what they'd seen. Perhaps someday, all humans

would live forever, but of the current generations—of the ones already alive in 2030—apparently no more than a handful would never know death.

Lloyd would find them. A message on the net, maybe. Nothing so blatant as asking anyone else who had a vision this time out to step forward. No, no—something subtle. Maybe asking all those with an interest in Dyson spheres to get in touch with him. Even those who didn't know what they were seeing at the time they had their visions must have researched the images since their consciousness returned to the present, and the term would have come up in their Web searches.

Yes, he would find them—he would find the other immortals.

Or they would find him.

He'd thought perhaps it had been Michiko that he'd seen on that snow-white plain far in the future.

But then the letter came, inviting him to Toronto. It was a simple email message: "I am the jade man you saw at the end of your vision."

Jade. Of course that's what it was. Not green marble—jade. He'd told no one about that part of his vision. After all, how could he tell Doreen that he'd seen Michiko and not her?

But it wasn't Michiko.

Lloyd flew from Montpelier to Pearson International Airport, and headed down the jetway. It had been an international flight, but Lloyd's Canadian passport got him through customs in short order. A driver was waiting for him just outside the gate, holding a flatsie with the word "SIMCOE" glowing on it. His limousine flew—literally—along the 407 to Yonge Street, and south to the condominium tower atop the bookstore and grocery store and multiplex.

•   •   •

"If you could save only a tiny portion of the human species from death, who would you choose?" said Mr. Cheung to Lloyd, who was now sitting on the orange leather couch in Cheung's living room. "How would you make sure that you'd selected the greatest thinkers, the greatest minds? There are doubtless many ways; for me, I decided to choose Nobel Prize winners. The finest doctors! The preeminent scientists! The best writers! And, yes, the greatest humanitarians—those who had been awarded the peace prize. Of course, anyone could quibble with the Nobel choices in any given year, but by and large the selections *are* deserving. And so we started approaching Nobel laureates. We did it surreptitiously, of course; can you imagine the public outcry that would ensue if it were known that immortality was possible but it was being withheld from the masses? They would not understand—understand that the process was expensive beyond belief and was likely to remain so for decades to come. Oh, eventually, perhaps, we would find cheaper ways to do it, but at the outset we could afford to treat only a few hundred people."

"Including yourself?"

Cheung shrugged. "I used to live in Hong Kong, Dr. Simcoe, but I left for a reason. I am a capitalist—and capitalists believe that those who do the work should prosper by the sweat of their brows. The immortality process would not exist at all without the billions my companies invested in developing it. Yes, I selected myself for the treatment; that was my right."

"If you're going after Nobel laureates, what about my partner, Theodosios Procopides?"

"Ah, yes. It seemed prudent to administer the process in descending order of age. But, yes, we'll do him next, despite his youth; for joint winners of the Nobel, we're processing all members of the team at the same time." A pause. "I met Theo once before, you know—twenty-one years ago. My original vision had dealt with him, and when he was searching for information about his killer, he came to visit me here."

"I remember; we were in New York together, and he flew

up here. He told me about his meeting with you."

"Did he tell you what I said to him? I told him that souls are about life immortal, and that religion is about just rewards. I told him I suspected great things awaited him, and that he would one day receive a great reward. Even then, I suspected the truth; after all, by rights, I should have had no vision—I should have been dead by now, or, at least, not walking unaided at a sprightly pace. Of course, I couldn't be sure that my staff would one day develop an immortality technique, but it was a long-standing interest of mine, and the existence of such a thing would explain the good health I experienced in my vision, despite my advanced age. I wanted to let your friend know, without giving away all my secrets, that if he could survive long enough, the greatest reward of all—unlimited life—would be offered to him." A pause. "Do you see him much?"

"Not anymore."

"Still, I'm glad—more glad than you can know—that his death was prevented."

"If you were worried about that, and you had immortality available, why didn't you give him your treatment prior to the day on which the first visions showed he might die?"

"Our process arrests biological senescence, but it certainly doesn't make you invincible—although, as you doubtless saw in your vision, substitute bodies will eventually address that concern. If we were to invest millions in Theo, and he ended up being shot dead, well, that would be a waste of a very limited resource."

Lloyd considered this. "You mentioned that Theo is younger than me; that's true. I'm an old man."

Cheung laughed. "You're a child! I've got more than thirty years on you."

"I mean," said Lloyd, "if I'd been offered this when I was younger, healthier—"

"Dr. Simcoe, granted you are sixty-six—but you have spent that entire span under the care of increasingly sophisticated modern medicine. I've seen your health records—"

"You've what?"

"Please—I'm dispensing eternal life here; do you seriously think that a few privacy safeguards are a barrier to a person in my position? As I was saying, I have seen your health records: your heart is in excellent shape, your blood pressure is fine, your cholesterol levels are under control. Seriously, Dr. Simcoe, you are in better health now than any twenty-five-year-old born more than a hundred years ago would have been."

"I'm a married man. What about my wife?"

"I'm sorry, Dr. Simcoe. My offer is to you alone."

"But Doreen—"

"Doreen will live out the remainder of a natural life—another twenty-odd years, I imagine. She is being denied nothing; you will be able to spend every year of that with her. At some point, she will pass on. I'm a Christian, Dr. Simcoe—I believe better things await us . . . well, most of us. I have been ruthless in life and I expect to be judged harshly . . . which is why I am in no hurry to receive my reward. But your wife— I know much about her, and I suspect her place in heaven is secure."

"I'm not sure I'd want to go on without her."

"She, doubtless, would wish that you would go on, even if she herself could not. And, forgive my bluntness, but she is not your first wife, nor you her first husband. I do not denigrate the love you feel, but you are, quite literally, simply phases in each other's lives."

"And if I choose not to participate?"

"My expertise is in pharmaceuticals, Dr. Simcoe. If you choose not to participate, or if you feign acceptance, but give us reason to doubt your sincerity, you will be injected with mnemonase; it will break down all of your short-term memory. You will forget this entire encounter. If you really do not desire immortality, please take that option—it is painless and has no lasting side effects. And now, Dr. Simcoe, I really must have your answer. What do you choose?"

•   •   •

Doreen picked Lloyd up at the airport in Montpelier. "Thank God you're home!" she said, as soon as Lloyd got out of baggage claim. "What happened? Why did you miss the earlier flight?"

Lloyd hugged his wife; God, how he loved her—and how he hated being away from her. But then he shook his head. "It was the damnedest thing. I completely forgot that the return flight was at four o'clock." He shrugged a bit, and managed a small smile. "I guess I'm getting old."

33

Theo sat in his office. It had once, of course, been Gaston Béranger's office, but his five-year term had long ago ended, and these days CERN wasn't big enough to require a Director-General. So Theo, as director of the TTC, had made it his own. Old Gaston was still around; he was professor emeritus in physics at the University of Paris at Orsay. He and Marie-Claire were still happily married, and they had a terrific, honor-student son, and a daughter, as well.

Theo found himself staring out the window. It had been a month since the great blackout—the Flashforward in which everyone lost consciousness for an hour. But they'd done Klaatu proud: not a single fatality had been reported worldwide.

Theo was still alive; he'd avoided his own murder. He was going to live—well, who knew how long? Decades more, certainly. A new lease on life.

And, he realized with a start, he didn't know what he was going to do with all that time.

It was autumn; too late to literally smell the roses. But figuratively?

He got up, let the inner office door slide aside, let the outer office door do the same, made his way to the elevator, rode down to the ground floor, walked along a corridor, passed through the lobby, and exited the building.

The sky was cloudy; still, he put on his sunglasses.

When he'd been a teenager, he'd run from Marathon to Athens. When he was done, he'd thought his heart would never stop pounding, thought he'd never stop gasping for breath. He remembered that moment vividly—crossing the finish line, completing the historic run.

There were other moments he remembered vividly, of course. His first kiss; his first sexual encounter; specific images—postcards in his mind—from that trip to Hong Kong; graduating from university; the day he met Lloyd; breaking his arm once playing lacrosse. And, of running their first LHC experiment, the jump cut—

But—

But those sharp moments, those crisp memories, why, they were all from two decades or more in the past.

What had happened lately? What peak experiences, what exquisite sorrows, what giddy heights?

Theo walked along; the air was cool, bracing. It gave everything an edge, definition, form, a clarity that had been missing ever since—

Ever since he'd started investigating his own death.

Twenty-one years, obsessed by one thing.

Did Ahab have sharp memories? Oh, yes—losing his leg, no doubt. But after that—after he'd begun his quest? Or was it all a blur, month after month, year after year, everything and everyone subsumed?

But no—no. Theo was no Ahab; he wasn't hell-bent. He had found time for many things between 2009 and today, here, in 2030.

And yet—

And yet he'd never allowed himself to make plans for the future. Oh, he'd continued to work at his job, and had been promoted several times, but . . .

He'd once read a book about a man who learned at age nineteen that he was at risk for Huntington's disease, a hereditary disorder that would rob him of his faculties by the time he reached middle age. That man had bent himself to the task of making a mark before his allotted span was up. But Theo hadn't done that. Oh, he'd made some good progress in his physics work, and, of course, he did have his Nobel. But even that moment—receiving the medallion—was out of focus.

Twenty-one years, overshadowed. Even knowing that the future was mutable, even promising himself he wouldn't let his search for his potential killer take over his life, two decades had slipped by, mostly lost—if not actually skipped over, certainly dulled, reduced, lessened.

No fatal flaw? It is to laugh.

Theo continued walking. A chorus of birds chirped in the background.

No fatal flaw? *That* had been the most arrogant thought of all. Of course he had a fatal flaw; of course he had a *hamartia*. But it was the mirror image of Oedipus's; Oedipus had thought he *could* escape his fate. Theo, knowing the future was changeable, had still been dogged by the fear that he couldn't outwit destiny.

And so—

And so he hadn't married, hadn't had children; in that, he was even less than Ahab.

Nor had he read *War and Peace*. Or the Bible. Indeed, Theo hadn't read a novel for—what?—maybe ten years.

He hadn't traveled the world, except for where his old quest for clues had taken him.

He hadn't learned gourmet cooking.

Hadn't taken bridge lessons.

Hadn't climbed Mont Blanc, even part way.

And now, incredibly, he suddenly had—well, if not all the time in the world, at least a lot more time.

He had free will; he had a future to make.

It was a heady thought. *What do you want to be when you*

grow up? The cartoon-character clothing was indeed gone. As was his youth; he was forty-eight. For a physicist, that was ancient. He was too old, in all likelihood, to make another major breakthrough.

A future to make. But how would he define it?

As laser-bright moments; diamond-hard memories; crisp and clear. A future *lived*, a future savored, a future of moments so sharp and pointed that they would sometimes cut and sometimes glint so brightly it would hurt to contemplate them, but sometimes, too, would be joyous, an absolute, pure, un-alloyed joy, the kind of joy he hadn't felt much if at all lo these twenty-one years.

But from now on—

From now on, he would *live*.

But what to do first?

The name rose again, from his past, from his subconscious. Michiko.

She was in Tokyo, of course. He'd gotten an E-card from her at Christmas, and another on his birthday.

She'd divorced Lloyd—her second husband. But she'd never married again after that.

You know, he could go to Tokyo, look her up. *That* would be a wonderful moment.

But, God, it had been so many years. So much water under the bridge.

Still . . .

Still, he had always been very fond of her. So intelligent—yes, that's what he thought of first; that wonderful mind, that sharp wit. But he couldn't deny that she was pretty, too. Maybe even more than pretty; certainly graceful and poised, and always immaculately dressed in the currently fashionable style.

But . . .

But twenty-one years had passed. There had to be some-one new after all that time, no?

No. There wasn't; he'd have heard gossip. Of course, he

was younger than her, but that didn't really matter, did it? She would be—what?—fifty-six now.

He couldn't just pick himself up and go to Tokyo.

Or could he?

A life to be lived . . .

What did he have to lose?

Not a blessed thing, he decided. Not a blessed thing.

He headed back into the building, taking the stairs rather than the elevator, two steps at a time disappearing beneath his long strides, shoes slapping loudly and crisply.

Of course he'd call her first. What time was it in Tokyo? He spoke the question into the air. "What time is it in Tokyo?"

"Twenty hours, eighteen minutes," replied one of the countless computerized devices scattered around his office.

"Dial Michiko Komura in Tokyo," he said.

Electronic rings emanated from the speaker. His heart began to pound. A monitor plate popped up from his desktop, showing the Nippon Telecom logo.

And then—

There she was. Michiko.

She was still lovely, and she had aged gracefully; she could have passed for a dozen years younger than her real age. And, of course, she was stylishly attired—Theo hadn't seen this particular look yet in Europe, but he was sure it must be cutting-edge in Nippon. Michiko was wearing a short blazer that had rainbow patterns of color rippling across it.

"Why, Theo, is that you?" she said, in English.

The E-cards had been text-and-graphics only; it had been years since Theo had heard that beautiful, high voice, like water splashing. He felt his features stretching into a grin. "Hello, Michiko."

"I'd been thinking about you," she said, "as the date the visions showed got closer. But I was afraid to call. Afraid you might think I was calling to say goodbye."

He would have loved to have heard her voice earlier. He smiled. "Actually, the man who killed me in the visions is in custody now. He tried to blow up the LHC."

Michiko nodded. "I read that on the Web."

"I guess no one's vision came true."

Michiko lifted her shoulders. "Well, maybe not precisely. But my beautiful little daughter is just as I saw her. And, you know, I've met Lloyd's new wife, and he says she's just as he'd envisioned her. And the world today is a lot like what the Mosaic Project said it was going to be."

"I guess. I'm just glad that the part involving me didn't come true."

Michiko smiled. "Me, too."

There was silence between them; one of the joys of video phones was that silence was okay. You could just look at each other, bask in each other, without words.

She *was* beautiful . . .

"Michiko," he said softly.

"Hmm?"

"I, ah, I've been thinking a lot about you."

She smiled.

He swallowed, trying to work up the courage. "And I was wondering, well, what you'd think if I came out to Nippon for a bit." He raised his hand, as if feeling a need to provide them both with an out if she wanted to deliberately misread him, letting him down gently. "There's a TTC at the University of Tokyo; they've been asking me to come and give a talk about the development of the technology."

But she wasn't looking for an out. "I'd love to see you again, Theo."

Of course, there was no way to tell whether anything would happen between them. She might just be looking for a bit of nostalgia, remembering things past, the times they'd had at CERN all those years ago.

But maybe, just maybe, they *were* on the same wavelength. Maybe things would work out between them. Maybe, after all these years, it was going to happen.

He certainly hoped so.

But only time would tell.

ABOUT THE AUTHOR

Robert J. Sawyer is the author of ten previous novels, including *The Terminal Experiment*, which won the Nebula Award for Best Novel of the Year; *Starplex*, which was both a Nebula and Hugo Award finalist; and *Frameshift*, which was a Hugo finalist.

Rob's books are published in the United States, the United Kingdom, Bulgaria, France, Germany, Holland, Italy, Japan, Poland, Russia, and Spain. He has won an Arthur Ellis Award from the Crime Writers of Canada, five Aurora Awards (Canada's top honor in SF), five Best Novel HOMer Awards voted on by the 30,000 members of the SF&F Literature Forums on CompuServe, the *Science Fiction Chronicle* Reader Award, *Le Grand Prix de l'Imaginaire* (France's top SF award), and the Seiun (Japan's top SF award). In addition, he's twice won Spain's *Premio UPC de Ciencia Ficción*, the world's largest cash prize for SF writing.

Rob's other novels include the popular Quintaglio Ascension trilogy (*Far-Seer*, *Fossil Hunter*, and *Foreigner*), plus *Golden Fleece*, *End of an Era*, *Illegal Alien*, and *Factoring Humanity*.

Rob lives in Thornhill, Ontario (just north of Toronto), with Carolyn Clink, his wife of fifteen years. Together, they edited the acclaimed Canadian-SF anthology *Tesseracts 6*.

To find out more about Rob and his fiction, visit his extensive World Wide Web site at **www.sfwriter.com**.